BURY HIM AMONG KINGS

BURY HIM
AMONG KINGS

Elleston Trevor

HEINEMANN : LONDON

William Heinemann Ltd
LONDON MELBOURNE TORONTO
JOHANNESBURG AUCKLAND

First published 1970
Copyright © Elleston Trevor 1970
434 79310 8

Printed in Great Britain
by Cox & Wyman Ltd,
London, Fakenham and Reading

To
DWYE EVANS

To this certain place were brought the bodies of six British soldiers, expressly disinterred from the unnamed graves of the battlefields. Torn unrecognizably by the manner of their dying and therefore lost to all identity, they were closed in coffins, each draped by the flag of the country in which they were born and for which they had died.

Then to this place was led an officer of high rank, his eyes blindfolded, to be left alone with the dead. Moving about, his hand outstretched, he touched the first coffin that he came upon, thus giving to the man within his everlasting name: the Unknown Warrior.

In the Abbey of Westminster, in London, these words mark his tomb:

Beneath this stone rests the body of a British warrior unknown by name or rank, brought from France to lie among the most illustrious of the land and buried here on Armistice Day 11 Nov. 1920, in the presence of His Majesty King George V, his Ministers of State, and the Chiefs of his Forces, and a vast concourse of the nation. Thus are commemorated the many multitudes who during the Great War of 1914–1918 gave the most that man can give, life itself, for God, for King and Country, for loved ones, home and Empire, for the sacred cause of justice and the freedom of the world. They buried him among the Kings because he had done good toward God and toward His house.

I

The Devil laughed and spun her round and she was near to fainting: the coloured lights went whirling about her head in a galaxy gone mad. Others dashed past, Hiawatha and Caesar and an Executioner; she reached out to them and tried to stop them but nothing would keep still; everything was racing and colliding and scattering away, faces and colours and lights, and the heat rose in waves against her, the noise beating at her until she nearly screamed or perhaps was really screaming, soundlessly as in a dream. The Devil leapt higher and hands took her from behind as she began falling.

The music stopped and laughter rose everywhere.

'Who was it?'

'Pam, I think. Poor—'

'It can't be *Pam*! She's Anne Boleyn – besides, *Pam* wouldn't ever faint!'

'Then it's Margaret. I can't tell Anne Boleyn from Lady Jane Grey!' A gusty laugh.

'You've had too much bubbly!'

'So's Margaret!'

'But the poor thing – we ought to help her!'

'Everyone *is* helping her!'

The throng was growing and those there first were trying to keep others away.

'Someone fetch a doctor!'

'Oh no, she'll be all right. It's the heat. Let's get some more windows open, come on!'

The band struck up again because someone had given them a signal, and the people drifted away and began dancing. The coloured lights revolved and Marco Polo hurled streamers across the heads of the crowd and they floated like rainbows through the air before they formed a web and shivered and broke as the dancers moved.

'Who's the Devil?'

'Vic Talbot.'

I

'He was making her dance too fast.'

'He's rather marvellous, isn't he?'

'Vic? Give me his brother, darling, any day.'

'I didn't know he had one!'

'But surely you know *Aubrey*? He's Harlequin, just over there.'

'Oh *that's* Aubrey Talbot . . . Felicity was talking about him earlier – she's absolutely potty about him!'

'Who isn't?'

'I'm not. I don't like them quite so tall.'

Two waiters struggled with the French doors: everyone was complaining of the heat, and people were already moving on to the terrace, the ragtime beat of the music drifting out with them to be lost in the August night. Candles were carried to the terrace tables, their flames flickering in glass sconces. A waiter tripped in a doorway and an unopened magnum exploded on the marble, the ice from the bucket cascading across silk and buckled shoes, the cheers of the young men covering the squeal of a girl alarmed by the breaking glass; the *chef du salon* hurried to the scene, gathering his staff.

The Devil tossed a streamer high enough to catch one of the chandeliers, and the Pope – not to be outdone by his arch-rival – threw one even higher, so that within a minute a competition was in full swing and the dancers were driven back as the leaping figures festooned the pendants with their coloured skeins.

Harlequin was not competing, but enjoying the game from a distance, hands on his hips. His mischievous young brother had started it so he ought to stand by in readiness to call a halt if the whole chandelier looked like coming down.

A group rushed past, Anne Boleyn among them.

'Hello, Pam!' he called.

''Lo, Aub'ey!' She was radiant and he felt proud of her.

It had meant something, the dropping of the 'r' from his name. The habit stemmed from her infancy when 'Aubrey' had proved too difficult; these days it was deliberate, though its meaning wasn't always the same; at this moment it was just a signal, perhaps the waving of the private Talbot flag above the heads of so many strangers.

'Where's Hugh got to?' he called through the din.

'Goodness knows!'

'Is he all right?' If Pam had no idea where he'd got to, she'd

2

have no idea whether he was all right; but Aubrey had meant 'go and see' and she would know that.

'I'd better rescue him!'

She broke away from her friends and started on a tour of the salon, smiling to those whom she knew among the chaperons and elderly uncles who lined the walls, fanning themselves and watching for misbehaviour – a scolding would justify their presence here where only youth should be. One of them alone looked any fun: General Sir John Kimmins, ramrod-straight and tapping a polished shoe to the music, a glass of champagne in his hand and one shaggy eyebrow lifting to the alert as Pam came past. They were the sad ones, she thought, the ones still young underneath the medals and the diamond studs and the double chins and the harsh obligation to look older than they felt or had ever wished to be.

'Good-evening, Sir John!'

'My dear child, how lovely you look!' His glass was raised in a toast to her. 'Anne Boleyn was never so fair, or Henry would have chopped off his own head rather than hers!'

'It's just that your eye is more gallant than his, I'm sure!'

It was all you could do for them. Passing on, she explored the alcoves and quiet corners, because Hugh wouldn't be dancing or throwing streamers at the chandelier. A young man with his good looks would normally be surrounded by the prettiest of the debs, but Hugh didn't know how to manage them and they were quick to sense it, so he was usually driven into corners by withered matrons eager to relive their youth. That was why Pam had said she must go and 'rescue' him.

Hugh was not a Talbot, but they counted him as one of the family: the grounds of the Manor adjoined those of Carisbrooke House and the Talbot and Sadler children had grown up together; besides which, Hugh was an only child and therefore lonely; besides which again, he had his parents to bear with.

'Oh Margaret! Do you feel better now?'

'Of course. It was so ridiculous of me—'

'It wasn't at all! It was my dreadful young brother acting the usual giddy goat. We'll put him up the chimney when we get him home, I promise you!' (The direst threat of the Talbot household, this, never carried out but fearful to contemplate.)

'No, it was just the heat, I think.'

3

Pam left her bolstered by her two attentive aunts, thinking: It was too much bubbly, old thing, and you jolly well know it.

She found Hugh on the terrace being bored by an earnest young Blue-stocking got up as a Quaker Girl, a garb that surely suited her. She had strong views on Lawrence and his 'epicene coterie', from what Pam heard as she neared them.

'*Hugh* . . . I've been looking everywhere for you!' A step back for the sake of manners. 'Oh I'm so sorry – you're busy talking.'

His shy smile was all the help she'd get; it was melting but utterly useless in this situation.

The Quaker Girl turned a myopic stare on her. 'We were discussing *Sons and Lovers*.'

'How marvellous! But whose sons and whose lovers? Do let me in on it!'

The stare was turned away, dismissing her; but she wasn't going. It was all or nothing once they got their hooks into poor old Hugh and you had to use the most basic tactics. (She had once said to him, in front of a thrice-divorced *marquesa* with a heaving corsage, 'But I never hoped to see you here tonight – surely you're still infectious?')

She said now: 'You did promise to dance with me again, but of course it's not important.' She turned away and heard his quiet voice:

'I'm sorry, but it's quite true. Will you excuse me?'

He caught up with Pam in the doorway; the movement of his Greek robes sent the candles flickering, and shadows leapt across the trellis.

'I'm starving,' she said. 'Let's go and see if there's anything left.' He never danced anyway.

'All right.'

'Of course, you don't *have* to. We just thought we'd rescue you.'

'I'm hungry too.'

That was a fib: he never ate anything except from politeness. She stopped suddenly and faced him. 'You did *want* rescuing, didn't you?' It was the first time the thought had ever struck her.

'She was very dull.'

Pam cocked her head to study his amused blue eyes. 'I'm not so sure.' He tried to lead her on again towards the buffet but

4

she wouldn't let him. When a new thought came into her head – which wasn't too often – she gave it her full attention. Perhaps he'd been interested in talking about the Lawrence novel. Myopic eyes were attractive to some people – they looked rather defenceless. Even an overblown *marquesa* might be amusing, if only for her Roman accent. 'Hugh,' she said with her dark head still on one side, 'wouldn't it be simply ghastly if Aubrey and I found out that all the time we've been rescuing you from people we've really been spoiling your fun?'

His smile deepened, lining his thin face attractively. 'You know you haven't.'

'You'd never say so!' She was annoyed with him now. There was more than shyness to old Hugh: he possessed the sort of reticence that people wanted to penetrate, and it frustrated them when they saw they couldn't; the secret curtain, concealing suspected treasure, was beyond their touch. In a way he was the reverse of Sir John: Hugh was a young man grown old behind the clear eyes and the boyish smile. Perhaps not old, but somehow estranged from youth. 'Wouldn't it be just as ghastly – I don't mean that, it's a stupid word, I mean really and truly terrible – if we all began losing touch with each other, the more we grow up?' Stupid again: 'grow up' was a childhood phrase. She was nineteen and Hugh almost twenty-one, and next week he was taking a post as a junior schoolmaster, miles and miles away in Dover of all places. 'I mean if we weren't able to understand each other any more.' Hugh was here, close to her, a kind of half-brother by adoption, not so wonderful as Aubrey and not such fun as Vic but all Hugh, totally Hugh and one of them, the one they always had to rescue at parties. He mustn't change; they must all stay as they were now, for ever, even if she had to blind herself to changes in the others, first small ones and then big. Perhaps this was something she must learn: that it was important to see people as you wanted them to be, not as they really were.

His smile was gentle, no longer amused. 'It won't happen,' he said.

'Oh, damn!' She took his hand. 'Let's go and stuff ourselves with *petits fours*!'

The game had caught on: there wasn't a single chandelier

without a web of streamers. At the buffet the corks were popping and now a huge yellow balloon went floating across the room, then another and another; hands flew up to touch them and the aerial armada was greeted with cries of delight as more came drifting across.

A waiter edged through the revellers, looking for the costume just described to him: 'Coloured squares like a draughtboard, and a black mask; a tall young gentleman, you can't miss him.' Harlequin, that would be.

'Mr Aubrey Talbot, if you please?'

'Yes?'

'Your chauffeur's outside, Mr Talbot, an' begs for a word with you.'

'Very well.' He made a last leap and sent two of the balloons colliding.

Pam and Hugh were at the buffet near the doors.

'Where are you off to, Aubrey?'

'Back in a jiffy!'

Kemp was standing alone near the entrance like a lost terrier, darting glances about him. There were no other chauffeurs in sight, for it was much too early for carriages.

'I'm sorry to disturb you, Mr Aubrey, but Sir William said how I was to come an' call for you an' your party – on account of the crowds, he said.'

'What crowds, Freddie?'

'Well, being Bank Holiday for one thing, an' then people are getting excited on account of the news, you understand. It's quite lively already in Trafalgar Square, an' I suppose Sir William doesn't want any upsets, specially as Miss Pamela's here.' He peered up at the black mask, a little disconcerted by it.

'It's orders, is it?'

'Sir William didn't seem to give us much room for manœuvre, by his tone.'

Aubrey put his hands on his hips. 'Well we've got a job on, Freddie. Do what I can, how's that?'

Watching him cross the hall again, Kemp knew well enough what he meant. Miss Pamela, for all her high spirits, would come like a lamb, but young Mister Vic was quite another case.

At the buffet Aubrey asked for a cup of coffee to be sent out, because Kemp was in for a longish wait.

'What's up, Aubrey?' Pam asked him.

'Freddie's here for us. Spectre at the feast.'

'But it's only just gone ten o'clock!'

'Not his fault, of course. Father's a bit worried.'

'Is it the news?' asked Hugh. He was looking pensive.

'The crowds are building up, it seems.'

'Then we'll go and join them!' cried Pam and popped a final *petit four* into her mouth, linking her arm in Hugh's.

Aubrey laughed. 'You know how to make it easy for me, old thing, but how do we prise Vic away?'

'*You* can manage him.'

'I'll have to. We can't let Father down.'

It was part of the idiom they shared: when dismayed by strict orders they had long learned to defend themselves by the pretence that they could ignore them if they chose – but they'd be 'letting Father down'.

Aubrey left them, looking about him for Victor.

'It suits him,' said Pam reflectively, 'don't you think? His costume.'

'Harlequin should be tall, yes.'

'I don't mean just that.' It was partly the way her brother walked, his heels rising a little higher than normal, his body poised and forward-sloping as if he held himself ready to meet both the known and the unknown with equal attention. 'He was born for moonlight and balconies, to leap from one to another without a sound.'

'I've never quite seen him as a cat-burglar myself.'

She laughed delightedly: a cat-burglar was not a wholly undesirable character, to her mind; it took daring to plunder the soft-lit boudoirs of the rich, and a rope of pearls glowing in a dark hand conjured beauty and danger in one image. She was nevertheless aware that if such a person were to disturb her in her own bedroom she'd probably club him with a hairbrush.

It was some time before Aubrey ran the Devil to earth, for he was nowhere among the guests: by bribery or coercion he'd persuaded the drummer in the band to 'let him have a go', as he put it.

'How am I doing, old boy?'

7

'You'll bust the thing!'

'It's a red-hot number so you've got to let it rip!'

They had to shout above the din and Aubrey knew that he would either have to get his brother away from his new plaything before talking to him properly or yell his message against his ear as briefly as possible. After his long search the second scheme had more appeal.

'Listen, Vic – we're going!'

'We're what?'

'Lea-ving!'

'Can't be done! I've got a clandestine rendezvous with Sophie Fuller on the terrace in half an hour!' He was having trouble in keeping time, his brow puckered and his bright eyes fixed on the conductor. 'You shove off and I'll catch you up somehow!' He shot Aubrey a sudden satanic grin and returned his attention to the business in hand.

Aubrey moved away, to lean against a column and watch his brother's antics; it wasn't the first time he'd been a willing spectator to tomfoolery: Vic gave a new dimension to whatever he did, bending his total energies to it and charging it with such concentration that it caught and held the attention of those who watched. But sometimes there seemed a feverishness to Vic's escapades that worried Aubrey; or rather it was his constant need for them that seemed feverish, the inability to pass a single day without some diversion ranging from a spontaneous prank to a carefully planned breach of the peace. Only his charm and his patent lack of any wish to do real evil had so far saved him from the wrath of Father or arrest by the police. Various friends had various explanations: it was natural high spirits, an excess of energy, a harmless means of self-expression. Aubrey didn't find it difficult to dismiss his occasional doubts: his young brother had been born with a good head of steam in him and the safety-valves to go with it. The worst anyone could say of Victor Talbot was that he suffered from chronic *joie-de-vivre*.

The moment the music stopped, Aubrey gave the family signal: the two notes of the cuckoo whistled softly. Vic looked round and saw him, giving the sticks back to the drummer on his way across.

'You know what? I'm going to *buy* one of those things! I've got a natural talent for percussion – that chap said so!'

8

He mopped perspiration with a flame-coloured handkerchief, bowing extravagantly to one of the girls who was still clapping his performance.

'You buy one of those things,' said Aubrey, 'and I'm going to develop a natural talent for making bonfires.' He put an arm round his shoulders and began leading him through the crowd.

'Where are we going?'

'Home. Our carriage awaits.' He glimpsed Sophie Fuller in squaw's plumage and steered Victor away.

'What's happened?'

'Nothing, yet. Orders from the All Highest, ours not to reason why. The streets are buzzing it up a bit and Freddie's been sent to take us home before there's any trouble.'

'Is there some sort of news then?' Victor swung round neatly to disengage himself from his brother's arm. 'Has the giddy thing started?'

'Not as far as I know.'

'Well I'm going to give Father a ring – dammit all, we've only just got here!'

'We've been here three hours and you've been close to bringing down the chandeliers and busting a drum and seducing Sophie Fuller on the terrace and you'll have to make it do for one evening.' The band had started a tango and he hurried Victor along by the arm but he freed himself again—

'Lay off me, will you? People'll think I've got sloshed on bubbly. Where's Pam?'

'Waiting for us.'

'She'll eat out of your hand, that girl. I think elder brothers are absolute hell, you know that?' He had stopped and was looking about him as if for physical escape, and Aubrey had the passing thought that one day, and for the first time, Vic would make his stand against authority. With it would go their childhood, and for this reason Aubrey had baulked more than one chance, during the past year, of letting Vic have his head. It would be a relief to him: the duties of an elder brother were irksome enough and he performed them without relish; but when Vic decided to establish his independence they would all three pass with him into adulthood, a status that he and Pam had as yet elected not to recognize. He already possessed his own key to the house and Pam could receive friends of her own choosing and visit whom she liked, subject only to 'chap rules'; but they had never availed themselves of privileges denied to Vic, the youngest. And Aubrey had an idea that once childhood was finished with, an era would dawn wherein demands would be made and effort required; and since making an effort of any kind was abhorrent to him he had so far refused to let Victor have his head.

He refused again now. 'You'd better face it, old boy. Pam and I are going, and you're going with us.'

Victor caught up with him. 'Well I'll talk to her first. I can't believe she'd leave just when things are starting to warm up, even for you.'

'It's not for me. We can't let Father down.' But he'd seen the chance, and took it. 'Besides, she wants to see the crowds on the way through town. Apparently things are even warmer out there – you never know, they might try overturning the car or something—'

'You think they would?' Vic's pace quickened. 'Well that's different! If we can overturn the odd bus or two it'll be fair exchange and we shan't have wasted the evening!'

Kemp was by the dark-blue Daimler holding the door open when they came down the steps, Vic in the lead.

'I'll drive, Freddie!'

'You won't,' said Aubrey and pushed his brother into the back.

'I've a damn' good mind to take a taxi!'

'You won't be allowed to drive that either. Keep a tight half-nelson on him, Hugh.' He got into the front with Kemp. 'I don't see any crowds?'

'They're in Trafalgar Square, sir, or they were when I passed through. I thought we might cut north an' go by Oxford Street.'

'Not on your life!' Victor was leaning forward and breathing down their necks, and Kemp glanced sharply to Aubrey for instructions.

'Let's try the Square.' Aubrey felt a vague excitement rising in him, and the night was still young.

The Strand was almost deserted but they met with groups of people near Charing Cross. The Square itself was milling with them, a sea of bobbing straw boaters, and Kemp had to pull up. Someone was making a speech from the base of the Column, and crudely daubed banners were dipping between poles among the throng below him: BRITAIN MUST KEEP ITS HEAD! BELGIUM IS NOT OUR CONCERN!

A group was pressing hard towards the Column beneath a flutter of Union Jacks, cheered on by the crowd as it was given gangway, and fighting broke out where the flags met the banners; the lone speaker went on shouting but could no longer be heard. Dogs ran yelping through the confusion and a bus was honking for room where people spilled on to the road. A banner went down and laughter mingled with the cheers. Coloured balloons sailed from an open char-à-banc and a man stood on its bonnet waving a bottle of beer: there had never been a Bank Holiday like this and they were all in the mood for it.

Aubrey said: 'Let's go down Whitehall – it's on our way if we leave through Chelsea.'

'It's the paintwork I'm worried about.' Kemp wasn't enjoying himself.

'It's not a rough crowd, you can see that.'

'Just as you say, Mr Aubrey.'

Along Whitehall most of the windows were still lit and police were in strength outside the War Office, where official cars were standing in a double row.

Pam said: 'I've never *seen* so many people!' Something in her voice made Aubrey look round at her. The brightness in her dark eyes was not all excitement: the sight of the crowds confused her, and Aubrey had seen her like this when they went on the roller-coaster at the fairground – she dared herself to stay on, at the same time longing for it to stop.

He said: 'We'll be home quick enough through Chelsea.' He wished now that he'd let Kemp avoid the crowds.

'I wouldn't miss it for anything!' She was gripping Hugh's arm as she stared through the window. Vic had the other one lowered and was leaning out and calling to people along the pavement.

'Not much hope down that way,' said Kemp.

Hundreds stood gathered near the Houses of Parliament and a line of police was filtering traffic to the left across Westminster

Bridge. The mood was less rowdy here than in Trafalgar Square and many stood with their heads turned to gaze up at Big Ben.

'Ten minutes,' said Hugh, and Aubrey looked round at him.

'What?'

'That's when it runs out.'

But they couldn't hear him because a bus had begun hooting just behind, and Kemp pulled the Daimler in to the kerb. Victor was out before anyone could stop him, joining a knot of Bank Holiday revellers who were prancing arm in arm towards the fringe of the crowd. In a moment they were all out of the car except for Kemp, Pam tugging Hugh along with her and Aubrey racing to catch them up. A man with a tray stood near the police cordon and they bought Union Jacks from him and waved them as they ran. They didn't know why they ran, or where: the excitement of the crowd had filled them of a sudden and too fast for them to question it; they looked for friends among the hundreds here, saw none but made new ones in the instant, laughing to strangers and waving their little flags as they capered, still in their fancy dress, towards the main body of the crowd. Here it was too thick for movement and anyway they were all out of breath, though Victor leapt at any young girl he could see, hoping to frighten her with his Devil's get-up and often fetching a squeal from the more timid among them.

Aubrey noticed that Hugh stood a little apart from them, his arms folded across the Greek robe and his head tilted to watch the great clock in the tower. Its hands neared the hour and Aubrey realized what he had meant when he'd said 'ten minutes'. The ultimatum was to run out at midnight, Berlin time – eleven o'clock here in London. He hadn't given a thought to it in the last few days; none of them had. The headlines had been so thick with threats and declarations and solemn political statements that he and Pam had stopped trying to make sense of them, while Vic never had time to look at a newspaper anyway.

The crowd seemed quieter now: nothing more than a murmur was on the warm night air. Somewhere a child was crying, wanting to be taken home; a flight of pigeons, wakeful still because of the movement in the streets, dipped from a parapet and rose to settle among the shadows of Westminster Abbey; a man on the steps of St Margaret's, hatless and with a brown paper parcel under his arm, began quietly singing 'Abide With Me'. Little by little even the murmur was dying away; and those who spoke, whispered.

'Aub'ey?'

He looked down into her frightened eyes; she took his hand, and Victor's, and raised her dark head to the tower.

When the first stroke of the hour came there was a hush over all; the weight of it boomed from the sky and the others followed in their thunderous order, each overwhelming the echo of the last among the ancient stones. Nobody had ever paused here to listen to the marking of the hour; there never seemed time to take such account of time's passing, in the trivial round of their city lives; but they listened now to the great clock and were silent while it boomed through the August night, knowing it told more than of the hour.

In the last stroke's dying there was left only their silence; down Whitehall and across the Bridge the traffic seemed to have stopped; the very lamps in the windows and along the Thames possessed a stillness in the vault of dark. Then a man's voice came like a spark to powder.

'*Down with the bloody Kaiser!*'

A cheer began from the heart of the crowd and was taken up and spread swiftly until the walls of abbey and church and parliament were filled and roaring with it while the coloured paper flags were sent waving as if to a sudden wind. The next moment it was carnival: a straw hat went spinning aloft and others followed until the lamplight flowed and whirled about their drifting yellow shapes; hearing the crowd's roar the traffic raised an answering fanfare with its hooters, soon to be joined by the sirens of river-boats and tugs along the Thames. A pack of college-boys, their hats still volplaning about the lamps, were leading a chant whose rhythm swelled from throat to throat: '*Down – with – Germany! Down – with – Germany! Down – with – Germany!*' Faster and faster the rhythm became until at last it turned to cheering that rose and fell and rose again with a note of ritual: discord had aspired to unison and now these voices were one voice, abiding, the cry of a people jealous of its name and of its land.

There was no reason here. They were met by common accord,

the more readily because it was high summer and holiday time; they were here to celebrate the chime of their city's clock and the past it swept away, the future it ordained. Of this, the future, they thought little, knowing it to be safe in their hands, as it had always been.

People began moving, their mood uncontainable by stillness. A Salvation Army band had struck up and a dog stood yelping at them, crouched and with its ears back. Soon there was singing.

Keep the home fires burning . . . though your hearts are yearning . . .

A pickpocket was busy where the crowd was dense, his voice even more joyful than the rest in a private celebration of his own. Newsboys came darting into the square with their red-chalked placards, their cries piping against the patriotic songs: '*Foreign Office official – ultimatum rejected!*' They were surrounded at once and coppers spilled on the ground in the struggle for the latest editions: London was hungry for headlines and the nation still uncertain until it saw its fate in print.

The papers were glanced at, passed about, and flung into the air.

'*If that's what they want then we'll give it to 'em!*'

A group of holiday-makers were joining hands and circling the Salvation Army band, singing until their breath exploded into laughter. An Irishman found a pacifist and put his point of view by hitting him with a bottle.

'Aubrey! Where's Vic?'

'Over there somewhere, organizing a war-dance!'

'Can we get him home before he's arrested?' She was in no hurry to go: since the mood of the crowd had run riot she had let herself be swept along by it, glad enough to have her fears dispelled; it had been the silence of everyone that had for a moment unnerved her, and the solemn boom of the clock. A little Union Jack was tucked in her dark hair like a Spanish comb and a corsage of streamers still clung to her Anne Boleyn gown. A perfect stranger in evening dress had asked her to dance with him and she had allowed him; a party of French chefs and waiters had sung the 'Marseillaise' until their breath was gone and she was hoarse from joining in.

'Hugh, do you want to go?'

'I'm enjoying myself!'

14

But Pam knew he wasn't. He'd just been watching people in the crowd, and not singing or anything. She didn't know how anyone could do that, not even Hugh; when they'd all sung 'Onward Christian Soldiers' she'd felt so exhilarated that she'd almost cried.

'Come on Aubrey, we ought to be going, or we'll get put up the chimney when we reach home!' She wasn't only thinking of Hugh; the hands of Big Ben were moving towards midnight and she didn't want to hear it chime again.

'All right,' he said. Her eyes were still bright but he could see that it wouldn't be long before her excitement turned to exhaustion. 'I'll want help with Vic, though; fetch Hugh and we'll all surround him and carry him bodily with us – it's the only way!'

They had trouble reaching the Daimler, though not with Vic. The crowd had been gathering in numbers for the past hour and now it was immense, flowing in from Millbank and Westminster Bridge and filling the roadway so that motor traffic had to be diverted along Victoria Embankment. Reserves of constabulary were being dropped from transports wherever their drivers could find room to pull up; but there was nothing they could do except to lend a hand with fainting-cases and lost children.

Aubrey and the others had joined hands and were having to force their way along, the boys protecting Pam as best they could; by now there were many in the crowd who were drunk or nearly so, and wildness was growing. An elderly man, believed to be a German, was being harried by a group of young bloods, and the police had been called to the scene; and Hugh, pushing his way with the others across the road, had his Plato's robe torn from the shoulder by a heavy fellow who for a moment clung to him in an effort to keep his feet.

'Can you see the car?' Pam was asking a little fearfully.

'It's not far now, don't worry.'

She had tried not to ask but hadn't managed: the crowd wasn't just a lot of people now; it was a creature itself, gigantic and shapeless and moving mindlessly without direction, swaying and surging about her frighteningly. She could climb tall trees and deal with horses and had swum right across the Serpentine – her brothers would vouch for that – but this crush

15

of half-crazed people enfeebled her and she thanked God she was with the boys and not alone as many young women seemed to be.

Some of the office windows along Parliament Street were open and clerks leaned from them to watch the mass below, one of them flinging torn-up paper that fell in a small blizzard; straw hats went spinning upwards in reply.

'I can't see it,' Aubrey said.

'Was it here?' It was difficult to get their bearings: the perspective of the street was lost.

'If it was here, Freddie must have moved it for safety's sake!'

They stood close together, resisting the press of bodies, then forced their way on again towards the buildings. Passing a shadowed doorway, Pam glimpsed a woman lying on the ground, her dress in disorder and a man sprawled on top of her; then they were past, but she had seen that a crowd was not human, but animal.

The heat of the summer night, already oppressive, was stifling here among the close-packed bodies, and constables and first-aid men were hard put upon to reach the fainting-cases and struggle clear with them.

A char-à-banc party came dancing arm in arm from the foot of Downing Street, paper hats bobbing and bottles of beer stuffed into their pockets, singing lustily—

'*My ole man's a fireman – now what do you think of that? 'E wears gorblimey trousers an' a little gorblimey hat!*' A bottle crashed to the ground.

'*What price the Kaiser?*'

'*Sod the Kaiser!*'

'*Amen an' bloody Hallelujah!*'

An elephant herd of double-decker buses stood honking, with the people on the top reaching to catch the torn paper that now drifted whitely from almost every window; a body of police was trying to clear the roadway, for the traffic was now cut off even from the Victoria Embankment.

'*Talbot! Talbot!*'

Aubrey, taller than the others, saw him first. 'It's all right – here's Freddie!' He waved with his free hand, his other arm round Pam to urge her along. Kemp trotted ahead of them with his elbow digging and prodding at all in his path.

"'Ere, whass the game?' A burly man swung a fist at him and Kemp gave him a foot behind the knee and he went down with his hat over his eyes.

The dark-blue Daimler was in a side-street with a constable standing guard: Kemp had brandished Sir William's name and although the man had never heard of it he thought he'd better be safe than sorry.

Kemp drove off as soon as they'd piled in, and took the quieter streets westwards and then south towards the River. 'I had to move the car, Mr Aubrey, or they'd've wrecked it, you understand.'

'You did very well. It was all my fault.'

'Oh, there's no harm done.' In an undertone: 'Miss Pamela not upset, is she?'

'She'll soon get her spirits back.' But he was angry with himself: Father had been right, and they should have gone straight home. He glanced behind him and got a rueful smile from her. 'You all right, Pom-Pom?'

'She's starving,' Vic said with an unsteady grin. It was always safe to say that about Pam.

None of them spoke again until they were nearing Chelsea. There was nothing to talk about except the crowd and the news of war, and the crowd had become ugly in their thoughts: Vic had at last found himself up against people who could play the Devil better than he did and it had sobered him; Pam had known real fear tonight, when Big Ben had chimed so ominously in the dark sky, when she had felt, later, so trapped by the crowd that she doubted if even Hugh and her brothers could save her, and when she had glimpsed the two writhing figures in the doorway, the naked thigh of the woman white in the shadows, the dark man so strangely humped: what could have come to their minds that they believed themselves, among a thousand people, to be alone? If mere news of war brought fever to the streets, what of the days ahead? She realized she was gripping tightly the hand that Hugh, with his usual gentleness, had given her to hold; and she tried to relax, go limp, and not to think any more. She asked him:

'Were you hurt, in the scrum?'

'Oh, no.'

'They tore your philosopher's robes, poor Plato. I hope they

17

left your philosophy intact.' She had observed him now and again, standing so still with the people milling about him, his head tilted attentively in almost a listening attitude though there'd not been much to hear that would make any sense. What had he been thinking when the clock had struck? And when they'd passed that doorway? Had he believed that love and a new life were being made in instinctive defiance of war's companion, death? It was the sort of thing that Hugh would think of: they often made fun of his solemn thoughts when they'd managed to drag them out of him.

They fell silent again; to talk about the war news would be worse than silence; besides, they weren't sure what it meant, what it would mean to them. For weeks there'd been rumours and official statements; the Press had made a megaphone for the proclamations and protests and denials shouted abroad by crowned heads and presidents and puppet governments, but it had all become so meaningless, and even Father's comments on the 'situation' were no more understandable than the editorials in his own newspaper, which spoke of 'sanctions', 'guarantees of neutrality', 'non-intervention' and the 'honouring of sacred obligations to mankind'. Of course it was clear that almost everyone was busy declaring war on almost everyone else, but that didn't necessarily mean there would *be* a war, or at least a war that would involve England. So they had finally become – as Aubrey had put it – browbeaten into boredom, and had sought refuge in the comfort of their own familiar affairs. But tonight the war news had become real to them, bursting over them in the stormy streets with the force of a sea-wave; and they had learned that to ignore something was not to banish its existence. Tonight England was in arms.

Somewhere by the quiet waters of the Thames where almost no one was about they came on a coffee stall and Aubrey asked Kemp to pull up. He brought a bag of currant buns back to the car and, as they drove on, Pam made a pretence of eating one for his sake. Victor, though not hungry, polished them off, and made a balloon with the bag but couldn't bring himself to pop it; there'd been enough noise tonight.

Towards Chelsea there was movement in the streets again: the artists' quarter was never early to bed and now there was something grander than their own designs to offer debate in the balmy night. Farther on there was quite a crowd and Kemp was already looking for a side-street when a constable signalled him to stop.

'What's happening?' Pam asked from the back.

'I can't rightly say, Miss Pamela.'

It was a different sort of crowd from the earlier one: people were cheering and calling out but in a different way, and a new sound was filling the street, rhythmic and insistent. The roadway was empty and the people made two close-packed lines along the pavement on each side, everyone waving little flags.

In surprise Aubrey said: 'They're coming!'

'Is it a procession?' Pam leaned forward trying to see.

Absently he said: 'You could call it that.'

The pipers and drummers came round the bend of the road and there followed the new sound they'd not heard before, of marching feet.

Kemp, his hands on the wheel, said: 'They'll be on their way to the station, then. Victoria.'

Pam spoke so quietly that no one heard her. 'So soon?'

The regimental band was abreast of them and the beat of the drums for a moment thundered inside the Daimler. Victor alone got out, his excitement aroused again. He stood with the other people, calling something, waving both hands.

It was a full company of more than two hundred men and they marched with a disciplined swing even though it was made difficult for them as the people broke from the pavements, mostly women, to press them with flowers and packets of chocolate and cigarettes, anything they could find at hand or bring from their houses, the younger ones linking arms for a moment with a man and leaving him with a kiss, the others forcing them to take their gifts and tucking flowers in their uniforms as they all went swinging past while their officers and sergeants did what they could to keep them in line of march and steady the step, themselves the most beset of all, their rank giving them prominence and the attention of the more daring of the young women. The boys and young men fell in with the soldiers to march alongside, white shirts open at the neck and faces brown from the long summer, plying them with shouted questions—

'*Where is it then, chum? France, is it?*'

19

'*You were quick enough off the mark, by God!*'
'*My brother's in your lot! Jim Foster − d'you know him?*'
'*I'm with you, boy, I'm signin' on tomorrow, I am!*'

They whistled and sang to the pipes and drums: *Glory, glory Hallelujah! Glory, glory Hallelujah!* Dogs ran barking among their legs.

The soldiers, thus hailed as victors before they had even neared the field, were drawn into the mood of Mafeking and called back in their own fashion—

'*Comin' with us are you then? Come on, keep up the step!*'
'*Well you're a nice girl, you are! Give us another one afore I go!*'
'*Hello Sally! You here to see us off or comin' with us?*'

They passed the dark-blue motor-car, one of them grinning and peering in at Pam. '*You're pretty, then! Wait till I come 'ome − I shan't be long!*'

A man red with embarrassment, trying to march with a basket of fruit on his arm. A bull-headed man with heavy boots, a flowered scarf round his shoulders. A boy, not yet a man at all, a crimson rose in his tunic.

Glory, glory Hallelujah . . . For his soul goes marching on!

Youths flocked into the roadway behind the rearguard platoon, waving their paper flags or carrying a walking-stick sloped at the shoulder, the young girls cheering them on; last came the children, skipping along and laughing, clapping their hands and blowing tin whistles fit to bust; people at the windows threw down sweets for them, too late to catch the soldiers. Then the road was almost empty and the first of the traffic was let through.

From the back of the Daimler, across Aubrey's shoulder, Pam saw a cripple move beneath a lamp-post and cross awkwardly on his crutches to the other side.

Victor appeared suddenly at the window, out of breath and bubbling over with it all. The young officers had looked as smart as anything and the girls had gone quite mad over them.

'You know, the whole thing looks like being rather fun, don't you think?'

Pam sat without moving. 'Get in, Vic,' she told him. 'We're going home.'

II

The beams of the headlamps were spread on each side of the
drive, bringing to sudden life the topiary creatures that peopled
the lawns: herons, peacocks, eagles with half-spread wings,
their shadows for a moment taking leave of them to go swooping
across the grass; then the Manor itself was thrown against the
dark sky as if by a magic lantern, a Lutyens façade of gables and
tall chimneys and white-painted casements, its angles and
cornices half lost beneath cascades of creeper. Those windows
showing light were mostly on the ground floor, and Aubrey
said over his shoulder:

'No one's gone to bed yet, so we shan't have to creep about.'
He was a little worried; his part-defiance of orders was trivial
enough: the worst that could happen would be a noisy dressing-
down according to tradition. 'Father wants to see you – he's
furious!' The time-honoured summons had never occasioned
fright: the 'fury' didn't last long and was even good fun to listen
to unless you had something really awful on your conscience,
and the next minute he'd be asking how your backhand was
shaping or what the concert had been like. What worried
Aubrey was that Pam might have been hurt in all that crush,
or badly upset, and that was what Father had tried to prevent.
It wasn't a very good show.

'The thing is,' Vic was saying, 'how are *we* going to get to
bed without being spotted? Because I'm damned if I'm stopping
up to listen to politics – they'll all be full of it tonight!'

'You're not using the window,' his brother told him quickly.
'That's an order from me.' Vic had come close to breaking his
neck last summer, climbing to his room well after midnight; as
it was he'd brought a whole mass of creeper down and of course
'Father was furious'.

'I've had enough giddy orders for the time being, thanks.'
Vic wished at once not to have said it but was too fed up to
apologize; the ball had just been getting into its swing when
they'd been sent for like a bunch of infants; the high jinks in

21

the square were enormous fun and then people had to get out of hand and spoil it all; and finally, just when he'd realized that a war could be a jolly good game if you put on a uniform to dazzle the girls, Pam and the rest had been as glum as cold pudding about it all the way home.

'There's Charrington!' she said now.

The big oak door was already wide open as the Daimler swung round the fountain-pond and halted at the porch. The butler stood framed for an instant, shielding his eyes from the headlights, then came to the car with his slight limp and crinkly lopsided smile, having no need to raise his voice above the quietly-running engine:

'I hope it was an enjoyable evening, Mr Aubrey?'

'Not bad. What's happened?' The Season was over but a few guests were still at the Manor and none had gone up to bed yet, and Charrington should have been too occupied to come opening doors, especially for them.

'Nothing at all has happened, only Sir William's a little put out, if you follow, as it's late.'

'Oh, Lord . . .' said Victor in a stage groan. 'A little put out' was Charrington's phrase for 'furious'.

Aubrey helped his sister out of the car and Hugh followed, bringing her fan which had fallen from the seat.

'I'll go and see him,' Aubrey said. It would suitably end such an evening and anyway it would ease his conscience.

'If I might suggest something, Mr Aubrey . . .' They stood in a silent group around Charrington, the big car's exhaust throbbing and tainting the warm night air, their young faces lit by the glow from the open doorway. It wasn't the first time they had consented readily enough to hear one of Charrington's 'suggestions', some of which had often saved them from trouble. There was perhaps a difference tonight: Aubrey was quite prepared for a dressing-down, feeling he deserved it; Vic knew he'd have no part in it, being the youngest and therefore not responsible; Pam, sunk in a mood of depression utterly strange to her, had no fears anyway that it would worry Aubrey over-much; and Hugh was of course not subject to Talbot discipline; yet despite this difference they were ready to listen to Charrington, perhaps from habit, perhaps remembering how often it had been worth it.

'It was quite some time ago when Sir William asked me if you were home yet.' His tone had the hush of conspiracy but the lopsided smile remained: the family was used to it but until a visitor understood that it was habitual they thought he must be enjoying a secret joke – some of the women callers would glance into the hall mirror fearing that something was amiss with their hat. Charrington was far from elderly but his smile crinkled one side of his face, and together with his lack of height and portliness it lent him the air of a wise and worldly gnome. 'I told him that you must surely be home by now, but that I'd go and make sure. Of course I'm kept busy with my lady's party in the drawing-room and he'll realize that.' An aside to Kemp: 'You can get off now, Frederick, but go quietly as you can and don't put the lights on again.' They stood away as the wheels crunched over the gravel. 'So if we were to go in without too much disturbance, it might seem you've been home safe and sound for quite some little time, if you follow.' Pleased though he was with his influence over them he never indulged himself. 'Well if you'll excuse me I must be getting back to the guests. Oh, I should mention that Major Sadler's here, Mr Hugh, talking with Sir William in his study.'

'Thank you, Charrington.'

The butler turned and crossed the lamplit porch with his barely noticeable limp. Nobody was certain how he had come by it but it had been darkly whispered below stairs that his father had beaten him, too young.

'Let it go at that,' Pam told her brother. 'I'm for sneaking up to bed without having to talk to Mother's friends, and I can't do that if you're going to brave the lion.'

'I'll leave it for the morning,' he said absently, and kissed her cheek. 'Sleep well, Pom-Pom, tomorrow's another day.'

Victor went into the house with her and Aubrey was alone for a few minutes, watching the robed figure of Hugh go flitting among the silent peacocks and eagles and past the summerhouse to the gap in the hedge that for years had been his private way between Carisbrooke and Ashbourne, between loneliness and friendship.

Voices came from the open windows of the drawing-room. They'd be mostly women in there and Aubrey decided that he wouldn't be saying goodnight to Mother unless he heard her upstairs before he turned in. Of two minds whether to 'brave the lion', he was at least sure that if he did, it wouldn't be to submit to any lecture but – more important – to ask Father's opinion on what was likely to happen, what kind of day tomorrow would really be, for all of them.

'You know which man I'll be backing, don't you? What did Lloyd George say only last December, only six months ago? To increase our armaments would be 'pure folly'! And at the same time Sir Edward Grey warned us that we were sitting on a powder-barrel! My God, Charles, it's not taken long to show us who was right!'

'It's Asquith we'll have to back,' Sadler told him calmly, 'like it or not.'

'Asquith! You know what *his* line is – maintaining what he calls the 'balance of power'. And just how much 'balance' is there in Europe tonight? It's more like a dozen monkeys jumping about on a see-saw – and I'll tell you this: they're due for a fall, the whole pack of 'em. Politicians, generals, emperors, all with their heads stuffed with suet and the false sense of their own omnipotence – you know what's happening tonight? The barbarians are grabbing the reins and setting out on a ride to hell, and who's in the cart behind them? All Europe!'

The telephone rang again and Sadler watched his friend take the call, his left hand knocking the receiver off and catching it in the same movement as if it were a conjuring trick of long practice, his wiry figure hooked over the desk and his attention fixed absolutely on the instrument, reminding Sadler of young Vic rather than Aubrey, who had more of his mother's ability to let the world go by.

'Sir William speaking, yes. Well I want Horder to tell me himself, so put him on.' It was typical of him that with a few seconds to spare he made use of them pressing the bell under the desk with his brightly polished shoe to summon Charrington. 'Horder?' He listened without interruption for fully a minute and with such attention that his compact body remained perfectly still, his gaze never straying from the massive globe that occupied one corner of the study; then he spoke with the same controlled energy with which he had delivered his opinions to Sadler just now: the words, for all their force and imagery, had been uttered almost in an undertone – the 'Talbot undertone' that in Fleet Street carried more weight than shouting could ever achieve. 'All right, Horder, now listen. You may be perfectly right and perfectly justified but this is the news page and not a platform for opinion. Did they reach you from the conference? All right. I've the actual draft here on my desk and you can take it down. Quote: *Owing to the summary rejection by the German Government of the request made by His Majesty's Government for assurance that the* – what? Assurance, yes – *that the neutrality of Belgium will be respected, His Majesty's Ambassador at Berlin has received his passports and His Majesty's Government have declared to the German Government that a state of war exists between Great Britain and Germany as from 11.00 p.m. on 4 August.*'

Quietly Sadler left the deep leather armchair and stood in front of the globe on its carved pedestal, patting his pockets as if hunting for something, not for his pipe and matches but perhaps, unconsciously, for a miracle: a tick of the clock retracted, a page of the calendar redeemed, and the last hours of this day reviewed by the gods and by their hand rewritten in form of reprieve. Europe looked small on the globe; it was the size of the storm that appalled him. It was certain now, of course: for weeks there had been so many doubts, so much confusion, and though he had been prepared to see the head-lines conveying the worst of news at any time from day to day, it had shocked him the more acutely for having heard it pro-claimed in almost an undertone and by his old friend, here in this quiet room at Ashbourne, a place that was almost as much his home as was Carisbrooke near by. *A state of war exists.*

'Oh, have they indeed?' William's tone grew even more controlled, and Charles found himself admiring the sound of it. He could, if he let himself, envy William for so many things – or perhaps it was only for one thing, one person, so important that it seemed manifold – but at this moment it would be for his strength of conviction, his sense of purpose that had left so many of his enemies defeated in the field before a shot was fired. 'Have they indeed?' – Charles didn't know who 'they' were, but he didn't think much of their chances. 'Listen, Horder. We accept the Neutrality League's advertisement precisely as it stands, a whole page and word for word, and we bring it out in the first edition on Page Three, is that understood? And if they feel any need for moral support, tell them the *Manchester Guardian*'s running it too – that ought to convince them.'

Sadler moved to the round table to look again at the advertisement; it was spread on top of the dozen or so press editions of the Talbot-owned *Courier* and was designed in heavy capitals with the heading fully one inch high:

BRITONS, DO YOUR DUTY!

Keep your Country out of a wicked and stupid war! The War Party says: We must maintain the Balance of Power, because if Germany were to annex Holland or Belgium she would be so powerful as to threaten us; it says that we are bound by treaty to fight for the neutrality of Belgium, who has been invaded, and that we are bound by our agreements with France to fight for her.

These reasons are false and these are the facts: If we sided with Russia and France the balance of power would be upset as never before; it would make the military Russian Empire of 160,000,000 the dominant Power of Europe. You know what kind of country Russia is. Our treaties expressly stipulate that we are not compelled to take part in a general European war to defend the neutrality of Belgium. The Prime Minister and Sir Edward Grey have both declared in the House of Commons that we have no undertaking to go to war for France. Nor can Germany annex Holland, Belgium or Normandy without gravely weakening her forces. It would thus be monstrous to drag this country into war on vague suspicions.

It is Your Duty to Save Your
Country from this Disaster!

Sadler turned away from the announcement with a sudden twinge of distaste. Even if these 'facts' were correct – and most of them were conjecture – there was something ignoble in canvassing the nation by means of a paid advertisement. If the Empire was tonight standing to arms could this kind of protest succeed? Wasn't there a stronger voice against 'disaster'? Ramsay MacDonald's perhaps, but who would listen?

' – And rewrite it this way. Heading: *The King and His People*. Subheading: *Loyal Scene before the Palace*.' Talbot glanced up as

26

the door was opened after a brief knock. 'Just a minute, Horder. Well, Charrington, are the children home yet?'

'Oh yes, Sir William, quite some little time ago. I couldn't –'

'Did they meet with any trouble?'

'I'm sure they would have mentioned it, Sir William. They seemed to have quite enjoyed themselves with –'

'As long as they're here. Please pour some more brandy for the Major.' He said into the telephone: 'Horder?'

Major Sadler shook his head to Charrington, who took his time going out: you could often hear things said in this room that nobody else would know about till they opened the papers next day. (There was a curious worn patch on the parquet just outside the door, where Charrington stood ostensibly as sentry in case Sir William wanted him. His status below stairs, already of the highest by nature of his position, became Olympian when there was news to be had. There'd been quite a to-do on his announcement that Douglas Fairbanks had gone up in a Zeppelin: Elsie had dropped straight on her knees in front of the sink to pray for him and Cook had cuffed her silly for calling on the name of the Lord in vain.)

Tonight Charrington paused only a minute or so, because Lady Eleanor might take it into her head to float away and cut some roses or go and see if Cleopatra had pupped yet, and he'd have to fill the breach; she was never good with guests.

' – No, exactly as I'm giving it to you. Quote: *The King and Queen drove from the Palace at tea-time yesterday along the Mall. Their Majesties were in an open carriage, and as they passed the German Embassy they were given a great ovation by the crowds. In the evening the singing and the cheering outside the Palace was unceasing* – no, put 'continuous', too many 'ing's. Yes. *And soon after nine o'clock the King and Queen appeared with the Prince of Wales on the balcony. The Royal Party remained for several minutes acknowledging the impressive demonstration of loyalty, and after they had gone inside the crowds dispersed in processions that filled the streets until after midnight.*'

Sadler took out his short pipe with the bitten stem but didn't fill it: he and Louise would be going soon and there'd be no time to finish the bowlful before retiring. He watched Talbot's well-groomed head and saw for the first time that he was beginning to grey at the temples. Sucking on his empty pipe

27

he wondered how the Queen had felt about the 'loyal' ovation, as a pure German; and King George for that matter – the Kaiser's own cousin. It would be a mad war, whatever else.

'All right, Horder. It it's anything urgent, yes.' He hooked the receiver and sat very still for a few seconds looking up at Sadler. His cleanly sculpted features would perhaps never change: they would take on the patina of age but not its shape; it was his expression that showed, tonight, the fatigue of the past weeks, the late conferences at his office in the City. Fatigue and something more. 'I wonder if it would ever have mattered, Charles. If there'd been too many 'ing's.'

'It won't last long. Give it till Christmas.'

Talbot left the desk and poured some brandy, gesturing to his friend, who shook his head. 'It's different for you.'

'Is it?'

'I mean as a military historian. It makes the whole business partly academic. Except for Hugh, I agree. He'll enlist, will he?'

'Of course.'

Sadler came from a long line of soldiers and he had himself fought in South Africa before malaria had cut short his active career; since then he had consoled himself by fighting on paper and to some purpose: his first book was still accepted as the definitive history of the Boer War. Talbot had never read a word of it except the dedication, which was to himself: the specially bound copy was in the shelves here, given pride of place for this reason alone. He didn't hate war: he despised it for its intrusion on the more useful affairs of men, believing it better to build a city than to burn it down. Maybe it had been a shade brutal to tell Charles that this war would be partly academic for him; but it was true enough: in a few weeks from now he'd be setting out the armies of Europe like a glorified chess game with the rest of the armchair warriors; and young Hugh would be out there somewhere on the field, the representative of the Sadler line with the onus upon him to find further glory for them all. And from what he'd seen of the boy it was going to take some doing.

'I don't mind telling you, Charles, I'm going to keep my boys out of it if I can.'

'I wish you luck with Victor, then.'

Talbot glanced at him and away. 'They'll listen to me.'

But Charles was right. They weren't boys any more: they'd remain his sons but would never again be children. You could keep them from tumbling into the fountain-pond and later stop them from pinching apples and later still forbid them to ride a motorbike on the lawn; but there'd be nothing he could do now if they chose to swop the last of their youth for a uniform. He might hope to dissuade Aubrey: he had more sense and disliked making an effort; but if Victor went at it with his usual bull-at-a-gate abandon then Aubrey would go along to look after him, that was certain.

Sadler put away his empty pipe. 'You don't think I welcome this war, do you?'

In a moment: 'No.'

William had actually needed to consider the question and Sadler was hurt by that little interval. 'You know me better than that. I had some excitement in Africa, saw a bit of life and a bit of action, enjoyed it as much as anyone else – but I was young then. Since they put me on the shelf with the rest of the old crocks I've had as much fun writing about it – it's a game, after all, war.' He raised an arm and smoothed the back of his head and Talbot noted the gesture: he wasn't being honest with himself and no amount of gesturing could cover the bitterness in his voice. 'I ended up a major, right? But I'm a paper general with my opinions on military matters quoted in the press. Fell on my feet, you see. Comfortably off, private means, a job to work at as long as I want to – *I* don't need this war.' He found himself looking at the big globe again. 'It's going to tear all Europe apart, you realize that? I'd put the clock back if I could, put a stop to it if I had the power. But if we're going to have it then we'll need to give it all we've got. There might be a quicker way to bring an end to it than by advertising in the newspapers, you know. Let the pip-squeak Hohenzollerns see the British Empire in the field alongside France and Russia and they'll have the sense to think twice about it.'

William put down his brandy still untouched; light from the desk-lamp sent its reflection swinging across the room. 'You know the size of our army, Charles. We've quoted your figures often enough in the past week.'

'The recruiting offices are already open. The first target's a hundred thousand and they won't stop there.'

29

William threw up his hands, turning away and turning back. 'A hundred thousand what? Boys. Hot-blooded young fools spoiling for devilry.'

Knowing where his thoughts were, Charles tried to help him. 'Don't underestimate them. They see this as a challenge to their generation.'

'Then it's the failure of our own.'

Stars pricked the dark above the mass of leaves; there was no moon that he could see anywhere. He waited, his haunches on the window-sill, one leg straight and the other crooked, his head tilted back to rest on the white-painted frame, the coloured chequer-pattern of his costume catching the late glow from the sky. As the minutes passed he wondered if the light had already gone on, unseen from here because of the leaves; then he saw it, a yellow oblong shining among their tracery. It winked once and remained. Had Hugh made the signal from long habit, just as he himself was here watching for it? In the beginning, when those leaves had been much lower and you could see most of the upstairs windows of Carisbrooke, the signal had been of great significance and Pam and Vic would crowd here with him to wait for it, unable to go to bed until they were sure that Hugh had leapt the gap from the outhouse roof to the one below his window without coming a cropper or disturbing his parents (they never knew which would be worse).

There came the time of course when there was no need for Hugh to perform his daring leap, but could walk in by the front door; and the suppers in the summerhouse with a pirate's cloak across the window to hide the candlelight had been transferred to the morning-room, no longer clandestine; but for years they'd gone on stifling their laughter as if no one must hear, and Hugh had still climbed to his room by way of the lower roof, saying it was quicker anyway. And there was nearly always the signal except when they were tired or he just forgot. Tonight it had a new significance, perhaps: in a week Hugh was leaving Carisbrooke for his schoolmaster's post at Dover, where he would be 'living in', so this late flickering light could mean that a part of him was unwilling to go.

Or that could be too fanciful; Hugh was so 'deep' that you

30

often found yourself reading into things a significance that wasn't there, when you tried to imagine what he was thinking.

Under the thin foot of his costume the floor was still warm from the summer day as Aubrey slipped from the window and crossed the room to give three short taps on the wall. *Hugh's home.* But tonight there was no answer: Pam must be already asleep.

The house was quiet; he'd never known such silence, or had never been so conscious of it as he was now. Voices came occasionally, floating up through the open windows of the drawing-room; and a door closed somewhere in the Kemps' quarters above the garages, a companionable sound that sometimes set him thinking, as he fell asleep, of the little man and his pale pretty wife. His relationship with Freddie – who was 'Frederick' to all but the younger Talbots – was in a lot of ways closer than usual between a chauffeur and his employer's son, and both had contributed to it without intention; it had become woven into the scheme of things at Ashbourne since he had first trotted into the main garage and come upon the top-heavy-looking Renault with 'all its insides out', as he put it then. Freddie had been stripping the engine – this was years before the long low Daimler had purred into the drive – and by the time it was reassembled Aubrey's own stubby hands were black beyond any scrubbing: he'd taken to engines as other boys took to fishing or stamps, and Freddie had been his guide and monitor, concealing – as he'd realized later – his impatience when the small trotting figure appeared to interrupt his work.

'I'll never get these valves back, Master Aubrey, if you don't stop pokin' about, now will I?'

'But you took them out to cure the fuffing-noise, you said! Well hasn't that cured it yet?'

'But they've got to go back or we shan't ever be able to go round an' round the Circus again.' That was Piccadilly and whenever they were driving in the vicinity they had to go round and round it three times, unless there was some grown-up with them (except Mummy – she'd always let them do it).

'But what about the fuffing-noise?'

'We shan't hear that again, because I've cleaned them.'

'They don't look very clean.'

31

'They were before you got your little hands all over them again.'

Freddie in his white overalls, only his hands ever dirty, and not often. The exciting smell of oil and petrol, the shine on metal things at first funny-looking and then familiar, the mysterious shapes and maps on the whitewashed wall, later to be known as gaskets and lubrication charts. A new world had opened for him and Freddie was its king.

But it wasn't until the day of the matches that he had come to know Freddie as a real person. It had been very frightening, and therefore never forgotten. He'd found the yellow box in the woodshed, left there by old Mr Willis; the flames were magical at first and had a fierce choky smell like the 'fizzworks' Daddy and Uncle Charles let off when it was November – they were little fizzworks themselves, really, a whole yellow box of them, and he scraped them more slowly sometimes to watch for when the flame burst out at the end where the red blob was stuck on – it was the blob that made them do it, you could see that. Then the big flames began, running up the bundle of straw string that Mr Willis tied the flowers with, and he blew at them all he could but it made them worse and the smoke got in his eyes and all he could see was watery red everywhere while the heat prickled against his face and the crackling noise began and got louder and louder as he stood trying to think what ought to be done, if it would be better to run and tell someone or try hitting at it. Then the voice was shouting – *'Quick then, come on, outside!'* – and hands came for him and lifted him away into the fresh air and dumped him by a bush where he sat sobbing with fright while thumpings went on in the woodshed and the terrible crackling stopped. He couldn't see anything because of the watering and when he tried to get up he found his legs were wobbling so he just sat there saying, 'I've done it, I've done it now, I have,' which was what Cook said when she burnt things, but only cakes, not whole woodsheds. Then there was another voice and Freddie ran past him suddenly and called out in his ordinary voice as if nothing was wrong at all – 'It's all right, milady, I was just burnin' a few oily rags!' There was something about 'smoke' and 'incinerator' and Freddie said, 'Yes, milady, I'm sorry!'

It was very quiet now and he could see better, and Freddie

wiped his face and helped blow his nose and then took him along to the garage and up the wooden steps. 'We'll have to clean you up a bit before anyone sets eyes on you an' that's a fact.' Mrs Kemp and hot water and soap and a towel with blue lines on it, her pretty hair in the sunshine from the window and her hands gentle, not pushing and rubbing at him like Nanny's did.

'But you said it was you, with oily rags!' His voice was muffled by the towel. 'It was me all the time!'

Freddie crouching in front of him and looking serious like when he was listening to engines. 'We don't have to go tellin' people that, now do we? But you promise me your word of honour you'll never touch matches again, eh? You see what they can do, don't you?'

'What's – what's it like now – in the woodshed?' His mouth felt all salty and loose.

'There's no harm done, but matches can do worse than that. You could burn the whole place down, all the house and the motorcars an'—'

('Hush, Fred, he's been frightened enough, poor lamb.' – 'He's got to learn, my lovie.')

The wooden steps again and the sunshine and the bright air that didn't smell of smoke any more: he felt better now, sleepy and calm, like you felt after you'd eaten too much cake and been sick, a wonderful feeling.

He hadn't dared go near the woodshed for a long time, and was surprised to see it still standing there among the bushes. Now it was gone altogether to make space for the third garage.

It was an odd thought that only last year had he repaid that childhood debt: odd because a six-year-old would hardly be expected to recognize a moral issue. Freddie had just driven him from town in the Daimler when he caught the wing on the stone amphora at the bottom of the steps by an inch of misjudgement. The damage was slight but it made an awful racket and he knew Father was in and must have heard it.

'Shift over, Freddie, I'm driving!' He was out in a jiffy and round to the other side, trying to climb behind the wheel; but Freddie was obstinate.

'I'm not lettin' you do that!' he said, quite shocked.

'Quick, man, shift over!'

'But it was sheer bloody clumsiness an' I'm not—'

Aubrey had to push him away from the wheel and was only just in time to be seen backing the car from the steps as Father came out and stood with his hands on his hips.

Freddie was in a quiet rage beside him, hugging his knees and rocking on the seat – 'Now look here, you're not to try an' make out—'

'Shut up, Freddie!'

Father must have been busy because there was no lecture.

'Aubrey!'

'Yes, Father?'

'You won't drive the Daimler again. Quite clear?'

'Yes, Father.'

'Furthermore you'll pay for the damage out of your own pocket.'

'Now Mr Aubrey—'

'Oh do keep quiet. Yes, Father – I'm very sorry!'

'Frederick, take the car to the garage!' It was this final order that had 'capped it all', as Freddie told him afterwards. Aubrey had tried to make him see the comic side – they'd both sat there at odds with each other while Father stood over them, a figure of wrath – but Freddie wouldn't have it. The real excuse for what he persisted in calling his 'bloody clumsiness' couldn't be mentioned: the Daimler, recently acquired, was much bigger than the Renault, and he was secretly frustrated by his small stature and refused to put a cushion behind him when he drove.

It was Father himself who had furthered the sympathy between the two of them, when not long afterwards Aubrey had whizzed home on his motorbike rather late for a tennis game and left his machine propped against the steps.

'Take that thing to the garage – how often have I told you?'

'Freddie'll do it for me while I'm changing!' He was halfway up the stairs with his long legs flying.

'Come into my study.'

It had been, looking back, a good lecture, and the vibrant undertone had set the glass front of a cabinet buzzing. 'Frederick is a servant. A servant is not a slave. He gives *service* and he gives it within prescribed limits. Service is valuable and sometimes much harder to give than the mere monetary recompense offered in return by his employer, who must redress the balance by looking after his servant, by seeing that he is comfortable in his quarters and even by advising him in his private affairs if such advice is sought. There are two other factors involved: consideration and dignity. A good master will give consideration freely, recognizing fatigue or indisposition or grave private preoccupations in his servant and telling him to rest. He will also respect his dignity and take care never to assail it by the making of thoughtless and trivial demands, implying that he is a mindless robot whose services are made available by pressing a button.' The panel of glass stopped vibrating for a moment. Both of them were standing and facing each other: Father never installed himself behind the big Directoire desk on these occasions, to leave the miscreant standing; the door was always carefully closed, safeguarding the privacy of censure. His heavy eyebrows lifted suddenly – 'I'm quite aware that "Freddie" – as you call him – is happy to trot about after you three children from his own goodness of heart, but I'm not having you encourage it by leaving your disgusting contraption draped across the front of the house and dropping its noisome oil on the steps for someone else to remove. Now cut along, you're late – and watch out for Gordon's drive: he's sporting a new racket so they'll be coming at you faster today.'

In the gloom of the room he heard Father's voice at this moment, a low vibration rising through the night's calm from the open window of his study, louder than usual – he must be on the telephone. This sound, and the door's closing somewhere across in the Kemps' flat above the garages, had stirred his memory. The glow of the sky was in the window and he undressed without switching on the light, his thoughts returning uneasily to the final hours of the day. He'd decided against seeing Father to ask him what was likely to happen; Uncle Charles was with him, Charrington had said, and he would have interrupted them: it was one of Ashbourne's traditions that when those two were together in the 'Lion's Den' you didn't butt in. Uncle Charles came pretty often, sometimes bringing Aunt Louise but mostly coming alone, wandering past the summerhouse with his hands clasped loosely behind him and the short black pipe jutting out, looking up suddenly as if disturbed in his own grounds instead of theirs – 'Hello, hello! Your folk about, are they?' In the earlier days he'd sometimes fished in the pockets of his Norfolk jacket to toss up an old golf-ball – 'Catch it and you keep it! Never mind, I brought it for you anyway, found it near the links, don't tell anyone.' Or Liquorice Allsorts for Pam, only a few in a small paper bag or she'd make herself sick. 'Don't let anyone see you giving 'em to her, she's not meant to have them.' A slow wink and a wiggle of his ginger moustache, which had always delighted them.

There'd been something pleasurable about these little admonitions at first, secrecy being a joy to the young; then as they grew up they realized without thinking of it consciously that Uncle Charles had secrets of his own that he didn't share with them – or sometimes couldn't when Aunt Louise was about: his sandy head with its freckled bald patch at the front would turn suddenly as the others – Aunt Louise among them – moved up to the next croquet-hoop, and he'd change the subject. It didn't occur to them to note which subjects seemed to be taboo.

They weren't sure even now about his reticence, though it had long been clear to them that he was 'kept on a tight rein', as Pam put it. There may have been evidence of something more but they weren't curious and it was 'none of their biz'. On the few occasions when Aubrey found himself thinking of it, an idea came to him that it was something to do with Hugh. The Sadlers, as a family, were simply *different* from the Talbots; seeing them together you got the feeling they were strangers met by chance, polite to each other and that was all. You'd never see the eyes of Aunt Louise soften, as Mother's did when Father was holding forth on a pet subject and boring everyone to a frazzle; and Uncle Charles could never manage that special look of Father's – half patience and half fascination – when Mother had just 'pruned' one of his prize rose-trees almost down to the roots. (Vic had once said in a rare moment of reflection: 'You know something I've discovered? Mother and Father are *potty* about each other. They seem to *enjoy* each other's faults!' Pam had told him: 'Perhaps they don't see them as faults,' and Vic had spread out his hands – 'Well that's what I mean! They're potty!')

Through the black tracery of leaves the oblong of light had gone out. Hugh was in bed, alone in Carisbrooke except for the few servants. He would normally have stayed for a while, after a drive back from town, but tonight he'd gone flitting across the lawn to the gap in the hedge as if he were expected home. Was it because Pam had been still upset by the fuss in the streets and Vic was in a foul mood and 'Sir William was a little put out' according to Charrington? Or because Hugh had known that his father was here and preferred to go home alone? Aubrey had never seen them turn up here together, either, although there was a sameness about the way they came: Uncle Charles through the wicket-gate in the orchard, Hugh through the gap in the hedge, each to be seen wandering across the lawn at any odd time but always alone, Hugh to ask if 'Aubrey and Co. had any plans', his father to ask as casually if 'the folk were about'. They came, he remembered thinking once, as if to warm their hands at a fire.

A door opened on the floor below. The doors in Ashbourne had identity, each with a tone of its own, and this was Victor's: the handle was loose because he was always halfway through before he'd got the thing open. Very far away there were human voices, calling out together; the faint sound made him uneasy: he'd seen enough of his fellow-humans tonight. These were probably the soldiers in the barracks or a crowd in the Park too excited to go home. It occurred to him that he ought to be excited himself: England was at war and these were great times and here he was quietly going to bed in the dark, his thoughts more on the past than the present. Did it mean so little?

The sound drew him to the window and he stood listening with the unpleasant impression that he was like a night creature, his ears pricked to catch the voice of the herd. They weren't singing but just calling out, some of them whistling; and a round of cheers went up. He couldn't distinguish any actual words, and his impression was strengthened: these sounds were animal; you'd hear them in a zoo at feeding-time. But he hadn't felt this in the crowd; it was he who'd asked Freddie to go down through Whitehall so that they could all share in the excitement; and in the thick of the people, later, he'd been yelling and singing and waving a flag along with the rest of them, God knew why. Now he thought of them as animals. Perhaps that was the answer: he'd seen how easy it was to be caught up in the mood of the herd, reason thrown to the winds. Imagine *one* man dancing down the street shouting and waving a flag: he'd be arrested! In a way it was a warning: tomorrow he was going to find himself caught up in a war, not just a crowd of people, and he must learn to stand back sometimes and take a good look at things, at himself and what he was doing, give cold reason a bit of elbow-room.

A new sound came and he turned his head. A voice at his door. 'Aub'ey?'

He crossed quickly and opened it and the light from the passage flooded in and for a moment dazzled him.

'Can't sleep, Pom-Pom?' He put his arm round her shoulders as he'd done so often in this doorway: she used to get nightmares from scoffing too much at suppertime.

'I've been talking to Vic.' She leaned her dark head against him; the air was warm but she was shivering.

'Have you?' This was why she hadn't answered when he'd tapped on the wall.

'He's going to join the Army.'

His arm tightened, trying to stop the shivering. 'You know old Vic – it's just a new craze and he'll change his mind soon enough.' But the distant voices still kept up, and seemed louder now.

'No. He won't. He meant it.' She was far from tears; her voice was quite calm. 'That means you'll go too. So it's all over now.'

'But that's nonsense—'

'No. It's over now. All we ever knew.'

III

Far across the green expanse of the lawns a white figure moved and Tom Follett looked up from the butterfly, squinting against the sun. Even from here he could see it was Lady Eleanor because of the parasol, and he began breathing quickly and looked down again at the butterfly and tried to tell himself she wasn't there.

A long way off he could hear tinkly metal sounds, Mr Kemp busy in the garages. Nearer, on the other side of the rose walk, Mr Willis was telling one of the under-gardeners to go and turn on the sprinklers, *but on'y in the shade, mind, down along the borders over there.*

Or you'd burn things. Mr Willis had shown him how a drop of water on a leaf with the sun shining through it could burn like a magnifying glass. He thought: When it flies away, I'll go and tell her. The sun was hot on the back of his neck; the broom, made of twigs, like the ones witches rode on, lay beside him, its tips green with the cut grass that clung to them. I wish I was you and I'd fly away. Or you and I'd ride off like the witches do.

He'd not had thoughts like that since he'd come here. The last two weeks he'd been so happy he couldn't eat properly or sleep properly because there was no time to think of such things with so much to look at and marvel on. At the Orphanage he'd had thoughts like that every day, wishing he was the bakerman's horse or a cloud or a bird so as to get away. But when he'd first come down this roadway – it was called the *drive* – and seen all the flowers and bushes like peacocks and then the house with its chimneys going right up to the sky a very strange feeling had come to him and it made him stop and shut his eyes for a minute till he'd got over it. It wasn't just because everything was so beautiful and green and wide after the red bricks and the hard mud playground; something was telling him he'd always be here now, all his life, for ever. Did people know things like this, of a sudden, and did it feel like it did with him, like drinking

39

all the sunshine up until you were giddy? A funny idea had come to his mind when he'd stood there: this was what it must feel like to have a mother.

Of course these things didn't last. Only two weeks and now he was going.

The gaudy wings were lifting softly up and down making shadows on the cool stone path; Mr Willis said this kind was called a Red Admiral and they did this with their wings to catch all the sunshine they could till they'd collected enough of it to fly with; it was like winding themselves up, he said. It must be true because suddenly it flew away and the warmth rushed into his throat and his eyes stung so he got up quick and just began walking across the grass, leaving the broom where it was. He'd tried two or three times to screw himself up tight enough to go and tell her but he'd not managed it so this time if he just kept on walking and didn't let himself think about it he'd be all right.

It seemed such a long way and by the time he'd crossed the first lawn – the big one, as big and smooth as a green lake – and the stone path and then the second one where the roses grew in a crescent (it was called an *arbour*) his legs were as tired as if he'd walked miles. Lady Eleanor was on the long cane chair, resting with her eyes closed; the lacy parasol made a pattern of little lights on her face and her sprigged-muslin dress and he thought how peaceful she looked, and young, though she was the mother of Mister Aubrey and the others. The cane stool was by the chair, with a rose-patterned dish on it, the spoon resting in the frothy puddle that was all that was left of the ice-cream. (They said she was delicate and ate a lot of ice-cream on doctor's orders but Mr Willis said with his quiet wheezy laugh that you'd never keep her away from it, doctors or no.) But she looked delicate, with her pale gold hair and her thin hands, like a china ornament. He stood with the sun hot on his back, wondering if she was asleep: she wouldn't have heard him come up on the grass. Perhaps he ought to go away again quietly or she'd get a shock if she opened her eyes and saw him there right in front of her; but that would mean having to get his courage up all over again and he didn't know how he could do it. Nothing had happened yet; everything was the same and he was going to be here for ever; but once he'd put it into words it would all be different. There was a shiver down his back in spite of the sunshine against it.

'What is it?'

He caught his breath; he'd been looking away from her at the white clouds in the distance over the chimneys and hadn't noticed her open her eyes; they watched him peacefully, pale blue in the shade of the parasol.

'I'm sorry to disturb you, ma'am.' (He couldn't ever remember to call her 'milady'; it had always been 'ma'am' at the place before.)

'Sit down,' she said gently. 'Sit on the grass and talk to me.'

'I'm goin' for a soldier, ma'am.' It came out in a rush and the sun seemed to go dark but he'd said it now and it was over with and he thought bitterly: Now I can start getting my ideas straight. (The Reverend Jones at the Orphanage had so often told him that, with his cold scaly hand tapping him at the back of his neck: *You're a young man now, you must realize, and you'll have to start getting some of your ideas straight, won't you?*)

'Sit on the grass,' she said. 'I can't see you with the sun in my eyes. That's better.'

He sat as respectfully as he could with his legs doubled under him. Mr Willis had told him: Her ladyship'll be asking you to sit an' talk to her if you go near, she likes talkin' to people, but you just tell her you've got jobs to do, polite, mind, or she'll be wastin' your precious time like she tries with everyone else. You can tell her there's waterin' to be done, for she can't abide seein' flowers suffer wi' thirst.

But that couldn't be helped: it was him that wanted to talk. Yet he'd nothing more to say now; it had been done.

'What did you want to tell me?' she asked vaguely, smiling to him.

It was easy enough the second time; there was a sort of nasty pleasure in it as if there was someone to blame. 'I'm goin' in the Army, ma'am.'

'But you're much too young.'

'No, ma'am, beggin' your pardon. I'm gone nineteen years.'

She watched him so steadily, her eyes half closed against the strong light, that he had to look down. 'That's still very young. You're Tom, aren't you?'

'Yes, ma'am.'

Her delicate fingers picked at her dress; he couldn't tell if she was thinking about it or giving her mind to something else altogether; you never could.

'What are we going to do with all those puppies that Cleopatra had, Tom? Was it five, or six?'

'Five of them, ma'am.'

'Yes. Now I'll tell you a secret. I'm going to give one of them to you, for your own. One of the boy ones. You could call him Alexander.'

'Thank you, ma'am, I'm sure.' A few days ago, before he'd heard all the talk and seen the giant posters in the streets and made up his mind, he wouldn't have known how to thank her, there wouldn't have been words, a dog of his own to belong to, something he'd never dreamed of. His rough fingers tugged at the grass as if he was trying to hurt it. 'But I wouldn't be here to look after it now I'm goin'.'

She nodded gently. 'But that's what I mean, Tom. You can't leave Alexander!' He didn't know how to explain; she didn't seem to understand; so he said nothing. She gazed at him with her faraway eyes for a while. 'And what do your parents say? Will *they* allow you to be a soldier?'

He looked up with a blank face, staring at her without meaning to; then he said with a kind of quick laugh on his breath, 'Oh yes, ma'am.'

She seemed puzzled. 'But why must you go?'

He stood up and faced her awkwardly with his thin wrists sticking out of his sleeves and his thin neck jutting forwards from his jersey, their young skin a deep pink, almost brown, from their two weeks of sunshine.

'A lot of people are goin', ma'am. Mister Aubrey and Mister Victor, an' others here.' Suddenly impatient with her he said, 'I'm as old as them.' He didn't want to be given puppies; there was enough to keep him here as it was, the whole world, here, without that.

'Yes,' she said slowly, and turned her head, the white parasol tilting. Starlings chattered along the eaves with their dry pebbly sound; the leaves of the creeper made a blood-red cascade in the hot afternoon light; many windows were open and at one of them a figure was hitched, cleaning the glass with slow movements as if in thought. Lady Eleanor turned her head away from the house. 'Yes, they are going too, I know.' She wasn't looking any more at Tom and her tone was measured in the way a child would have when reading aloud. 'You must remember that there is always a place for you here when you come back.'

He'd not thought of that. Once in uniform and marching away like you saw them all over London now, you'd be gone, that's all, just gone.

'Thank you, ma'am.'

She said nothing and he shifted his feet but she didn't look up at him again so he just turned and went all the way back and picked up the broom and took it to the shed where it belonged.

The bright sun sparked on the brass trumpets as the band went thumping past the crowds, the beat of the big drum sending phantom cannon-fire through the chasm of the street where it seemed a wind stirred all the little flags though the air was still; and behind the band came the army, an undisciplined flood of boys and older men in open shirts and starched collars and black clerical jackets and pepper-and-salt suits – a bobbing tide of cloth caps and boaters and trilbies and bare tousled heads flowing between the ranks of the whirling flags and the bright-eyed faces of the girls. Fifteen minutes ago the band had set off from the barracks with a handful of youths strutting after it and now the whole length of the street was filled with them and still their number swelled as the Hamelin music led them on and the people blocking the pavements cheered them as they went their way, singing and laughing and waving to the girls while in their wake the streets grew empty as if robbers had been here.

At the Town Hall the band left them, marching away at ease with the trumpets slung and dangling, caps coming off and handkerchiefs mopping at the sweat; the August sky lay inert across the roofs and in the bronze light they stood and talked and swopped cigarettes and loosened their collars and hooked their jackets at the shoulder, the clerks, milkmen, chemists and accountants, the boys, the men, the sons and the lovers herded together in the heat of noon, a rag-tag army, renegade from the business of the capital and committed to the business of war.

Its god stared down at them, his finger pointing. *Your King and Country need YOU!*

'All right, mate, we're comin'!'

'Well why don't they bloody well let us in?'

'You in a hurry are you, chum? I been here since nine this mornin', not had a peck to eat!'

'Bastards, I say!'

'What d'you expect? There's thousan's here, they can't—'

'I mean them German bloody bastards! You wait till we—'

'Oh *them*. Ne' mind, we're on our way.'

'Well why won't they let us in?'

The news of Mons had brought many of them here. Until today the war had been a paper thing, a summer storm of posters in the streets, a carnival staged for the parks where the brass bands played and the youths of the city were paraded and drilled with walking-sticks and wooden guns slanting at their shoulders, puppets in an open-air charade; now there was word from across the sea: *Disaster at Mons. British Expeditionary Force driven back by massed German armies. Losses feared heavy.*

The war was real.

'I've got a brother out there.' A fag-end dropped, a foot smudging it out.

'Thought you'd keep 'im company, did you?'

'If it ain't too late.'

The double doors swung open again and they surged forward and again were held back.

'What the hell are they playing at in there?'

'Why don't we try Kensington?'

'It's worse there. I passed it earlier – like a flypaper. We'll just have to stick it out.'

A woman came dodging among them, her eyes darting and her thin hands pushing them aside. '*Billy! Billy!*' They tried to give her room.

'Hey, there's your Mum!'

'*Sh!* Don't let her see me for God's sake!'

'You'll catch it, you will!'

'Shuddup, can't you? Face the other way.'

A bus came nosing past and they were pressed against the wall of the Town Hall, swaying and trying to keep their feet.

'Pity on me corns, eh mate?'

44

'Sorry – it's such a frightful crush, isn't it?'

They pressed their hands along the side of the double-decker to save getting pushed against it.

'Who's he, then? That toff?'

''Ow should I know?'

'Blimey, they take all sorts, don' they?'

'Kitchener's not fussy.'

Billy! Billy!

'Take my advice, you'll go off home like a good boy.'

'You give me away an' I'll bash you! Once I'm signed on there's nothin' she can do, see?'

The conductor of the bus grinned down at them from the upper deck. 'I got room for one more on top! Anyone want to change 'is mind?'

'Come on down along of us an' be a man!'

'I signed on a week ago!' The bus lurched and he gripped the rail.

'What you doin' up there then?' They had to yell at him now as the huge thing gathered speed.

'They got no uniform yet – no rifles, no nothink! You're wastin' your time, you lot!'

'But didn't they let you—'

He was too far away now, waving to them, his ticket-punch flashing in the sun.

'Well that's a bloody turn-up, that is!'

'Don't you worry, we'll get in there if we have to break the doors down!'

'Say, you guys should get yourselves organized, for Christ sake!'

'Where are you from then, chum?'

'The States, where else? Look, is this the only place in all London where you can sign-on?'

'Well there's Buckingham Palace – ask for a bloke called George an' mention my name.'

'You kiddin'? I'm Sam Quincey, who're you boys?'

'Wiggy Bennett. This is 'Arry Ross.'

'Put it there – pleased to meet you – but you know somethin'? You really should get yourselves organized, huh?'

The big double-doors opened again and those on the steps struggled through.

The room was large and all the windows were open but it was like breathing treacle in here and there was hardly any space you could find to stand in. Posters covered the walls, swords and Union Jacks and pictures of soldiers marching. THIS IS OUR FLAG! TAKE UP THE SWORD OF JUSTICE! YOUR KING AND COUNTRY NEED *YOU*! Flies buzzed round the white china lampshades and at the three desks the recruiting-sergeants stood with their batons, sweat running down their faces.

'All right then, come on, you next! Name?'

'Sid Marks—'

'Marks, Sidney, come on, get it right!'

At the next desk they were being handed the Bible to touch and all the others craned to watch what was going on. They listened fascinated to the mystic ritual that would turn an ordinary man into a soldier of the King. A middle-aged officer with rimless spectacles and the pinched face of a parson was reading from a sheet of printed paper:

'I swear to serve His Majesty the King, his heirs and his successors and the generals and officers set over me by His Majesty the King, his heirs and his successors, so help me God!' He glanced timidly across their watching faces. 'Now please repeat those words after me. I swear to serve . . .'

Their obedient drone filled the room.

'Name? Come on, don't worry about what's 'appenin' over there! *Name?*' He'd been at it all day and he'd be at it all day tomorrow and the next day till this lot was done and then there'd be another lot and another lot after that, you got sick of the sight of them, worse than sheep at a sheep-dip, some of them swearing they was nineteen years old and staring you in the eye as bold as brass, my God, they'd not got their nappies off yet, poor little perishers, some of them swearing they was under thirty, you could see the dye running down from their hair with the sweat, what had come over them, that age, playing at soldiers? 'Come on, religion?'

'I don't rightly know—'

'Church of England then. Trade or profession? Come on, 'ow d'you earn your livin'?'

'I'm a rag-picker—'

'Refuse-dealer. Right, you next – name? Come on!'

46

They stood assembled in the presence of their flag and from the wall their god stared down as he did from a thousand street-corners of their city.

A CALL TO ARMS

An addition of 100,000 men to His Majesty's Regular Army is immediately necessary in the present grave National Emergency. Lord Kitchener is confident that this appeal will be at once responded to by all who have the safety of our Empire at heart.

'Name? Come on then!'

By Christ he could do with a beer.

Suddenly she was among them, a plump shabby woman all in black with the brim of her hat turned down low at the front so that she had to hold her squat head back like a bird with a heavy beak as she peered about her.

'You can't come in 'ere, missus!'

Her big black eyes discovered him and she waved the piece of paper for him to see. 'I've brought it, Sergeant, like the officer said!'

'You can't—' Then he remembered. She'd been here three days ago, and not the only one – you'd think that every mother's son in England was running away from home. 'Beg pardon, sir, will you – er—?'

'Yes, Sarn't. Take this desk and keep some sort of order.' He eased his way to the edge of the close-packed throng. 'Follow me, madam, will you?'

She waddled after him, white of face and with her large eyes looking at no one. In a corner of the room he found her a dusty chair but she wouldn't sit down; the heat and the struggle of getting here had left her panting but somehow she found breath enough to deliver her troubles almost without a pause, fanning a smell of perspiration towards him with the piece of paper—

'You wasn't the officer I spoke to before, he was another one, much thinner an' wore glasses, but you'll do, I know you'll 'elp me. Me name is Mrs Bennett an' me son Wilfred come 'ome the other day an' told me as 'ow 'e'd joined up in your army, an' 'im me only boy an' me a widow, see, an' I knew it was this place because I found the bus-ticket in 'is pocket, after,

47

an' the officer told me, when I come 'ere, there was nothin' to be done unless o'course my Wilfred was under the age, which 'e *is*, if you was to look at 'im you'd see for yourself—'

'Yes, Mrs Bennett, I understand.' He took out his handkerchief and held it to his face as if to dab at the perspiration, taking a deep breath of filtered air. 'They asked you for your son's birth certificate? And this is it?'

She offered it to him tentatively, half afraid to trust him with something so precious, her large black eyes fixed on him in mute prayer. He glanced at the date and turned the certificate towards the light, finally to hold it higher against the flat glare from the windows.

'You can see for yourself, sir, can't you?' Her whisper was desperate.

He looked down, giving her back the certificate. 'Mrs Bennett, I quite understand your feelings, as a widow with only one son; it means you'll have nobody else at home with you for a while.' He forced himself to hold the gaze of her dark and now hopeless eyes, conscious of his prescribed cruelty. 'But you must have friends and other relatives, good neighbours and other people like that to help you, I'm quite sure. You should try to feel proud that your boy has answered, of his own free will, the very desperate call of his country. We need these brave young men, you know, if we're to beat the Germans; and the more there are, the sooner they'll be home again, you see that, don't you?'

In a moment her voice crept out: 'I thought, with the certificate, you see ...'

He obliged himself to put his hand on the moist and fleshy arm, turning her gently towards the doors. 'Mrs Bennett, someone has made an alteration on the certificate, and it's easy to detect. If you'll take my advice, you'll burn it and report it as lost, and apply for another copy. You may want it on future occasions, and it'll save you a lot of trouble.'

The doors were letting the next group inside and he cleared a passage for her as best he could. The new arrivals gathered about the desks, straightening their jackets and ties, aware of officialdom here.

'Name? Look sharp now!'

'Braithwaite.'

48

'What? Spell it to the officer!'

A boy with a red face, still puffing from the battle in the doorway, eyed the beefy sergeant across the heads of the others. 'My oath, if they're all like him I think I'll cut and run while the goin's good.'

'*Sh!* He'll have your balls off!'

'That's what I mean.'

Another bus went past the building, its noise drumming on the windows.

'Right – name? Come on!'

'I want to enlist in the 3rd Battalion, Duke of Lancaster's Regiment.'

'Like to pick an' choose, would you? Come on, let's 'ave your name an' quick about it!'

'There's no need to shout, now, you've got no authority over civilians.' A short man but stocky, arms folded and his bright eyes prepared to stare the sergeant out. 'Just see if there's vacancies in the 3rd Duke of Lancaster's and put me in with them an' you can shout to your heart's content. Bargain, is it?'

The big room was hushed. His mild tones had carried to every ear, and even the sergeant lowered his voice, maybe realizing how effective it could be.

'If you want to enlist in 'Is Majesty's Armed Forces then you can give me your name an' details, right? If you don't want to enlist then you'll find the door over there, right? Now what's it to be?'

The officer at the desk had stopped writing, conscious of the hush throughout the room. 'What's the problem, Sarn't?'

'This man wants to pick 'is regiment, sir. 3rd Dukes. I've told 'im—'

'All right.' He turned to the civilian. 'You've got a brother there, or friends or something?'

'Yes, sir.'

The officer dragged a different exercise-book across and steadied the pot of ink. 'They're under complement, yes, we can fit you in with them.' He took up his pen.

'I've got your word, have I, sir? It's important to me.'

'Good Lord, if we get any more like you we'll still be here when the war's over. Look, here's the battalion and regiment, top of the page, fair enough? Now let's get on with it.'

49

'Thank you, sir.' He looked dutifully to the sergeant.

'Name?'

'Kemp.'

'Christian name?'

'Frederick.'

'Age?'

'Twenty-nine.' He began staring the sergeant out.

'You sure?'

'Quite sure.'

'Trade or profession?'

'Gardener.'

'Right, stand—'

'What's his religion, Sarn't?'

'Religion?' He was sweating with anger: the short-arsed little bugger had so narked him he'd clean forgot about religion and the bloody captain wouldn't let it go, not him. 'Come on!'

'Protestant.'

'C of E, sir. Right – stand over there with the others. Next! Name? Sharp now, we've 'ad our time wasted enough as it is!'

Kemp found a place among the packed bodies and stood with his arms folded and his eyes on the chipped plaster dado of the wall. Well he'd done it now: another few minutes and he'd be leaving here a soldier. Gwen had woken up crying in the night and he'd tried to tell her what was in his mind: the British Army was being smashed up at Mons, men like himself with wives like Gwen, and they wanted help out there and they'd got to have it and quick. Certainly there were crowds of boys round the recruiting-stations every day but that didn't mean some of the older men couldn't go and help them did it? Did she want everyone to stay home and let a bunch of kids go out there and take on the whole of Germany?

He'd gone on a lot about it, trying to make her see, but all she said into the hot damp pillow was: 'You're going because the boys are going. To look after them.'

She meant the Talbot boys. 'Isn't that just what I'm tryin' to say, love? They're two of the kids I'm talkin' about, an' who's goin' to look after them if some of the older men don't go out there with them?'

She'd said, with a certainty that would have made a denial

50

look foolish, 'You'd never have wanted to join up if those two weren't going to. Just those two.'

Now he was here among the 'kids' he'd talked about, a lively lot and younger-looking than even he'd imagined, some of them with down on their chins, too young yet for a razor blade, their eyes full of wonder no matter what they looked at, even that poor old windbag with the stripes on his arm. Thank the Lord there were a handful of grown men here to make up the weight or you'd get a nasty feeling that the only ones the army could get its hands on were those too young to know what they were doing. The Talbot boys weren't here, of course: they'd put in for commissions right away, the day after they'd all got back from the fancy-dress ball, and last week they'd been sent their papers and Mister Victor was so cock-a-hoop that no one could have put on a glum face; Mister Aubrey wasn't so noisy, you wouldn't expect it, but he'd cleaned up his motorbike till you wouldn't know it from new – they were allowed to use them if they wanted to, on home stations.

'I've never seen such a shine on her, never!'

He'd given his easy smile. 'You can do a lot with some Brasso and a bit of pride, Freddie: You taught me that. And it's all the rage, where I'm going, to shine everything up.'

'Mister Victor seems pleased.'

'He's hysterical! I'm only going along to keep him out of trouble.'

'That a fact?'

'Well no, not altogether, I suppose.' He was folding the dusters and stowing them back in the tool-kit. 'We've got a war on our hands and the sooner we get out there the better.'

It was then, in that split second, Freddie had made up his mind. It had been bothering him ever since the boys had put in for service and he couldn't very well talk it over with Gwen because the thought of leaving her was the biggest argument against it; on the other hand, those poor blokes were getting what looked like quite a pasting over in France and the posters were up all over the town, you couldn't avoid them, couldn't help thinking you shouldn't be driving about in a Daimler and cooling your heels outside Harrod's and Fortnum's while there were those men fighting as hard as they could to keep the

Germans clear of the Channel; it made you feel ashamed. On the other hand again, he was well over thirty years of age and they wouldn't take him on if they knew, but that wouldn't stop you getting in if you'd made up your mind, as he'd learned quick enough when he was talking to the other chauffeurs in town. So he'd been on a see-saw for the past few weeks, as you might say; then there was the day he'd seen Mister Aubrey fretting away at his motorbike, and that was that. Twenty-one, but still a boy for all that, studying at the University, no different from school, really, nothing much on his mind but enjoying himself in the garage with a few spanners and an oily rag, flying off to parties and dancing half the night. Yet it had come out as calm as you like – 'We've got a war on our hands and the sooner we get out there the better.'

It had been a kind of revelation, like when you find yourself in a church and look up and see the coloured windows suddenly. It was the 'we' that had done it, the sooner *we* get out there. *They'd* not started the damn' war, boys like him, but they saw it had got to be stopped and they were quite ready to go out there and do it.

He looked down from the chipped dado to the faces around him, all of them keen as mustard to 'do their bit', as the posters put it. Say one thing, you could find yourself in worse company than this.

'Name? Come on!'

Poor old devil, too old for soldiering any more and busting himself for a beer.

Trade or profession? He'd said gardener, not chauffeur, or they'd have him traipsing up and down in lorries behind the lines; he'd have to be where the young Talbots were, right at the front, if he was to look after them properly.

At the next desk they were touching the Book.

I swear to serve His Majesty the King, his heirs and his successors and the generals and officers set over me . . .

The gold hair streamed from the brush, whispering.

'You'll send me to sleep, Kitty.'

'Should I stop, milady?'

'Not yet. Another ten times.'

Kitty smiled and raised the silver brush, catching sight of

52

her own face in the mirror and thinking, I'll never be as beautiful. Her hair was just brown and not nearly so fine as this. She swept the brush down again slowly, drawing out the soft waterfall whisper. Her mistress lay still on the *chaise-longue*, delicate hands sleeping in her lap, small feet curled on the silk brocade.

'Just another ten, Kitty.'

The girl smiled again. She always said that. Kitty herself was as artful in the same way every morning, especially in winter when the floor was going to be cold and the water cold in the jug, counting silently up to ten before she pushed down the bedclothes and braved it all . . . and then another ten . . . until sometimes her father came in, smart in his striped butler's waistcoat, clucking and 'looking daggers' and fetching the big jug and pretending he was going to pour it over her as she tumbled out squealing.

The brush sighed through the gold, leaving a shine of candlelight; at this hour it was always candles, never the electricity.

'More tomorrow, Kitty.' It was better than saying they must stop: that would be unbearable for them both, almost especially for the girl, who knew that the last slow stroke of the brush meant the ending of the day; tomorrow would be as nice but why couldn't a day go on and on for ever? Then there'd be no water-jug or breakfast in the noisy kitchen with Cook bustling and Elsie chattering about Douglas Fairbanks until she was chased out to do the grates.

'Goodnight, milady.'

'Sweet dreams, child.' The pale blue eyes watched her in the mirror. 'Are you warm enough in bed?'

'Oh yes, thank you.' This question, so often put to her at this hour, didn't seem strange even tonight when every window was wide open so that one could breathe; it was true that Lady Eleanor never seemed to know what time of the year it was (Cook had to make ice-cream even when the frost was spiky on the window-panes), but that had nothing to do with the question; it just meant sleep well, be comfy, see you in the morning.

Kitty slipped to the door, the little rose on her bodice blooming and fading from candlelight to shadow; perhaps it was why everyone thought milady was 'a little vague at times' – it was because they didn't understand that it wasn't what she said that counted, but the meaning behind it.

When the door was closed Eleanor took the vellum diary from the bureau, finding the pen and pausing to wonder at the blue and amber iridescence of the ink-coated nib, then writing with the fluent strokes about whose sureness there was nothing vague at all.

I bring you a troubling day, as they mostly are, of late. Victor going loudly about the house, not boisterously in his usual fashion but almost angrily as if in defiance of us all. Has he for so long been straining at his childhood leash, eager for freedom? It is how he thinks of it, I know very well – as freedom; I shall pray against his disillusionment, but perhaps uselessly, for it is inevitable that with his young life burdened by the harsh commands of generals, colonels and their like, he will wish back again the days when the gentler entreaties of an elder brother appeared so onerous. Even it might be hoped that he will shy so fiercely at military discipline that they will push him out as an incorrigible nuisance. My fears are greater, alas, for Aubrey; he gets on so well with people and so enjoys obliging them that they will find the most irksome of tasks for him. All I ask and pray is that both, in the days of judgement now upon us, may be spared.

Light fanned suddenly across the ceiling and she heard the sound of the car. Frederick was bringing William home, so very late again, from his office, and perhaps for the last time, since Frederick had enlisted and was awaiting summons. Even Tom had offered his child's heart and puny sinews to the service of the country.

I must confess to you that today I did two very stupid things – I would call them cruel save that cruelty implies intention. Young Tom, who came here so recently from an orphanage, approached me with the news – half-doleful and half-brave – that he is 'going for a soldier', as he quaintly put it. First, I offered him a puppy – you remember that Cleopatra littered a week ago – hoping to tempt him from his thoughts of leaving us; I should have seen that his young mind was already quite made up, and that it would only be hurtful to offer him a gift he must refuse. Second, I took him for another of our undergardeners, their looks being alike, though I had his name correctly, and asked if his parents would allow his going to the war. Was he hurt more by my ignorance of him or by the reminder of his being an orphan? I dare not think. Yet the boy, for all his scrawny looks and mildness, has endurance in him, for he made no attempt to point out my error. Perhaps, after all, those valiant men in France will welcome so stout a brother-in-arms.

It hadn't rained in the night but the trees were weeping at daybreak, their leaves gathering the mist and dropping tears along the paving-stones where the paths bordered the lawns.

The household was up early and Cook's shrill tones were heard before their usual time as she chased the rest of the staff from 'her' kitchen before they'd had time to enjoy a proper breakfast. There was no extra work for them today: the last guest had gone and no more were due; it was simply that Cook habitually took upon herself the duties of herald, so affected was she by the moods of the household, and at times of drama or excitement her cries would frighten even the starlings from the roof.

Sir William was off to Fleet Street before eight o'clock, driving the Crossley himself: in the past week the official *communiqués* from the battle fronts had become confusing and the staff of *The Courier* had their work cut out to sift fact from conjecture, to substantiate the wildest reports and to present the best picture they could of the events across the Channel without letting it be seen that their readers were, by governmental order, to be misled. At a conference yesterday Sir William had called an under-secretary 'a disgrace to his post' and walked out, leaving someone else to shut the door. The information services were at war with themselves, one faction pointing out that it was news of disaster that filled the recruiting-stations, such was the mood of the country, another claiming that reports – however true – of heavy losses would spread alarm and despondency. In answer to his chief editor's inquiry as to the outcome of the conference Sir William had said in his leonine undertone, 'We can print what news we like, providing it's not the truth!' Charles, now working in the Bureau of Propaganda, had been the first to enlighten him on this state of affairs, drawing on his military knowledge and giving him, in the privacy of William's study, an estimation of the Allied fortunes that differed tragically from official reports. Their forces, driven back from Liège, Mons, Charleroi and the Marne by the more massive German armies, were everywhere on the

55

defensive; but the truth of these catastrophes must be withheld or at best made palatable by talk of 'strategic withdrawals', a 'well-ordered straightening of the line', and 'resolute holding-actions'; so for William it was the more galling to have Charles's experienced opinions at his service while the edicts of the Defence of the Realm Act decreed them unprintable in terms of the 'public good'. 'By God, Charles, if England's strong enough to send her sons out there by the hundred thousand then she's strong enough to be told what's happening to them! Or are we just throwing them into the sea and turning our backs on them – is that what they deserve?'

An hour after the Crossley left the Manor it was followed by the Daimler, the early sun glowing on the dark-blue bodywork as it turned through the gates and vanished. From her window Pam watched it go; Freddie was at the wheel and her brothers in the back (Aubrey had been forbidden to drive it since he'd bashed the stone vase by the steps). She'd meant to go with them into town but had slept too late and they hadn't disturbed her. For this she was angry with herself to the point of tears: there weren't many days left for her to be with them, and they'd think she didn't care.

In the big car there was silence for most of the way and the only conversation was between Aubrey and Kemp. Victor was in the same mood that had lasted for weeks now and people were getting bored with him, choosing to let him talk if he felt like it but not responding; for almost any subject was soon turned to 'the big day' that was coming, by which he meant the day when he'd be ordered to report to barracks.

Aubrey had told him once, in a rare moment of impatience: 'We know you're going, and so am I – in case you're forgetting it – and you may have the Hun on the run single-handed before you've been out there a week; but despite the pain in the neck we can sometimes be to our family they're going to miss us, and they're not looking forward to "the big day" as much as you are. So for the sake of decency just dry up about it in front of the others, there's a good chap.'

It hadn't done much good but there were times when Vic seemed to realize for himself that he was hurting people, especially Mother, and did his best to talk about something else. But the mood in general remained, and Aubrey found

56

himself trying to fathom it. You'd call it defiance, but what had the kid got to feel defiant about? Father had made his expected attempt to talk them out of going but only in the form of his own opinions, not as an order that had to be defied.

'You know what's happening in the world? You'll please suffer me to explain.' They were in his study, each in an arm-chair: there was no suggestion that they were 'on the carpet' for anything they'd done wrong. 'The world has come into the hands of barbarians. I don't mean the Kaiser – he's a Prussian peacock full of his own fine feathers but from the most informed reports he's been dead against going to war. And I don't mean our own King George, a peace-loving chap if ever there was one. I mean the rag-tag-and-bobtail gang of cut-throat dictators and presidents and pint-sized kings and their puffed-up generals who think that by turning Europe upside down they can come up with a bigger chunk of territory than they've got at the moment. Put it briefly, they're going to start a fire and loot the place while everyone else is busy putting it out. These dangerous grab-alls are supported by armies – conscript and volunteer – of men who can't see farther than the flag they're waving in front of their noses and who think this war is going to be like the last – a torchlight tattoo with proud banners and flashing sabres and a bucketful of brass medals at the end of it.' He swung away and swung back, looking down at them in turn, his silence subduing them. When he spoke again his voice was a low vibration. 'It won't be like that, this time. You will both be lucky to come out of it alive.' He looked down, away from them. 'I don't pretend I can stop your going. I think you'll go. But don't rush into this lunatic's nightmare with any visions of a glorious crusade. Don't let yourselves be swept up by the hysteria without stopping to *think*. Give it a few days. Give *me* those few days. That's all I ask of you both.'

Aubrey had been the more affected by this appeal; Father had confirmed his own self-counsel of the night before when he had stood alone in his darkened room and seen that if he were to be caught up in this war he must learn to stand back and take a good look at things, give reason a bit of elbow-room. But, leaving the study together, they'd not spoken a word, and by the end of the day Vic had put in for a commission. Aubrey had used those few hours as he had promised himself, lying among the sweet grasses of the orchard, its leaves shading his eyes; but his thoughts couldn't stray far from a central theme: if Vic enlisted he'd have to go too, and would have to go at the same time in the hope of their staying together in the same unit. All he could do for Father was to understand that he wouldn't be rushing into it with any visions of glory but simply the idea of looking after his young idiot brother.

'Where first, Mr Aubrey?'

'What? Savile Row.'

Today was the final fitting unless Vic wanted something altered again: he'd been driving old Cosgrove mad up to now, changing his mind about the shade of the cloth and the cut of the lapels and the colour of the silk lining, until Aubrey had told him in front of the tailor: 'We're going to a battlefield, not a fancy-dress ball.' Cosgrove was working late at night as it was, with half his customers yelling out for uniforms.

Kemp opened the glove-compartment and found a cigarette, watching them go into the shop before he lit up. They wouldn't have minded; that was why he didn't take it for granted; what wouldn't do for Sir William wouldn't do for them either, that was how he looked at it. Normal times he didn't think to catch a smoke on the sly like some of the drivers did; but it was meant to calm the nerves and he'd enough on his mind just now. The thing that worried him the most was whether he'd been firm enough with that officer: it was all very well him saying the Lancasters were under complement and he could fit him in, it still wasn't a certainty.

He drew the smoke into his lungs. They'd look well, them two lads, in their uniforms, Mr Aubrey was the height for it and his brother had what you'd call an athletic figure, what with all his tennis and dashing about. They'd be proud of them at the Manor. Never so proud as he'd been of himself, though, couple of days ago when he'd mentioned to Mr Aubrey as how he'd been to sign on – that'd surprised him, that had.

'But you never told anyone! What gave you that crazy idea?'

'Well I dunno, sir. I'd feel a bit useless hangin' about the place with everyone out there doin' their bit.'

'Then we might see something of each other.'

'Bound to. It's the same battalion – 3rd Duke of Lancaster's, that's what you told me, isn't it?'

'But what marvellous luck! You know, it won't be so bad out there after all!'

Been really pleased, you couldn't mistake it. Made him feel he'd done the right thing. But there was still the worry: if that blinkin' captain didn't make sure he was put in the 3rd Dukes the whole thing would go for nothing, because Gwen was right as usual, he'd never have chucked up a damn' good job after all these years with people who'd looked after him and Gwen as if they were in the family, never in his life, if them two boys weren't going.

Should have been firmer with that blasted officer, told him it'd got to be the Dukes or nothing, take it or leave it. He tossed the fag into the gutter. Calm the nerves? They made you a bloody sight worse.

'Charles, how *can* you say that!'

'I've said it.' He scraped the ash from his pipe into the onyx bowl on the sill of the window-bay, a habit he knew she disliked. He did a lot of things she disliked but was under no illusion about it: they were not gestures of independence but of revolt. 'What did you expect me to do? I can't *order* the boy to enlist, can I?' This was the third argument they'd had since Hugh had gone off to his school at Dover just as he'd planned and as if the war didn't exist.

'It's becoming so embarrassing!' Louise turned away from him again and pouted in profile against the windows, a little trick she'd adopted since changing her coiffure to the Grecian style, which he much admired. It sometimes occurred to him at times of despondency – usually during the period of depression after a bout of malaria – that the one consolation to temper his manifold regrets was that he had married, at least, a beautiful woman. 'In Fortnum and Mason's this morning Lady Wendholme said she'd heard that Hugh had joined one of the "élite" regiments and was eager to know which one. What could I say?'

'What did you say?'

She turned as if slighted. 'That he was still not decided.' She kept her voice low because of the servants, her rose-bud lips discreetly ejecting the words like stones discovered in glacé cherries.

59

'Sounds rather lame,' said Charles, putting his pipe away. He'd stay another five minutes and then make the excuse of work, some of which he brought home from the Bureau of Propaganda. There was no hope of reaching any kind of accord; they shared the contention that Hugh should enlist – should *have* enlisted weeks ago – in Charles's own regiment; they differed only in that Louise thought he could do something about it while he knew there was nothing.

'What would *you* have told her?' she demanded.

'Who? Sophie?' The use of the name was natural, not deliberate; they'd been on Christian-name terms with the Wendholmes for a long time but titles so fascinated his wife that she derived a thrill from pronouncing them; even Eleanor was 'Lady Eleanor'. 'I'd have told her that our son is against war, against killing and therefore against enlisting. At least it's honest – no one could say anything so unpopular if it weren't the truth.'

The sunburst clock gave its delicate chime and he turned his head, a little pointedly. She didn't notice. 'I'm less concerned with the truth in this instance than with the family name – your own name, Charles.' Her long dark eyebrows were poised in studied surprise: it was the only feature to lend imbalance to her looks, spoiling the grace of her straight nose and high cheekbones; or perhaps it was that the eyebrows were both mobile and eloquent and thus drew attention. 'I think you once told me, with pardonable pride, that the head of the Sadlers has been a soldier through more generations than you can remember; and now your own son – ours, if you choose – has broken the tradition. I do wish I could make you understand—'

'You know how I think of it.' Calmly promising himself that he'd shortly excuse his retirement on the plea of work, he was none the less provoked by her insistence, reminded of what he wished to forget. 'And you know what my duties are – as a "soldier".' She was bored by his bitterness that he was unfit for active service, so often did he show it. 'My job is to persuade young men of his age to fight, spending my day and half the night thinking up slogans for the posters and trying to find the best way of expressing the simplest idea – that every Englishman worth the name should serve his country. D'you imagine my colleagues and the friends at my club don't see the irony of it, knowing my own fit young son is dodging the war?' He patted his pockets suddenly, looking down, saying more quietly, 'Not dodging it, no. I must take care not to—'

'You forgive him so easily, Charles, don't you see?'

'Forgive him?' His sandy head jerked up. 'What should I do – condemn him? He's condemned himself as it is; a man of his age runs the gauntlet whenever he walks down the road. Half a million volunteers already in training or France – there aren't many civilians about, you know that.'

'But it's his own decision!'

'And he's willing to take the consequences.'

Her hands flew, wings beating at the bars of his obstinacy: 'Has he thought of the consequences to *us*? The daily embarrassments and humiliations—'

'Why should he, Louise? We're thinking of ourselves, not him. Have you spent a thought for *his* humiliations? He disappointed us when he refused to join the Officers' Training Corps at school, and when he chose to teach at some godforsaken place in Dover when he could have applied for a junior post at Downside – "lowering the standard", you called it and I agreed. He's sensitive enough to know he's let us down and he's having to live with it, alone.' He found himself halfway to the door, angry with her and as usual unable to conceal it. 'You know something, Louise? These people who—'

'I'd be obliged if you'd lower your tone, Charles. The servants—'

'I'm less concerned with others' opinions than you are, and if anything I say is overheard and passed about it might do some good. These people – if you'll hear me out – who say "of course my son's been a great disappointment to me" don't ever stop to ask themselves whether the shoe might not be on the other foot. Or perhaps you feel that Hugh enjoyed an ideal childhood?'

He left her. From that point in the argument they could proceed only to the hurtful recriminations that so often lingered in the darkened room after the bedside lamp was turned out, or were ended – no, postponed – by the throwing down of a napkin at the breakfast table, the scrape of a chair.

Climbing the staircase he thought half aloud: *We will not discuss it again.* They were both now accustomed to daily reminders of Hugh's fall from grace; well, they must ignore them. He didn't give a damn for others' opinions and he must therefore help Louise to dismiss them with the same ease. Today's scene had been coming for a long time and both had known it: this morning the Talbot boys had finished their end-of-training leave and were due for France, and had come, naturally, to say goodbye, both handsome in their uniforms, Aubrey with his easy stride and confident gaze, Victor with his eagerness for battle.

'How gallant they looked,' Louise had said. 'How very gallant.' And of course within a minute they were talking of Hugh.

We will not discuss it again. He shut the door of his study on this resolve and tried to work, but an hour passed before he began writing. Discussion could be banned easily enough: one had but to keep one's mouth shut; to discipline private thought would be more difficult.

In the dusk the flag above the Castle could still be seen moving in the soft September wind, and gulls wheeled perpetually across the white bulwark of the cliffs below it. From here, not far from the docks, he could see the School, one of the lights coming on in a window; it was a distinctive building with sharply descending roofs in the Swiss-chalet style that in fact gave it its name – Chalet School.

He had come down here two or three times to the little park when the working-day was finished, to sit for a while in the bandstand where the wooden collapsible chairs were stacked and chained together until the next Sunday. *The Band will Continue to Play throughout September*, the paper notices said, *Exigencies Permitting*. A long word, he thought, for war.

He felt the boards trembling under his feet as another convoy of lorries came round the park towards the dock area; standing packed together, clinging to the uprights and each other, the soldiers sang in the dusk, waving to anyone who chanced to see them go by. *Ooohh, I do like to be beside the seaside . . . I do like to be beside the sea!* The wind blew the smell of exhaust-gas across the park, where flowers were still in bloom, their colours fading as the light grew low.

The shape among the hills, of the Chalet School, was almost

62

lost now but he saw its outline as clearly as ever in his mind, though it looked fragile enough, a little seat of learning, its few lights steady in the gloom below the great bastions of cliff and castle whose walls echoed the unceasing drum of wheels and soldiers' songs.

Ships clustered in the bay, awaiting their human cargo and the dull load of the guns, their lights uncertain in the choppy sea.

A seat of learning. Pompous enough as a phrase but he didn't think of it as that when he was teaching – or trying to teach – the boys, competing for their attention with the more exciting and more explicit rumble of the lorries in the town below; he thought of it in that grandiose way only when he looked up at it from here, when he saw it dwarfed by the mightier shapes of castle and battleship. You had to keep faith in what you were doing and wave your own little flag.

Aubrey understood. It had surprised him when Aubrey had said: 'Well if every man jack of us goes off to the wars there'll be no one left to teach the next generation about peace. You stay where you can do the most good, old boy – any damn' fool can pick up a rifle and shoot a man dead.' It had been kind of him to say that. Vic of course had seen it – as he saw most things – through his own eyes: 'Oh, you'll be out there with us before long, you know – you won't be able to resist it!'

The wind fluttered the paper notices on the bandstand and sent the gulls lifting high against the cliffs and then drifting away, their wings held still. The dark was nearly down.

They'd exchanged a few letters, he and Aubrey, and Pam had written rather a long one, her pride in her brothers overcoming her acute sense of loss – the loss of their childhood and the fear of loss to come, so that the letter wasn't uncheerful. There was nothing in it about his own answer to the war; was that because she felt that whatever she said it would seem like judgement, or because she knew that the opinions of others didn't worry him?

The last letter, from Aubrey, had been just a few lines to say they'd 'soon be off' and that he'd write next from France.

He left the silhouetted cage of the bandstand and walked between the flowers, black now in the starlight, and wondered if that was why he'd come down here tonight, as close to the embarkation area as one could go, in the hope of seeing them on their way. A thin hope: the streets were filled with troops at every hour by night and day and they were two among thousands.

It's a long way . . . to Tipperary . . .

Boots rang on the hard road, loudening from the town's centre. In the first few weeks the people of Dover had cheered them and pressed gifts on them and children had run beside them, the motor-traffic honking by way of salute and farewell; then there had been too many and the novelty lost its shine; now you heard only the wheels and the boots and the singing.

It's a long way . . . to go . . .

Self-sufficient, banded together in the anonymity of their uniform, they called their own farewell. If people, he wondered, had so soon grown bored with them, how long would it be before the whole war became no more than an irksome background to their more urgent private affairs? The carnival was over: the cheering and flag-waving and hero-making were past now, like a fever dying; would people come to wish that in those mad midsummer days they had stormed the offices of government, instead of the idle streets, to demand that peace go on?

Their boots rang and their song echoed from the walls and as they came past him in their swinging khaki ranks he saw the excitement in their faces and the brightness of their eyes in the light of the lamps. They at least had no doubts.

The brother of a pupil had visited the School not long ago to say goodbye, and had proudly shown everyone the special message from the King, printed these days on cheap paper and distributed as souvenirs to the men who passed through the town.

I have implicit confidence in you, my soldiers. Duty is your watchword, and I know your duty will be nobly done . . .

They swung past with their rifles at the slope, their heads lifted, the heavy packs pulling at their shoulders.

I shall follow your every movement with deepest interest, and mark with eager satisfaction your daily progress . . .

The rhythm of their march would never end, for there were others behind them, a hundred thousand, ten times a hundred thousand; the heart of a country was beating in the night.

Indeed your welfare will never be absent from my thoughts.

They marched singing to the sea.

IV

The vaulted roof of the station made a sound-trap for the uproar below and the rail traffic officers stood on crates and swung their megaphones to focus their shouted orders but even their megaphones were silenced from time to time by the roar of steam as an engine got into motion and dragged its load away into the steel-grey drizzle of the morning.

'Fifteenth Manchesters to Number Three and cross by the subway! Twenty-second Royal Irish Rifles to keep station! That party there – get back from the edge of the platform – train arriving!'

Steam billowed upwards to the grimed skeleton of the roof and formed a cloud that crept towards the open end. Buffers rammed steel on steel and recoiled and rang again with their springs flexing and shaking off dirt. Another whistle shrilled and a young rail-traffic officer went pelting past a line of close-packed troops to the swarm of men milling below the clock – *'Will you keep clear of the edge you bloody fools there's a train coming in!'* His R.T.O. brassard had slipped and was round his wrist and he caught it before it fell; his white face ran with sweat while the troops stood huddled in their greatcoats against the chill gusts that swept through from the goods-yards to the north.

A colonel hooked at his arm. 'Take care whom you're addressing and try to get things organized!'

'I'm sorry, sir – I've not slept for days and you can see what we're up against – could you possibly—'

'Right. *That sergeant!* Get your men clear in both directions and single file *at the double!*'

Most of the R.T.O.s were fighting-officers back from sick-leave or recovering from wounds and some had the knack of handling massed troops and some didn't.

The mouth of the station grew dark as a locomotive drew in under a pall of dirty steam, its fireman swinging from the cab and yelling for gangway. Rain drifted in on the wind and men stood with their backs to it.

'Tenth Battalion Royal Engineers – stand by to entrain!'

65

Doors were banging and a French porter grabbed at a Yorkshire boy asleep on his feet and falling as the great wheels rolled to a halt – '*Tu veux te tuer, toi? Alors!*' He helped them sling their kit through the doorways, arms like hams and a barrel chest, his smock long torn away by the press of men and equipment. '*Allons-y, mes braves – à la guerre!*'

In the station, in the goods-yards, in the weed-thick sidings, in the soot and the rain and the steam and the day-long and night-long pandemonium they stood packed or shifted or paraded in phalanx of platoons, companies, battalions, whole regiments, two thousand of them waiting for the trains, always two thousand though the trains came in and were filled and came again, never the same two thousand but always here, waiting to be taken to the war. Beyond them to the north lay the sea, its rain-grey horizon mottled with the shapes of the troopships and destroyer escorts out from England and crowding at the docks.

'*Third Duke of Lancaster's to assemble in the station forecourt – quick as you can, please!*'

Somewhere in the gloom a tide of khaki began flowing to the open end and through the curtain of rain, the officers and N.C.O.s going ahead to guide them or falling back to cover the rearguard.

'C Company to the left and keep together now!'

'Mr Talbot! Have you got your party?'

'All present, sir!'

'Take them round by the sheds and cut back to form up behind B Company!'

The rain touched their faces and the wind drove it inside their collars but it was better out here by far, you'd got some air to breathe.

'Pick up the step, now!'

You couldn't pick up the bloody step over railway lines and clinkers and weeds as high as your knees but never mind, you could put up a show.

'Station forecourt, is it? Means they got some taxis for us instead, now ain't that nice!'

'You've got some 'opes, you 'ave.'

'No talking now! Pick up the step!'

''Ow can I wi' thistles in me boots?'

.   .   .

They marched two miles and two miles back because there was no room in the station forecourt: it was part of the dock area and jammed with wagons and guns and convoys of R.A.S.C. vehicles and ambulances; cavalry companies wheeled about and staff-cars blocked the gates.

'It's perfectly simple,' said Barclay-Smith, 'there's more stuff coming in than going out.'

'That what it is? Then you better tell the Colonel – he obviously hasn't realized.'

A man got out his mouth-organ and a sergeant told him to put it away quick. It meant Col. Pickering was somewhere about, and their talking fell away.

They marched again as best they could across the lines and past the signal-box, and halted again. The wind was cold but the rain had stopped and they stood trying to wipe their collars dry.

'Where do we go from here?'

'Back where we started, mate. They're only shiftin' us about to keep us warm.'

'You know something? You boys should get yourselves organized!'

'Oh my Lord, we thought we'd lost you, Sam. They said you'd fallen off the boat.'

'Who, me?' Sam Quincey gave them his big white grin. He wasn't a man to fall off anything: he liked to be jumping on.

'You see any girls around here, huh?'

'Do I see any *what*?' Percy Stokes blinked through the wan afternoon light at the signal-box and the coke-dump and the waste of weeds and then looked at Sam as he looked at most people, his intelligent-monkey's face set in a frown of fascinated incomprehension. 'What d'you think this place is, an open-air *Folies Bergères* done up to look like a wet Sunday?'

Corporal Kemp came past, picking his way neatly over the rubble, his equipment as tidy as if it had just been issued. 'We've got a train, what d'you think of that? All to our little selves.' He went on his round with the news.

'You jokin', Corp?' But he was out of earshot.

Percy Stokes looked towards the station. 'Well he was and he wasn't.' He gave his sudden stage-laugh, a maniacal outburst that ended as abruptly. 'Can you see what I see?'

67

It was a *ramassage* train, a species concocted by distraught French traffic officials whenever they could find anything with wheels on it and an engine to pull it along. This one was out of a train-spotter's nightmare: half a mile of passenger-coaches, goods wagons, horse-boxes, timber-trucks and guards'-vans, crawling up to the waiting troops in a cloud of steam tinged with bright orange by the flames of the fire-box. A cheer began at one end of the battalion and was taken up as the engine-driver gave an answering blast with his whistle.

Barclay-Smith stood laughing like a fool. 'Top marks for inventiveness – but what is it?'

'I'm not gettin' in that bloody thing till they've put the fire out!'

'You'll not go far if they do!'

Sergeant Kilderbee jumped to the top of a coke-heap and cut the cheering short. 'All right! Every man on board in thirty seconds! Sharp now, before anyone sees us!'

There was a rush for the footboards because his meaning was clear enough: some bright spark in the battalion had got wind of an empty *ramassage* train and commandeered it without asking for orders and if they didn't take possession they'd be stuck here for days.

'Sharp, now, look lively! Quincey, give a hand to Follett with his kit! Where's Corp'l Kemp?'

'Three more for this one, Sarge!'

Steam blew past them on the wind. A mass of men was gathering by each passenger-coach but they were sent along the line to whatever truck they could find.

'Coaches for the officers an' the 'orse-boxes for the troops, that's bloody democracy for you!'

'Well what d'you expect?'

'Some bloody democracy!'

Percy and Sam were in first with their kit and reaching down to help the others and Tom Follett dropped his entrenching-tool and Tuffnel grabbed it for him while Oscar gave Smithy a bunk-up and tumbled in after him: they were the same group, these, that had formed by the slow alchemy known best to recruits at a training-camp, where men meeting as strangers and with nothing in common but their uniform instinctively sought and sensed the response in those who would

68

become their friends. In the bewildering weeks of drill and parades and calculated oppression designed to crush their individuality they had kicked back, at first singly and then in their little groups, and had saved themselves. You could make them stand like skittles and number off and slope arms and salute, but you couldn't choose their friends for them; each had rescued from the onslaught of shouts and threats and pinned notices the precious distillations of his own private spirit, to offer them freely to those who saw good in them, felt need of them and finally accepted them, and all with nothing said in words. They had come to know each other, many of them, better than their own brothers.

Nor was their comfort in each other expressed except in ridicule. Oscar Phipps, his eyes lifted in a stare of concentration, was struggling with a new tune on his mouth-organ in the corner of the truck, and Percy jerked his head.

'Oscar, there's something wrong with your breathing – you can hear it a mile away!'

The line of trucks jolted and was still again.

'You blokes see what it said outside, did you? "*8 Chevaux – 40 Hommes*".'

'What's that mean then?'

'Means how many the truck can hold. Eight horses an' forty men!'

'Where they goin' to put the horses then? There's no bloody room in here!'

'Listen, Wiggy, if anyone comes along, you get on your hands an' knees, they won't know the diff'rence!'

Percy was in the doorway looking along the train in disbelief. 'You know what my father is? He's a stationmaster. Now what would he think of this lot, eh? Three coaches, ten dog-kennels, two rabbit-hutches an' a tin piss-house, now what'd happen if he strung this lot together at Clapham Junction, eh, they'd ask for their money back!' He came and sat on his kit, his feet stretched out between Sam and Tuffnel. 'That's a fine moustache you got there, Geoff. Take much growin', did it?'

That one was always good for a laugh: Geoff's moustache was the pride of C Company. At the training camp he'd appeared on parade with a shadow on his top lip and Sgt Kilderbee had been quick enough to notice.

69

'Lost your razor, Tuffnel?'

'I'm growing a moustache, Sergeant.'

'Then you can think again. Report back to me after parade with a clean shave.'

The order was obeyed but next morning there was a written application in the Orderly Room for 921 Private G. K. Tuffnel to see the Commanding Officer, No. 2 Platoon.

Kilderbee was on to it first. 'This application. Personal reasons?'

'Yes, Sergeant.'

'Give it a name, then.' Kilderbee eyed the dutifully blank face and wasn't deceived by it. Tuffnel was one of the quietest, never in trouble and liked well enough in the ranks, but there was something about his reserve that put you on your guard; in a battle of wits this was the kind of man who'd win by giving you enough rope to hang yourself. 'If it's something I can do for you without troubling Mr Talbot it'll save everyone's time.'

'I want permission to grow a moustache, Sergeant.'

Kilderbee's face went stiff. 'Now just listen to me, Tuffnel. We're forming a battalion here and we're in a hurry. Colonel Pickering and the rest of us have got to make soldiers out of eight hundred civilians and put 'em into battle where they're badly needed. If you didn't have a bit of intelligence I wouldn't waste my time telling you, but if you had a bit more you'd see for yourself that we've all got our work cut out – Mr Talbot included. So you can just forget that application and turn your mind to more important things, understand?'

'I'm sorry, Sergeant—'

'*Don't* apologize to an N.C.O! Mean you refuse?'

'No, Sergeant, but I've a right to insist.'

Kilderbee's mouth formed a slit and his eyes were half-closed. There was nothing he could say to this man. The camp was a shambles still: no proper hutments or washing facilities, no rifle issue or even uniform for a lot of them, the officers and N.C.O.s hard put to it to make a show of authority when the lads could see nothing but muddle wherever they looked. No wonder they played the goat like this.

'Report to the Orderly Room at 0900 hours tomorrow. I'll be taking you in myself.'

The company office was littered with paperwork and Lt

Talbot was on the telephone, his face patient but strained from overwork. Kilderbee hadn't much time for this young chap, far too lenient with those below him and too obliging to those above, that was how all this mess of paper had got in here, shoved on him by the Colonel.

'If there's no choice,' he was saying into the telephone, 'so be it. No, I don't mind – if you want a thing done, as they say, ask a man who's busy.' He hooked the receiver and collected his long legs under the desk 'Sar'nt Kilderbee?'

'921 Private Tuffnel, sir. Application for interview.'

The lieutenant cocked an eyebrow at his tone. It wasn't often he heard anger in this sergeant's voice and it was obvious something pretty bad had happened. He rummaged among the papers for the application form but couldn't see it. 'Go ahead, Tuffnel.' He looked up at the correct blank face with its rather pronounced jaw-line.

'I'd like to grow a moustache, sir.'

'Well why don't you grow one?'

The private went on staring in front of him, two inches above the officer's head.

'Permission to speak, sir?' Kilderbee was like a wooden post and his mouth opened and shut by numbers.

'What? Yes, of course.' The sergeant must be in a fury about something, to play it as regimental as this.

'The growing of hair on the upper lip is forbidden, sir.'

'Oh, is it? Then why did you let this man apply?'

Kilderbee had to pause before he could answer, to get control of himself. Blame the selection boards: they only asked these kids four questions – what school did they go to, what was their father's income, could they ride a horse and what wine would they drink with fish? Get all four right and you'd got a pip on your shoulder and a Sam Browne belt. They didn't tell you not to tick off a senior N.C.O. in front of a private, not them.

'Permission may be granted in special circumstances, sir.'

'I see. If there's a scar or something. You haven't a scar, Tuffnel?'

'No sir.'

'Have you any special reason for wanting a moustache?'

'No sir.'

The lieutenant looked from one to the other, untroubled by

71

the strained silence in the small littered office, then noticed the application form among the stuff on his desk. He cast an eye over it and dropped it on to the mess that had long since overflowed from the waste-paper basket.

'Permission granted.'

The man's eyes glanced down two inches and up again, perhaps in surprise. 'Thank you, sir.'

'All right, Sar'nt.'

Kilderbee looked straight at him. 'Confined to camp, sir, fourteen days?'

'Who, Tuffnel? Why?'

'Required by regulations, sir. No man to be seen in a public place during the period when—'

'Yes, I see. All right, Tuffnel, are you willing to do fourteen days' C.B.?'

'Yes sir.'

The lieutenant studied the blank face with its stubborn jaw. 'Well you've asked for it. Off you go.'

Kilderbee quivered. '*Party* – abou-out – *turn*!'

As Tuffnel moved, the lieutenant said quietly: 'All right, Sar'nt, he's dismissed.' He waited until the door was shut before he looked again at Kilderbee. 'Stand easy, for God's sake. Now tell me what the hell that was all about, will you?'

The sergeant let out a long breath. 'With respect, sir, me and the rest of the N.C.O.s are trying to turn a bunch of lackadaisical civilians into a body of first-class fighting-troops and I told Tuffnel as much, but he chose not to see it. If we let these lads worry over what they've got on their upper lip instead of how to load a rifle and thrust with a bayonet I don't see how we're ever going to knock some shape into them.'

'Yes, I know we're up against it – no organization from the top and all that.' The lieutenant uncoiled himself wearily from the desk and leaned at the open window, taller than the sergeant by a head. 'But you chaps have got a great deal of discipline into these boys and you're working them pretty hard – as you must, I quite see that. And they don't spend the *whole* of their time shoving their bayonets into sandbags; even the Army gives them time to themselves and it's in those odd moments they grab the chance of remembering they're

72

people.' He studied the sergeant's face as he spoke; its expression remained implacable but there was a certain distinction in the face itself that was woefully absent in that of Sgt Knight in the same company, a traditional bullet-head with none of this man's education. Kilderbee could at least understand what you were saying, though whether he approved or not was quite another thing. 'This boy Tuffnel thinks a moustache would suit his uniform, or he wants to please his girl-friend, or he feels he's a man now and wants to look like one – whatever his reasons are they're damned important to *him*. And they're not our concern. We let him grow the thing or we don't, and I saw no point in refusing. We don't want clockwork machines out there, Kilderbee, we want men with some pride left in themselves as individuals.' He looked away from the stony face and sat down again in front of the mass of reports and rosters and indent-forms. 'You want to say anything more?'

'No, sir.'

'Fair enough.'

Kilderbee came to attention. 'If I might just mention it, sir, I think that application form dropped off the desk, didn't it? It'll have to be completed with a report on the interview an' details on any decision taken, an' sent on to—'

'Good of you to remind me, but it can stay right where it is. It's not the decisions that take the time, you know, it's the paper-work. Young Tuffnel's going to be sporting a full-blown Kitchener moustache before I've finished writing reports on it, if I'm fool enough.'

The rest of C Company had never known exactly what had been said at the interview but events gave them a clear enough picture: for the next two weeks Geoff Tuffnel was confined to camp and Kilderbee had pushed him on one fatigue after another, chasing him round the place like a parson trying to drive the Devil out of his parish, and the beginnings of a fine straw-yellow moustache had established themselves to the point where Geoff was declared fit to show himself in public.

They'd gone into the town together on the evening of the fifteenth day, he and Percy Stokes. 'Well you must've wanted that thing badly,' Percy had said.

'Not badly, no.'

Aubrey came away from the carriage window.

'A damn' close thing,' he laughed to the others.

The battalion was on the move, dispersed among its weird collection of rolling-stock, and a cheer had resounded as the engine got up steam. A senior R.T.O. had come trotting up from the station, waving papers with much show of menace, while the Adjutant – by good luck sighting him – had sprinted to the locomotive and somehow got the driver into action. The R.T.O. was last seen engulfed in soot and sparks, still waving his papers, his shouts drowned by the chorus of cat-calls from the last truck in the line.

'Is the Old Man on board?' asked Lt Coxhead, putting his feet on the seat opposite.

'No, he cadged a lift from a staff-car.'

'The Lord be praised!' Coxhead's fear of Col. Pickering showed itself by repeated questions as to his whereabouts.

Lieutenant Lovell was handing round his cigarette-case, a rather impressive thing of heavily chased silver – a present from his parents on the day he left for France; his youthful wish to have it admired cost him dearly in Player's. Julian Lovell, the son of a bank manager in Kensington, had attracted Aubrey from their first meeting at the training-camp and already their friendship was closer than most others among the junior officers, though Aubrey didn't know why. It might have been that although Julian harped a lot about 'decency' in its moral sense, his views were genuine; in the confusion of the early days when responsibility seemed heavy to a raw subaltern he made his decisions and delivered his judgements in terms of 'the decent thing to do' as distinct from – and sometimes even in opposition to – King's Regulations. It got him into trouble, of course, but that didn't change his convictions, and perhaps it was for this that Aubrey admired him. Of their group, one or two subs were already trying for quick promotion by the simple means of licking the Old Man's boots; several others were too scared of the Colonel to do anything except keep out of his sight; and the rest kept a copy of K.R.s under their pillow as a magic talisman: 'Do everything from the book, old boy,' as Coxhead put it, 'and you can't go wrong.'

Julian snapped his beautiful cigarette-case shut and took a light from Aubrey. 'Three empty seats here and the other ranks crowded into horse-wagons.' His handsome face was frowning as he leaned away from the match and blew out smoke. 'Not quite cricket.'

Coxhead grunted. 'And where would I put my feet?' He stretched out luxuriously, unbuttoning his tunic and watching the last of the raindrops trickle down his polished shoes. 'Most of 'em have never known any better, so why worry?'

'Then it's time they did.'

'Oh for God's sake, Julian, you can't have a war and a social revolution at the same time!'

Julian laughed – and this too was something in him that attracted Aubrey: a readiness to dismiss his convictions in company when he saw they were boring to others. 'All right, we'll deal with the war first, then we'll get women the vote to start off with.'

'So long as they'll vote for me, old fruit.' Coxhead's passionate *affaires* were legendary, though few envied him: among the chaperons of London there was a price on his comely head and by all reports he'd twice escaped the horse-whips of outraged fathers.

Watching his companions Aubrey thought again of Noël, who must have made just this kind of journey and to the same destination, as carefree and as confident as they were now. He and Vic had been at Epsom with him – a bit shy but good fun when you could winkle him out of his shell – and he'd spent a week with them at Ashbourne, 'a charming boy,' Mother had said, 'and so *knowledgeable!*' (He'd helped her replant some Thibetan orchid bulbs that he'd seen her busily putting in roots uppermost.) Aubrey had later run into him a few times at Oxford but that was all, and he still couldn't understand why the shock had been so acute when they'd heard the news; Pam had been very upset, though she'd known him only for the one week when he'd stayed, and had gone all the way out to Reigate by train to see his parents. The worst of it was that the news had come when he and Vic were waiting for their orders for France. It was, he supposed, the first time the casualty lists had taken on meaning for them: unless you'd actually known someone they were just a list of names. Now there was Capt. Noël Lindsay, M.C., killed in action.

The carriage jolted to a sudden shunting of buffers and they were thrown forward against the empty seats.

'My God,' said Percy Stokes, 'we've hit a cow!'
They picked themselves up.
'Bloody elephant, more like!'
Their equipment was all over the place and Sam dived for the candle before it set something on fire. It was Barclay-Smith who'd produced the candle: he'd got enough in his kit to stock the Army and Navy Stores and without it they couldn't have played cards because the only daylight was from gaps between the boards. Smithy was more than just organized: he was a one-man calculating-machine-cum-statistics-bureau and there were so many items in his kit that weren't official issue that he had to distribute them among his friends for safe keeping whenever there was an inspection: slide-rule, stop-watch, thermometer, pedometer, inclinometer, magnetic compass, altitude meter and various gadgets they couldn't even give a name to. Before joining up he'd been apprentice to an instrument-maker and his boss had told him to take his pick – 'It's little enough to offer a lad who's off to fight for his country' – and Smithy had made a clean sweep of the stockroom. The idea of fighting for his country hadn't in fact occurred to him; he'd have stayed on at the works but the chivvying of his friends who'd signed on out of boredom with their own jobs had finally got on his nerves and he'd hit on a compromise: the fascination for measuring things had absorbed him as a civilian and he could go on being absorbed as a soldier, and once in uniform his friends would leave him in peace. He hadn't reckoned on people like Sgt Knight or the frustration of fatigues but he learned a very simple trick for dealing with them: he measured them. The bellowing of Sgt Knight, reduced to a precise number of decibels on the meter in his hand, lost its fearfulness and became a matter of interest; and the force required, in terms of foot-pounds, to shift ten full sacks of potatoes from the ration-cart into the cookhouse (height of the cart, height of the cookhouse step, and distance between them being vital factors) made the actual effort irrelevant.

He was crouched at this moment by the candle, peering down his long thin nose at a brass chronometer. 'The way it works out,' he told Sam, 'is that we've averaged twenty kilometres an hour since we left Boulogne and it's now ten minutes past five. That means we'll reach—'

'You can't do that,' said Sam flatly. He was always trying to catch Smithy out.

'Can't do what?'

'You can't know how far we've come. This damn' truck's got no windows in, right? So you can't see any signs with distances on, right? So you're kiddin'.' He grinned in delight about this because he'd never managed to catch Smithy out before.

'You'll just have to take my word for it. That means we should reach—'

'Con-man, huh? No dice. We reach where we reach when we reach there, son, even Sam Quincey can guarantee you that!'

Percy Stokes gave his sudden maniacal laugh. 'Go on, Smithy, he wants it in writing.' He couldn't see how Smithy was going to do it but he had a blind faith in his ability and wanted to hear it justified. 'Leonardo da Barclay-Smith will now reveal all!'

'He can't, man, he's kiddin'!' Sam rocked on his haunches ecstatically, his white grin shining in the candlelight.

'Well I don't mind.' Smithy put away his chronometer. 'I just thought you'd like to know when we should reach St Omer, that's all.' He got impatient with people who took him for some kind of conjurer with a card up his sleeve; the figures were there and you couldn't alter them.

'Okay,' Sam said, 'an' when's that?'

'Twenty to seven, if we keep up the same speed.' He gazed past his long thin nose at the dim-lit interior of the truck, thinking of what to measure next.

'Or midnight,' laughed Sam. 'It's anybody's guess!'

Percy blinked at him, worried. 'Can't you shut up for a minute?' He turned to Smithy. 'D'you mind just telling me how you work it out? We'll forget this transatlantic son of a cattle-thief – I'm asking you to tell *me*.' It was an affair of honour now; Smithy didn't care a hoot if Sam didn't believe him but they'd never hear the last of it if they left it like this. 'I suppose it's a kind of sixth sense, is it?'

Smithy's head swung to look at him, shocked. 'Of course not! I was timing the gaps in the rails, that's all.' He shifted his position impatiently. 'Look, these rails are nine yards long – I paced one of them out, at the station. You can hear when the wheels pass across the gaps so all you want is a stop-watch, and I happen to have one. We've been doing a rail every one and a half seconds, on the average, which is forty rails a minute or two thousand four hundred rails to the hour, and with nine yards to a rail that's twenty-two thousand yards an hour, or twelve and a half miles, which is twenty kilometres. We left Boulogne at ten past four and it's now ten past five. According to the signposts in the road outside the station it's fifty kilometres from Boulogne to St Omer, and we've done twenty so there's thirty to go, which means another one and a half hours if we keep up this speed, so we should reach there at twenty to seven, which is what I told you, isn't it?'

Percy's sudden hyena-laugh had the ring of triumph in it. Sam sat staring at the long-beaked Limey with his eyes almost crossed – it had brought the sweat out just listening to the guy. '*Ho*-ly *Jee*-sus . . . Okay, boy, you get the cigar, huh? But gee, it's a darn shame, ain't it?'

'What is?'

'Well there's just one little thing that's goin' to bust the whole o' that schedule wide open. We just hit a cow, didn't we?'

The rain drummed on the roof of the truck and ran down the sides, seeping in through the cracks in the timber and trickling across the floor. The candle still burned but most of the talk had died away and the cards were back in their box. After the sudden halt the train had picked up speed again and many were sleeping, lulled by their boredom and the monotony of the wheels. Those still awake had made seats for themselves with their boots and haversacks and groundsheets to avoid the puddles on the floor. The wind whistled between the boards and brought the rain in with it.

'Tired are you, mate?'

'No, I was just thinkin'.'

'Sorry you joined?' Wiggy said it with a quiet laugh but it wasn't so funny. This wasn't soldiering.

'Oh no. I had to join.' It had never come to his mind that it had been a mistake, once he'd decided on it; the Red Admiral had been there on the path in the sunshine, that was one part of

78

his lie, then it had flown off and he'd walked across the grass into the next part of his life, this part he was living in now; it was silly to wonder if it had been a mistake. He looked at the little bunched-up face of Wiggy Bennett in the candlelight. He liked Wiggy; a friend as nice as him made up a lot for not having the puppy. Would she christen one of them 'Alexander'? That would be nice, as if she remembered him. He said, 'Are *you*?'

'Eh?'

'Are you sorry you joined?'

'I s'ppose not. We'll 'ave better times than this. But my Mum didn't want me to, poor ole girl.' He pinched out his dog-end and put it in the tin with the others; nine or ten dog-ends and you'd got yourself a whole new gasper, bit of paper and a bit of care. 'Of course she knew I was meanin' to do it, all along.'

'Did she?' said Tom.

'Too true she did. First thing I knew she was dishin' up me dinner on the plates we kept for best, the ones with no bits chipped out. "Who's comin', Mum?" I asked her, an' she said nobody was comin', it was just that she thought we ought to use 'em more, she said, the best ones. Nex' thing I knew there was a hot-water bottle in me bed, August, mind you, when you couldn't so much as breathe. "What's this for, Mum?" I asks 'er, an' she says it's nice an' warm when the sun's out but the nights are turnin' chilly. Mind you, I'm like a cod on a slab all winter, got no flesh on me, see, but that wasn't why she did it, poor ole girl. But it was no good, I'd thought it all out. I got no Dad, see?'

'Haven't you?' said Tom. 'That's funny, because—'

'Eh? It's not, y' know. There's no—'

'I didn't mean—'

'There's no money, see? She goes out scrubbin' steps for a few shillin' an' I picked up what I could but it wasn't so much. I'm a rag-picker, me, or I was an' you don't get rich on that, you can go from door to door all bloody day an' turn in twenty pound o' rags on the scales but they tell you they can't use it, the stuff's 'alf-rotten, but they'll give you a bob out o' the kindness of their hearts, the bastards, take advantage of you, see? So when the war come it was a big chance for me an' I took it, quick. A shillin' a day, regular, all me food an' clothes an' everythin' I could ever need, even an overcoat – I'd never 'ad

79

overcoat in me life before – an' me room empty so she can take a lodger in, five bob a week when she's lucky an' the seven bob a week what I send 'er regular – 'cause what 'ave I got to spend it on? I got all I need.' He drew his neck into the collar of his greatcoat against the draught from the cracks. 'Of course I couldn't tell 'er what was on me mind, she wouldn't've listened, see? She wanted me to stay 'ome safe an' sound, that's all she was thinkin' of. You know what she went an' done when she knew I'd gone an' signed on, eh? She tried to make out I was under the age, but they twigged 'er.' He sniffed a dew-drop off his nose. 'Poor ole girl.'

Tom pulled his thin wrists deeper into his sleeves and said, 'Well, things are better for her now.'

'Eh? They are an' they aren't. Trouble is, she worries, always 'as done, you can't stop 'er. Your Mum worry, does she?'

'Well, I expect they all do.'

'Natural, I s'ppose.'

'Yes.' He hadn't thought about this before, and it pleased him. There was no one to worry over what happened to him, and that was nice. He'd wanted to say goodbye when he'd left, but Mr Charrington said Milady was resting and he'd never even seen Sir William except from a distance one day in a white Panama hat, and there didn't seem to be anyone else about so he'd just said goodbye to Mr Willis and come away.

'Blimey, I couldn' 'alf do with a cuppa.'

'A what?'

'Cup o' tea. Couldn' you?'

'Yes. It'd warm us up.' There was one person he'd have liked to say goodbye to and that was Mr Charrington's daughter, Miss Kitty; he'd seen her quite a lot, sitting with Milady in the garden, sewing things, always with silks and laces on her lap, her head bent over them and her little hands busy, ever so slender she was; of course she'd never noticed him, except once when he'd had to go quite near with the barrow: she'd looked up, kind of startled, with her eyes very wide open, and then looked down again quickly with a smile that meant it'd been silly to be startled. He'd always remember how she looked that day. But of course he couldn't ask Mr Charrington if he could say goodbye to her, what next! And besides, she wouldn't even

80

know his name, there were so many gardener's boys about the place – Mr Willis was always 'sending them off' and getting different ones because they'd 'got no mind to learn anything', so he said.

'Wouldn' it?'

'I beg pardon?' Wiggy had been saying something and he'd not been listening; he often did that, found himself thinking about the people at Ashbourne Manor.

'I said it'd be better if we was marchin', wouldn' it? At least it'd keep us warm.'

'Well I expect we'll have to, later on.'

'Too blinkin' true.'

He'd have to stop himself thinking about the people there; he was in a different life now. But he'd seen Mr Kemp once or twice at the camp and it reminded him every time; he'd thought of going up to him, once, and saying who he was, but Mr Kemp was a corporal and it might seem he was trying to curry favour. He'd seen Mr Talbot as well, several times, the tall one, not his brother, always very smart and of course getting saluted a lot, being an officer. Milady and the other people must be ever so proud of him.

He turned his head to say something to Wiggy about Mr Talbot but saw he was falling asleep, a lock of wet hair hanging down from under his cap and his hungry-looking face screwed up against the cold. Draughts came through the cracks and drips of water were tugged in, and soon the remains of the candle got blown out and they rattled on in the dark.

The rain had given over by morning and the sun was a pale blob in the sky when they tumbled out of the barn to go on parade. The train had left them at a village near St Omer and they'd marched to their billets, and now they thought they were going to march again, until they saw the buses.

'My God,' cried Percy Stokes, 'we're back in Piccadilly!'

There were dozens of them all in a line, bright red London double-deckers and with the advertisements still on – *Pear's Soap* – *Dewar's Fine Old Whisky* – *Oxo* – and they looked just like a bit of London swept up and dropped here in the night among the poplars, except that their destination boards said *Ypres* and *Somme*.

81

A cheer went up in the morning air and Sgt Knight cut it short but they couldn't keep still or stop talking; they weren't long from home but already they missed it and here was a reminder they'd never thought to see; a lot of them laughed in simple delight and a few were silent in unconscious thanksgiving – the Londoners, these, born and bred there among the smoky streets – because a part of all they had known had followed them out here to colour the flat grey foreign land and drive its strangeness away; and one man wept as his mother had wept when she'd seen him climb the swaying steps with one hand on the rail and the other waving to her till the bus turned the corner and was gone.

'*Right!* First party on board an' up top an' leave your equipment below! Second party inside an' downstairs! Come on now, we've not got all day!'

Everyone tried to get on top and the steps got jammed with struggling bodies and caps were knocked flying and mess-tins rang against the rails while the sergeants waved their arms and bellowed above the din.

'*Get that staircase clear will you! You're boardin' a bus, not stormin' a bloody castle!*'

'This one's full up, Sarge!'

'*Then take the next one, it's goin' to the same place, isn' it!*'

The first of them moved off, lurching under its load, and the long red line began breaking up as the others lumbered after it along the sharply cambered road, and there was no stopping the cheering now: you might just as well give a bunch of kids a bag of sweets and tell them not to eat any. Those on the top decks wouldn't sit down: they were too busy waving to their chums and pulling at the leaves of the trees as they passed. Some of them staggered up and down the gangway calling out, a mess-tin for a ticket-punch: 'Fares, please! Fares, if you please! Now then, lady, you can't bring that dog up 'ere, it'll on'y poop on the floor!'

'Conductor, do you stop at the Ritz?'

'No, guv'nor, I can't afford it!'

'Oo – conductor! This nasty man's interfering with me!'

'Then shut yer legs an' pinch 'is fingers, ducks! *Any* more fares, please?'

They went swaying along the road with the wind on their

82

faces and the leaves blowing past, their laughter flying away behind.

There'd been no hope of the officers commandeering their own bus: it had been every man for himself.

Julian Lovell was squeezed in by the piled equipment on the lower deck, his legs drawn up to save his smart brown shoes from getting scratched. 'The idea's practical, of course, but whoever thought of sending these things out is also a first-rate psychologist – I'd say the morale of the whole battalion's gone up by ninety per cent!'

The singing on the upper deck had the sound of a bank holiday outing instead of a movement of troops. *Hello, hello! Who's your lady friend? Who's the little girlie by your side?*

'It doesn't take much,' smiled Aubrey, 'to make a soldier happy.' Yet he didn't share in it; his solemn vow to stand back sometimes and listen to the small voice of reason was becoming irksome to him, yet the habit was established and hard to break. Only days ago these gay red buses had plied the streets of London and only weeks ago these boisterous young men had ridden on them to work and back or to the shops or to see their girl-griends, their clothes brushed and their smart hats devilishly tilted; now they rode in them, all in the same drab brown, to a foreign field where they would kill and be killed by young men like themselves; and whoever had thought of this idea might well be a first-rate psychologist, but he also had a sense of the macabre.

'Something on your mind, old boy?'

'M'm? Good Lord no! Why should there be?'

'I just wondered.'

It wasn't the girl I saw you with at Brighton,
So who – who – who's your lady friend?

They marched twelve miles in five hours in column of route across the flat bleak countryside, sometimes halting to rest or to draw back from the tree-lined road to let a convoy go through, forming again four abreast and marching on, the lance-corporals and corporals among the men, the senior N.C.O.s and officers at stations alongside, the Commanding Officer, Second-in-Command and Adjutant on horseback, a ten-yard gap between the platoons and a twenty-five-yard gap between the companies, eight hundred men in step at a hundred and fifteen paces to the minute and in full marching order, each man with a nine-pound rifle and seventy pounds of pack: greatcoat, groundsheet, blanket, spare boots, haversack, full water-bottle, bayonet, entrenching-tool, iron rations and sixty rounds of ammunition.

'*Pick up the step!*'

Since noon a few score of them had dropped out and lay on the edge of the ditch with the sweat drying on them and their faces to the sky. The rest marched on.

Sometimes the Colonel reined in and watched them from the saddle as they went past, his beautifully groomed chestnut swinging its head and showing the whites of its eyes. 'That's it, boys, keep it up!' He flicked dust from his immaculate breeches. His plump face was a healthy pink from the wind and the gentle exercise; his eyes were smiling. 'That's the style! Keep it up!'

They didn't look at him; they looked at the bobbing pack of the man in front. They'd seen other battalions on the march, seen them yesterday from the buses, and knew a lot of commanding officers chose to march with their men. Not this one, not bloody Pickering.

The N.C.O.s did their worst and their best, each in his own fashion. Regimental Sergeant-Major Blossom worked like a sheep-dog, shouting, rallying, dropping back to check the rearguard platoon, extending his step and overhauling them as far as the leading company and checking it and dropping back, his head thrown up and his neck-muscles standing out like rope – '*Le-ef*'! *Le-ef*'! *Le-ef*' – *Hipe* – *Le-ef*'! *Get the step an' keep the step an' jus' let it carry you on!*' – an old campaigner, Blossom, Regular Army man, South African ribbons and a Military Medal and a couple of gold wound-stripes on his sleeve, a man you could curse with respect.

Not like bloody Knight: '*Come on, you crummy lot of two-legged sheep – call yourselves soldiers, do you? By God, I've seen bloody ducks waddlin' better'n' you do! Now get yourselves smartened up an' try to look like members of 'Is Majesty's Army!*'

They never knew where Sgt Kilderbee was because they couldn't hear him; you'd see him right up at the front of the company and then suddenly he'd be beside you and then gone again before you could look round. 'Tuffnel, take that man's rifle. All right, Follett, we know it's hard going but we've got to get there and it's not long now. Barclay-Smith, your pack's shifting – someone help him get it to rights.'

A man on an inside file went down with a crash of equipment and they tripped and staggered about him and Kilderbee was there in the instant. 'Quincey! Gilmore! Get him to the ditch and loosen his collar and leave him there – someone take their rifles, quick now!'

The rest marched on, picking up the step again and closing the gap, going forward with their eyelids drooping, with their shoulders rubbed raw under the harness, with their feet burning in their boots.

If it's more than another mile then I'm done.

I'll get there if it kills me. I'll show bloody Knight.

I can't go on. But I can't drop out. Have to go on.

'Le-ef'! Le-ef'! Le-ef' – Hipe – Le-ef'!'

Their boots lifted and fell. Their bodies had turned to lead and the lead had gone into their boots. They were boots on the move.

A jingle of harness.

'That's the style, boys! That's the style!'

Go an' get fucked.

The packs bobbing and never still. The sky reeling and never still. Their boots never still.

'You all right, Tom?'

'Yes.'

'You sure you c'n manage?'

'Yes.'

A man pitched forward and bruised an eye against the pack of the man in front and staggered up straight again and picked up the step.

Eleven miles and the sun sliding down the last of the scummy sky, rain on the wind again and the yellow leaves whirling all the way down from the poplars, smudged out by the boots.

'All right, lads – there's one more mile to go, so keep it up!'

A man fell away from an outside file and lay sobbing. The rest went on.

'Wiggy! Give me that rifle, come on!'

'I'm all right.'

'Don't be so bloody obstinate, man!'

Sergeant Kilderbee was there. 'Bennett! Don't give it to him, give it to me. Quick now!' Most of the N.C.O.s were carrying rifles by this time; R.S.M. Blossom was festooned with them and it made no difference to his step, they might have been matches. '*Le-ef*' – *Hipe* – *Le-ef*'!' They cursed him for doing what they couldn't.

Three of the C Company subalterns carried a rifle apiece – Mr Lovell and the Talbot brothers – sloping them smartly at first and then letting them trail because you couldn't fool anyone over this last mile: they were all dead beat except for that bastard Blossom.

The greater part of the 3rd Battalion, Duke of Lancaster's Light Infantry, entered the village of Bailleul near the Belgian frontier a little before dusk, and there halted for the night.

Some of their number slept in billets and some under canvas, a groundsheet beneath them, and these were awakened first though it was still dark. They lay for a long time, puzzled by the trembling of the earth, some thinking it must be their own bodies shaking for an unknown reason, perhaps in reaction to the fatigue of yesterday's march.

A few threw off their greatcoats and went into the open air, feeling it cool against their faces; there was no wind; they noticed that the air smelt stale and bitter. Standing uncertainly and still drugged by their long sleep they listened, looking upwards at the dark and then eastwards at the red of dawn.

Forms moved near them and they realized that others had come to stand here under the uneasy sky. More of them, awakened, came from the tents and turned, as they had, to watch the redness in the east.

'Dawn, is it?'

'No.'

The sky throbbed with colours, the sour light flickering against low cloud. The horizon seemed on fire over there. The ground trembled; the air trembled, smelling of exploded chemicals. The hollow drumming shook the far sky and they stood together excited and afraid.

'The guns, is it?'

'The war.'

86

V

A few hours after dawn a convoy of empty lorries began moving in on the camp from the west. The battalion stood paraded in a half-circle on the dewy field and Col. Pickering was raised on an ammunition-box, fresh-faced and immaculate, his cane tucked behind him, his brightly gaitered legs slightly apart, bending forward from the waist now and then to give emphasis to the more important phrases.

'Your performance of yesterday was a disappointment to me. Of our total complement more than seventy men fell behind during the march, including two lance-corporals and a corporal. This is not good enough. It indicates a readiness to give up when things become a little hard. To give up, behind the lines and in safety, is to lose self-respect and the respect of one's comrades. To give up, in battle and in danger, is to lose one's life and to hazard the lives of one's comrades. So you must never let yourself give up. Never. *Never!*'

The first of the lorries was bumping over the asphalt track beyond the tents; the others followed and turned off in formation to halt in echelons. Some of the men watched them, uneasy; they would have liked better to march there, to the east, as if of their own free will; but the convoy had come for them.

'Listen as hard as you can to me and not to the noise over there. Tonight we are going into the front lines. For the first time. Not into battle, but into danger. Our job is to hold the lines, that is all. To hold them. We shall find ourselves in a fairly active sector – you heard, I know, a great deal of business going on earlier this morning. That is just routine. When we are there we shall follow a routine of our own: we shall show courage, and be steadfast; we shall resist with valour, if we are attacked; we shall prove ourselves a worthy successor to the battalion we are relieving. So that when it is said that the 3rd Dukes know how to take it on the chin, we can answer – "But that's only a matter of routine!"'

Not all were listening. There were some who knew that once in the lines their gallant commanding officer would keep to his dugout, just as on the march he kept to his horse. Some refused to listen on principle, seeking comfort in a private act of insubordination under his very eyes. Some were distracted by the crawling line of field ambulances in the rearguard of the convoy.

The Adjutant was handing the Colonel some papers.

'It is my duty to announce to you that at Etaples yesterday the execution of sentences by court martial was carried out in the prescribed manner, by a firing-squad, in respect of three private soldiers and one junior officer. They had severally deserted their units in the presence of the enemy and from motives of cowardice. I am not obliged to read you the details of these crimes and their inevitable consequences, but only to acquaint you of them. I am confident that no officer, N.C.O. or soldier of the 3rd Duke of Lancaster's Regiment will invite such a fate.'

The convoy lumbered eastwards. There was no singing, and no laughter.

'Did 'e 'ave to tell us?'

'Tell us what?'

'About them poor bastards.'

They clung to the uprights, swaying, the wind tugging at their greatcoats.

'He said it was his duty.'

'Duty be fucked, 'e could've kept it till some other time, couldn' 'e, instead o' tryin' to scare the shit out of us before we got near the line.'

The convoy lurched to a halt and they were pitched forward, bruising themselves and cursing. A cavalry squadron went clattering past with pennants crackling in the wind. Two staff-cars followed, three brigadiers and a general and their aides-de-camp sitting back with their legs crossed, one smoking a cigar. In the next ten miles the convoy was stationary more than it was moving, leaning from the steep camber while more cavalry was let through; and in the approaches to Ypres it was slowed to a walking-pace by other convoys, staff-cars, ambulances, wagons, gun-limbers, field-kitchens, horses and mules, while despatch-riders swerved waspishly through the confusion and M.P. contingents yelled and gesticulated, trying to sort out the traffic. Most of it was moving east and was ordered past the battalion convoy to leave it covered in dust.

'Don't they want us, then?'

'We'll get there, don't you worry, all too bloody soon.'

They lurched together, trying to keep their feet in the grinding trucks while everyone else hurried past. Everyone else seemed to have priority, an urgent appointment to keep in the battle-zone, and they felt like so much rubbish, to be carted in fits and starts and dumped when their journey was over.

'You know what he was sayin', Wiggy, about us havin' courage an' bein' steadfast an' that? Well he got it out of a book, d'you know that?'

'You read it somewhere, then?'

'No, I don't read books, much.'

'Then 'ow can you tell?'

'I just know, that's all. It come out too bloody smooth, some'ow.'

Dust billowed about them as a munitions team rumbled past, the horses dragging at the shafts.

Somewhere south of Ypres they were ordered out of the trucks and paraded in the field by the road, to set off on foot in double file, A Company leading. They marched through the fading light of the early October afternoon, sometimes halting and taking to the ditch to let traffic through.

A gun-battery was unlimbering in the concealment of an orchard, the last of the yellowing leaves eddying about the gunners as they sweated to set up their positions before dark came down.

'We must be near.'

'Eh?'

'That's the third battery we've passed.'

'Near what, then?'

'Christ, the front line! Isn't that where we're goin'?'

They'd no time for each other, and wondered why, wondered where all the fine cocky eagerness had gone. Some of them knew.

'That dolled-up bastard starts the day by tellin' us we gotter be brave or get fuckin' shot by a firin'-squad an' then we're loaded up like fuckin' cattle an' tipped out 'ere like somethin' the dog sicked up.'

'Sorry you joined, mate?'

'You can shut your mouth for a start.'

They marched through the dusk.

'*Companee . . . Companee . . . Hult!*'

The N.C.O.s came past, pressing them to the side of the road, and they saw a party of men coming down from the east, a rabble of filthy uniforms with no one in charge, some of them limping, holding each other up, staggering blindly through the twilight helping each other along, with stretchers rocking in their midst, their blankets dark with blood and their bearers drunk with fatigue, their heads lolling and the khaki ripped and stained with blood of their own, a face staring up at the silent men who watched them go by, bone-white and with an unlit cigarette hanging from a nerveless mouth, a head with clotted bandages instead of a face, an arm dangling and swinging to the movement as the bearers tripped and tried to steady their feet, tried not to fall. A man reeled and another threw an arm round him and half-carried him along, one foot dragging and its boot scraping on the roadway. A boy-officer walked alone, his tunic flapping and his wax face staring in front of him with the vacant look of the mad as he marched his body along for fear it would otherwise fall. None of them spoke; the strength left in them must take them as far as the medical post and until they reached it there was nothing they wished to speak of.

Their shuffling died away.

The two leading companies were already re-forming on the road and Kilderbee and Knight were at work. 'Right, double file an' quick about it! Stop gawpin' like bloody apes an' get into line!' Their orders were quiet and had an undertone of anger. 'Come on, get those feet moving! *Le-eft right* – pick up the step!'

The anger was also in the men and they marched with an obstinacy that had not been present before; they were thinking for the first time of the enemy somewhere beyond the darkening ridge ahead of them; he had become real and they were angry with him.

'*Left – right*, pick it up – pick it up!'

'Is it far now, Sarge?'

'You tired or somethin'?'

'No, I'm not tired.'

Kilderbee caught the man's tone and turned his head. 'Rarin' to have a go, are you?'

'That's right.'

He gave a grunt of a laugh. 'God 'elp them, then.'

But there was nothing to do when they reached there and the anger had to dry on them like sweat and turn sour.

The enemy was not here, though this was as far as they could go because of him. Moving among them in the gloom of the early night to marshal them through the maze of the entrenchments R.S.M. Blossom sensed the mood in them and knew what a shame it was, what a waste. Bloody Pickering had done his best to put the fear of God in them with his talk of firing-squads and they'd slunk up the line like a mob of convicts but since they'd clapped eyes on those poor beggars they were different again, different men altogether, you could feel it like a fresh wind blowing. Give 'em orders now to fix bayonets and charge and they'd go through a brick wall, through a mountain, there was an army here and its blood was up and you could win a war with this lot, one hand behind your back and your boots still clean.

'No talkin', now, an' keep your eyes about you. Follow the man in front of you and remember the enemy's got listenin'-posts everywhere.' It was a shame and a waste but you couldn't send a signal to the High Command saying you'd got a bunch of lads here in a mood to murder. 'Keep down low an' don't think just because it's dark the snipers can't see you, they can see through a sack o' soot.'

The surface of the land was unbroken by any movement, its folds and ridges of clay spreading from the hills to the flat horizon under the ashy light from the sky where stars clung among thin cloud, but below ground level a battalion went into the line and a battalion came out.

'What are you lot?'

'3rd Dukes.'

'God bless you, then.'

'What's it been like?'

'Can't grumble. He's quiet tonight.'

Men squeezed past other men through the network of narrow channels, their equipment catching and swinging them round before they could free it, their feet sliding on the clay-filmed duckboards and their hand going out to touch the man in front. *'Ang on, Charlie, I'm caught up.* D Company in Rest. Lamps winked along the communication trenches and faces passed through their light. A Company in Reserve. *Keep moving, no noise now!* Clay, sandbags, telephone-cable, the tail of the man in front, the blind leading the blind. B Company in Support. *Look out – sniper!* A man pushing through with a spiked German helmet on his head, grinning like a schoolboy. *Where d'you get that, then? Bought it in Berlin, what you think?* C Company in the front line. A kid covered in clay and asleep on his feet, a chum shoving him along. The smell of damp, of burst latrine-pits, chloride of lime, tobacco-smoke, sweat, cordite and a bitter-sweet smell that was strange to the new battalion and too well known by the old, the smell of the dead.

'Right, remember your positions. No noise now.'

'Sar'nt Jackson!'

'Sir?'

'Get that party sorted out, they're blocking the gangway!'

'That you, Oscar?'

'It's me. This the front line then?'

'Fucked if I know. Where's Sam?'

'Say, you see any girls around here?'

'Thought you was lost, mate.'

'Corp'l Kemp! Is your wiring-party ready?'

'All ready, sir.'

'You know the drill, but wait for the order.'

'Mind that telephone-cable there!'

''Ow can you? It's like bloody spaghetti!'

'This the front line then?'

'Don't keep on askin' me that, fer Chris' sake! You 'opin' it is or 'opin' it isn't?'

'I just want to know.'

A parachute-flare burst very high and floated to cast its acid light across the lines and they stood frozen in it, dazzled and exposed and feeling themselves to have been caught in an act whose purpose was still not plain. Figures in a tableau, their shadows stark against the clay and the sandbags, they felt hypnotized, powerless to move until the fierce white light went out.

First-Lieutenant Talbot, commanding No. 2 Platoon, was standing near the angle of a traverse watching his men. Officially speaking, he thought uneasily, the 3rd Battalion of the Duke of Lancaster's Light Infantry were holding the line; but the truth was that they were huddled here in a wet ditch on foreign soil, untried, uncertain and in some measure afraid. He heard Sgt Kilderbee somewhere along the trench beyond the next traverse.

'Blake – sentry. Mayhew – sentry. Follett – sentry. Rest of you stand fast.'

The shadows crept higher against the clay walls and in another minute the light floated below the parapet and the trench was blotted out. The lieutenant waited for thirty seconds so that their eyes could accommodate, then gave the order.

'Stand to!'

He could hear them moving and the voices of the N.C.O.s beyond each traverse as the order was passed along.

'*Stand to . . .*'

Some of the men were clumsy in the dark, butting their boots against the fire-step, knocking their rifles, and Sgt Kilderbee heard them and was moved. They were like infants learning to crawl; how many times had these lads climbed the fire-step on Salisbury Plain? He didn't dare think; but that was only in training and there'd been one thing you couldn't make them forget: that they'd been play-acting, sticking their bayonets into sacks of straw and firing into cardboard and charging at dummies. But this fire-step was real and they knew it and couldn't even find the bloody thing without tripping over it first. Give them a week and they'd climb it in their sleep; their training was over now.

'*Stand to . . .*'

Private Follett pulled his rifle up and laid it across the sandbags, his spindly elbows crooked in the aiming-position and his thin neck poking from the collar of his uniform. He could see nothing in front of him; the night, after the bright flare, was darker than ever; but he knew that enemies were over there, and that if they tried to come near he would shoot at them.

His body leaned at the very edge of the front line and there was nothing between him and them, and closer than this he wouldn't let them come. He felt this, not in words in his mind but in a kind of warmth, a kind of strength, in his body; and it was this that she hadn't seemed to understand, looking up at him from the shade of her parasol and saying he was too young; and he couldn't explain. The posters on the walls had said in great big letters: *Your Country Needs You!* He'd stood in the street sometimes just staring at them, and thinking. There'd been no one he could talk to about it but that didn't matter, there'd never been anyone he could tell things to, and he was used to thinking them out for himself. But it must be true, what it said: his country needed him. Nobody had ever needed him before, and now it was a whole country! He couldn't believe it at first, but inside, from the very first one he'd seen, he'd known it must be true. A whole country.

He held his rifle steady. The sandbags on the fire-step had crumbled a bit because of all the soldiers who'd stood here before, and he shifted his feet to where it was more solid. They'd gone now and he'd taken their place, standing here between the enemy and England.

His young cheek was pressed against the cold butt of the rifle, warming it.

A sentry turned his head as Cpl Kemp came down the trench at a businesslike trot.

'You seen Mr Talbot?'

'Which one, Corp?'

'Senior.'

'I think 'e's along at No 3 machine-gun post.'

It was an hour since stand-down and their eyes had grown used to the dark, and the corporal kept up his pace through the next traverse, checking the sentries on his way.

'Mr Talbot?'

A figure detached itself from the others in the M.G. post. 'That you, Freddie?'

'Yes, sir.' A small lamp burned here on the ground and their faces were subtly altered by rising shadow. 'You know there's a raid on, sir?'

'Tonight?' He'd heard a rumour but had dismissed it; the

battalion had only just got here and no one knew the terrain at first hand.

'I'm on it,' said Freddie. 'Been taken off the wirin'-party.' He seemed ready to say more, but stood licking his lips as if hoping to be prompted.

'You must have volunteered.' It couldn't be a full-scale raid or he'd have been briefed about it. Some hot-headed ass must have put the idea to Capt. Bailey and got his permission. 'What the devil made you—' but he broke off and stared down at the worried face in the lamplight. 'Oh, Christ . . .' He started along the trench towards the Company H.Q. dugout with Freddie trotting after him. 'My brother, is it?'

'I thought you should know, on account of—'

'Bloody young fool!'

The raiding-party was already assembled when they got to the dugout, six men and a corporal, their faces blackened with the burnt cork and a belt of bombs at the waist. Victor was with them and Aubrey drew him aside.

'You could have told me first,' he said in a bitter undertone.

'Why?' Vic had a tin mug in his hand and drained it off: there'd been a tot of whisky issued all round. 'Cheers. Come to wish us luck?' His eyes were bright in his sooty face and his tone was mischievous.

'You've never seen that ground by daylight, you know that.' He realized it was the first time he had ever felt anger towards Vic, and he knew why. His authority as an elder brother had gone and there was nothing he could do to stop this happening; his slight seniority in rank meant nothing either: Vic had gone straight to their company commander, who'd agreed to the stunt. 'What the hell is Bailey thinking of?'

'Winning the war, old boy. Isn't that the general idea?' He tossed the mug and made a pretence of catching the last drop on his tongue.

Aubrey was shaking, and for a moment couldn't answer. He'd known this kind of thing would happen sooner or later: in the past he'd dismissed his brother's feverish need of escapade as a natural *joie de vivre*, dodging the effort of trying to understand it; from now on he must recognize it as a problem that had to be licked. Vic had dangerous toys to play with now and they could turn his mind to *joie de mort*.

'Those are good men you're taking out there with you, Vic.'

'The best.' The special-issue dagger that was slung from his waist flashed in the light as he turned away.

The voice of Capt. Bailey sounded from the dugout, telephoning a coded report to the Colonel on the raid-party's readiness, and as Aubrey swung round his path was blocked by Freddie Kemp.

'Leave things as they are, Mr Aubrey, eh?' He spoke with a soft intensity. 'He'd never give you permission – it's too late an' we're all briefed an' there's no room for another officer. We don't want *all* of us to go out there, do we now? He'll be all right with me.' His stare was steady.

Aubrey was in a mood to push past him but he held back. Impulsiveness had a high price, here. He was no more experienced in warfare than Vic, and less than Freddie, who had earned his stripes for his quiet efficiency in the advanced combat course. There was small hope of his doing anything for Vic tonight if things got out of hand, and at home there'd be two telegrams instead of one.

He said to Freddie: 'Did you ever tell Mrs Kemp why you joined the army?'

'Funny you should ask, sir. It was her that told me.' He smoothed the soot on his face with careful fingers; even covered with the stuff he managed to look neat and tidy. 'The objective's only a couple of prisoners an' it won't take long, and anyhow the captain says not to press matters if it gets too lively.'

There were breaks in the ridges of the land where shells had furrowed their way into the clay and they had gone forward in a crouching walk to within a hundred yards of the wire; now they lay prone.

There seemed no light in the flat low clouds above them yet there was a diffused glimmer at ground level and the coiled wire lay sketched across the horizon. From the charts handed over by the retiring battalion they judged themselves to be roughly midway between an advance listening-post and a hump of ground south of it, where the trunks of smashed trees stuck up blackly from the skyline. Vic spoke softly.

'All right, Stevens?'

'A minute to get me wind, sir?' The corporal had lost his footing on the way here, tripping and going down because of the weight of the bombs.

'Take your time,' Vic told him. The covering-party of ten riflemen had followed them out but they wouldn't be worried by any delay: there'd be nothing for them to do until the fun began. It was almost a pleasure to lie here for another minute or two, savouring the foretaste of the whole thing. It would go all right, he knew that. This was his lucky day: he'd had a job talking Bailey into the stunt and if Aubrey had got wind of it earlier he could have talked him out of it again; it was only the Old Man's continual gassing about 'the minimum standard of enterprise and initiative without which no officer is worthy of his commission' that had made Bailey agree. There was nothing Aubrey could do about it now – and that thought alone was a tonic. It was something he could enjoy getting used to: making his own way through this war as a full-grown man and not as someone's younger brother.

A war was a wonderful thing in a certain way; you could win fame in peacetime, work for a professorship in something or other, play at Wimbledon, drive a racing-car, go on the stage, but it was damned hard going and you could spend half your life at it and not necessarily succeed; but in a war you could get there overnight, screw yourself up to do something that other chaps might funk and with a bit of luck you'd get a mention in despatches or even the M.C. – and that wasn't just fame, it was *glory*!

'He's there, sir. Masters.'

'Right.'

Masters was to start the thing off by obliterating the listening-post.

He couldn't hope for a ribbon tonight, of course; this was just an impromptu raid and they'd bag a couple of Huns or they wouldn't. But he'd have to get one before the war ended – most people said it'd be over by Christmas – or before he went home on leave. An inch of purple-and-white silk stitched on just here above the pocket, all perfectly simple.

He moved his head to the left. Masters on the extreme flank near the observation post. Then Blount, Cpl Stevens, himself.

To the right: McFarlane, Hicks, Tuffnel and Freddie Kemp. Everything seemed to be all right and now he felt the sweat breaking out while his heart throbbed against the ground, thumping away as if he'd been running. He was swallowing frequently but it was all perfectly simple, forget the actual risk and go hell for leather, never mind about Aubrey's extra bloody pip, just concentrate on getting through.

'When you're ready, sir.'

They were all waiting for him and the sweat was pouring out and he could hear his breath hissing on the clay under his face – oh God, could your body be afraid and not your mind? This was why it was so magical, an inch of coloured silk: people knew how much you'd had to pay.

Rage took him – he'd been deceived: it wasn't all perfectly simple. Cpl Stevens was watching him, wondering at the delay, and with a savage jerk he got the revolver free and fired the single shot into the air. Masters put his bombs into the listening-post so fast that the rest were hardly on their feet before the flash lit the dark on their left flank and Tuffnel could see Lt Talbot silhouetted against it as he began pounding over the pocked and littered ground between Hicks and Cpl Kemp and straight for the enemy line with the Mills bombs jumping in their canvas belt and the clay flying up behind his boots. There was nothing to be heard from their left; the idea was that Masters would wipe out the listening-post at the start in case they had a light machine-gun and tried to cause trouble with it, and if there were anyone still alive he'd drag them home for interrogation. Masters could look after himself anyway; he was one of the veteran draft that had joined the battalion at Armentières after a month in action and ten days' rest. The main assault-party was to keep going and cut the wire and storm the front trench, get an idea of the enemy strength and snaffle what prisoners they could. It had looked all right on paper and Tuffnel thought they had a chance or he wouldn't have volunteered, and this was better than spending the night stived in a hole in the trench with the rats keeping you awake.

'All right . . . Down!'

They threw themselves flat and their fingers hooked at the release-pins and they began counting. Some shouts had gone up from the enemy line when Masters's grenades had exploded and there was already some pot-luck rifle fire coming from the parapet towards the right. *Two . . . three . . . four . . .* They kept prone, their eyes swivelled upwards under the edge of their cap-comforters to judge where the opposition seemed heaviest. *Five . . . six . . . seven . . .* A machine-gun started tacking away and they shrank against the earth instinctively but it didn't know where they were. They threw on *eight* and brought their arms forward to protect their heads and waited. They'd sent in two each, throwing in unison and concentrating on one point, and it wasn't possible to count the bursts: there was just a big ragged percussion and when the fragments had stopped whining they heaved themselves up and started forward again. A lot of noise had begun and the M.G. was joined by another but their own people had been waiting for that and the mortars were opening up to lob their bombs well ahead and on each side where the maps showed the machine-gun posts to be.

'*This way!*'

The flank-men swerved in against the orange light from the mortar-bombs and Vic waved them on to where he'd seen the break in the wire; it didn't look big enough but they hadn't expected to do more than this with fourteen grenades and it was all they'd get. Someone went down and there was a shout – '*Trip-wires, look out!*' – and they broke their run and began throwing again, each man for himself and aiming directly into the trench. Vic jumped a wire and slung his last grenade and was through the gap and running blind, the explosions bright against his eyes and their sound coughing heavily in the confines of the trench. He couldn't assess what was happening now: the mortars were still pumping the stuff in beyond the first trench to leave it clear for them and distract the opposition and the night was going slowly mad as if an ammunition dump was blowing up. The fumes choked him and he tripped and swore and staggered on and knew that he shouldn't be here and wouldn't be here if Aubrey hadn't forced him into it: he actually saw his brother's face in front of him for an instant; then a flash burst and he reeled and the rifle swung again and he kicked out, realizing he was on the edge of the parapet and a Hun was firing almost vertically up at him; he kicked again and felt the impact on the bastard's head and then he was going down and clinging to what he could to break his fall.

Freddie had raced in from the flank and was already here, clubbing a white-faced German who was trying to release a bomb; Cpl Stevens came over the sandbags feet first and crashed down and lay on the splintered duckboards with blood gushing from his neck. The trench had caved in badly here and bodies in field grey were strewn among burst sandbags; the cordite fumes drifted in a slow fog, choking and blinding them as they groped through the debris trying to find some survivors to take back. Vic saw movement and was about to warn Freddie when he recognized the black face under its cap-comforter: it was Blount, lugging a Hun through the smoke towards the slope of earth where the sandbags had collapsed.

'You're wastin' your time,' Freddie was calling, 'he's a goner!'

Blount let the man drop, laughing stupidly, and Hicks came through the gloom, bloody but energetic – 'There's nobody left in this one, sir, I've been right along it!'

Vic wheeled round and started towards the traverse but heard Freddie calling – 'Signal, sir! Signal!' Pale rose light was tingeing the smoke and he looked upwards and saw the flare from their own lines curving and falling beyond the smashed parapet.

'Right – we get out! Where's McFarlane?'

'They got 'im on the wire, sir.'

'Tuffnel?'

'He's up top still.'

There was nothing they could do for Cpl Stevens; Freddie found his paybook and some letters on him and took charge of them, following the rest up the slope of earth.

Vic drew some clean air into his lungs. 'Spread out and run like hell!'

A machine-gun was tack-tacking to the north and as they began running they could hear its sound loudening as it traversed. White light flooded the ground soon after they'd cleared the gap and the trip-wires, and rifle-fire started up from a point nearer their run; the flare was parachute-type and lit them efficiently and as the first of the bullets began threading among them they dropped and crawled to the shell-holes.

•   •   •

It was past midnight when Aubrey saw the first two coming in, but even with the observer's fieldglasses he couldn't recognize them. The covering-party of riflemen were still out there hoping to protect the rest. He went steadily along the sap, controlling his stride and carefully remembering the places where he must crouch because of his height and the risk of snipers. He refused to think. For two hours he had been shut in with his thoughts and had found a dozen ways in which he could have stopped Vic going out and now he refused to think any more. Above him the whole sky whispered, *Is your brother dead?* Along the main trench he passed three sentries and refused again, refused to ask them who had come in.

Captain Bailey was there, not far from the dugout, telling Kilderbee to withdraw the riflemen. An M.G. was still busy and their cover was so poor that it would be a matter of time before they were picked off where they lay.

He passed a man slumped against the parapet and heard him say, 'He's back safe an' sound,' and turned, realizing it was Freddie.

'Is he?' His voice was surprisingly cold and he was aware of it and tried to add something more appropriate but could think of nothing. Freddie had straightened up but his once-neat face, streaked with sweat and the remnant of the soot, looked loose with fatigue. 'Sit down, for God's sake. Have a rest.' He walked on and saw Vic going into the dugout, Bailey's arm round his shoulders. The first of the covering-party were dropping over the parapet, their clay-heavy boots clumping on the duckboards.

In the dugout a lamp burned and in its light the captain's face had a pallor, though he was doing his best to seem casual. As Aubrey ducked through the doorway he was giving Vic some cognac in the dented silver cap of a whisky flask. 'Won't you join us?' he asked Aubrey with rueful formality, and found a couple of mugs among the litter of maps and jam-tins and biscuits on the ammunition-box that made his table. Vic didn't look up; he sat slackly with his back to a pit-prop, his shaking fingers round the brandy. Aubrey had difficulty in recognizing him; it wasn't the young sharp face that was strange, despite the burnt cork and the shadows from the roof props, but the slack defeated attitude: he had never seen Vic tired before and certainly never defeated.

He accepted the mug from Bailey but didn't drink. 'You all in one piece?'

Vic swung his head up, his reddened eyes focusing. 'Oh, hello. Yes, I'm all right.' He looked down again and drew the shaking cup to his mouth.

Aubrey said to the captain: 'Where are the rest?'

'There aren't any. Your brother, and Corporal Kemp.'

Vic lifted his head. 'Masters didn't come in?'

'Unfortunately not.' Bailey answered with an undertone of defiance that showed he felt mostly responsible. 'Never mind, you livened things up.'

'Any prisoners?' Aubrey asked remotely.

The captain put his tin mug down with a little bang. 'Don't ask for jam on it. Your brother's back isn't he?' He glanced across Aubrey's shoulder. 'Come on in, Corporal Kemp!' He reached for the bottle. 'We'll need some details. I'm told you actually saw Corporal Stevens dead in the enemy trench and McFarlane hanging on the wire. Now what about—' He broke off as Kemp put a grimed hand to his tunic and dropped a little pile of Army paybooks and private letters on to the table; on top was a creased photograph of a young girl in a wedding-dress.

'We didn't find Tuffnel, sir. He's the only one we're not sure about.' The regulations were strict: the next-of-kin weren't informed of a death unless the evidence left no doubts. He glanced at Mr Victor but he seemed too shaky to make any kind of report. 'Blount an' Hicks were with us as far as the shell-hole where we had to lay up for a bit on account of the flares. When it was dark again there was a bit o' noise from the German line and we could hear their voices. One time, we were certain it was a party comin' to follow us up, try gettin' their own back.' He looked reflectively into the tin mug for a moment, then jerked the spirit into his mouth and put the mug down, sucking in the fumes. 'Blount an' Hicks didn't like it, but Mr Talbot held them back till we'd got a plan. There was one bomb left among the four of us an' we were goin' to use it to give them some cover if there was a rush made. They began runnin' the minute they were out of the shell-hole – they'd been told to crawl – an' a machine-gun got them, like it was bound to.'

Captain Bailey said thinly: 'You mean they panicked.' It seemed he found the responsibility too much for him and wanted to share a little, even with the dead.

'They were too confident, sir.'

The rebuke was clear enough and it sparked off the anger that had been rising in Aubrey over the last minutes. He didn't want to hear any more. 'Trench rounds,' he said tersely. 'Better luck next time.' He turned and ducked below the lintel and went with his slow stride along the darkened trench, passing the sentries and the men who slept or were huddled sleeplessly, their rifles beside them. His anger was strange to him and felt more like an illness; he couldn't ever remember feeling angry, even as a child; nothing had come to touch the peace he'd known for the world, the small and secluded world of Ashbourne where life had seemed one long summer – too small and too secluded, he knew that now. It hadn't prepared him for this, the world of war, and he'd better start sizing it up. War magnified everything: two hours could last a lifetime and your brother could die a hundred deaths while the minutes leaked your hope away; a simple decision by one man could mean life or death to others. War was a vigilant and ever-wakeful thing, a watcher that missed nothing, taking your quiet word and shouting with it, taking your idle hand and killing with it; whatever you said, whatever you did, was magnified to the proportions where only a world gone mad could make room for the consequences you never meant to bring about.

Standing alone for a time and watching the flash of the guns lighting the low clouds farther east, Aubrey knew he must start doing something he'd always managed to avoid until now: he'd have to start making an effort.

A shadow moved. 'Sir?'

'Well?'

'I think I can hear something.' The sentry had left his rifle on the parapet and was standing to attention in front of him.

'What like?'

'Hard to say, sir. Some sort of movement out there.' He was only a kid, as so many of them were. The distant flashes gleamed on the sweat-film of his cheek.

'Never leave your rifle. Go back to your post and keep a sharp look-out. It's probably rats.' The boy only wanted someone to talk to.

Captain Bailey would take full blame, of course – Pickering would see to that. He'd let himself be talked into a hopeless operation by an irresponsible young sub, and the Colonel had allowed it on the chance of snatching a wink of approval from High Command: this was his battalion's first night in the line and even a half-successful raid would have looked well in despatches; even one captured Hun would have made it almost worth-while – Intelligence was always itching to get their hands on someone to interrogate. In addition the stunt had been mounted with complete disregard for every rule in the book: exaggerated reliance placed on the element of surprise and the mortars used to distract the enemy at a late stage instead of blowing the wire and softening up the resistance first. Result: six dead and no prisoners.

Someone was coming slowly down the trench in the feeble light, his boots slurring on the duckboards, his bare head tousled; dried clay fell from his torn uniform and he was wiping the black from his face with a filthy handkerchief, and there was a familiarity in the gesture that Aubrey recognized.

Vic almost collided with him, his thoughts elsewhere. For a moment he stood peering up; then out of the exhaustion he summoned a tone of defiance and his voice was sharp. 'Well? Why don't you say it?' He felt himself swaying and with a jerk of impatience straightened up and went on towards his dugout.

An hour later a sentry heard sounds nearing the trench and called a challenge and was answered by an English voice, and Tuffnel came sliding over the parapet, to reach up and drag a heavy bundle across the sandbags. It lay sprawled at his feet.

Sergeant Kilderbee was fetched and by the time he arrived they'd thrown water over the big Hun's face and he was trying to stand up. '*Kamerad . . . Kamerad . . .*' The insignia of a senior N.C.O. were half-hanging from his sleeve. Others stood about, brought here by the disturbance – Sam and Percy Stokes and two of the medical orderlies – and Tuffnel was unbuckling the big canvas belt he'd kept his bombs in.

'Is he wounded?' asked Kilderbee.

'No, Sarge. I had to club him, that's all.'

'Right, two of you as escort. Take him to the Colonel. Look sharp.' They fetched their rifles and Kilderbee got a cigarette from his tunic and thrust it at Tuffnel, striking a match. 'I know your sort. You want a moustache an' you get one, you want a prisoner an' you get one. Pig-headed sort, that's you.'

VI

The shelling had eased up during the past hour, though there was still an occasional *crump* from the front-line area a mile to the east. Another stretcher-party came blundering through the mud towards the Casualty Clearing Station, their backs bent against the rain.

'Poor bastards,' said Harry Ross, and tried again to light his fag, but it was too damp.

'Never mind,' said Tom, 'it's our turn in the line tonight.' He watched the stretcher-bearers through the fringe of water that dripped from the edge of the corrugated iron.

Percy Stokes jerked a frown at him. 'What d'you mean, "never mind"?'

'I'd rather be up there myself, really, than sittin' here listenin' and' watchin' them go by.'

Percy's quick eyes were almost crossed in his effort to understand this line of reasoning. 'Well you know the way.' He lifted the jam-tin again to look at the flame. It was an hour since Sam Quincey had come doubling under the edge of the shelter with the tommy-cooker – 'Okay fellers, we got some combustion! Tea in ten minutes!' They'd gathered round the stove and put a match to the tablet of meth. but now only Percy had any faith and even that was slipping. 'Where d'you scrounge this thing, Sam?'

'Huh? The stores.'

'Well they won't miss it.' He put his finger into the water.

'Don't scald yourself,' said Geoff Tuffnel dryly.

'Eh? I'm tryin' to break the ice. I think this water's colder than when we started an' we've used half the tablets. You know what I think this thing is? It's for keeping stuff cold in summer. So when the sun comes out an' the butter starts meltin' we'll have the answer.' He sat back on his haunches and blinked at the haze of December rain across the shell-torn fields. An edge of icy wind cut down through the gap between the corrugated iron and the tarpaulin and Harry Ross squelched outside to do

106

something about it. 'You know,' Percy said, 'the cave-men lived more comfortable than this. Haven't made much progress have we?' He looked round for diversion. 'Where's your mouth-organ then, Oscar? Come on, chew us off a concerto.'

'I'm doin' a letter to Mum.'

'Be in time for Christmas then.' It was only the first day of the month but Oscar needed time to do a letter because he never knew what to say, and people had to help him. 'What've you put so far?'

'"Dear Mum."' He sat hunched in his greatcoat and pressed against Wiggy Bennett for warmth, though Wiggy had none to give him: he'd wound his cap-comforter round his face with just his eyes showing.

'Well she'll know who it's for,' nodded Percy.

'Shall I put that it's rainin'?'

'Never get past the censor, I've warned you about that before. If it's raining it means there's not much visibility, so our batteries are having to fire blind without any help from the observers, an' that means we can't have any plans for mounting an offensive.' He dipped his finger into the water again.

Oscar sucked his pencil. 'Better not put that it's rainin', then.'

'You'd be exposing the intentions of the High Command.' Percy blinked around him. 'Geoff, don't sit there doin' nothing. Nip out an' bring in a prisoner – we could put him in boilin' water, if we had some boilin' water.'

Geoff gave his slow token smile. They were always telling him to do that. Their platoon commander said Tuffnel was recommended for the Military Medal and the Colonel said he was sure to get it. They were all sweating on it now.

A heavy one came down somewhere between Reserve and Support and they heard it before it fell and sat waiting and avoiding each other's eyes; then the ground shook and the tarpaulin was ripped away from the iron sheeting and the rain-haze turned brown as the pulverized clay drifted down. Far away they could hear the faint cry: *Stretcher-bearers!*

Geoff and Smithy went out to fetch the tarpaulin.

There was a time, Tom thought, when they would have all got down and covered their heads; it was funny how quickly you got used to things. There'd not been much shelling farther west when they'd first gone into the line but up here it had been very bad, ever since they'd come. Some of them couldn't seem to get used to it, though; last night he'd heard one of the boys sobbing for a long time, going on and on, alone somewhere in the dark trench, breaking his heart. He'd gone over to him and sat with him till he fell asleep.

'Five-nine,' said Harry.

'You must live here,' Percy told him.

Oscar bit into his pencil. 'Shall I put as 'ow we 'ope it won't rain again tomorrow, then?'

Percy looked shocked. 'What! It'd seem we were all watchin' the met. reports, hopin' for the weather to clear so we can go into the attack. Talk about revealin' information to the enemy, I don't know how you can play such a dangerous game, Oscar. Before you know it you'll get shot for a spy, an' then what's your Mum going to do without all those lovely long letters to read?'

Oscar frowned at his limp bit of paper. 'Better not put that, then.'

Smithy came in from helping Geoff with the tarpaulin and got on to his knees, pulling his issue knife from the edge of the puddle by the duckboards and sticking it in again an inch higher, measuring the distance with the top joint of his thumb; his long sharp nose, red with cold, hovered over his brass chronometer.

Percy's gaze was concentrated on him. 'Is my bath ready yet, nurse?'

'You know how it works out? Two inches an hour, and the duckboards an inch and a half above the surface of the water. So we've got forty-five minutes before we have to start bailing out.'

'There's a factor you ain't considered,' Sam grinned cheerfully. 'I float.'

The express-train rushing of an H.E. began filling the air and they listened to it as it loudened and someone called out sharply – 'This one's not for us!' From where he sat Geoff Tuffnel could actually see the thing, a shadow curving fast through the haze, gross, stinking, evil, plummeting beyond the ridge to the west where men would be running or diving flat. Light burst half a mile down the line near the transport park; then the ground shuddered.

'Tch!' exclaimed Percy, 'isn't it shockin'? You'd think they'd find somethin' better to do, a day like this. Haven't they got any cards?'

The tarpaulin flapped but didn't blow away: Geoff and Smithy had put more sandbags on it.

Oscar nibbled his pencil. 'Shall I tell 'er we're makin' some tea?'

Percy dipped his finger. 'You jokin'?' He lifted the tin to see if the flame was still going. 'I should just put "Dear Mum" – you've got that part done already, haven't you, so we can go on to the next bit – "I hope you get this letter, and be sure to let me know if you don't. Your loving Oscar." There's no vital military information there, so you've done it on the censor at least.'

Oscar's pencil began worming its way across the damp shred of paper, but in a moment it stopped. 'Wait a minute, Perce. If my Mum *don't* ever get my letter, then 'ow will she know she's got to let me—'

Percy's stage-demon laugh echoed from the corrugated iron. 'You're bright today all right, Oscar! Now before you get writer's cramp why don't you just get out your suck-an'-blow kit an' give us a tune?'

'Jeeze,' said Sam, hugging his knees and staring at the rain, 'you know we get droughts where I come from, huh? Months on end, all you get to see is dust an' tumbleweed, you know that?'

Tom looked up from his notebook. 'What's tumbleweed?' It sounded a pretty name and perhaps old Mr Willis had never heard of it, and he could tell him in a letter.

'Huh? Oh it's just a weed on the prairie, Tom, an' when there's no rain the roots go dry an' the wind pulls 'em out o' the ground, so they go rollin' an' tumblin' 'way across the land.' He sat staring at the rain, not seeing it now.

There is an American soldier with us, wrote Tom, *and he tells us about his home.* It was a difficult letter and he'd never dreamed of writing it before the miracle had happened. They'd been coming out of the line, the time when Geoff had captured the German, and Cpl Kemp had spoken to him.

'Follett!'

'Yes, Corp?'

'Where have I seen you before?'

They were peeling the muddy covers off their rifles and cleaning them; Tom often watched the corporal when they were doing this, enjoying the way he touched and squinted at the metal parts as if he'd made them himself.

'At the training-camp, I suppose.' He'd seen the corporal looking at him sometimes and looking away. Tom had never smiled at him or anything, to mean he recognized him, because that part of his life was over and he didn't want to be reminded of it.

'Before that, I mean. In civvy street.' He put his steady bright eye to the barrel and squinted along it, using the pull-through again.

Tom didn't know how it happened; it was as if someone else was saying it for him because he'd made up his mind a long time ago not to mention it. 'I was under Mr Willis at the Manor, so you might have—' But he couldn't finish because he suddenly had to swallow hard and a kind of warmth was spreading all through him and he shut his eyes quickly.

'That's it!' he heard Mr Kemp saying. 'That's it!'

It was a very strange feeling and he wondered at it and felt almost frightened, not knowing himself, not knowing that all the time he'd been holding back his secret from Mr Kemp a part of him was longing to tell it; and now he'd done it without meaning to, as if he couldn't stop it coming – and suddenly he could smell the cut grass, a sweet green smell that went right down in his chest, and thought for a minute that when he opened his eyes he'd see the tall chimneys there. All he saw of course was the smashed roof of the barn where they'd sleep tonight, and Mr Kemp with his steady eyes on him before he looked away and started polishing the bolt with his bit of four-by-two.

'Miss the place, do you?' There was a roughness in his voice. 'So do I, boy.'

'Yes.'

'Never mind, this lot won't last for ever, then we'll be back there. Well fancy me not recognizin' you right off! Mr Talbot know you're with us, does he?'

'I don't think so.' He wanted to go on talking and listening and never stop; now he'd let himself bring it all back to mind he couldn't have enough of it – it was as if he'd been hungry.

Suddenly he was saying – 'She said there'd always be a place for me there, she told me herself. Do you think she meant that, Mr Kemp?'

'Well of course.' Funny, hearing it again, 'Mr' instead of 'Corporal'; the kid was back there at the Manor in his mind. He recalled old Willis telling him about the 'new lad' – came from some orphanage. 'The firs' little beggar that's shown willin' to learn a cowslip from a chrysanthemum an' don't leave me barrows all dirty.' He said: 'If Milady says there's a place for you then it's safe as houses.'

'Is it?' Tom wasn't meaning to speak, it was words rising up from deep inside. 'I've got a place there? *I* have?'

The trouble with miracles was that you couldn't just sit there while they happened, something had to bust, and he was suddenly covering his face and though he squeezed his eyes shut so tight that it hurt, nothing could stop the tears coming and he just sat crouched and ashamed, fiercely ashamed, while their salt ran warm on his lips and he tried to stop shaking; he felt his rifle being taken from where it had rested across his feet, clear of the mud, and heard Mr Kemp saying, 'If we don't get this nice an' clean before Sergeant Knight comes an' puts his nose down the spout he'll have a fit, now what've we got in this barrel? Tch-tch! Lump o' clay, three field-mice an' a turnip, this won't do now, will it?'

Dear Milady . . .

That had been weeks ago and he'd only just screwed up enough courage to write a letter. He'd lain awake so many nights since then, listening to the guns and the rats and the sentries pulling off their gloves and blowing on their hands, thinking of all the reasons why he mustn't do such a thing – a gardener's boy wasn't meant to write letters to a lady and she wouldn't even know who it was from ('And what do your parents say, will they allow you to be a soldier?'), wouldn't remember him at all. *But he'd got a place there . . .* and he belonged to the tall chimneys and the potting-shed and the smell of cut grass, just like the Red Admiral did; and the time came when he'd asked Sam how to get a notebook and Sam had given him one from the stores, which he called 'Woolworth's' in his laughing way; and every day he'd found himself sitting with it on his knees when they came off fatigues or sentry-go or church parade, and now it was happening and his hand wasn't steady and he knew he'd want to tear it all up afterwards and would have to try not to.

There is an American soldier with us and he tells us about his home. He wanted to ask how to spell the weed Sam had told them about but he might laugh at him. *He says there is bad drought where he is from, which would not suit Mister Willis, I am sure.*

He looked up at the others. Oscar had tucked his piece of paper away and was sitting with his mouth-organ against his lips – Oscar had puzzled-looking eyes whenever he wasn't playing it, and his lips folded over it like a horse with a lump of sugar – and Percy was bent over his tommy-cooker making magic signs and saying 'Abracadabra' and Harry Ross was laughing at him. She wouldn't want to know about that, and it would take too long to explain. Pop Jarvis was hunched up fast asleep, clasping his rifle, a raindrop sliding down his face from a leak in the roof; he could do that easily, just doze off and wake again; 'Sleep is meat an' drink to a man,' he'd said once, 'an' you must get it while you can.'

There is a friend of mine called Pop Jarvis, and we call him Pop because he is older than all of us . . .

He looked younger, though, when he was asleep, his brown lined face almost smoothed out. Perhaps he wasn't so old but had been such a long time in the war, right from the beginning in August until now, getting on for Christmas-time: he was a 'Mons-man' and had a gold wound-stripe on his left sleeve, and he knew all about how to go on as a soldier. It had been Pop who'd made Frank Adams feel better, for a while anyway, the first spell they'd had in the line. Frank had been shivering with fright because of the shells, and Pop had talked to them in the dark trench, telling them how to keep their rifle-bolts clean by using a worn-out sock, and how to keep a wood fire going with Army biscuits when there was no more wood, and how they should cut the bottom off their greatcoats to stop the mud making them heavy, all that sort of thing. Frank said he couldn't sleep on account of the cold, and Pop Jarvis had loosened his boots for him and put some empty sandbags over his feet; then he'd got a tin and some dubbin and a bit of four-by-two as a wick and put a match to it, making a night-light for them all; and that was when Frank had stopped shivering, staring at the flame and then at Pop smiling at him with his wise sort of face. They'd all felt better, not only Frank; the shells didn't stop going over but somehow they were outside now, lost in the dark and nothing to do with them, safe down here with their own little light to keep things away.

Frank wasn't with them now; he was up in the dugout helping them with the roof, which had caved in because of a shell; perhaps he'd heard Pop saying, 'They never come down in the same place twice.' He and Sam had agreed they were going to look after Frank tonight when they went into the line; he was getting worse, not better.

She wouldn't want to know about poor Frank.

I will close by hoping you are well, and Sir William and – her name had jumped to his mind, Kitty's, as it did so often, but he daren't write it down – *the other people there with you. Yours very respectfully, Tom Follett.*

Percy balanced another tablet on the end of his bayonet and eased it under the tin, dipping his finger into the water. 'Well I never, it's got the chill off! I think science is marvellous, don't you? Couple of tons of methylated spirit an' you've got a cup of tea!'

On the second day in the line they could still hear the piano. It had been playing all yesterday and now Aubrey paused on his way through the trench and stood listening; it was mostly Schubert and was played quite well, though the piano sounded old and they'd taken the back off to increase the volume.

Nigel Coxhead had been provoked by it. 'If we can get any kind of a bearing on it I'm going to start up mortars.'

'Why?'

'Well, I mean they've got such a bloody cheek. They know we can hear it.' The German line was less than eighty yards distant in places.

'They may think we enjoy it,' Aubrey had smiled. 'As a matter of fact the Sonata's a favourite of mine.'

'What, fifty times a day?' Nigel's good-looking face was doughy and his eyes red-rimmed. The lack of feminine company made him morose and in Rest he finished every evening with a half-bottle of cognac. 'You're too damn' tolerant, old horse, that's your trouble.'

113

This morning a lark sang, high over the blackened stumps of what had been Liancourt Wood, where the last of the mist was thinning under a pale sun; its fragile notes were so different from the hard twang of the piano that the ear was untroubled by any discord as the bird accompanied the man. Each seemed to proclaim that this was a morning for peace.

Aubrey went on, his step slower, unwilling to disturb the mood of the hour by his own movement. Men slept here and there, exhausted from their night duties; others stood leaning on their rifles, straightening as they saw him coming.

'Good-morning, Tom! All's well with you?'

'Yes, sir!'

The boy's eagerness touched him. Freddie had told him a few weeks ago there was 'a lad from the Manor' here. Aubrey had found out his name and spoken a word to him the same day, asking if 'all were well' with him, and though they seldom met, the phrase had become established like a password between them, to mean they both knew of a place where the trees were not blackened stumps nor the earth a wilderness.

Another link with home was in his hand now as he walked on: he'd cut this ashplant from the spinney beside the orchard, the week when he and Vic had left, and had come to cherish it.

The crack of a rifle came again – he'd heard it before from the dugout and assumed it was a sniper, but laughter followed this time and he wondered what could be going on. Beyond the traverse he saw a group of men, and Vic nearing them from the other direction on his rounds. They seemed to be taking it in turns to fire at something, and the laughter came again, this time cut short as they heard Vic's question.

'What's so amusing?'

Aubrey climbed the fire-step and took a cautious look across No Man's Land; ridges of shell-torn clay hid the enemy line but a man with a sack was dodging about on the surface where the communication trench had obviously been blocked by bombardment.

'It's their postman, sir. We're tryin' to make him drop his letters!'

Vic's head lifted and he gazed across the clay ridges, then took the rifle from Tuffnel, dragging at the bolt; the men stood back, delighted to share their game. The field-grey figure was trotting obstinately towards his front line, the sack of letters swinging. The shot cracked and the postman stood strangely erect for a moment and then fell slowly on to his face; a break came in the lark's song, then it was resumed.

Vic thrust the rifle back at Tuffnel, whose face was expressionless.

'In case you've forgotten, we are at war.'

Towards dusk a salvo crossed the lines from a battery of British twelve- and fifteen-inch guns and C Company was alerted while Capt. Bailey telephoned Battalion H.Q. to ask what was on. After a few minutes the heavies fell silent and a group of Quick Dicks began barking away from their position nearer Reserve, then their light vibration was overlaid with the bump of 4.2's as the German artillery opened up in reply.

A watery sun floated beyond the British lines, its colour melting into the haze until the horizon was stained with red. Crows drifted blackly across, seeking trees that had once been here.

The earth had lost its stillness and the duckboards trembled; tin mugs vibrated in the dugouts and the fieldglasses that Julian Lovell had hung on the wall began slowly swinging. He looked at Aubrey, his eyes questioning, and Aubrey shrugged.

'Bailey's finding out.' There had been no orders of any kind.

The first of the 4.2's were falling well to the west and some lighter material followed them in to explode above the Support area. From the open trench Sgt Kilderbee saw an air-burst shrapnel shell making its double detonation, a puff of yellow smoke billowing from the cloud of green, the steel splinters blossoming in the last light of the sun. 'All right, take cover,' he told the men nearest him, and sat on the fire-step with his back against the clay and in the lee of the blast. The bits came whining down to pick at the sandbags, wicked stuff, some of it sharp as knives. When it was over he got up and started towards the platoon dugout, running into Lt Talbot.

'It's nothing for us,' Aubrey told him. 'H.Q. says the new battery's just shooting itself in.'

'Just our luck, sir.' The gunners called this kind of thing an artillery duel but it was the poor bloody infantry that copped it in the end. A big one landed close and they both stood still; the light of its explosion flickered across Aubrey's face as he shut his eyes against it, and Kilderbee felt glad to be with him; there weren't so many that'd take a close one as calm as this – Col. Pickering would have been in that dugout before you could see his arse go through the door. He was quite pleased with Mr Talbot of late; there'd been a time when he'd not gone much on him, too easy with people by a long chalk, but he was steady enough out here and you could count on him and that was saying a lot. 'Inspect the rum, sir?'

'I don't think so, no.' It was a duty he always chose to neglect, and the sergeant had only asked as a formality. The rule was that when rum was issued an officer must be present to see that no abstainer gave his share to another man who'd already drunk his own, especially when the battalion was warned for action; but he'd too much respect for them to play the schoolmarm, watching them while they were trying to enjoy their tot; and drunkenness in C Company was rare.

Kilderbee had disapproved of this at first: the lieutenant was still too easy in his ways and couldn't seem to change the ideas he'd held at the training-camp – 'Out there, Kilderbee, we'll want men with some pride left in themselves.' But after a time the sergeant had seen there was no advantage taken at rum-issue, and sensed it was partly because the men knew the rule and knew Mr Talbot was ignoring it as a gesture of his confidence in them. They'd do a lot for their Platoon Commander, that was plain: the few words you overheard when you were on your rounds told you more than a month of Battalion Orders. This was why, he'd sometimes thought, Mr Talbot was a first-lieutenant while his brother was still a one-pipper, dashing about the place trying to win the war on his own without a thought for the men.

'Better watch this one, sir.'

Aubrey cocked an eye at the sky and nodded, hitting his arm – 'Come on!' They ran for the dugout. It was a heavy five-nine and the only good thing about them was that you could hear them coming and get a rough idea of where they were going to land; this one came with a slowly-rising roar that began vibrating in their chests and they drove their feet at the duckboards and second by second forgot everything except that the sky was filling with sound and the earth was their only shelter; and then fear broke out in them as they plunged through the doorway and threw themselves down, the primitive and necessary fear of the mole for the eagle, the living creature's last defence that will find ways of survival and the strength to pursue them, the nerves galvanized and the blood racing and the mind numbed to enable the body to look after itself unencumbered by the conflict of choice and decision.

Someone shouted, someone outside or already in here with them, no words, just a shout, perhaps their own, a sound thrown against the bigger sound in instinctive challenge. Light blazed and the dark streamed with colours and the earth staggered, shrugging their prone bodies away while the night gaped and the wind screamed and snatched at them, its breath foetid with nitrous gas; a timber crashed and rain began: a rain of metal and earth and unknown things breaking away and flying up and falling, whirling in the new dark coming down, the new silence, their heads singing with it, the new shape, their raw hands groping and trying to learn it and find a way out, a way back.

Earth tumbling. Shouting again. Not shouting, it was a whisper close to the ear, magnified, greeted by the senses athirst for known things, familiar things, the voices of others. '... Right, Kil'bee?' The stink of chemicals, the breath rasping in a throat full of razor-blades. 'Kilderbee, are you all right?' Memory, the way back: it was Mr Talbot's voice, they'd come in here together.

'I'm all right. Are you?' A weight was across his hip; he could hear Mr Talbot grunting as he dragged at it; it was a timber prop and together they got it clear and Kilderbee stood up. A cry from the distance – *Stretcher-bearers!* He said, 'We'd better get out there.'

The trench was blocked at the place where they'd been standing: they just walked into solid earth and had to climb and go down the other side. Some stuff had come down farther along the front line and the flash of the guns cast a nervous light across chaos where dark figures ran and stumbled and carried each other, falling and getting up, losing their way because the trenches were blocked and gapped and broken and nothing remained familiar.

Stretcher-bearers!

Men ran blind and others stopped them, showing them the way to the aid-post where the M.O. and some orderlies worked by the light of candles and a paraffin lamp.

'Where's Harry?'

Some kept to their shelters, the holes in the wall of the trench where they had been sleeping or waiting for stand-to, and as each new explosion roared they braced their limbs against it and against the shuddering earth as if to keep it still. A man went past on his hands and knees, moaning and trailing blood across the tilting duckboards and someone dropped from a hole: 'Come on, son, lift up then an' onto me back.'

A kind of answer came, a bubbling from where a mouth had been, and weak arms felt for the rescuer with the uncertainty of the infant seeking its mother's body.

'Lift up, then, get your arms round me.'

Whistles blew and Sgt Knight ran crouching along the parapet, cursing, dropping as a *minenwerfer* sailed lazily through the dappled dark with its brute blunt shape turning and glinting in the flare of the guns as it wobbled to earth and the earth fountained and took fire.

Stretcher-bearers!

'Where's Harry?' Friends looked for friends, knowing many were buried and unable to call out.

An N.C.O. went lurching to a dugout where an officer was trying to sandbag a telephone as linesmen searched for the break, their reels scraping along the clay.

'Mr Yates has just been killed, sir!'

'All right.' What else could you say?

Two men dug at a smashed traverse with their entrenching-tools. 'They said it was an artillery duel.'

'It's bloody not. Everybody's in it now, that was a minnie jus' come down. Who's under this lot, then?'

'I dunno. I just saw a foot.'

A stretcher-party made its way across open ground, plodding and unmindful of the menacing sky; you couldn't go by the com-trench, it wasn't there now; you couldn't know where the next one was coming down and fifty-fifty you were as well off here as over on the left; you couldn't stop, and that was something, you'd got a job to do.

'Geoff!' A white face loomed from shadow. 'He's gone!'

'Who?'

'Harry.'

Geoff stood still and saw the ginger hair and freckles and the laughing eyes and the name in gold on the board that would never be anything at all to do with them, though it was their name, Harold Ross.

Light burst and a man screamed and earth silenced him.

The bearers were everywhere, their arms red from wrist to elbow. 'My kit?'

'What's that, chum?'

'You got my kit?'

'You'll not be wantin' that, now. A Blighty one, you've got!'

'There's everything in it, though!' Brass chronometer, compass, stop-watch, slide-rule, everything. They didn't understand.

In No 3 Platoon trench Lt Lovell picked his way over the wrecked duckboards and heard coughing and looked up and saw Capt. Bailey staggering towards him from the dugout, eyes staring from his blanched face, hands clawing at the air, his body jerking, the coughing sound going on and on with the rhythm of words, the teeth bared in the shape of laughter, the head lolling.

'Are you hit?' But he could see that it was nothing that could answer; it only looked like Capt. Bailey. Drumfire beat across the sky and light flickered like an electric storm.

At the far end of the trench some sandbags had been hurled across leaning timber and here Frank Adams sheltered. He had never been drunk but this was what it must be like: you saw things clearly through a lot of confusion, and small things seemed important. He smelt of sweat though the night was cold, and he knew that he'd messed his drawers at some time when they'd all been trying to run clear. He didn't know where Sam and Tom were; they'd promised to look after him when they went into the line; they mustn't find him yet. He had made a hole through the sandbags, just big enough for his arm, and now he sat shivering, the fear not letting him move yet, though he knew he would do it.

He heard men passing, one of them coughing all the time and the other talking to him, telling him it was all right, they'd go and find the dressing-station and see the M.O. there. The coughing sounded peculiar.

A bump came and they were calling for stretcher-bearers again; the ground shook and he felt for the hole in the sandbags, afraid that their shifting might close it up. He could smell the gunpowder smell as the blast-wave blew past his shelter, and it was this that brought it all together in his mind, the dark and the death and the way they didn't seem to worry about it, all the others, marching up to the line and laughing, some of them, knowing what might happen. How could they do that? It wasn't something you could ask. But he'd had enough now and his stomach sickened whatever he looked at, a rifle, a boot, a man's face. Everything was so big and hard, and noises were heavy; men were like horses here, leather on them and hard brass buckles, their heavy boots creaking, the strong wood of the butt and the cold metal, their voices loud, the sergeants with their square bodies and knuckly hands and their strong necks stiff in the rough khaki; there seemed to be no soft flesh any more, no whispering or the long calm of an evening, the rush of tall grasses, a white cloud drifting; and nobody minded, they were all busy, banging and polishing and shouting, driven by something inside themselves, a hard metal engine, and making loud jokes at the roaring in the rain, *that one's not for us, no ball, Jerry!* They didn't think of death, they couldn't, to go on like that; or they thought of it as something they wanted, heavy steel exploding against their hard marching bones in a kind of marriage, their laughter blowing away in the mad stink of the wind; he thought of them as he moved at last, listening, and knew he'd never understand them any more than they could understand him, *there's no call to be afraid, lad*, and felt about in the dark and found it, cold under his fingers, *but why isn't there, don't you know we'll all die?* There was shouting a long way off but he paid no attention, pulling the metal ring of the grenade and starting to sicken again as he pushed it through the hole in the sandbags, keeping a grip on it, his arm blocking the hole as he thought of all the trains and all the lorries grinding with their great heavy wheels and bringing more men, and more men, from the places where there were children and leaves and white linen to here where their hard spades dug at the frozen ground and their guns poked out to kill with, what made them come? It was said you never felt it, only later, but later there were nurses and morphia and the sweet drinking in of the day-long knowing, the knowing that you would never have to come here again, but oh God the waiting was bad and he kept wanting to pull his arm back through the hole but made himself stay as he was, his breath held and his teeth biting together and a noise starting in his chest like a puppy crying, his left hand already numb as if it knew and it banged and he screamed.

It had taken an hour to clear the communication-trench and some of the bearers were using it now; the shelling was easing up but an enemy mortar battery was sending stuff all the time and there wasn't only yourself to think of, there was the poor sod on the stretcher.

Aubrey had been through twice with a man on his back and was taking a third down now, with two of the men just ahead of him, their stretcher made of duckboard slats and a groundsheet.

'Am I hurt bad?'

They jogged over churned clay, slipping. 'You're okay, pal, it's nuth'n the Doc can't fix, so you just think good'n' hard about how it'll be when the nurses tuck you up, huh?'

Linesmen with lamps pressed back for them, keeping their wires clear.

'I tell you what my father is, did I? He's a station-master, Clapham Junction. I don't know—'

'Am I hurt bad, am I?'

'Now don't interrupt. If you were hurt bad I wouldn't trouble telling you about my father, would I? I don't know how he stands it, all those trains and the people complaining at him all day long, chronic it is, enough to get on your tits. You know what I'd do if I was my father? Get into step can't you, Sam, you're catchin' me in the balls every time. I'd line all those trains up end to end from Victoria to Balham an' take the engines away, then when the people started saying we were half an hour late an' still hadn't moved off I'd tell 'em they've not left Victoria yet an' here they are already in Balham, we can't go quicker than that!'

The man under the blanket rocked as they clambered upon rubble. 'How far is it? How far is it now?'

'Dear me, you're as bad as those people at Victoria, you are.'

'Not far now, son,' Sam told him, and slowed his step again; Percy was running out of the last of his steam and he hoped to Christ he wasn't just going to fold up and drop everything.

Aubrey slowed with them; the man on his back had passed out and the smashed leg was swinging and he tried to find it with his hand, and managed. A big one rushed above them and they stopped and stood with their heads down like oxen, shutting their eyes as the world flashed and the ground danced; the fine rain of the debris began touching their faces and the air turned sour; then they went on again.

The walking wounded trudged down from the line with the slow resignation of the losing team leaving the field; there was no hurry now. One of them, his left hand a great clotted bandage, walked with the arm raised to help stem the bleeding; there was peace on his young face. Some had been given a lighted cigarette and they passed them among the others. 'Did old Smithy catch it bad, then?'

'Not from what I could see. It was his kit he was most concerned about.'

A wry laugh, the tone tender: 'He'll be lost without that.'

The front trench was surprisingly crowded; despite the weight of the bombardment there had been only three direct hits. Some mortars were still thumping and the odd heavy lumbered across but the party was over and these were just the people who never knew when to stop: they lingered, pulling the last few crackers. A sniper had found a vantage point and was amusing himself trying to pick off the walking wounded. The air was still, and tainted with the morbid alchemies of war: exploded chemicals and the putrefying flesh of long-dead bodies hurled from the earth, chloride of lime and excrement, and the earth itself, its body winter-stale.

'Who's got a fag, for Christ's sake?'

The silhouettes of rats rippled across the skyline of the sandbags, attracted to new odours. Spades bit into the sullen clay.

'*I want this trench cleared in one hour from now! Come on, jump to it!*'

'Sod 'im.'

They struck softness, and went gingerly.

'Hear the news did you Charlie?'

'Eh?'

'They got a direct hit on Battalion H.Q., with the Colonel inside an' all!'

A hand leaned on a spade. 'You mean fuckin' Pickerin' got *killed*?'

'I heard Peach Blossom tellin' the officers.'

'That bastard *dead*? Then 'oo-bloody-ray an' bless the Lord Jesus what's answered all our prayers!'

'Come on, get stuck into it there!'

The sniper whipped a bullet whining through the dark.

'Who's got a fag?'

VII

In all London the coldest places were the railway stations and at Charing Cross the people stamped their feet and took another turn, their noses red and their breath clouding and their hands in pockets and muffs; from inside the crowded buffets – you'd never get in there, it wasn't worth trying – they wiped the steam from the windows again and peered out at the clock.

The Dover train was already an hour late. A little man in a bowler hat made a show of consulting his fob. 'They're quick enough takin' our lads away,' he said loudly to no one, 'but not near so fussy bringin' 'em back!'

The chill December fog hung below the great arch of the roof, and the lamps dimmed away in the distance, yellow and smothered; a crowd hemmed in the hot-chestnut man near the main exit and he was making his fortune, half cooked and half rotten, penny a bag, but they didn't complain: they only wanted to stand near his brazier.

Then everyone was craning suddenly and the murmur swelled and people grabbed at their children while the porters struggled to clear the edge of the platform; and within the passing of a second after so much waiting the shape of the locomotive – only half-believed – was creeping massively below the lamps, its formal ugliness dragging its linked and sooty load and releasing by its mere presence the qualities of longing and of love.

Can you see him?
They all look alike!
A little girl jumping up and down.
Stand on this box, darling, I've got you tight!
Wave, then, an' he'll see us first!
Blue eyes brimming above a handkerchief.
You mustn't go on so, he won't want to find you crying!
Is Daddy here? Is Daddy here?
A hand gripping a hand, praying in silence.

Can you see him yet? Can you?

Him. The one man in the world. Hundreds of him, already leaning from the windows, waving.

'*Mind the doors there please! Mind the doors!*'

The engine-driver was hooked over the grimy rail, wiping his moustache as he looked along his train, smuts in his eyes, an oily rag in his hand.

'Shut off, Jack?' called the fireman.

'Eh? Ye', shut off.' By cripes, you felt you'd done something these days when you brought one in; used not to be like this, before.

The doors banged back and boots hit the platform and the women pressed forward with a cry, the world new-made, or waited unmoving, smiling, seeing in every face for an instant his face, everywhere, and sometimes nowhere, the smile dying.

''Allo there Mum!'

'Oh Jimmy . . . Oh, *Jimmy* . . .'

Winter had gone.

Julian found his cap and put it on dead straight as he always wore it. 'Who's meeting you, Aubrey?'

'No one.' He got his ashplant from the rack.

'Why ever not?'

'What? Well, I didn't tell anyone which train I'd be coming on. Stations are ghastly, aren't they?'

'The modesty of the man! They'll never forgive you.'

Nigel Coxhead was already off the train and they saw him in the arms of a girl in Red Cross uniform, lost to the world.

'Good Lord, is that the Moira he was telling us about?'

'Trust old Lothario,' laughed Aubrey, 'isn't she an absolute beauty!' For a moment he couldn't look away; it seemed so long since he'd felt a young girl's arms, and it hadn't meant very much at the time; this, he thought, was what it should have been like, should have looked like, and what it might mean if it happened again.

It was difficult to leave the carriage: they were near the front end of the train and half the British Army was tramping its way past to the exits, lumbered with rifles and equipment.

'Holy *cow* . . . just look at all those *girls*! *Yahooo!*'

'Sam,' said Percy, grabbing his arm, 'you are now in the capital of the civilized world where women are women an' not wild mustangs, so put your lassoo away an' try to behave like a soldier of the King. Not that they're much better, but—'

'They're like *flowers* everywhere,' Sam told him, staring at the pretty furs and dresses colouring the earth-dark backcloth of khaki; his voice was soft with awe, and Percy glanced at him.

'And there's notices everywhere not to pick them, so come on, Sam.' Their plan was that Percy and his young brother Nick would share the front room and leave Sam a room of his own upstairs, Mum and Dad staying where they were, though they'd offered to move to the back just for these few days. The letters had been going to and fro for months, while Sam had kept saying: 'You got a woodshed, huh? Then that's for me!' Percy was now alarmed by the picture of arriving home with his 'gentleman friend from the States' festooned with a garland of girls; Mum and Dad weren't stuffy but they'd never seen an American yet.

'Hey gee . . . look at *this* one!'

'Sam, remember you're an ambassador of your country while you're here, and—'

'Well hello there, babe! You lookin' for someone?'

'Yes!' she said eagerly – 'my brother!' She was fair and had eyes like a china-doll's. 'Have you seen him? His name's Bernard.'

'Bernard who, sweetie?'

'Cooper. He's in the—'

'Well look, Miss Cooper honey, I'll be your brother, just give me a try, huh?'

'Sam,' groaned Percy, who had never seen such charm got up in khaki.

'Well *you're* saucy, *you* are!' Her laugh was a peal of small bells. 'No, I must find him an' I know he's here somewhere because a friend of his said he was on the train, so—'

'Look, dolly, why'n't we do a deal? If I find your brother, will you see me tonight?'

Her laugh was delightful. 'Well you *are* a scream! Are you American?'

'I'm *all*-American, ma'am! So it's a deal – now what's he look like, this guy Bernard? Tall? Short? Handsome, I know that, with a sister as lovely as you.' He gazed into the china-doll eyes and she wriggled skittishly, glancing aside to Percy.

'Is he your friend?' she asked, giggling.

'He was.'

'Now you just stay right there, sweetheart, while I jus' turn this whole darn train on end an' tip brother Bernard out at your pretty feet!'

Percy sat down on his kit and closed his eyes.

The platform was less crowded now, though a lot of people lingered, clinging to each other, laughing together about nothing, some trying to get into the buffet, eager to celebrate with a quick one before the bar was closed.

Tom Follett had stayed in his carriage till all the others had got out; there was nobody meeting him and he was in no hurry. Dumping his kit on to the platform and bringing his rifle, he saw two officers go past, Mr Lovell and Mr Talbot, and wondered what it would feel like to be going there, through the big gates and past all the peacocks and herons and eagles and right up to the house, with all the people smiling because you belonged there, and Cook doing something special in the kitchen and the dogs barking and jumping round your feet – they'd be getting on now, the puppies, nearly three months old, Alexander and the others. He wouldn't be going there but that didn't matter so much because he knew at least what it felt like to belong, like Mr Talbot did, though of course in a much smaller way. 'If Milady says there's a place for you,' Mr Kemp had told him, 'then it's as safe as houses.'

He'd thought of those words ever since, saying them over to himself sometimes, dropping to sleep; and one night on sentry-go when the line was quiet he'd carved them along the clay with the point of his bayonet, every word, and then scratched them out again so nobody would see in the morning. You did silly things sometimes.

'You diggin' in at the Y.M. are you, Tom?'

'Yes, I expect so.' You came to know things about each other in the trenches, whether you had anywhere special to go on leave and things like that.

'So'm I! Come on with us, then, eh?'

'All right.' He picked up his rifle.

Thin bespectacled young men in Salvation Army uniform sheepishly accosted the soldiers with cheap leaflets, ashamed of their poorly printed message but sustained by their sense of duty towards their brothers-in-arms, who in their innocence were surely unaware that the Disease was Dangerous and that the Sole and Single Prevention was a Clean and Wholesome Way of Life.

'What's this then? Oh, Christ. Here's me, not seen a woman for months, an' here's you in the middle o' London an' no more use to 'em than a bloody catkin – no justice is there?'

Flappers in slinky furs cast their bold glances at the subalterns, electing the loneliest. 'Do excuse me, but are you being met?'

'Er – actually no.'

'How ripping! Just tell me where you want to go – I've Daddy's car outside and we're here to look after you.' A dazzling smile. 'It's our little contribution to the war effort, you see!' You weren't really in the swim without a young officer on your arm, slightly wounded for preference to add a touch of saintliness. 'Now where *are* those dratted porters?'

From the opposite platform a troop-train drew away with cheers from those of its passengers who had yet to see France; the rest stood quietly at the windows waving to no one, to the grime and the fog and the lamps of the London they loved.

'Askin' for her brother. Your mob, isn't 'e?'

'Who?' asked Geoff Tuffnel.

It wasn't the girl with the china-doll face; this was a different one, asking for a different name.

''Arry Ross. That right, Miss?'

'Leave it to me,' Geoff said dully, looking her over. Thin, red hair and freckles, yes, this would be Harry's sister, though she hadn't his same laughing eyes: she was worried.

'I can't find him,' she said, too quickly, wanting to hurry on again, to go on looking.

'Is your name Judith?'

The green eyes lost their misery. 'How did you know?'

He said tersely: 'I'm a chum of his. He talks about you. About all the family. He's coming on the next train.'

'Is there another one today?'

He got his rifle and took her arm, surprising her by his firmness. 'It'll be a long wait. We'll go and have a nice cup of tea in the buffet.' She didn't resist. 'I'm Geoff Tuffnel, same company.' He glimpsed Wiggy Bennett trotting past the big Kiwi Shoe Polish advertisement, a crumpled brown paper

128

parcel on his arm; that would be the German spiked helmet he'd picked up a week ago on wiring-party, and Geoff thought vaguely – wanting to think of anything except what he was doing now – of old Wiggy putting it on the mantelpiece for his Mum to admire.

'Why,' she said, 'Harry told us about you in his letters. You did something brave, didn't you?'

'No. Come on, we'll have to barge our way through this lot. You just keep tucked in behind me.'

The buffet was packed but he hardly broke his stride as she clung on to his canvas equipment – it was like following a bull through a field full of sheep, though they made way for him without him seeming to touch them. He even got two chairs and one of the small iron tables, and she studied him when he was fetching a waitress, his straight nose and strong-looking jaw and fine moustache, and the ribbon on his coat: this was the boy Harry had told them about all right, though he'd denied it.

'Two coffees, please, miss, and two small brandies, quick as you can but I know you're busy.'

'I don't think I want brandy,' Judith said.

'Warm you up, you've been out on that platform over an hour, Southern Railway for you, same as it always was.' He didn't smile but there was a smile there, she thought, in his rough tone and the way he took her hands on the table and rubbed them slowly before she'd time to draw back. 'How's London, then? Sooty as ever but we miss it out there, the ugly old thing.'

'London's all right.' She tried to draw her hands away because there were people looking but he went on rubbing the warmth into them; it was like being captured by a friendly bear. And they were talking, both of them, about London and what was going on there, 'You go to the picture palaces much, do you? What's this new comic like, Charlie Something? Chaplin, that's right, they say he's a real turn, we get the papers out there, of course.' And she told him about how they were draining the lake in St James's Park so the Zeps wouldn't know where the Palace was, by the reflection. 'Well I never,' he said, 'all those poor ducks! What are they keeping them in now – buckets?'

She picked up her glass of brandy, her green eyes watching

him as she wondered what he'd do if she refused to drink it –
she'd only tasted it once before in all her life, at Christmas-time
last year – but before she knew what was happening he took it
from her and poured it into her coffee: 'That's where it'll do
most good, in there an' down the hatch.' They were talking
again – he wouldn't let a minute's silence go by – and she told
him she was a munitionette at the National Factory in Silver-
town, 'that's why my face is yellow,' though he said he'd never
noticed, 'it's the T.N.T. gets on our skin, they call us "canaries",
but we get a pint of milk given to us free every day, they look
after us like that.' They began talking about Harry and how he
was keen on motorbikes but Geoff seemed to get off the subject
till they'd finished their coffee and she was feeling the warmth
all over her. 'You know the best medicine for cold weather all
right, I'll admit that much.'

'How old are you, Judith?'

She was surprised. 'I'm gone seventeen. Why?' He really did
ask her the most daring things.

He nodded. 'Gone seventeen, and working in a factory, eh,
well you're learnin' a bit about life, I suppose, this rotten war
we've got.' A gentleman had just left their table and Geoff got
up and came round and sat beside her; and she saw his face
had changed, he looked almost frightened of something though
it couldn't be that, a brave boy like him. 'It's rough on so many
of us,' he said, 'this war, people losing their pals and their
relations, look at the casualty lists, but we'll all get over it quick
enough, at least we're all together in it, that's a big help, and
we can look after each other no matter what happens, no
matter how bad things look, just for a time – you'll be able to
remember, when there's bad news about, that we're all
ready to help each other an' —'

'Geoffrey,' she heard herself saying from somewhere deep
inside, 'you're not trying to —'

'There isn't another train, Judith, he's not comin' back.'
His arm went round her thin shoulders but she shrank away
and he let her go and his head dropped as if it was his fault
somehow. What had happened to the telegram? They couldn't
have got it. 'He was a wonderful kid, Harry, an' we're proud
of him and we always will be —'

'It's not true,' she screamed but it was a whisper.

'He wasn't badly hurt like some of them, that's one thing, first he was with us an' then he was gone,' and then her ginger head was against his chest and he was holding her and staring back at the people, damn them, till they had to look away, none of their blasted business.

The joke went off well for Julian: he saw her first and just had time to swing up a brilliant salute and say – 'Miss Lovell, I believe?'

Aubrey stood away while they hugged each other; she'd dropped her muff in the excitement and he picked it up and stood with it, feeling a bit embarrassed: mauve velour wasn't quite right for his uniform. He couldn't see her face because her squirrel coat had a high collar and she was reaching up, but he knew she wasn't bad-looking from the photo Julian had shown him.

'Oh, *Julian*! Are you all right? Mother's not here – she came but it was so dreadfully cold waiting and I packed her off again, I knew you'd understand—'

'You shouldn't have come either, old thing, but oh Lord it's good to see you! They all right at home?'

'Daddy tried to come but it's accounting-time – oh heavens, where's my muff?'

'What? Oh, this is Lieutenant Talbot – my sister Diana.'

She turned and he knew that a photograph is nothing until you have seen the original; only then can you look at it again with recognition. At this moment the cold had brought a glow to her skin, pinking the tip of her nose, and in her excitement her eyes were alive with light, a flash of kingfisher-blue among misty lashes, and she was smiling, suddenly shy – 'I didn't know you were here—' as if they already knew each other; then not another word she could think of when she'd been full of so many.

He was presenting the mauve velour muff carefully balanced in the middle on his upturned palm, so that she could slip her hands in, and she laughed softly, conducting the trivial rite, and he said: 'I'll leave you two children in peace.'

'Nonsense, old boy – we'll share a taxi, come on!' Julian picked up his valise but they didn't seem to be listening and he had the odd feeling that he, not Aubrey, was the stranger here.

'Or do you want to give your people a ring first, say you've arrived?' The doors were slamming and a guard passed under the lamps, green flag tucked under his arm and boots creaking, his breath blowing grey before him. The long train was empty and the platform almost deserted now, the few people talking like actors at rehearsal on a half-darkened stage.

'I'll ring them from somewhere else.' They started for the exit, passing a young corporal and his girl who stood silent and alone in the middle of the grimy platform, her head on his shoulder as if sleeping, his arms round her, his hands cupping her at her slender back and his mouth tender against her hair, renewing their love unspeaking and unmoving, lost in its spell.

How can they bear to part again, Aubrey wondered, people like these? The idea was strange to him; it was a thing he'd never considered. A pair of M.P.s trod circumspectly past the advertisements, blancoed gaiters correctly adjusted and caps tilted forward on their bullet heads. 'I was so upset,' Diana was saying, and the buffers beside them began clanking and they had to bend their heads to listen. 'I came on to the wrong platform, the one over there.' A small hand flashed out of the muff to point, as a child will do, unsure of being able to explain. 'It was full of soldiers getting into the train, and two of those people, military policemen, were struggling to catch a man.' Steam roared in the distance and the wheels beside them rolled, the carriagework creaking. 'They caught him, and pushed him into the train and slammed the door on him.' She was looking up at Julian as if hoping he'd say she was mistaken or it must have been just horseplay; and Aubrey saw how deeply troubled her eyes were, a darker blue. 'Why didn't he want to go?'

'Oh,' her brother said lightly, 'some of them get as far as the station and then panic, that's all. They're all right as soon as they move off.' A boy in brand-new porter's uniform went dodging past with his trolley, weaving among the scattered groups, whistling his toy along.

'But they're all volunteers, so can't they change their mind?'

'Once they've joined up they're in the Army, old thing.'

'You make them sound like prisoners!' Her fair brow was perplexed, and Aubrey wondered how she could have remained so protected from reality in six months of war – or were they all like this, the women of England? Despite the casualty lists and hospital trains did they believe it was every young man's dream to march away like a wooden soldier and fall dead for God and Country?

'Oh, come,' laughed Julian, 'not quite prisoners! Young horses, if you like, and some need breaking in.' Meaning to reassure her, he knew he'd sounded callous; in the past they'd been of one mind about injustice and had gone crusading all over the place, and the only time they'd failed to agree was when she'd tried to enrol him as the first masculine Suffragette.

'That's not like you, Julian!' She looked at him quickly, perhaps wondering if it had at first escaped her that he had changed physically too after all these months.

'I know,' he said ruefully, 'I didn't quite mean it.' He glanced at Aubrey for help.

'Growing up is painful, isn't that what you mean?' A stocky private was leaving the crowded buffet, a girl with him, her head lowered as if trying not to weep; at this distance it looked like young Tuffnel but he wasn't sure. 'And this war's forcing a few of us to do it quickly, sometimes in the shape of a military policeman.' It sounded pretty lame, but then what else could you say? That poor devil had probably seen a hospital train or had a girl: there might be some who *couldn't* bear to part. The real answer was the one that smoothly shrugged off every act of cruelty and despair: 'There's a war on.'

They had reached the forecourt of the station and suddenly he was looking again at London – the windows of the Strand and the grey finger of the Column, ghostly in the fog, where the bank holiday crowds had shouted and danced and waved their paltry little flags. They'd got what they wanted: did they want it still?

'I expect,' he heard Diana saying, 'it's time I grew up too; then I'll understand.'

Suddenly angry, his tone brought surprise to her eyes. 'No, stay as you are. We'll all need your compassion one day – don't let that go too.'

It was a shock seeing the ambulance in front of the house and for an instant he thought his senses tricked him: the guns had hurled this familiar bit of debris after him as a souvenir; then Pam was across the porch and into his arms while he was trying to pay the taxi, the Red Cross brassard showing whitely on her sleeve.

'It's mine,' she said as the taxi rounded the fountain pond and grumbled away. 'Isn't it smart? I drive it.' Her dark hair was cut short in a bob, and was she taller? 'I wanted you to be proud of me.' She was pressing his arm as if to confirm what her eyes believed: Aub'ey was home. 'Oh, damn! I'd meant to be wearing my cap, I look quite stunning in it for an old horse-face. You all right, Aub'ey, not hurt anywhere?'

'You're taller,' he said. They walked together into the house. Others had heard the taxi.

'Not so fat, that's all. I still scoff what I can find but the work's got me into condition. Why isn't Vic coming?' Aubrey had telephoned from a hotel on his way, though Julian and Diana had wanted him to use theirs; it would have meant talking to their people and his wish to be home had become almost feverish.

'The luck of the draw,' he said, and had no time to reflect on his lie before Charrington came limping across the hall, fuming because he'd been engaged at the back of the house and hadn't heard the taxi; and Lady Eleanor was suddenly with them, floating from the drawing-room to become lost in Aubrey's tall embrace while Pam went rattling on –

'We've telephoned the office and of course Father was furious that you didn't say when you'd arrive – you'll go straight up the chimney when he gets here, providing he doesn't bust up the Crossley in the fog – I was still talking when he simply dropped the telephone and you know what he drives like even when he's not in a hurry! Oh damn,' she said softly because Mother looked so heartbreakingly happy in Aubrey's arms, and she went into the morning-room for a quick blub.

Charrington wanted to bring the whole staff above stairs but Aubrey said not to disturb them, and went off to see Mrs Kemp first of all to tell her Freddie was in top form and was due for leave in three weeks' time, 'while the decorations are still up and there's some Christmas pudding left, trust him to wangle that,' and he left her before the first tears came – everybody seemed to be doing it and he found it depressing. It was just as bad in the kitchen and Cook stood by the pastry-table trying to hide the big iced cake she'd made as a surprise, a wooden spoon in her floury hand and the tears glinting on her fat crumpled face, 'Oh it's *wonderful*, Mr Aubrey,' while little Elsie uttered soft tremulous moans, 'Oh it's *wonderful*, it is,' and he gave them a cheerful wink and got out as fast as he could.

'I've never seen everyone so deliriously happy!' Pam told him when he was back in the drawing-room fiddling at the piano. 'What price Christmas after this!'

'Happy? They're all howling their eyes out!'

'Well of *course*, how else can we express ourselves? Women *adore* howling, didn't you know?' She wondered why he was so pensive, just standing with his long fingers picking out chords, the light on his fair hair and his quiet eyes in shadow; there were lines on his face she hadn't seen before, tiredness-lines yet more permanent-looking than that; and he was thinner, as she was, and for the same reason. What was it really like out there? He'd never tell anyone, just as she'd never tell anyone what it was like when another train drew slowly in, oh God, another one, with the ambulances backing up and the smell of the gangrene coming at you, a nightmare smell, *careful with this one, he can't stand much more,* and the women who came to watch from a distance behind the barriers, some already in black, perhaps wanting to get used to it so that when he too was brought home like this there'd be less shock to get in the way of what they'd have to do, and the poor little probationers shivering more with nerves than the cold, *don't make such a fuss, Nurse, just cover his face,* and sometimes a different train at the platform opposite, right opposite, slowly going out with their fresh young faces at the windows and their hands pressed to the glass, their bodies whole and the pity in their eyes no more than passing because they knew this couldn't happen to them. The trains were so slow, coming and going, so sure. But this was nothing; all she saw was the consequence, splinted and bandaged and tidied up, of what Aubrey had been seeing out there: and now she wondered why he was standing so pensively, his gentle fingers trying to remember the notes he must have thought so many times he'd never play again, and nobody here to do her the service of slapping her stupid face.

'You're getting it,' she said tightly.

'Am I?' He cocked an eyebrow, smiling, pleased, and she turned away.

'Sit down to it and use both hands. I've got to go and take this outlandish rig off to look decent for dinner.'

'It suits you, Pom-Pom – you look all the rage.'

'You always were a hypocrite.' She even slammed the door hoping she'd pinch her fingers in it.

Aubrey hitched himself at the Queen Anne stool, for a moment touching the cold keys and then giving in to melancholy now that he was alone: was it always like this the first time home on leave? He knew they'd wept on seeing him because he was from the past and they'd let themselves believe those days were back again; and because they knew it wasn't true; and because, anyway, it wouldn't be for long: he'd be back in France before Christmas. Would it have been kinder not to come at all? The fire murmured in the hearth; he felt its heat on his face; but the ivory was so cold under his fingers and he couldn't remember the chords because there were too many other things in his memory since last he'd played them, the thin crack of the shot breaking the lark's song as the field-grey figure stood suddenly erect, as though surprised, before toppling. *In case you've forgotten, we are at war.* No, you little swine, that wasn't war, it was an act of murder, and your own men witnesses. Worse, your own brother. The flames sent light flickering on the carpet and across the knitting on the hearthside stool, knitting of all things . . . in this house where the days had been so brief that there was never time to shut a door or go up one stair at a time, voices piping from room to room and feet pounding to pursue the little urgencies of a peacetime world, each minute quicksilver. It was Mother's, the knitting; and he smiled, his dejection easing: it was her 'war-work', she'd told him vaguely, comforts for the men in France; but her knitting would be like her gardening – a 'masterpiece of inspired recklessness', as Father had once said, surveying the sturdy crop of onions among the daffodils – and if any man in France had a dwarf's foot and a giant's leg those socks would fill the bill. Yet these roses, scarlet in the silver bowl, were hers too: you could never see roses without thinking of her; they were everywhere in this house and on every dress she wore, and when

136

Father brought her flowers on his way home from the office they must be of this same kind: carnations would hint almost of unfaithfulness.

He heard the bath running, a vibration in the ceiling: Pam, hurrying to be downstairs again, not to miss anything. He should go and change: he was still filthy from the journey, but had no mind to go. Was this, then, what he'd come all that way to do? Sit sullen and alone at the damned piano?

He was on the stairs, one at a time, when the headlights passed across the mirror in the hall; even then his father was up the steps before he could open the door and they nearly collided under the iron-framed lamp, taking each other's hands and standing and saying nothing, their eyes meeting and holding as they tried to bridge the gap and nearly succeeded, each finding something new in the other's face and knowing that memory was not at fault: they were both a little changed. Sir William noted the lines on his son's mouth, not of maturity but of enforced experience, and knew they were permanent: this war wasn't a passing sickness but a process of ageing, the months crammed into weeks. Aubrey saw with a shock the white of the temples that before had been scarcely touched with grey, and knew that you didn't have to be at the front to feel a war like this: it sufficed that your sons were there.

'I'd have been at the station, you know that!'

'I'm glad you weren't – it was perishing cold and we got in an hour late. You're looking fine, Father.'

'I know what I'm looking but you've not changed, more of a man, that's all.' They went in and Charrington took the black astrakhan coat, his puckish lopsided smile showing his pleasure; it had been a week after the boys had sailed for France when the casualty lists had lengthened day by day and Sir William had told him: 'If by any chance a telegram arrives I want you to open it yourself and telephone me at the office, and don't show it to anyone else until I get here.' He said now: 'Well where's the champagne?'

'We thought we'd wait for you,' Aubrey told him.

'There was no need for that—' but he was quietly pleased – 'get it popping, Charrington!' He shot his cuffs, looking at Aubrey: 'Now tell me why Vic's not with you.'

'It wasn't general leave – the names went into the hat.' It

had sounded too casual and his father's eyes glanced away and back, and the strong undertone deepened.

'Didn't you see your commanding officer, what's his blasted name? Two brothers on separate leave, what next?'

'We lost the C.O. just before leave came up.'

'Got an adjutant, I suppose?'

'Well there'd been quite a lot going on, and it wasn't easy to get much sense out of people.' The tone still wasn't right: it didn't matter how often you rehearsed a lie that you'd no heart for telling.

His father glanced round to make sure Charrington had gone. 'I take it he's perfectly unharmed?'

'Oh yes—'

'Then I'll thank you for a straight answer. Why isn't he with you on leave?'

'He refused it.' The relief was immediate, surprising him. It hadn't been too bad on the journey: he'd been with Julian and Nigel and they'd talked the whole time and he'd managed to forget about Vic; the depression had settled on him in the taxi, after Julian and his sister had been dropped off and he was alone. Vic had been fit and in good form when he'd left him, but coming through the gates his excitement of being home had been dulled and he'd felt himself to be the bringer of bad news. And the only way out was to lie. Now it had been spoken, and rejected, but in his relief he saw the tightening of his father's mouth and knew that the hurt wasn't healed but only passed on. 'He asked me to give his love to everyone at home.'

'Civil of him.' He put his arm round Aubrey's shoulders and they went into the drawing-room. 'Enjoying himself, is he? Going at it hammer and tongs, well, that's always been his way.'

'He's got the idea that the war won't last very long.'

'Has he indeed?' His tone remained deliberately light. 'So he wants to acquit himself while there's time. Commendable ambition, though you can tell him from me there's no need to hurry. We don't have to mention this to anyone; it might be misconstrued.'

There were Union Jacks over the gate of No. 21 Cooper Street, limp in the lamplit fog; and he saw a heavy figure pacing on the pavement, turning and pacing back as he neared.

'Is that you, Geoff?'

'Dad? How's tricks?'

He'd felt badly about it later. All he'd put in the telegram was *arriving some time Tuesday* and they told him Dad had been up at six and hanging about the whole day, only coming in for a peck of food and then off again, up and down the bloody pavement, it was awful to think of, when he could have told them the time of the train within an hour or two. There'd been a reporter traipsing up and down with him half the morning, a boy from the local rag hoping to take his photograph; and Mr Tomkins had been along to say he'd got the Boy's Brigade Senior Band all standing by to play him along the street and up to the gate. One thing, he'd been let off doing that, in fact he couldn't have done it in any case, imagine it, didn't bear thinking about.

They'd not known what to do, of course, whether to book tables at the King's Arms for middle-day or whip round Hobson's the grocers to see what they'd got in tins so Mum wouldn't have to cook for nothing if he didn't turn up till late. The place had been full of the neighbours most of the day and some were still here, sitting wherever they could find a perch and going through the crate of Celebration Bass that Dad had got in – Dad didn't care for it, never touched a glass, it was the local wallop for him every time, but he'd got it because of the name and was pleased he'd thought of that.

Two or three of them were half-seas over by now and when Mum said she'd got to go and bring the washing in Mr Griggs took the hint and got the last of them out of the place, a real gent because he was the worse for wear himself and wouldn't have minded staying – 'And I will say again, on behalf of us all,' swaying about a bit with one hand on the hat-stand, 'that we are conscious of the single – the signal honour that you and your proud family 'ave – have afforded us on this memorable day . . .' Mr Griggs was president of the local Rotary and when cold sober could bring the house down, give him any subject you please.

Little Eth was still on the edge of the table in the parlour, swinging her legs and drawing her finger across the ribbon on his tunic for the hundredth time, 'it's like a little rainbow, isn't it, Mum?' and Geoff thought it was funny how a kid could see something in a scrap of coloured cloth because she'd been told it was important; but then everyone was like that, come to think about it. He found it hard to make sense of anything these days: one minute you were lugging a perfect stranger through the mud while a lot of other strangers were trying to kill you for doing it and the next minute your kid sister was playing with a rainbow and half the neighbourhood had gone off with a skinful; but what was the connection? He'd gone out there because there'd be no chance of any sleep in the trench, what with the rats all over you – the best thing was to do night duty when you could and kip down in the daytime when you knew it was only your chums knocking about and not some pink-eared little perisher trying to nibble you down to the bone – and the object of the operation was to bring in a prisoner so that was what he'd done. He'd not gone out for a medal so why give him one? What a brave boy am I, written all over his chest, it made you puke, but when he'd told 'Major Blossom he wasn't going to wear it he'd hit the roof – 'For one thing you'd be improperly dressed an' for another thing you owe it to the Colonel, there's many a commanding officer what wouldn't have taken the trouble he did to make sure you got your due, so you got to grin an' bear it, boy, stone the crows, anyone'd think it was a birthmark you'd been told to wear.'

Old Peach Blossom was lying in his teeth, that baby-faced bastard Pickering had been after credit for the battalion – in short, for himself. Kilderbee was no better, 'It'll encourage the others, can't you understand that?' Been proper sharp with him. But what sense did it make? Were they trying to win this rotten war so everyone could go home or to win a tin medal so they could strut up and down like feather dusters?

Come all this way and the caper was still going on, they wouldn't let him alone. 'You mean you never *told* your own Mum and Dad?' Mr Hicks had kept on asking him, 'not even in a *letter*?'

'Well I forgot.'

'You *forgot*?' He looked round at them all, acting amazed to get another laugh while Dad had filled his glass again, prouder than ever.

But it was true, near enough, he'd *wanted* to forget, put it that way. The presentations had driven him off his rocker, hanging about in Brigade Support for a whole day behind canvas screens with everyone looking so pleased with themselves and the Divisional Commander two hours late because he'd got stuck in a convoy – that was the tale, but he'd overslept, more like. Then his own chums wouldn't give him any peace, *Lo, the Conquering Hero Comes* on Oscar's mouth-organ, and Percy Stokes keeping on at him, 'Excuse me, but there's fifty German generals outside an' they've heard you're in this area so they want to give themselves up to save any trouble – they say they'll bring their own handcuffs an' won't make any noise.' A real trial, Percy.

He'd thought it would be all right if he said nothing in his letters but Dad's foreman at the works had seen it in the papers – apparently there were lists printed now and again – and of course the local rag had got wind of it and the cat was right out of the bag.

'I could cry,' Mr Hicks had said, with a trickle of Bass down his gristly chin, 'when I think what you – what you brave lads are doing for us out there ... I tell you, I could cry ...'

'Don't take it to heart then, Mr Hicks, come on out and join us, always a welcome.' He'd not meant to say it but he was getting really fed up and George Hicks was quite young enough to sign on.

'And who'd keep the trams going' – his unsteady arm swept out and nearly brought the Coronation mug off the mantelpiece – 'all over London, eh?' He was a senior driver on the City run, as he'd tell you quick enough.

'People can walk, can't they? Got no kit to carry.'

Someone had coughed a bit loud and Dad had called out, Any more beer? so he'd shut up and got through a couple of bottles himself, sauce for the gander. But there were a lot of people like George Hicks about the place, the papers were quite hot on them, calling them the 'self-styled indispensables' and the 'parasites on the body of our warrior nation' and all that. Geoff didn't agree – you could join up or keep out of it just as you pleased, it was meant to be a free country, wasn't it? But what got his back up were the pigeon-chested little Cuthberts in their spats and celluloid collars who tried to make out they'd be in the front line quick as a flash if they'd not got the trams to keep going.

Never mind, they were on their own now, and he picked Ethie off the edge of the table and swung her up till her head sent the lampshade rocking and she squealed with laughter; this was what he'd come home for, just Mum and Dad and little Eth like it had always been.

'I've got your tub all hot, Geoff!'

'Have you, Mum?' He went into the scullery where the steam was like in a ship's boiler-room and there was a big new cake of Lifebuoy and two thick towels folded on the stool – he couldn't take his eyes off them because they were so white and pure-looking; you never saw anything white over there, it was all mud-coloured, even your handkerchief was khaki.

'Tch! Look at me,' he said as he tugged his boots off, 'I'm like a blinkin' sweep. I should've popped in at the public baths and that's a fact.'

'Should you, Geoff?' Her eyes were very bright. 'I think you're clean enough for this house,' and she went out.

He wallowed in the tub like a pig in clover and then went upstairs and put his blue suit on, and the smell of the mothballs took him right back to Saturday nights when he'd put it on to go round to the slate-club to watch Dad, who'd been darts champion and beaten the Elephant and Castle two years running, a record. Then he combed his moustache and looked at it in the glass and thought for two pins he'd shave it off except that old Kilderbee would be disappointed – it was a sort of secret joke between them now and they got on fine: he'd soldier anywhere with that sergeant.

Dad had been up the road to 'see about tonight' and he was back now; Geoff's door was ajar and he could hear the plans being made – it was to be the King's Arms, the table in the corner by the fireplace and only Uncle Sid and Aunt Mabel invited, no one else, keep it very quiet so they could see something of each other and enjoy themselves, and Mr Edgby the manager said the drinks were on the house, including champagne with the cold chicken and whatever they wanted afterwards – he'd try to see they weren't disturbed but of course he couldn't guarantee 'it wouldn't end up like Mafeking Night once the boys heard there was a hero in their midst', and Mrs Banks was coming in to put Ethie to bed and stay till they got back.

They were already in their best – they'd been in it all day, not knowing when he'd come – Mum in her art-silk frock with the big cameo and Dad in his dark grey double-breasted, and when Geoff went down they were standing together against the drawn curtains, waiting to surprise him with their plans.

'We – er – we thought we might just trot along for a bite at the King's Arms, what you say, Geoff? Just us and your Uncle an' Auntie, that's all, nothing—'

'That'd be a treat for me, that would, a real big treat. But I've got to go somewhere else tonight.' He should've gone down when he'd heard them talking about it, but Dad had got everything lined up already and this seemed the only way, come right out with it and hope they'd understand. 'Could we leave it till tomorrow?'

They all stood awkwardly listening to the tick of the tin clock on the mantelpiece; then Dad cleared his throat and said very heartily, 'Of course we can leave it till tomorrow – can't we, love? I should've realized you might have got other plans.' His wink looked dreadfully false, as if half his face was paralysed. 'Is she nice?'

And Mum said quickly, 'Oh I'm sure she is!'

'I've got no plans like that.' He bit his lip, angry with himself, got the whole thing the wrong way round like a bloody idiot because he was afraid they wouldn't do it. 'Listen, I'll give it to you straight – a chum of mine got killed out there and his family's only just been told, and I'm asking you to go over there with me and talk to them a bit, try and comfort them. No one's got your kindness, no one in this world, and it's not far, only a tu'penny bus.'

He was sitting on the bench.

The park had a pond in it with ducks on: he used to throw bread for them on Sundays when he was here; and the houses were all round the edge of the park, with a road and lamp-posts. The trees were bare now, though, and it was dark and he could smell the frost on the grass, and wondered what the ducks did when there was ice on their pond; perhaps Mr Willis came and broke it for them with a stick, he always took trouble to see the birds and animals were all right – 'Now there's a nest by the pottin' shed, Tom, with a hen thrush in it. She's sittin', got eggs. We can't stop usin' the path, but you'll want to go by quiet, an' don't stand there an' stare at her for she won't like it, look at her casual in passin', see, but don't you stare, for that's how stoats catch 'em, starin' till they're silly with it.'

Another taxi came round the road and went through the big gates and he watched it; the bench where he was sitting was right opposite the gates and when the motor-cars went in there he watched for their lights to show up the peacocks and eagles, which seemed as if they were moving in a slow kind of dance, because of their shadows.

'You'll go an see my missus, won't you now,' Mr Kemp had said. 'I've sent her a letter an' there'll be a bit of a bed for you over the new garage, where we keep the deck-chairs an' that.'

But it didn't seem right. He'd come here last night as soon as he'd got cleaned up at the Y.M. Hostel but he'd just come away again without going in. Two weeks he'd worked here, that was all, and that was six months ago; they wouldn't even remember who he was, except for Mrs Kemp and then only because of the letter; you couldn't just show yourself here after six whole months and ask for bed and board, it wasn't right.

But there was nothing to stop him sitting here where anyone could sit, and look at the place. There must be a party this evening, there'd been five motors and three taxis so far, and some of the people in them had uniforms on – they'd be friends of Mr Aubrey, perhaps Mr Lovell and Mr Coxhead, he couldn't see much in the lamplight. It was so very strange to think of them all in there instead of where he'd seen them last, mud up to their knees and shells bursting and everything; come to that, it was strange to be here himself, the night so quiet and the light on that lamp-post over there so steady: it'd burn till morning and nothing would make it go out. This was another world.

He could hear dogs barking and the whimper of pups, excited by the noise of the motors and asking to be let out to join the fun. Alexander. He pursed his cold lips in a whistle for Alexander, a very soft one so nobody would hear. You did silly things sometimes when you were alone, and the thought of the puppies was making him smile so he had to stop whistling because his mouth was the wrong shape now.

When it was too cold to sit any more he walked right round the park, coming back and crossing the road and getting up on

144

the low mossy wall and sitting there, tucking his greatcoat under him so as not to get a cold bottom. He could see the porch of the house from here, right in the distance across the lawns, and the people going under the big iron lamp as they went in, with Mr Charrington opening the door for them – he was actually looking at Mr Charrington! The thrill of it shivered down his back and he gave a little short laugh, surprising himself; it had been a wonderful idea to come here; this was better than a seat at a theatre-palace, he could see the tall chimneys black against the frosty stars and the windows all lit up, and someone drawing the curtains high in the house – that might be her, doing it, it might easily be! Hello Kitty . . .

He sat thinking of her, a bit troubled because he couldn't remember her face after all this time; it was funny how you could think of someone – he'd thought of her often out there – without seeing their face in your mind. How could that be? Perhaps faces weren't what you remembered most; he thought of her as prettiness, with her hands sewing, the silks and laces on her lap; she was slender, he'd not forgotten that; he thought of her as slenderness.

'Now what are you up to, soldier?'

He nearly fell off the wall.

The badge on the big helmet shone silver: it was all he could make out because the bull's-eye lantern was full on him, dazzling. 'Come on down, now!'

He was tall, with a heavy moustache, his nose red with the cold.

'I was looking at the house.' He'd grazed his ankle scrambling down, and it throbbed hotly.

'I know that.' His breath clouded out from his bright teeth as they stood under the lamp-post. 'You've been watchin' it best part of an hour, first on the bench and now up there. What's your business?'

'I've got a place here.' He was suddenly thinking of when he'd scratched the words on the clay with his bayonet.

'What does that mean?' There was no reply. 'You from the barracks, are you? Or on home leave? Let's see your pass.'

Another motor came round and Tom peered at it past the constable in case it was someone he recognised, and when he looked up he saw the constable's eyes on him, narrowed and steady in the shadow of his helmet. He gave Tom his pass back with a careless jerk of his hand, like giving a dog a biscuit. 'Hangin' about for one of the maids, are you?'

'No.'

'Then what's your business here?' He sounded impatient suddenly, and Tom realized he should have said 'yes' so that he'd go away.

'I told you. I've got a place here.' It should have worked like a magic spell but of course it didn't. He had to tell him how he'd been taken on last summer and how Mr Kemp had said he'd be coming back here when the war was over. It didn't sound truthful, somehow, when it was all put into words: it was like telling someone what you'd dreamed.

'Then if you know these people, why don't you go in an' see them, 'stead of hangin' about?' His voice went thin and sarcastic suddenly like the Reverend Jones's used to at the Orphanage. 'Or wouldn't you be welcome, for some reason?'

'I don't think they'd remember me.' He was miserable now, because everything was spoiled; and he wondered if the best thing wouldn't be to run off and have done with it. 'I mean they'd remember me, but—' It was so hard to explain, and he looked past the dark bulky uniform to the frosty emptiness of the park.

'Now look here, my lad!' His white teeth glinted in the lamplight, sharp as a dog's with a bone, and his grip came on Tom's arm as if he knew what was in his mind. 'You can't have it both ways – either you're known here or you're not, an' it's easy enough to find out, so I'm takin' you along the station on suspicion of loiterin' with intent or I'm takin' you in those gates to see what they've got to say about you – now which is it to be?'

VIII

'What a marvellous cigarette-case!'

'Do you like it?' said Julian. 'My people gave it to me the day I left for France.' He took a cigarette and snapped the case shut, holding it for her inspection.

'Well they know how to choose presents!' She touched the heavy silver chasing. 'May I have one?'

'Oh, I'm – I'm so sorry.'

She glanced up, pleased with his shocked face. 'I drive an ambulance, did Aubrey tell you?' *And if I can drive an ambulance, old boy, I can smoke a cigarette.*

'Honestly? How – er—'

'How very Amazon of me.' She accepted a light and noted that the more elderly guests were watching, their chins well tucked in. 'If we join the Women's Legion or the Land Army we're called Amazons. Do I look so unfeminine?'

'Hardly that!' *Nor very feminine either,* Julian thought: *but what did the word mean anyway? With her dark bobbed hair and almost olive-black eyes she was damned attractive: a most important feminine quality!*

'I'm teasing,' she said. 'But we get fed up with people thinking that women are only good for having babies and the vapours. You've been out of London for quite a time – a lot of us smoke cigarettes these days, it's catching on.' *Not perfectly true: the few friends of hers who'd tried one were either sick or shown the door by their fathers; she'd asked Julian for one of his because he was such a beautiful tailor's dummy and looked easy to shock. Besides, it would keep her mind off the food: the double doors between the drawing-room and the dining-room had been opened to let the guests wander through to the buffet, and she only hoped they wouldn't scoff everything before she could decently follow.*

'I think your sister's dazzling,' she said.

'Diana? She'd love to hear you tell her so.'

'I bet everyone does, specially the men.'

147

'I – don't quite know.' She caught his slight quick frown: he was one of those young men who took the strong protective role, regarding their sisters as bits of Dresden china. Thank the Lord, Aubrey wasn't like that! He'd always regarded her as a *person*. But perhaps she could see Julian's point of view; Diana did look rather fragile; far livelier than a bit of china, certainly: but fragile. She was over by the piano at the moment, stuck with a chinless young subaltern and in need of early rescue.

This thought sparked memory off and Hugh flashed into her mind and she felt the pang again, the bitter remorse, a melting kind of pain. She hadn't dared tell Aubrey yet; but he'd have to know.

Things were getting noisy in here: people were drifting back from the dining-room to talk; they were mostly young – this was in honour of Aubrey's homecoming – but Charles and Louise had looked in, of course, and a few others of their age were here, some with sons overseas – you could pick them out easily: however they talked and smiled they weren't wholly here with you; they'd left part of themselves at home in case there was a telegram. Pam had gone out of her way to talk to these, trying to cheer them up, safe in her knowledge that Aubrey was here and Vic not in action; but she knew of the falseness underlying her charity: when Aubrey went back she wouldn't be able to squander her reassurances so freely; she'd need them for herself.

Even Lady Waring was here, when she could have telephoned an excuse; sitting upright on the fringe of Mother's adoring entourage, her calm lace-gloved hands composed on her lap, she looked often for the tall figure of Aubrey and smiled, seeing him, smiling not to him but about him, about his being here, safe and home from the war. 'I did so hope you'd want to come,' Pam had greeted her, 'you know what a soft spot my brother has for you! Do tell me how David is – Aubrey says you get a letter from him every day!'

'He has been reported missing.'

'David . . . ?' Your heart lurched; it always did.

'But things are so confused over there, and I'm sure he'll write again soon.'

'Of course he will. Of course.'

Don't make such a fuss, Nurse; just cover his face. But the trains

148

didn't bring them all back, not even those hellish trains: they didn't all come home to be healed or amputated or to die in decency and peace with the soft voice of a woman for goodbye. The trains were her abomination and after three months on the ambulance convoys she still wasn't inured to them: two scheduled arrivals every day and often more, coming in at any old time on priority signals – nine, once, within the same twenty-four hours, after the battle of Ypres – sliding like the dark filth of a nightmare under the cavernous roof, slow and sure and inevitable. But for some people they weren't the worst. Telegrams were the worst.

David? She hadn't known him very well, any better than she'd known Noël Lindsay: her brothers had so many friends; but she remembered him all right, long legs and a raucous laugh, a duffer at tennis but with an inexhaustible fund of jokes. Missing. Where? Over there: it was all you ever knew. Of course David would be writing again soon. Of course. But it made you wonder if you should stop smiling when you greeted someone, just in case, or should wear half-mourning so as not to hurt unwittingly by negligence; black was the fashion this winter.

Crossing the hall from the cloakroom Aubrey saw a policeman and a soldier at the door, with Charrington holding them at bay and looking mystified.

'What's the trouble?' Aubrey asked him.

The constable was new to this beat but he could recognize the son of a house when he saw one, and his salute was as presentable as the police were ever taught. The soldier's was far smarter.

'This young man claims to be known here, Mr Aubrey. I was just asking his name.'

The boy stood like a neat scarecrow, too thin for his uniform, his cold raw face in shadow below the lamp; and for an instant Aubrey was at a loss until he mentally filled in the background of clay, sandbags and the light of shells. Tom Follett. He felt sudden resentment: did the boy have to turn up here looking so pinched and forlorn on the night of his homecoming party? Yet he knew the thought was false: he was only rationalizing his resentment, unwilling to admit the truth.

Tom had brought the war here with him, the clay and the sandbags and the light of shells; and for these few days Aubrey longed for the luxury of forgetting it.

They heard laughter rise from the drawing-room and he noticed how quickly it subsided, not lingering as in the old days six months ago; it was as if people were looking over their shoulders as they laughed, afraid of waking someone: perhaps the dead. Noël, and probably David, and the dead to come. The war was here already in this house: young Follett hadn't brought it.

'Why it's you, Tom!' His mean thought had shamed him and he must make amends. 'Come along in!' He offered the boy his hand and he struggled with his woollen khaki glove, caught unawares. The constable's face was open in surprise. 'You too, Officer – come and warm up while you tell me your troubles.'

'There's no trouble, sir.' He sounded disappointed. 'This young man seemed interested in the house, an' I thought it best to enquire, like.'

'You did perfectly right. Charrington, what about some hot whisky?' The constable made the required protest but Aubrey dismissed it and left the two of them in Charrington's good hands.

His mother deserted her friends the moment he told her that Tom was here. 'But wherever has he been? Mrs Kemp was expecting him last night!' Aubrey watched her float ethereally through the guests, a red rose at her waist. She had a fondness for Tom, it seemed: she'd had a letter from him, 'so nicely written, and telling me all about his friends out there'.

'Empty glass, Nigel?'

'I'm fine, old fruit. Enjoying myself no end.'

It was obvious enough. This was Coxhead's element and there wasn't a girl in the room unaffected by his dark and rather intense good looks, though he was still with Moira, the beauty in the Red Cross uniform who'd met him at the station. They'd arrived together in a cab and without a chaperon – London society was changing very fast, thought Aubrey, and for the better – and Nigel had introduced her as his 'fiancée', though she wore no ring. She wasn't, from close to, strictly beautiful: her features were too irregular; but there was a sensuality in her low voice and her heavily lidded eyes that was immediately arresting: an orchid was like this, flamboyant, defiant, its colours too rich for innocence. Aubrey would have put her down as predatory if it hadn't been clear that Nigel absorbed her utterly.

'A red-hot number,' Pam told him later, not troubling to keep her voice down.

'Where *did* you pick up such engaging slang, Pom-Pom?'

'It's American.' They were at the buffet and she reached for another *pâté*. 'You know there are flowers that eat flies, don't you? That's what she reminds me of, and one day she's going to eat Nigel.'

'He'll probably enjoy it,' Aubrey smiled.

'Of course. He's hungering for it – *Götterdämmerung à la carte*.'

'You'd better make up your mind who's going to eat who!'

'I expect they'll take it in turns, a bite at a time. Poor old Charles is going through the brandy—' she switched suddenly – 'have you noticed?'

'"Uncle" Charles?'

'I don't call him that any more. Sometimes I feel like his mother, or I mean I feel a mother's – oh, anxiety for him. Do I mean anxiety? He's losing his grip, you know. On Louise. They have awful rows these days.'

'Do they?' he said, to give her time. By her tone, by her reluctance to meet his eyes, he knew she had something on her mind. Vic? He didn't think so. Everyone had accepted his story that Vic had 'just been unlucky', and Father wouldn't have told her the truth: he was too hurt for that.

'I've been trying all the evening,' she said, 'to talk to Charles, but he seemed to be dodging me. Then a minute ago he came over and said very solemnly, "I am proud to see your brother here" – meaning you of course – "I am proud for your father." That's why he's drinking too much.'

Aubrey could see him through the open doors, standing alone, a balloon glass in his hand. Louise wasn't in sight; she might even have gone home. He suddenly realized that Pam was standing beside him looking as alone as Charles, no longer interested in the ravaged array of dishes, and no longer talking.

'What's up, Pom-Pom?'

She raised her dark head and her eyes glistened. 'I've been a bitch, while you were away. A thorough-going, rotten little bitch.' She looked down, tearing at her nails. 'You're not going to like this, Aubrey.'

He laughed gently, certain that she was exaggerating whatever was on her mind, as she always had. But his laugh died quickly, like the laughter he'd heard from the hall, earlier, and for the same reason: the war was everywhere, not only in Flanders; it was just over your shoulder, wherever you were, and to laugh was to tempt the fates. The war brought hurts that even Pam couldn't exaggerate.

'About Hugh, is it?'

'Yes.' She wouldn't look up at him. 'He'd come up from Dover for the week-end – he does, sometimes – and Charles took us for a meal at the Trocadero with Louise and a few friends. I – I was dancing with Hugh, and we were just talking about the war – I don't even *remember* what we said, what *he* said, can you imagine that? It's because I want to forget. The papers had been full of the new battle – Ypres, this was – and I was frightened sick that you and Vic were going to be in it.' She lifted her face quickly as if to assure herself that he was here still. 'I know I'm telling it all upside down, Aub'ey, but I can't help that. And I don't even *know* what Hugh said. All I know is that I slapped his face and told someone to take me home.' The tears came, slow on her upturned face, and she got her handkerchief. '*Why* do I always have to bloody well snivel?'

'He must have understood, old thing.' But she hadn't exaggerated. For her this was very serious. Trivial enough, God knew: a girl had slapped a man's face in public, while most of London listened to the troop-trains going out and lived in daily dread of a telegram. But inside this dark young head – still a child's, for all its ability with an ambulance – it was unthinkable that she had done this to Hugh. With her own hand she had put out the brave candle she had always hoped to keep bright: not childhood, but its faith in constancy. Hugh had been a third brother to her and even when they were young they'd never been, the four of them, the kind of family where a slapped face was all in the day's work; however humiliated by a thoughtless word, they were able to withdraw, quickly to forget it or laugh it off. This was the affinity she had ended after all those years, cheaply and in a public place.

'He'll have forgotten,' Aubrey said, 'by now.'

She flared. 'He thinks more of me than that!'

'But he'll want to forget it, just as you do.'

'I haven't seen him since then. He's been home several times – Charles told me – but he didn't come through the hedge, or even ring up.' Her eyes were dry again but she tore slowly at her crumpled handkerchief with hateful fingers. 'It wasn't what he said, so much – probably something about it being wrong to go and fight in a war: he feels stronger than ever about that—'

'It was because you were worried—'

'Yes, oh God, yes, about you and Vic and thousands of others – those foul trains coming in all the time. And the stupid thing is that he's right, you know – the world's a madhouse, suddenly – but I wasn't in the mood to hear it said.' She was staring past Aubrey through the open doors. 'Charles forgave me, for making a scene like that, but he shouldn't have, it made it worse. He should have stuck up for his own son.'

'Did you tell him so?'

She turned quickly – 'How did you know? Did he—'

'No. I just thought you would. You mustn't blame him for not having Hugh's kind of courage.'

The idea was new to her and she considered it gravely. 'Courage? But Charles is an old soldier.'

'A soldier's a man in uniform, and sometimes that's all he is. It's easier to dodge bullets than do what Hugh's doing.'

She faced him thoughtfully, her mind at the brink of revelation. 'Could you do it?'

'No. Never.'

It happened when Aubrey noticed Diana alone for a moment. She was gazing into the massed scarlet roses in the silver bowl on the piano, her fair head tilted attentively as if they were in conversation, she and their quiet blooms; and he held back, not wanting to disturb her. Her dress was the same mauve as the muff he'd picked up from the littered platform, and a mauve ribbon caught the knot of hair at her slender neck.

He would have been content to watch but suddenly a flash of blue came and he was looking into her eyes.

'I didn't want to disturb you.'

153

Mischievously she said: 'I saw your reflection in the bowl.'

'You're not a young woman to be caught unawares.' She seemed surprised and her eyes changed quickly, their colour clouding. 'You're wrong. I was born unawares.' There was hesitation on her lips, then she just said: 'Your house is full of roses.'

'My mother loves them.'

The crash was light and musical but it silenced the whole room and he saw Charles standing there, tilting on his heels and looking down in solemn bewilderment. It was a Staffordshire piece, a shepherd and his lass, now in bright fragments. He supposed Charles had caught it with his elbow in passing. His mother's voice came in the heavy silence, her tone dancing:

'Oh Charles, I'm so *very* glad. It was a present from Aunt Sophie and I've always disliked them both!'

Laughter came quickly but as Diana turned back to him Aubrey saw the shock still in her eyes, though she was saying, 'She even has roses on her dress, and they suit her so.'

'Have you talked to her?'

Charrington was limping up to gather the fragments, and people were speaking again, over-loudly.

'For a long time.' Diana managed to smile. 'Or rather I listened. She really is such a lovely person.'

Charles was making his apologies, standing over Mother with a dignity made pathetic by its difficulty: he was fast losing his feet. In a moment Father took him out of the room, arm in arm to pretend engrossed conversation; and it was now that Aubrey realized something that he prayed Pam would never discover: at that dinner-party she had hurt Charles far more than his son.

'You've captured my mother's interest,' he told Diana. 'She's been asking me about you, but . . .' He shrugged regretfully.

'There's nothing to know,' she said with a touch of bitterness. She had a way of narrowing her eyes, as if trying to focus on a thought that was too close, or too far away, to have the shape and meaning that she knew it should. 'Your brother's not here this time, so Julian tells me. Victor, isn't it?'

'He was unlucky.'

'Julian says he's great fun. Always – always game for adventure.'

'Well he's in the right place now.' He didn't want to talk about Vic; and she didn't want to talk about herself, though she seemed almost desperate for someone to listen. At the station yesterday she hadn't been so feverishly preoccupied, and he wondered what could have happened in the interval.

'Your – your sister's delightful, Lieutenant Talbot. It must have worried your parents when she proposed to drive a Red Cross ambulance.' It was a question, by her tone, and her eyes were serious, demanding an answer; he felt also that it must be the *right* answer – not necessarily the truth but the one she wanted to be told. He found himself wishing he could guess it, but there was no clue.

'No, but the Red Cross must have been worried' – he smiled – 'because I'll bet she drives like a fiend. Would you care to call me "Aubrey"?'

'Thank you. And you may call me "Diana".'

Her courtesy was old-fashioned in a girl so young, and he wondered – as he had wondered yesterday – how she could have remained so protected from the realities of a world changing so fast that 'old-fashioned' had been customary only six months ago. Her parents' influence, of course, and her brother hadn't escaped it: he'd smiled to see Julian just now, waiting for the roof to come down while Pam smoked one of his cigarettes.

Suddenly it connected in his mind: her strict parentage, her half-fearful admiration for Pam, and the bitterness when she'd said, 'There's nothing to know.'

'Have *you* proposed driving an ambulance, Diana?'

'Oh no!' The light blue eyes were appalled. 'I could never manage that!'

'Then what *have* you proposed?'

She stared at him for so long that he wondered if he'd affronted her, breaking one of the traditions that had fallen with this Autumn's leaves.

'You're – you're very intuitive,' she said.

'Or too personal? Perhaps I shouldn't have—'

'I'm going to run away.' She was wide-eyed and her breath had quickened.

'I beg your pardon?' He tried not to smile.

'I'm going to run away from home.'

155

His first thought: 'Does Julian know?'

'No.' Her small hand was on his arm. 'And you mustn't tell him.' Her fingers were strong, for all her slightness. 'You won't, will you?'

'You may change your mind,' he said. He was aware already of responsibility and it irked him; all he had wanted to do was to be with her for these few minutes, to be eased in his mind by her freshness and innocence after the months of wearying horror; now he was committed, a conspirator in a childish escapade.

'You will please not tell my brother.' Her soft lips were compressed and her eyes had narrowed again.

'How old are you?'

'Twenty. I'm not an infant, you see.'

'Where are you going, if you run away?' He felt for a cigarette. 'D'you mind if I smoke?'

'Please do. I realize that for you, just back from France, my troubles are absurdly small. That's because you don't know the whole story – and I'll spare you that. All I ask is that you don't tell Julian – or anyone.'

'Will you be going far?' Julian was a good chap, and the responsibility he felt was to him, not Diana. He probably ought to know that his young sister was off on some desperate enterprise; he could spend his leave in worse ways than helping his family through a patch of trouble.

'I shall remain in London,' she said flatly.

'Are you going to be a nurse?'

'You really are intuitive.'

'No. Lots of young girls are doing it. I suppose your people are dead set against the idea?'

'They think I'm not strong enough for the work.' She said it without criticism.

'I can understand that.' A small head on a slight figure, delicate wrists and the neatest of ankles: she just wasn't the right material. Pam had told him something of the military hospitals in London: 'The driving's nothing – you've got to keep your wits about you, that's all. It's the nurses I admire – my God, you need to be a horse to be a nurse, and that's only the physical side. I nearly faint sometimes when I'm helping with the stretchers from the trains, then I remember that all

156

I'm doing for these poor wrecks is giving them a ride: it's the nurses who've got to live with them from then onwards, whole wards full of helpless pain. I don't know how they do it.' He told Diana: 'I believe things are pretty rough, you know, in the hospitals.'

Her miniature hands hung clasped in front of her and for a moment she looked helpless, but her tone was crisp and reminded him of a kitten spitting. 'I'm cursed with the appearance of a Dresden doll – fragile and rather vacuous – but I—'

'Hardly vacuous—'

'Thank you for your gallantry but I'm serious.' Her sharp little teeth came together and he saw tears of frustration suddenly – 'Can't you see I'm serious? Don't you know how useless I feel when so many men like you need help?' She paused, wishing not to have said it. 'I don't mean like you. I can't imagine you ever being different from what you are now, tall and confident and quietly invincible.'

'We're all invincible,' he said, 'on leave.' He found an ashtray. 'Won't your people let you give it a few weeks as a probationer, to try out your wings?' A few weeks' scrubbing out the wards and even this little spitfire would know when she was beaten. Hadn't it occurred to them?

'It's not a question of "letting". I won't bore you by describing the atmosphere in the house when I talk about nursing, but I love my parents dearly, and that's what makes it so hard; they make me feel I'm deserting them.'

'But you'll remain in London, you said.'

'For my training. Then I'm volunteering for duty overseas.'

He felt a jolt of misgiving. 'You mean France?'

'I hope so. We can't choose where it will be – we just volunteer for a posting.'

He found himself looking for Julian, and saw him near the fire talking earnestly to Lady Waring. 'I see,' he said abstractedly. He would have to tell him about this, or the poor chap would be crazy with worry when he found out too late.

'I want your word, Aubrey.' She'd been following his gaze. 'That you won't tell him.'

He looked down and saw the steady challenge in her eyes, and wished she were less lovely than she was, because it distracted him and he ought to be thinking straight for Julian's sake, and maybe for her own.

'It's not my concern, I know—'

'Yes,' she said, 'it is. We're strangers, and I've burdened you with an unwanted confidence – though I'll never understand how I let it happen. But Julian is your friend, and by his letters I know how enormously he admires you; and he won't thank you for not telling him about this, if one day something bad happens to me as a result. So I realize how much I'm asking of you.' Her fingers were on his wrist again and he was conscious of their warmth. 'But nothing is going to stop me; I've spent too many sleepless nights to have any doubts left. So if you tell my brother, I shall still do what I plan to do; but you'll have made it more painful for me. And for him.'

He was reluctant to answer, either way, and remembered his resolve, standing alone in the dark trench watching the distant flash of the guns, that he must start making an effort to accept responsibility. But that had been in Flanders, in the war, far from the imagined peace of home. Yet no one here was at peace. Pam, her heart trying to heal from the hurt she'd given someone else; Charles, who would rather face a bombardment than the more subtle agonies of derision on every side; and this spirited child setting out deliberately to wound those she 'loved dearly' because her greater need was to heal the wounds of strangers.

He said: 'When are you leaving home?'

'Next week.'

'While Julian's still on his leave? I would have thought he deserved—'

'I arranged it deliberately.' It was said slowly, like a confession, and he knew that the bitterness in her tone was against herself. 'He'll be here to help my parents get over the shock.'

He stubbed his cigarette out impatiently, of half a mind to take her by the hand and lead her straight across the room to Julian and let them battle it out; he was hesitant only because he might be doing it for his own sake and not theirs, simply to rid himself of the responsibility.

'Why don't you just sign on as a probationer, all open and above board? Why do you have to "run away"?'

'Because if they knew which hospital it was they'd make a

158

scene – or my father would – and take me away again.' Very softly: 'I've had enough scenes.'

'You'll keep in touch with them, I suppose?'

'Of course. Without telling them where I am.' He couldn't judge whether the anger in the amethyst eyes was for him or for herself. 'You think I'm heartless, don't you?'

He said: 'If I were to march you straight over there to your brother, would you listen to him?'

Pain furrowed her brow and for a moment she closed her eyes as if to shut him out of her mind. 'I can see,' she whispered, 'that it's no use. I was stupid to tell you. But I've had to fight this alone for so long . . . and you seemed so – so easy-going in your manner.' She looked up at him with a kind of surprise, as if he'd been changing before her eyes into someone different. 'Or I was judging you by Julian's letters – "easy-going" is a phrase he uses so often about you. I didn't know you were such a – responsible person.' She gave a little frown: 'Have I said something amusing?'

'I'm always amused when I learn something new about myself. Ignorance seems ridiculous at such close quarters, but I'm rather good at it.'

She hesitated, but didn't pursue it; she was too worried by what he had half-threatened. 'Do you intend to take me across to my brother?'

'No. I think you meant what you said: it wouldn't stop you; it'd only make things more painful. What day will you be going?'

'Tuesday.'

It was very difficult, because as he looked across the room again he met Julian's eyes by chance, and Julian smiled to him. He looked back to Diana. 'Then I'd better not see him again till then, or I'd be tempted to tell him.'

She drew a slow breath. 'So you're not going to?'

'Not until you've gone.'

'But you need never tell him that you knew!'

'Of course I must. He's my friend. For a few more days, at least.'

'I think that's enough now, Kitty.'

'Yes, milady.'

159

They hadn't spoken while the brush drew down the long gold hair; in the glass Kitty had seen that her mistress's eyes were closed, though there was no sleep on her face: often she would simply doze off, but not tonight. The light in the room was colder than usual, sharper, because the electric lamp on the escritoire was going instead of the candles; and this had happened only once before in Kitty's memory, on the night when the 'boys' had left for France. Sometimes there was sadness in candlelight, milady had said.

'Are you warm enough in bed, Kitty?'

'Oh yes, milady, thank you.' She hesitated at the door, trying to think of something cheerful to say, then went out in silence, deciding it was best.

The light brought peacock colours to the crust of ink on the nib.

Already the house seems empty again. He is such a big person and had filled it for those few days with his incomparable presence. Dear William said goodbye to him here – there is a greater understanding between them, I notice; is this because Aubrey has matured by force of circumstance or does mere absence bring, like fondness, an increased affinity? One thing I know: they conspired to keep from me the truth that Victor could have come home with his brother had he wished. Have we already lost a son, not by an act of war but by estrangement? How selfish we are to expect that our company is held as dear by others as we hold theirs! I would console myself by talking to William about it, but he would be hurt to know I had divined the truth from which he has tried to shield me; so we must both say nothing of it, withholding the comfort of our shared dismay so that neither shall be hurt ... It won't have escaped you that such ironies have come to frequent your pages; the more brutal the times the more sensitive we become, hoping perhaps that the bullying Fates won't see us in our silk cocoon. A feeble enough defence, but the alternative is that we too shall become brutalized.

Aubrey rode in state to Charing Cross, beside Pamela in her ambulance. I half-wished they would strike some lamp-post a suitably glancing blow, to bring him home again as a light casualty for a few more days; yet how far has a mother gone towards spiritual ruin when she craves the presence of an injured son, rather than bear his absence whole in limb? But I mislead you: I'm frightened of the guns, that's all, and what they may do with him now. His ship sails tonight from Dover, and I have never known such terror in my soul.

This morning, before leaving, he played for us at the piano; the winter rain beat at the windows, and sometimes he glanced up at them as if acknowledging that beyond the warmth of those last minutes with us he was awaited by a winter of his own.

A draught came sighing musically below the door: someone had entered the house from the terrace behind. It would be Charrington, seeing to it that the hearths were stocked before William came home.

I must tell you that Tom — my thin brave Tom — also took his leave of us today. He has been busy with Mr Willis these days past, felling and chopping dead wood for the hearths. Betweentimes Cook lured him into her domain 'to feed his poor little gizzard', as she put it, then to chase him out again, herself disabused, with the warning that such an appetite would be his downfall. He has also managed to speak more than once to Kitty, and is, I believe, deeply under her spell.

The pen was held still, her fingers for a moment lacking courage. Then she dipped it into the inkwell with a care that falsely spoke of indifference.

David Waring is now reported killed in action. I told no one until Aubrey had gone; our leave-taking was sad enough without poor David's spirit beside us to see him off.

A light swell ran, rolling through the harbour-mouth and lifting the sterns of the dark grey ships, bringing the creak of ropes. Rain slanted in the fickle wind and the cry of gulls was sharp and then fading as the gusts shifted, deflected by the cliffs.

'You nearly missed the boat, old fruit!'

Aubrey had found them on the aft deck, where the light of naphtha flares shone across the wet tarpaulins.

'Where's the rest?' He was still out of breath, and the rain clung like hoarfrost to his greatcoat.

'Down on C Deck,' Nigel told him. 'Did you get enough time for anything serious?'

'No.' It was the easiest reply; he hadn't been seeing a girl anyway, but Nigel wouldn't believe that.

Julian's cigarette-case flashed in the bleak light, and Aubrey accepted one. 'Thanks. You all right?' There'd been this kind of sea ten days ago, coming over, and it had bothered Julian.

'Fine. If it doesn't get any worse.'

They exchanged a few more words, each eager to hear it

reaffirmed in the other's voice that they were back on a friendly footing. The first time Aubrey had telephoned Julian it hadn't been too good. Diana had left home the day before and Julian was still very upset; he'd rung off with distant politeness while Aubrey was trying to explain. But he agreed they should meet, two days later; and Julian had conceded that it must have been 'damned difficult to do the decent thing', and Aubrey's relief had been greater than he'd expected to feel: a measure of the value he set on their friendship.

There had been a note from Diana, dated Tuesday of that week. *I am writing this in the mean little cubicle that is now my home, and have already learned the true meaning of loneliness – it is to be among strangers. I am also overwhelmed, of course, by all the doubts so easily dismissed when my small ambition was driving me on. I have written to Julian, beseeching him to understand the grave dilemma in which I placed you. Having incurred your dislike I realize it will mean nothing to you that in sharing – however unwillingly! – in my plans you gave me great comfort in the days before I 'took the plunge'. For this I shall be for ever grateful, and will think of you and pray for you when you are back in France.*

The rain hissed slanting into the dark sea.

Poor little devil . . . It hadn't been easy for her to do what she thought was the right thing. There were plenty of girls of her age all over London, dressed to kill and hunting for officers to give them a good time. He wanted to write to her, but of course had no address.

'Seaman, can you find me a life-jacket? I was late on board.'

The smell of ether was on the wind: alongside there lay a hospital-ship, white overall and with a green band, her big red crosses marked by lamps. The last of the wounded were being taken off, and one by one the ambulances were moving away to the rail-head. He thought of Pam.

'She's still punishing herself,' he had told Hugh. He'd telephoned the Chalet School from London, and they'd met in a pub here at Dover an hour ago.

'I didn't know. I'll write to her.'

Their conversation was fitful, and they both watched the time, and neither tried to pretend they were the same two people who'd sung and cheered with the crowds near Parliament that summer night.

Hugh's face was drawn and he glanced round when anyone came into the bar, as if constantly prepared to meet a challenge.

'You finding it hard going?' Aubrey asked him flatly. He risked missing the boat and he wasn't in the mood to spend these few precious minutes in strained small-talk with a friend he'd known all his life.

'A bit.' The faint smile, wrinkling the corners of his eyes, looked more like the Hugh he'd known: pensive, amused, but at no one's expense. 'You get a lot of your friends cutting you.'

'Well it's their loss.' He noticed that the barmaid was enjoying a game of her own, eyeing him with moony admiration and then throwing a cool glance to Hugh until Aubrey turned his back to her. He'd seen this kind of disdain for young civilians many a time in the streets of London, but hadn't thought until now what it must be like to be its target. 'You haven't lost Pam, I can tell you that. She can't forgive herself.'

'I know she did it on an impulse.' The smile came again. 'What doesn't she do on impulse? I would have rung her up, you know, but then I decided it'd be best to leave things as they were. We become oddly cut off, Aubrey, and we start thinking – or I do anyway – that it's better to lose friends than embarrass them. So it seemed a sort of opportunity.'

'Write to her, then. Because you're wrong. Don't go on hurting the poor kid.' It would be good for Hugh as well to put it all down. Diana wasn't the only one who was finding it hard to do what she thought was right.

Hugh asked: 'Was it for Pam you came to see me?' He drank from his glass, perhaps to make it easier for Aubrey to lie if he had to.

'No,' he said carefully. 'I wanted to see you anyway.'

'I'm glad.' The *whoop-whoop-whoop* of a destroyer piped faintly from the sea. 'You'd better be going, hadn't you?'

'I'll finish my beer, but you don't have to talk.' Hugh was too keen to give his friends 'opportunities' so that they were spared 'embarrassment'.

'There's my father, too,' he said.

'He's old enough to see someone else's point of view.'

'Not really.' He played with the cardboard beer-mat, running his nails round its edge. 'It's not a question of age. Cement sets pretty quickly. He told me, you know, that he didn't understand my conviction. He said he respected it but couldn't understand it. I think that's as much as I'll get from him.'

Aubrey remembered Charles, his solemn bewilderment as he looked down at the broken ornament; and an odd saying came to him from far back in his memory, the words, not at the time understood, of a childhood nurse: 'He seeks solace in drink.'

'He was bearing up perfectly well when I saw him last,' Aubrey said, a little too quickly.

'Was he?' His tone chose to disbelieve it. 'What about you, Aubrey? We haven't talked about you.'

There were already paper-chains across the ceiling and a coy sprig of mistletoe above the door; and a fragile gilded ball, dangling from holly against the mirror, began tinkling as if a lorry were going by; but there was no lorry.

'There's nothing to say about me. I've just followed the crowd for the sake of comfort.'

'Comfort?' The ball shook, rattling on the glass; and the talk in the bar fell away.

'What's that?' asked Aubrey.

'Don't you know?' Hugh watched him steadily. 'It's the guns.'

'All that distance?'

'They're nearer than you think. They don't give me much peace.' He found some money and put it on to the bar.

'This was my—'

'Let me do it. At least let me do that.'

The grey ship lifted and fell.

'They're running.'

'Eh?'

'The engines. Won't be long now.'

'Full of Christmas cheer, you are.'

Percy Stokes was by the rail, his hands spread along it like an admiral's. 'Right – heave to and hard abaft there! Scupper the lockers an' splice the mainbrace or I'll have you in irons, you motley lubbers!' He cupped his hands. '*Belay there!*'

'Put a sock in it, Percy, you'll 'ave us chucked off!'

'Well you wouldn't complain, would you?'

'Hey, can you see that little brunette doll, right by the red cross amidships? She's lookin' this way right now. Gee, I'd like to—'

'Oh my God,' said Percy, 'don't you know when you've had enough?' He blinked at Sam in horrified fascination.

'Did he find a girl?' asked Wiggy.

'Did he what? Have you ever pulled winkles off a pier? You don't know what it's been like, that's a fact. "Where are you off to?" my Mum says, first day we were home. "Oh," I tell her, "I'm going to show my American friend a bit of London – the Palace an' Tower Bridge an' the Horse Guards an' all that." And what happens? We get slung out of the Dance-Drome, Peckham, because he was trying to do the Boston with three girls at once an' when Sam does his version of the Boston it's more like a Roman orgy, then we're in a taxi and a copper pulls us up along the Strand an' tells the driver he's overloaded because Sam's gone an' packed six of 'em in with us and half of 'em are in a state of disarray as you might say, and there's my Mum an' Dad barricading themselves in the house because the front path's jammed with chorus-girls screamin' out for Sam to autograph their garters, and you ask me did he find a girl? Ten days' grievous mental strain, that's what I've been through, an' I'd've put in for sick-leave if I could've found the strength.'

'Hey, she's lookin' this way again!'

'Then I'm divin' overboard, it's the only solution.'

Whoop-whoop-whooop.

Geoff Tuffnel stared through the rainy dark at the flicker of signal lamps. There must have been hundreds of ships here in the harbour and standing off in the roads; the water was a restless field of stars. 'We've got a naval escort of six destroyers,' he said. 'Mr Lovell told me.'

'Are we expecting trouble?' asked Tom from beside him.

'Making sure we don't get any.'

They could feel the vibration underfoot.

Wiggy shrank deeper into his greatcoat. 'I've never been so perished. 'Ave you ever been so perished?' Wiggy felt the cold. ''Ere – you know 'ow much I got for that Jerry 'elmet, eh? Ten bob! Ten shillin'! An' it was bashed about like a piss-pot in a shipwreck. Ten bob – I can't get over it!' And all because Mum wouldn't have it in the house. 'What happened to the man that wore it?' she'd asked him. ''E snuffed it, I suppose,' he'd said. 'Then you can take it out of here, quick as you like.' He was quite upset; it was a real posh ceremonial full-dress affair, patent leather and a metal spike and badge, proper dog's dinner, and he'd had to smuggle it past all the M.P.s because you weren't meant to bring home souvenirs, and now she wouldn't have it in the place. But he'd had a fit when the bloke at the shop offered him ten bob. It was in very poor condition, he'd said, otherwise he could have made it fifteen. The place was chock-a-block with the kind of stuff you saw all over No Man's Land – bullets, nose-caps, badges, knives – stuff you took for rubbish. Rubbish? It was a gold-mine! Rag-picking? That was for mugs. He was in the antique business now.

The rain made a ring of haze around the lamps. On the quayside humped figures stood by the capstans, staring up at the bridge. Along the packed decks the men stood huddled in the lee of the rafts and open boats, their collars against the wind.

'Harry's got a sister,' said Geoff.

'Eh?'

'Harry Ross. I met his sister. She was waiting for him at the station. The telegram had gone astray.'

'Bloody Post Office for you. They should be more careful these days.'

'Her name's Judith.' He spoke mostly to the wind.

'Is it?' They couldn't quite remember what Harry had looked like. You forgot things quickly with so much going on.

Mum and Dad had been wonderful. He'd known they would be. Judith had cried a lot, then Mrs Ross had made a big jug of cocoa – took some doing that, finding the right tin and counting out the spoonfuls as if it mattered – and they'd stayed till gone midnight. Been a lot of questions of course: had he been with Harry when it happened? Did he suffer? What was the place called? Was that where the cemetery was? Yes, he'd been beside Harry when it happened; he didn't suffer, not for so much as a second, a bullet clean in the head.

'We're castin' off!'

'Are we?'

Because it was no good telling them the truth. He didn't even know the truth. It might have been one of Harry's legs

166

he'd dug out of the sandbags; it might have been Harry on that stretcher under the blanket, moaning till he died. It didn't matter. The big tin with the blue label, six spoonfuls and don't forget the sugar, that was what mattered now. You'd got to start again.

He'd seen Judith twice more. 'I'll never forget the way you told me, Geoffrey.' Red hair and freckles, yellow little face because of the chemicals, too thin, nothing but skin and bone, she didn't eat enough. 'Nor will I.' Let him never have to do that again.

The heavy lines hissed into the sea and the capstans rattled. The deck shook to the engines. Somewhere men were singing softly, 'Holy Night'.

Tom felt the wind on his cheek. It was blowing from the north-west, from London way. Wind was news, going from one place to another, from where you wanted to be to where you were. Mr Charrington would be putting logs in the hearths, like he always did before Sir William came home. They'd cut a whole lot, Mr Willis and him, enough to last through Christmas. That was a nice thought.

Bells rang and there was shouting and then the big grey ship dropped her stern as the screws bit at the black water. Along the rainswept decks the men fell quiet, turning to face the land. Lights winked from the destroyers as they formed station out to sea.

'Farewell Home an' Glory.'

The planks drummed beneath their boots.

Write to Pam. You don't lose friends that easily. Not you.

Nurses in cloaks waved from the white ship.

'Goodbye, Dolly, be good!'

The logs would last all through Christmas, and there'd be Kitty's face in the firelight. The light he'd helped to make.

Pans rang at the galley portholes and gulls swooped.

Judith's name on the wind.

''Appy Christmas!'

The ship turned, and England fell away.

IX

'*Stand to!*'

It had not been dark in the night. Mist lay in the hollows, pooling across the ravaged corn and flowing among the leafless stumps of the wood; and the moon's light glowed in it and made whiteness everywhere, so that the sentries had been, all through the night, uneasy, shouting their challenge at rats and the broken trees and the movement of the mist itself. All through the night a man had moaned, his sound now loud, now faint, now here, now there, as if he were nowhere, as if it were no more than the disembodied moan of man against his fate.

A party had gone out more than once to find him and had come back with nothing, but the sentries heard him still.

Day broke and rose light touched the folds of mist, seeping through the corn; the corn was a heavy sea, its waves piled and frozen to stillness, its hollows ringed with the upthrown earth of summer and inhabited by the living of yesterday, their blind faces lit by the first dawn that was not for them.

In an hour the mist grew sparse and the red of poppies burned, and the sun's light stole among the shadows of the corn, sparking on twisted metal and the worn brass lacehole of a boot, finding a hand and failing for ever to warm its cold curled fingers. Rats moved heavily, abroad for greed, their hunger long since satisfied; above them larks climbed the neutral air to scatter their careless music.

'*Stand down!*'

Boots clumped on the duckboards. A man yawned.

'You know what day it is?'

'It ain't pay day.'

'It's August the fourth. We been at it a year.'

'Roll on.'

'It's for the day after tomorrow,' Capt. Diplock told them. He reached for the brandy; the shadow of his arm was cast by

168

the candle for a moment across their faces. 'Any more for any more?' They nodded and passed their mugs.

'They can't do it,' Aubrey said indifferently. 'The men are dead beat.'

'Including me,' grunted Julian.

There were some French 75's banging away from somewhere beyond the salient, and sometimes a Big Willie gave a thump, looking for the troop concentrations the balloons had reported earlier.

'The men are dead beat,' nodded Capt. Diplock, inhaling the fumes from his mug, 'and there's heavy wire reported right across the sector, and the guns can only give us token protection because they're hard up for shells, and I've got a fat dose of hay fever.' His red eyes glowered at the candle. 'Be all that as it may, *mes amis*, the day after tomorrow at precisely oh-five-three-oh ack-emma we are to provide the second assault-wave and follow B Company to their doom.'

His face looked extraordinary. By daylight it was permanently askew, one cheek tugged back by a surgeon – presumably following a war-wound though nobody had ever asked him – and the ear on that side half shrivelled; here in the dugout he sat obliquely to the candle, the only source of light, so that he resembled a red-eyed waxwork rescued from a fire.

'They'll call it off,' said Aubrey. He tilted the ammo-box and hooked his thumbs in his pockets, staring through half-closed eyes at the marigolds. 'They'll have to.'

Diplock blew his nose again and sipped more brandy.

'The Old Man's been chivvying Brigade since we first got warning. I may inform you that he's wasting his time. Our fine friend Brigadier-General Mainwright is out for a spot of personal glory, and it's to be our honour to provide it.'

'He can come,' Aubrey said wearily, 'and get it for himself.' In the Gentlemen's Relish jar the marigolds blazed quietly. Fresh-picked, he thought, fresh-picked. They'd been growing along the parapet, all in a row. You'll have to get rid of them, he'd told the men, they're a perfect marker for snipers. So it was done. But they'd been proud of them, the only bit of colour in this rotten deadly hole, and even the Hun had left them alone though he could see them all right, couldn't miss. It had been a proper garden there on the parapet, and the men had thought things couldn't be so bad if they could bother with growing a garden. But it was done. He'd seen Tom's face for a moment, though; it was Tom of course who'd brought the seeds and planted them, no one else would do a thing like that. Now it was done, and he'd brought the flowers for the dugout and some for Freddie Kemp. They were from the Manor, he'd said, the seeds.

'Officially,' the captain said, 'it's a sideshow with limited objectives, to test the enemy's strength.'

Julian helped himself to some more brandy, past the point where he could call it a night and turn in. Soon he would be drunk. He didn't do it often. He knew when he did it. When they were warned for action.

'Unofficially,' Aubrey reflected aloud, 'it's going to be a massacre.' Now they'd been picked, they'd start dying, the marigolds. Who would outlive them? Not everyone.

Julian raised his mug. '"Yesterday this day's madness did prepare . . . tomorrow's silence, triumph or despair . . . Drink! For you know not whence you came, nor why. Drink! For you know not why you go, nor where."'

'True enough,' said Diplock rheumily, and drank.

The smart young soldier stood at the French coast reaching across the Channel to the reluctant civilian. COME, LAD, LEND US A HAND! Some wag had brought it back from leave and hung it outside a dugout in Support, and someone else had got a bit of charcoal, copying the lettering quite well. DON'T BE SO DAFT, MATE, STAY WHERE YOU ARE!

When Geoff Tuffnel saw it he said: 'It's not the ones who won't join up that I can't stand, it's the bastards who buy you a beer and slap you on the back and tell you how much you're doing for King and Country.'

'It's your ribbon, Geoff.'

His jaw came forward. 'No, it's not.' You couldn't even mention it these days. 'They do it to anyone in uniform. They'd push their own kids out here if they could, soon as they learned to walk. London's full of 'em, the whole country is. The papers put 'em up to it – "Our gallant lads victorious again", that sort of rot. They'll do anything for us so long as we go on giving 'em a bit of excitement. We're the biggest performing circus they've ever seen.'

'Ne' mind, chum, I'd rather be me than them.' You found yourself agreeing with old Geoff, of late, just to keep out of trouble.

'Now look here, you people, haven't you any jolly old fatigues to do, what?' Percy had joined them, picking a speck of dust off his brand-new lance-corporal's stripe. 'Fetch my charger will you, my good man? I'm going to review the enemy lines, they're too frightfully untidy for words.'

'Is it still on?' asked Barclay-Smith. He'd rejoined them at Easter with a smart wound-stripe. But they missed old Oscar.

'Is what on, my man?'

'The attack.' They said the C.O. was sticking his neck out trying to get it cancelled and they hoped to Christ he succeeded, because if *he* didn't like the look of things they must be bad. Col. Forsyth was a V.C.

'Well now,' Percy stroked his chin, 'Haig didn't mention anything to me in the mess last night, but he probably didn't want to bother me with trifles, like the considerate fellow he is.'

'If you've got no news,' Gilmore told him, 'have a heart an' shut your gob for Chris' sake.'

Percy looked at him loftily. '*Such* a common person.' But he shut up. Dicky Gilmore was new and had never seen action and he'd got the wind up and didn't mind who knew it. He wasn't the only one; there'd been a stream of blokes on sick-parade the past three days till the order had gone up: any man reporting sick without a genuine complaint was straight on a malingering charge.

It wasn't the idea of action that worried them. It was what Pop Jarvis had overheard the captain saying on the phone when he'd passed the dugout. 'We'll have a go, but we've not got a bloody chance.'

It was late afternoon when Vic found his brother in No. 2 Platoon dugout.

'Did you send for me?'

Aubrey looked up, his strained face for a moment blank while his memory adjusted. 'Oh hello, Vic. Take a pew.' He glanced over the letter he'd been writing. 'What was the exact message you got?'

Vic hooked his leg over the crate that served as the visitor's chair. 'From Salmon?' He didn't quite cotton on. 'He said you wanted to see me.' There was a whole lot of papers spread over the table: Aubrey went in for that sort of thing; his own den looked much less busy, because any bumph arriving went straight into the rubbish box.

'Condolences to the bereaved.' A five-nine had come down in Support last night and made a mess. Aubrey crumpled the letter and dropped it into the littered ration-tin. 'D'you ever get them right first time?'

'I never do any.'

'Ah.' Aubrey shouted for his batman. 'How's it all shaping?' he asked Vic. 'Cigarette?'

'The chaps are a bit windy.' His sharp young face didn't have its usual tension; for once it was he who looked relaxed, not his brother. 'I dunno who started the scare about this stunt but he wants shooting.'

Salmon came and Aubrey asked him: 'What message did you give Mr Talbot?'

'Your compliments, sir, an' you wanted to see 'im.' His dull suety features showed surprise.

'The correct message was that I was looking for him. Get it right next time.'

As the man went out Vic drew on his cigarette, watching his brother obliquely. In this company a first loot didn't 'send for' a second loot: he just let it be known he was 'looking for' him; and in this case he and Aubrey held equal command, each with his own platoon; but how could you expect an amiable peasant like Salmon to recognize a nicety as fine as that? Old Aubrey was getting as bad as Father.

'I don't think anyone "started a scare" about this stunt at all,' he told Vic quietly. 'It's simply common knowledge that we're going to need a lot of luck. As for B Company even luck's not going to save them.' He put one foot on the rim of the heavy ration-tin but the attitude seemed forced and he didn't, Vic thought, look any more relaxed. Perhaps it was because most of the strain was in the eyes, where it couldn't be hidden.

'You're not windy too, surely?'

Aubrey cocked an eyebrow. 'Of course. It'd take a damn' fool not to be.'

Vic shrugged. 'That's me.' He was getting a rough idea why his brother had wanted to see him.

'No, you're not a fool, Vic. The chances you take are calculated. The trouble is, you still take them.'

'Oh for God's sake, we've had this out before.' It was only a week since he'd organized a patrol to winkle the snipers out of Les Marroniers village, and Aubrey had got into a fine old state because they'd lost Sgt Knight and been ambushed on their way back. Capt. Diplock had called it 'an ill-starred enterprise' but Aubrey had accused him of 'culpable reckless-ness' and stayed in a huff for days. 'Is this what you fetched me here for? The usual lecture?'

Aubrey pinched out his cigarette carefully between his shoe and the rim of the tin, dropping it in. 'There's another thing about the chances you take. You have to screw up your courage first; it's not just a blind swipe. You *make* yourself—'

'Look, there's a war on, isn't there? Diplock knows that much.'

'He's not your brother.'

'Thank God for that.' Vic felt the tension coming back into him, the special kind of tension that only Aubrey could create: the feeling that he was being watched and would have to justify whatever he was doing. He remembered – quite often, these days – an odd thought that had struck him once, years ago, when he'd been going slowly up the stairs in disgrace an hour before his usual bedtime. 'However old I grow he'll always be older than me.'

Aubrey's eyes were on him, not so much hurt as puzzled: you looked like this at a face you remembered but couldn't place. 'What did I do to you, Vic? When did it happen?'

'You didn't do anything.' He got off the crate and it rocked to stillness with a stupid irrelevant sound, providing argument for neither. 'Mind if we talk about something else, if we've got to talk at all?'

Aubrey looked down and said dully: 'No, we don't have to talk. You've got a lot to see to, and I don't want—'

'I didn't mean—'

'Oh that's all right.' The field-telephone had started ringing

173

and it was a moment before he realized it ought to be answered. 'Talbot, Two Platoon.'

Vic turned and stood in the doorway, where a patch of bright colour showed: earth had crept between the timbers and now a wild flower grew there, deep yellow; and he thought vaguely how impudent it was, how useless, to be growing there.

He was angry with himself because he'd not been able to put what he felt into words; he'd tried but had only blurted out something beastly. Aubrey had done nothing to him, ever – at least he'd admitted that much. Aubrey had done nothing wrong in his life, nor even made the effort. Pick up a racket and it was his game and set, that was Aubrey. No one questioned it; they'd learned to expect automatic and effortless success from him and he'd never let them down. The only thing wrong with that was that it left you struggling away for nothing: do your damnedest and the most it would get you was second place.

'Why can't A Company send some people?' Aubrey was asking on the telephone.

Some men sweated past the dugout dragging wire, their gauntlets and puttees ripped, some R.E.s helping them.

'Tell 'im about it?' one of them was saying, 'You'd 'ave to shoot 'ole in 'is 'ead an' shout through it afore that bastard'd listen.' The barbs gouged at the dried mud and brought flakes away.

Who was the 'bastard'? Vic wondered. Not the Colonel, he knew. Forsyth had brought a new strength to the battalion – the 'Gentleman V.C.' was the name he'd got for himself within a month – but now they were back in the bloody-minded mood of Pickering's time.

He listened to Aubrey's steady tones. 'I'm not sending any men from my platoon, and you know why.' The enemy lines were too close for free speech. 'You can ask Captain Diplock and when he comes back to me I'm telling him the same thing. Try the R.E.s, they've had a new draft in.'

When Vic turned back, his brother was sitting hunched at the littered desk, fingering his closed eyes. For some reason it angered him: the invincible Aubrey shouldn't look like this.

'Mind if I shove off now?'

Aubrey blinked up at him against the sunlit entrance. 'I

want to say this before you go. Tomorrow we'll be up against it and we'll have to fight to survive. Try to be content with that. Don't *ask* for trouble this time or by God you'll get it.' His hand touched a paper. 'I find these letters difficult to write, although they're to strangers. I don't know how I could ever send one to Ashbourne.'

The poppies were black in the starlight and the stumps of the wood leaned darkly against the glow of distant fires, their columns a ruined temple roofless under the sky.

It was said that Norville was burning down.

Often the ground shook and men slept fitfully, sometimes speaking for the sake of company.

'They're hungry tonight, the guns.'

The night was warm. Last summer there had been fireflies here; the wood had been known for them.

Twice they'd heard Mr Talbot and the captain arguing.

'If we get any sleep tonight it'll be thanks to 'im.'

Oscar had played his mouth-organ for them a bit and they'd listened with silly smiles on their faces because they'd thought for months now that he was dead, ever since Neuve Chapelle where he'd been posted as missing. After base hospital he'd been sent up the line to a different regiment by mistake – it happened a lot. He'd only come in this afternoon, quiet as ever, and couldn't understand why they'd asked him to play a tune for them, thought they were joking.

Tom shared a hole in the trench with Pop Jarvis. Old Pop was spark out, of course; nothing could keep him awake if he wanted to sleep. 'Sleep is meat and drink to a man,' he'd sometimes say. Tom watched a patch of stars, thinking that if Kitty happened to be looking at the sky too, this minute, she'd see them herself; it made her so close. Today he'd put a Scarlet Pimpernel in her letter, to show her what sort of flowers there were here; but it might not interest her; she'd not answered his first two letters. But he'd go on writing to her sometimes just for the pleasure, even if she never answered, even if he threw them away instead of posting them; it was wonderful writing to Kitty.

The starlight touched the tips of the sentries' bayonets.

'Seen Tosh, have you?'

'Not since stand-down.'

'Said he wasn't goin' to have any. Not this time.'

'Easy to say.'

'No, he's got it worked out. A bash at the rum-jar so they'll cop 'im for bein' drunk when warned for action.'

'Christ, he'd get six months.'

'That's what 'e told me. Six months peace an' quiet, be'ind the lines, 'e says, while you silly sods are still 'ere with your guts 'angin' on the wire.'

'He'll never do it.'

'Surprisin' what you'll do these days.'

Light spread above them blindingly.

'What's Jerry lookin' for?'

'Trouble. What else is there?'

Before midnight Capt. Diplock came past on his rounds, full of brandy and hay fever. A sniper tried to pick him off as he went through a traverse but he didn't so much as duck. 'You'll have to do better than that,' they heard him say. He was all right, old Dippy, go a long way with a bloke like him.

The last-minute duplicates were still coming in to Platoon, a lot of them *Read and Burn*, and Aubrey was alone in the dugout going through them. The stress was on security but you couldn't mount the smallest offensive without making it obvious in the rear: only this morning a war-correspondent from *The Courier* had asked him for 'anything interesting' since his father owned the paper and would welcome 'special copy'. He'd sent him to the Colonel and wished him luck. The rest of the stuff was routine and he made a heap in the tin and struck a Swan Vestas, watching the flame take hold.

'Playin' with fire again, Mr Aubrey?'

Turning to see the short neat figure in the doorway he thought: What will all those years have led to? Only tomorrow?

'Hello Freddie. Come and have a drink.'

Aubrey poured some brandy, his eye catching the envelope on the table. He and Julian had known her address since January. *Miss Diana Lovell, Annexe to 3rd Nursing, St Mathias Hospital, London EC2.* All he had said was: *Some business afoot. I just want to tell you again how much I admire you for choosing the hardest road. It has been an inspiration to me. Will you always remember that?*

'Cheers,' Freddie said. 'No news, I suppose?'

176

'It won't be cancelled, if that's any news. Unless the weather breaks.'

Freddie looked from the doorway to the high clear stars. 'No chance of that, sir. Tomorrow's goin' to be a lovely summer's day.'

A company runner came dodging through the early mist with the captain's watch a little before 0500 and the platoon commanders set their time by it. The barrage had started up a few minutes ago and the German batteries were replying. From the support line C Company could see low air-bursts finding the range of the front-line trenches where B Company were waiting to go over; then a heavy four-point-two sailed across the pale disc of the sun to reach Support and send a fountain of sandbags and timber whirling high, and from that moment telephone communication with Battalion ceased.

The second-assault trenches here were crowded but orderly. Stretcher-bearers stood with their poles furled into the canvas and a medical aid post had been set up and manned near Queer Street Redoubt. At precise intervals a unit of battle-police – stronger than usual because confidence in this operation was low – was deployed and ready to follow the fighting-troops in their hundred-yard rush on the front line and see them over the top, shooting or arresting any man who refused action. They stood quietly, looking at no one.

Breakfast had been finished an hour ago and there had been a rum-issue on orders from Col. Forsyth. At the height of the barrage a man was seen lurching over the duckboards with his rifle trailing, shouting or perhaps singing against the noise of the guns. Sgt Bruce caught him and threw him towards one of the battle-police.

'Arrest that man. Get him away quick!'

He didn't resist but they were rough with him.

''E done it, then.'

'Eh?'

'Tosh. Like 'e said.'

They looked away.

The British guns had faltered twice and each time it had seemed they would stop altogether. The men glanced at one another with anger in their eyes.

'Call this a barrage? Fuckin' disgrace.'

It was said that the batteries were short of shells.

Sergeant Kilderbee stood near the redoubt watching the men, noting those who looked like needing help. Young Follett was white about the face: the scene with the drunk had upset him. He didn't seem to understand what the M.P.s were doing here either, kept looking round at them.

The barrage was thinning away.

Aubrey looked at his watch. 'All right, Sar'nt.'

'*Fix bayonets!*'

Some of them were clumsy, their hands too weak where a minute ago they'd been strong, and a man dropped his bayonet and it struck his boot point-downwards and he yelped but none of them laughed, they cursed him.

In the light shudder of the guns a man was heard sobbing and a corporal went to him and spoke sharply but he couldn't stop. The battle police were on the watch now, their blunt heads turning slowly and their holsters unclipped.

'You all right, Sam?'

'Who me? I'm dandy. It's what I came for, ain't it?'

A stretcher-bearer hitched up his brassard, proud of its bright red cross and proud of what he would do today; but this was his first action and it was all that kept him from fainting: his pride.

Percy saw him and passed him a fag already lit. 'That four-poster's no use to me,' he said indignantly, 'it's got no pillow!'

Regimental Sergeant-Major Blossom was coming down the trench, his moustaches meticulously pointed and the South African ribbons aglow on his chest. 'All right lads, only a few minutes more so hold steady now!' One of the M.P.s had left his foot in the way of Blossom's boot and he swung on him with a voice that would have carried a mile. 'Stand up straight, you idle bastard! There's no need to look like a sack o' coke jus' because you're not one o' my fightin'-men – you're not fit to lick their boots!' He swung away.

Geoff Tuffnel faced his front again. 'I feel a lot better now.'

'Geoff?'

'What?'

'Look after Wiggy if you can. He's so small.'

The guns were lifting and Cpl Kemp threw a last look and saw Mr Aubrey standing perfectly quiet with his ashplant in his hand as he studied his watch and then the whistles were blowing as the two hundred men of B Company swarmed from the front line in a dark wave against the mist, their cries drifting back to the support trenches where the second-assault troops held steady and watched them go and heard the sudden rattle of machine-guns from the enemy lines and now the whistles shrilled close at hand as the signal came and Blossom was first over the parapet with the senior Talbot after him and then Kilderbee and Sgt Bruce and Tuffnel – Quincey – Stokes and now the whole of Two Platoon in a tide of bobbing khaki spreading across the sun-baked clay towards the front-line trenches.

The shelling had left a litter of burst sandbags and wrecked duckboards and they dropped clumsily over the parados to stumble and collide with each other, their boots finding the softness of fresh cadavers where the shells had come in, but for a moment they were sheltered from the hail of the machine-guns as somewhere ahead the first assault-wave drove into it through the shivering corn.

'Hold fast, lads! Wait for the signal!'

They could see nothing beyond the ragged wall of the trench. Some had been hit on the rush from Support but most were untouched and stood leaning on their rifles, surprised and angry with their loss of wind and the weakness of their legs, only now willing to admit to the fatigue that had been building up through the weeks of strain and the constant demand for working-parties that had robbed them of sleep. They stood crouched, hearing and sometimes feeling the wind-rush of the bullets above their heads, the strays that were passing between and beyond the men of the first assault-wave as the guns chattered, traversing and traversing back without a pause.

A man wiped sweat away, his eyes forlorn. 'Poor bastards.'

'Them or us?'

They heard screaming from across the corn and it made the waiting worse; they had nothing to do that would take their minds from fear. The air was deadly above them.

'Still goin'?'

'We got to, 'aven't we?'

They met each other's eyes and saw no comfort.

'Jim.'

'Yes?'

'Look, if I cop it, will you tell—'

The whistles were sounding.

'*Come on the Dukes!*'

Many missed their footing on the broken clay and their friends helped them, pulling them up by their rifles; a bayonet caught a man's face and opened it to the bone. They left the trench as if it were a ship sinking, as if they sought safety.

'*I can't . . . I can't . . . Don't make me go . . .*'

The battle police were working, pushing at those who needed help over the parapet, dragging at the few who cowered and whose legs were simply unable to bear them. A man clambered up the parados and began running blindly back the way he had come and a pistol cracked once.

'*Come on the Dukes!*'

They were moving faster, finding their feet and breasting the yellow corn, their eyes narrowed against the glare of the sun, their heads held low as if in shame for those who had sent them here to run through this summer field once known for its fireflies.

Tom was hanging back still, stumbling, one hand held out as though needing to touch this moment so that he could understand it.

'All right, Follett – come on, boy!' Sgt Kilderbee was with him, an arm at his thin shoulders.

'It isn't right – it can't be right!' Tom called out in his bewilderment, but managed better now.

They ran together through the field, the man and the boy.

Dust clouded behind the wave of troops.

'*Keep spread out! Don't bunch!*'

It was Aubrey who saw the captain go down, his twisted face turned for an instant towards the sky before the corn covered him. A strange thought came: *he'll never get over his hay fever now.* Julian was somewhere on his left, yelling encouragement to those near him. He didn't know what had happened to Nigel Coxhead. He ran on with his platoon, a clear thought coming now: with Diplock killed he was left in command of the company, but what difference was that going to make? There was nothing he could do but keep on running. The enemy wire was in sight and the men were bunching because the inadequate barrage had gapped it in only three places; it was there that the machine-guns were concentrated.

There seemed to be men standing still, close to the German line, standing and doing nothing, some leaning forward, idle, their rifles resting beside them. They formed a line along the wire and only a few moved; all were quiet but for one man whose face no longer had shape, and from its bright colours a scream came and the wire quivered as he struggled on its barbs, dislodging a companion who danced loosely and toppled away. They were the men of the first assault-wave, the few score among the two hundred who had come this far, and they had not seen the wire in the sun's glare or they had run into it believing they saw a gap. The others of their company were among the corn, moving only when the boots of the second wave disturbed them or when enough of life was left to be dragged on all fours away from the monotonous rattle of the guns. Some of these carried wounds so grave as to be numbing, and moaned only because the sun was hot on their backs and the effort they had made had burned in their bodies, leaving them thirsty.

The troops of C Company crowded the gaps in the wire and fell there while the bombing-parties hurled their explosives towards the machine-gun posts; others came, shouting at the enemy until they were spun and hammered by the bullets and pitched down across the bodies of their leaders; yet others pressed on, mindless and beyond courage, the time for thinking long since passed and death so close as to be discountable.

Smoke drifted from where the bombs had gone in, and the guns nearest the gaps fell silent. Rifle fire still crackled from the ridge beyond the wire but Aubrey had yelled for Bruce and Kemp to detail covering groups and they were putting out calculated bursts of rapid fire while the rest went through the gaps to charge the German line.

'*Hold off the bombers! Hold off!*'

The early fear of the morning had turned to rage and in the reeking shambles of the trench there was no quarter given: these men, the remnant of the second assault-wave, had seen a whole company wiped out and their own friends heaped dead and dying in the few gaps that the inadequate barrage had been able to make for them, and it was for their bayonets to give them solace and they took it bitterly and with a strength that had been beyond them an hour before.

Aubrey found them already in possession of the line when he brought in the stragglers; many he didn't recognize as the men he had known at this day's dawn: Quincey, the amiable American, his bayonet bloodied to its hilt and his eyes still hating the field-grey dead at his feet; Tuffnel, the first in the battalion to be honoured for his almost casual courage, cursing the men of his own country while his boot smashed and smashed again into the dead face of a German boy whom he could have loved more than all the generals of the British High Command; Freddie Kemp – even he – watching him with the dull eyes of a man whose faith had been lost to him by the mere carelessness of his earthly gods. They were gathered here to celebrate their victory: a field of withered corn where the dying moaned, and a line of wire where scarecrows dangled on parade.

Some had not changed. Blossom. Kilderbee. They had known war of old and had accepted it.

'Are we to go straight over, sir?' Blossom was a man of routine. The remnants of the second assault-wave had captured the front-line trench and were held ready to proceed against the rear positions. Capt. Diplock had been lost and Lt Talbot was in temporary command of the company. It was a matter of routine and all he needed were orders.

Aubrey stared at him. His eyes stung with sweat and something had gone wrong with his arm: his ashplant felt sticky and he couldn't grip it properly. He asked:

'How many are left, Mr Blossom?'

'We lost p'r'aps half our number, sir.'

Rifle fire was spreading overhead from enemy Support. The land rose to a crest, eastwards, and a machine-gun farther back was raking the vicinity of the wire in an attempt to assess any response.

'I want two runners.'

The R.S.M. raised a shout. Kilderbee was foraging among the dead for their water-bottles, Kemp passing them along the line.

'Freddie.'

'Yes sir?'

'Go and find out if—' Aubrey stopped short. 'It doesn't matter.'

'I saw him come through the wire all right. He was—'

'I said it doesn't matter. Get that water dished out.'

Blossom was back with two men but Aubrey didn't look at them, giving the duplicate messages to the R.S.M. 'When they get through they can stay there. Give them covering fire.'

Someone had got one of the machine-guns reversed and Kilderbee ordered rifles to the parados but a German observer in a forward redoubt saw the two men go over.

'They're hit, sir.'

'Get me two more.'

This time he made himself look at them. A boy with a harelip and the reserve of the facially afflicted; a taller man beside him, his eyes flickering and the colour gone from his face.

He said to Blossom: 'Covering fire.'

Of the eight runners sent out one got through to the battalion lines. It was not known how many were sent forward with the reply before it reached the trench.

Your request to withdraw is not granted. Your orders are to mount the immediate assault of the enemy Support and Reserve at whatever cost.

Aubrey recognized Col. Forsyth's writing but knew they were not his personal orders. The Brigadier had stressed that he should be kept fully informed at all stages of the operation.

'Give this man some water.' He couldn't find the message-pad because his hand was trembling with anger. The numbness in his other arm was spreading; Kilderbee had wanted to fix a tourniquet but the flow had stopped now; it was just that the muscles were useless.

'Mr Blossom, write this for me, will you?'

The machine-gun was giving sporadic bursts to draw their fire, and clay pattered on to the message-pad as Blossom wrote in elaborate capitals.

I repeat my request for a covering barrage enabling me to withdraw. Please fire green if request granted. It is otherwise my intention formally to surrender my forces to the enemy in one hour from now, that is at 0735.

.   .   .

A white Very signal curved above the battalion lines.

'There's a runner got through, sir.'

'Yes.' There had been six. He wondered how many more he could have sent out; where was the line drawn? When did it become murder?

Kemp trickled some more water on to the swab and went on wiping. Another volley of rapid fire opened up as a warning to the enemy to keep off, but it wouldn't be long before they realized the trench was thinly held.

'It's a bullet, Mr Aubrey. Gone clean in.'

'Leave it, then. Got some iodine?' Then he saw Vic suddenly, recognizable only because the change in him was one of degree: he looked more than ever like a cocky buccaneer, his shirt open and a bandage round his head; but his eyes were jumpy and he couldn't keep still.

'So you're all right,' Aubrey said.

'Blossom says we're withdrawing,' Vic said with an edge of disbelief.

'We're going to try.' The iodine stung and he bit on the pain, enjoying it after the numbness; pain was life. 'Is that your blood all over you, or someone else's?'

'Why aren't we going on?'

'Is that what you've come to ask?'

'Of course it is!' His hands flew about helplessly and he stared with bloodshot eyes at his brother.

Aubrey put on his tunic again, Freddie helping him. 'Then there's something else you should know. If they won't give us a barrage to get us out, I'm surrendering.'

Freddie packed up his field dressing, turning away, busy with it. Somewhere a man screamed and the sound knifed through the sunshine to cut at the nerves.

'*Kilderbee!*'

'Sir?'

'There'll be no more attempts to bring the wounded in!'

Vic stood in front of him, a curious smile on his mouth. 'The Duke of Lancaster's? Surrendering? Christ, we've got half a company left!'

'You want to see the rest of them dead too?' Aubrey hadn't meant to shout. Perhaps he'd not shouted at all, it was just the lightheadedness, he'd lost some blood.

'No wonder you're always nagging me not to take risks!' Vic's eyes were feverish and Aubrey saw that he'd been keyed up to killing-pitch in his first sustained action and couldn't stop, couldn't face the inertia while his nerves were still galvanized. 'It's because you've no guts,' Vic said savagely, 'and you don't want me to have any either!'

'Not really.' He didn't want to talk; the anger inside him was itching for an outlet – he knew why Tuffnel had smashed at the German boy's head – but it would have to wait; it wasn't for Vic.

'So we chuck it in, do we? You've called off the attack?'

Kilderbee gave the word and another fusillade crackled across the parados.

'Half a company,' Aubrey said wearily, 'against a whole battalion, uphill and into the sun? You'd call that an attack?' He wished the sun would go in; the trench was full of cordite fumes and the flies were clouding on the dead, a beautiful metallic blue.

'Better than being a prisoner with a tin bowl!'

Aubrey studied the young wild face. 'You'd rather die, wouldn't you?'

'Of course!'

'Then you're a fool.' But it reminded him and he called to the sergeant.

'Sir?' The stony face presented itself, eyes hooded.

'Kilderbee, I want you to pass this along. Make sure they all understand. If we're refused a barrage we shall put up white flags but I don't intend forcing anyone to become a prisoner of war if he prefers a quick death.' Suddenly he was nauseated by the buzzing and called to Freddie – 'Corp'l Kemp, do something about those bloody flies can you? There should be some lime somewhere.' He looked back at Kilderbee, for a moment wondering what he was doing here. 'Oh, yes. I shall give a signal – red flare – some time before I surrender, and anyone who wants to take his own chance of getting back to our lines can push off. They know the odds. Two runners got through out of fourteen.'

Another machine-gun had joined the first and a man fell back from the parados in perfect silence until his rifle hit the ground. Kilderbee swung about.

'Two rounds rapid! *Fire!*'

The fumes drifted in the sunshine.

'Those who decide to stay,' Aubrey said in a moment, 'will give covering fire for the others until there's no more ammunition.' He was vaguely aware of his brother's presence and was again reminded of something that had to be said. 'Mr Talbot here will in any case be staying until we surrender. That's quite clear, Kilderbee?'

'Yes sir. Do we—'

They weren't expecting it and Aubrey missed him the first time as he jumped for the parapet but the sergeant was quicker and between them they pulled him down as one of the machine-guns traversed close and its fire ripped along the sandbags in a series of dull percussions on the dried clay.

'*Let me go – you've no right—*'

Light flashed against Aubrey's eyes and at first he thought he'd been hit but it was just the sudden effort, that was all. His good arm was locked round Vic's leg and Vic was trying to kick him away but he held on, the light pulsing in his head.

'I've got him, sir.'

The gun was traversing back and they had to keep low. Pulverized clay floated bronze in the sunlight.

'Two men,' Aubrey grunted. 'Keep him under guard.' His brother's face was turned to him, distorted with hate. 'Don't let him try again.'

They were paraded soon after 0900 hours in the shade of the medical tents. The smell of the barrage was still on the breeze but they didn't notice; it was the smell they lived with.

'Blake?'

'Sarn't!'

'Durnforth?'

'Here, Sarge!'

'Follett?'

Right in the distance they could see a smudge of green through the haze beyond the rear; that'd be trees, ones with leaves still on.

'Gardner?'

Two bearers came at a shambling trot towards the tents and

186

they watched them. The man on the stretcher was strapped to it and shouted in delirium, struggling to free himself.

'Pay attention! Anyone see what happened to Gardner?'

They could smell the ether from the tents.

'Ingleby?'

A man eased a fag out; the packet had got crushed flat because he'd crawled all the way; the delicate paper was split. He licked it and smoothed it over with his finger.

'Jarvis?'

'Saw him hangin' on the wire. Can we have a smoke, Sarge?'

'Yes. Keep a look-out, mind. Stokes?'

Sergeant Bruce looked up.

''E was on a stretcher,' somebody said.

'Right. Surridge?'

A man struck a match.

'Taylor?'

'Got 'is foot blown off.'

'Sure of that?'

'If it's all the same to you, Sergeant, it's not som'thin' you can make a mistake about.' The tone was sullen, as many of them were. They didn't mind fighting so long as they'd got a chance. Today there'd been no chance.

'Right,' Bruce nodded. He was Sgt Knight's replacement, been with them six months now. Any other time he'd have slapped that man on a charge for a remark like that; today he'd kill anyone who touched them. 'Report to the major and give him what details you can.' He saw the Adjutant coming past on his way to the C.C.S. 'Watch your fags then, quick.'

'Who are your people, Sergeant?'

'Two Platoon, sir, C Company!'

The captain's face was quiet with concern. 'The whole platoon?'

'Yes, sir.'

He was making a quick count. Fourteen men. There'd been sixty when the whistles had blown. He looked away. 'Carry on, Sarn't.'

They brought their cigarettes out of their cupped hands.

'Tuffnel?'

'Sergeant.'

'Williams?'

He made a cross.

'Woods?'

He made a cross.

'Right, you can fall out. An' don't forget, if you've got definite information on anyone missing, give it to the major.'

They sat in the shade for a time, not speaking. For each of them there was something private in what they had just done together, and there were things they had experienced this sunny morning that they didn't want to talk about, now or perhaps ever.

Pop Jarvis, hanging on the wire. *Sleep is meat and drink to a man.* You'll not go short of it now, chum. Little Arthur, sitting in the crater looking at the end of his leg. *Where's my foot gone? Where's it gone?* Puzzled, more than anything. Bobbie Tanner, hooked over like an earwig you'd trod on but speaking plain enough. *Tell Dad not to hit her any more now I'm gone.* They didn't get on, he was always putting in for special leave and never getting it.

'Give us a light, mate.'

They turned their thoughts to the rumours that were going round, consoling themselves in talking of the fate of others.

'Mr Talbot's come in. The young one.'

'He'd get through anythin', that little bugger.'

'Well, he was lucky this time. Corporal Kemp brought him in on his back, half dead.'

'Better than nothin', i'n' it?'

'You know what I heard Peach Blossom say? Half that stuff was from our own batteries, fallin' short.'

''Ckin' gunners.'

'I dunno about that. I reckon they put up a right old barrage, better than the one we went over with. Wouldn't be here otherwise, would we?'

'That's right you know, Alf. They chucked everything in. Made up for the first time, like.'

'You think we'd've surrendered, do you, if they'd not pulled us out?'

'Bet yer life. Talbot meant what 'e said. I was there when ol' Peachy took down the signal.'

'He's for the chopper, that boy.'

Geoff Tuffnel turned his head. 'Who is?'

'Mr Talbot. Refused orders, didn't you know?'

'Yes,' Geoff told him evenly, 'I heard.' His head swung again as the clink of harness sounded. A red-tab was dismounting near the C.C.S., two aides with him. 'But who says he's for the chopper?'

'Well, I mean it stands to reason, mate.' He'd caught the challenge in Geoff's tone, and wished he hadn't started this. 'He was told to press on, 'stead of which he brought us all back, or what was left. Ask me, it'll be a court martial an' reduced to the ranks, the least they'll do to him.'

They watched the three officers. One of them turned towards their group and they began cursing him under their breath; then the red-tab said, 'All right, Morton, leave them be.' They went on smartly to the main tent.

'Brigadier, ain't he?'

'That little bastard?'

'Christ, I got a kid at 'ome taller'n' what 'e is!'

Geoff Tuffnel watched the officers until they were out of his sight. 'Court martial,' he said slowly, 'an' reduced to the ranks, eh? An' you think that's right?'

'Course I don't, but what can I—'

'Sitting here like you are now, safe an' sound, and you think that's right, what they'll do to him?'

They watched Geoff covertly, worried by his tone; it was so quiet, like the first faint thunder when you were far from home.

'No, I don't think it's right, for Chris' sake – I've said so, haven't I? But what d'you want me to—'

'If they try that on a man like him, I'll start a mutiny. I give you my word. And I want to know who'd be with me. And I want to know now.'

It was not possible to talk inside the medical tent since the wounded were still coming in, so they retired to a patch of bitten grass by the transport park and were standing in a small group: Brig. Mainwright, his aides-de-camp, Col. Forsyth and Lt Talbot.

Mainwright was a short man with a white cavalry moustache, his rather square head set permanently forward as if to meet challenge wherever he went, perhaps even to seek it. His lack of height may have told him instinctively that this was essential; at middle age he had also perhaps begun to fear the easy confidence of younger men, and relied on his force of bearing, learned in the saddle and on the field, to override it. His voice was not loud, but its slightly high pitch seemed to express protest at the incompetence manifestly rife among all of lower rank. It was said in the mess that he had divorced his wife for not keeping the silver clean.

'Lieutenant Talbot, I am advised by the Medical Officer that you have just had a bullet extracted from the arm and should be allowed to rest. Colonel Forsyth tells me that you knew of my arrival and elected to present yourself. That is so?'

'Yes, sir.' The sling was comfortable and the anaesthetic had left him strangely clear-headed: he was conscious of seeing with great sharpness each blade of grass, the seams and stitches of the immaculate uniform in front of him, the tiny veins gathered in the corners of the small pebbly eyes that gazed at him from the shadow of Mainwright's cap. The two aides, he noticed with the same clarity of thought, were young for their rank and taller than average, perhaps chosen by the Brigadier for his immediate entourage to show that youth and height in a man were of no consequence and that he was their superior.

Colonel Forsyth, lean, watchful, his face leathery from the African sun, the Victoria Cross prominent among his several ribbons, had the attitude of a referee, his quick eyes flicking from one to the other as they spoke.

'I also understand that your brother has been wounded.'

'He's alive.'

'We're to be thankful for that. A withdrawing action,' Mainwright said deliberately, 'is inevitably more costly than a bold frontal attack, as you have now learned.' The smell of ether coming from the lieutenant reminded him that he was not long out of the anaesthetic. 'Tell someone to bring chairs,' he told his aides. 'I must inform you, Talbot, that Colonel Forsyth here has done his best to minimize your responsibility in this shocking affair, and you may later wish to thank him; the fact remains that you alone must be held entirely to blame.' Studying this young fellow as he spoke, he saw no emotion in the rather withdrawn face; but there was intelligence in the eyes and they watched him steadily back, to the point where he preferred to look away. 'This is not an official enquiry, of course. You'll be obliged to answer for your actions in formal court martial at a later date; but it's never too soon to give a man the chance of explaining himself before the memory of events loses its freshness, you understand me?'

'Yes, sir.'

Mainwright glanced down after a moment. 'I don't seek your gratitude for this. The fact is that a man in your position needs all the help he can be given, even by those whom he has most affronted.'

Morton was back with an orderly, and with a slight smile offered the Brigadier a chair back-to-front, knowing he liked to straddle it cavalry fashion; it was his favourite pose for the war-photographers, his arms folded across the back of a chair and his riding-crop dangling confidently, a reminder to those at home that the situation on the Western Front was well in hand.

'Sit down, Talbot. I want you to relax.' This young officer was to be broken, and he felt again the sensation that had stirred in him early this morning when he had visited B Company in the front line: the feeling of awful power, of the responsibility in his hands for those subject to his decisions. They had watched him, those young boys, with looks of sublime obedience as he spoke to them and gave them a little of the courage that had brought him through so many campaigns. They knew that the decision had been his, to send them against the enemy, to hurl many among them to their death, and that a word from his lips could countermand his own order and stay the Reaper's hand. One boy had looked at him with such pleading that surely it would have broken the resolve of a weaker man; the young soldier had stood as if naked before him, a sacrifice to the Lord of battle, and he had been obliged to look away, thanking God that his power was not of that kind: these were his legions, not his slaves, fine intelligent young men who knew that his duty suffered him to think first of the war and its waging, and second of these beloved lives who were perforce its instruments. Impossible of course to make them understand the weeping of his heart as he had sent them across the parapet.

His crop dangled from his hand. 'Now what possessed you, Talbot? Speak your mind. Was it sudden panic?'

'No sir, it was sound reasoning.'

One of the aides sucked his breath in.

'Reasoning? To refuse my express orders to take your men forward against the enemy?' He wasn't sure that Talbot realized what he was saying; he seemed too calm. 'We have an ugly word for that kind of thing. Cowardice. You doubtless know you could be shot for it.'

'Not really, no.' Aubrey felt Forsyth's glance switch to him again. 'When a unit's engaged in action the commander's expected to advise H.Q. about local conditions. In this case I was satisfied that my remaining forces were going to be butchered to a man if I pressed them on, and I naturally assumed you'd accept my word for that, since my record's perfectly good.' There was shouting suddenly, muffled by canvas, from some poor devil in the medical tent; the casualties weren't all physical: quite a few had lost their reason out there. Aubrey looked at the little round eyes in front of him and felt nausea. Mainwright couldn't help what he was, but he'd have to be stopped.

'You wish me to concede—' the tone took on a slight shrillness – 'that a junior officer, finding himself by chance in command of a company, "assumes" that the general whose meticulous planning has mounted the operation will follow his "advice" without question in mid-course of the battle? Surely I have it wrongly?'

'I'm not asking you to concede anything, sir.'

'So your opinions brook no argument?' Something like a laugh escaped the Brigadier's mouth and the crop was gripped with sudden strength, his knuckles whitening.

One of the aides got up from his chair in a gesture of silent outrage. Col. Forsyth didn't move. Another field ambulance was rocking to a halt near the C.C.S. and in a moment its dust came blowing across the withered grass.

'Morton, do sit down and spare me your embarrassment.' The tone was controlled again but the words were sharp and whittling. 'Lieutenant Talbot, I want you to realize your position. You are to be charged with flagrant defiance of orders at a most critical time, with unqualified refusal to press forward a prescribed attack and with an attempt to surrender your forces to the enemy on your own personal initiative. Can you imagine how it will go for you when judgement is passed on you by the court? Your name dishonoured and your career ruined, if indeed you're not put before a firing-squad. Yet you have the impudence to suggest, when my only thought is to help you, that you were virtually in charge of today's action, and not I.' His eyes had become bright and his voice almost gentle. 'Doesn't it occur to you that a plea for mercy would be more fitting to such a case?'

Aubrey found himself looking past the Brigadier to the dun-brown canvas of the medical tents. Part of his mind was with his brother; the M.O., his shirt stiff with blood and his eyes already weary, had said only: 'He's not actually going to lose anything, but it's going to be a job, that's all I can say for the moment.' And part of his mind was floating quite detached from this time and this place, looking with cold judgement at the war as a whole, the race of man as a whole. You had to stand back sometimes and reason things out, or you'd be done for.

There were some good leaders in this war but the little Napoleon in front of him wasn't among them. He was danger-ous, a disease.

'Can we finish our talk in private, sir?'

'I see no reason.'

Aubrey knew that Mainwright would regret it but he'd been given his chance. 'Your operation,' he said, 'was certain to fail, in terms of ground gained and lives lost, even before it began. We all knew that. Colonel Forsyth himself tried to persuade you to cancel it.' He was speaking quietly but was aware that the anger he'd refused to vent on his brother was now coming out and doing something to his voice; and as he listened he recognized the undertone, the one he knew so well. 'There was nothing I could do about it myself, of course. But once we were in that trench we were out of your reach and I had the chance of saving some of those men from certain butchering. This I achieved. It wasn't your fault or mine that our covering barrage fell short in places. The thing is that I've brought back close on sixty men who'll be fit to fight again.' He looked across the wasteland where the lines made furrows in the haze. 'They'd have been dead by now.'

The leather crop was quivering.

'I refuse to listen to—'

'You'll have to, before long.' His chair went over and caught one of the aides across the shin and suddenly they were all on their feet. 'By God, I'll tell all England!'

'You're out of your mind!'

'No, sir. If you give me the chance of a full-scale court martial I shall publicly accuse you of the wilful and wholesale killing of your men, front page and banner headlines. In a month from now your name will be the most hated in the country.'

X

Across the street the rain dripped from the chestnut leaves; below them was the giant figure of a white-haired woman with her arm encouraging a young man in a brown suit: GO! IT'S YOUR DUTY, LAD! Fat bright conkers had burst from their shells along the pavement, some to be crushed by the buses.

'You can see him now, Captain.'

He came away from the window. Along the corridor he asked her: 'Wasn't this a hotel once?'

'Oh yes. The War Office commandeered it.' She sounded tired and he had to walk slowly beside her. 'By the sound of things they'll have to commandeer a few more.'

'You don't get much peace.' The papers were full of the new Franco-British offensive at Loos, and yesterday morning he'd actually heard the barrage, standing in the garden at Ashbourne.

'Who does?' she said wryly, and took him to the wrong ward and had to ask someone the number before they found the right one.

'How is he, Sister?

'Oh, he's fine. It's slow going, with abdominals, that's all. You're his brother, aren't you?'

'Yes.'

'That's good. He wants cheering up.'

Vic laid his book down listlessly as they came in, his hollowed eyes focusing. As the sister went out he said dully: 'Well what d'you expect me to look like?'

Aubrey found a chair, annoyed that the shock had shown in his face; it wasn't only the waxy white of the arms sticking out of the blue pyjamas and the hollowness of the eyes; this was just a paper portrait of all that life and energy he'd known; the resemblance was still there, but that was all.

'They tell me you're making fantastic progress.' The M.O. at 93rd Field Hospital had in fact been pleased – 'Multiple

contusions, intra-abdominal lesions and a perforated duo-
denum, and if that doesn't mean anything to you I'll just say
the mortality rate is somewhere around eighty per cent.'

'Less fantastic than yours. Congratulations.' His speech
sounded stiff but there'd been no damage to the face. 'Signal
H.Q. that you're ready to surrender and they make you a
captain.'

'I'm replacing Diplock, that's all. There's a shortage on.'
Vic wouldn't have heard the whole story; in the first three
weeks he'd been under the knife a dozen times and in any case
the thing had been rapidly hushed up by orders from on high.
'Sick of reading yet?' He put the new novel he'd brought where
Vic could reach it.

'My God' – his laugh was grating – 'I could tell you a bit
about "human bondage"!' He dropped the book beside him.
'But they do their best for me here. Worked off their feet, poor
bitches. I suppose,' he said thinly, 'you saved my life out there,
didn't you?'

'It was Freddie who brought you in.'

'Was it? There's one thing, I'll never go short of a wet-nurse
with you two around.' His eyes, shadowed from weeks of pain,
moved restlessly, picking on objects but not going once to
Aubrey. 'You know you'd never have turned me in as a
prisoner, don't you? Christ, can you see me waving a little
white flag at a bloody German?' He said suddenly – 'Father's
been here several times, but when he asked about you I played
the gent. Thought you should know.'

'Should know what?'

'That I didn't mention your little plan to give up the
fight.'

Aubrey said in surprise: 'D'you think it would worry him?'

'Well it's nothing to be exactly proud of, is it?'

Aubrey got up and stared from the narrow window. 'Pride?'
he said with contempt. 'I could have killed sixty good men out
of pride.' The scene from this window was the same: the
cascade of leaves in the September rain, the righteous mother
urging her son to go and get smashed to blazes. This was the
one the troops hated the most, the one they never brought back
from leave as a joke. How many mothers were there like that in
reality? One would be bad enough. 'What are the nurses like,

pretty?' He knew there was nothing else they could talk about. They'd nothing in common. They were merely brothers.

'It'd be no good to me if they were, would it?'

Aubrey turned quickly. 'You weren't hit there. The M.O. assured me.'

'Even went into that, did you? Tell me, how are my tonsils?'

Aubrey came back to the bed. 'I don't hear any untoward vibration. How do they feel?'

'They've been full of tubes for a month. What's Ashbourne looking like?'

'A lot of strange faces there. Most of the women staff's in munitions now, or on the land, and poor old Charrington's trying to whip the "temporaries" into shape. Willis has been ploughing up the flower-beds and planting cabbages, and Mother's put some along the south wall, convinced they're climbers.'

For the first time Vic's face softened. 'Then they'll have to be. Someone had better warn them.'

'You see a lot of her, I expect.'

'She camped here the first week, brought her own bedclothes and a tin of toffees. Before she left we were all getting ice-cream instead of the usual tapioca – she's presented a freezing-machine to the hospital.' His white hand rested on the Maugham novel. 'Thanks for bringing this.'

His eyes had closed and Aubrey knew that Mother had never seen this young face as he'd seen it today himself, stiff with hostility and spite. That was for him alone.

'I'll go now, Vic.'

The dark eyes came open. 'All right.'

'Father's dining me at his club tonight. Any message for him?'

'He wants to show you off. His elder son, a gallant captain.' He was wearying and the remark sounded forced, as if he must keep the spite alive, his only strength. 'I suppose you're on sick-leave, are you?'

'That's what they called it.'

'For a pin-prick in the arm . . .' His smile was a mere flattening of the lips. 'Only you could manage that. Never a peacock in your way.'

Aubrey had picked up his cap and the scarred ashplant, but turned to look down again. 'Never a what?'

'A bloody peacock.'

There was a note of bitter satisfaction in his voice as if it pleased him not to be understood, and Aubrey sensed a distinct warning that he mustn't go yet, that this was somehow important.

'Give my regards to Father.'

'Of course.' Aubrey didn't move. The idea of 'peacock' brought only one memory into consciousness: when they'd been very young he had taken the reins in the governess-cart for the first time, trotting the pony down the drive at Ashbourne when by chance Mother had been on the steps with some of her friends, saying goodbye to them. As he came bowling smartly round the fountain-pond they'd all clapped their hands for him, calling something about 'Jehu'. He remembered feeling rather good about this impromptu ovation, though if he'd known beforehand that so many people were watching he wouldn't have had the nerve to do such a thing. Vic had been there, strait-jacketed in his starched sailor-suit (the one he 'loaved' so much, 'I loave it, I do'), his small hand secure in Mother's to keep him away from the carriages. His frustration at being a mere tethered spectator at this impressive event must have flowered in secret, for soon afterwards he'd persuaded their governess (a fool of a woman with squeaky boots) to get out of the cart near the gates and leave him in sole command. Aubrey had been with Father on the lawn being shown how to swing his first real tennis-racket while Uncle Charles threw him the ball, and they'd all looked up when the sounds of trouble began. The peacock (blind in one eye due to a fight in the mating season) was pecking uselessly at the gravel when the pony surprised it, and the big gaudy tail was immediately spread, surprising the pony. The consequences of this mutual alarm were out of all proportion: the pony, bolting, forgot that the cart was wider than its own galvanized flanks and dragged it through the rose-arbor before wrecking a wheel and pitching Vic among some blue hydrangeas. Of course 'Father was furious' and the governess received wages in lieu of notice that same night.

The smallest impressions remain etched on the memory, though they are believed forgotten, and Aubrey realized that the place where he had been destined to remember the peacock was this narrow room, more than thirteen years later, with its peeling white paintwork and the view of the chestnut tree and the boy here in the bed nursing his hate for a brother.

Vic had never forgotten.

'A peacock,' Aubrey said, thinking how absurd it was. An eagle, a tiger, a wild bull – anything better than a stupid ornamental bird as a symbol for all this hate, for all those childhood humiliations that a younger boy must suffer at the innocent hands of an elder.

'It's nothing you'd understand.'

'No.' But he understood at last the scraps of paper he'd sometimes found in the nursery or under his 'favourite tree' (they'd each had their 'own' tree, and his had been the tall ash in the spinney beside the orchard, a branch of it now in his hand), the notes in red crayon, *I hate you.* They'd not worried him. Little Vic was always bothered by people who wouldn't let him have his way, especially the governess – 'I hate her. I *loave* her!' The notes had stopped, as they grew older, and he'd forgotten them, as he'd forgotten the peacock, until now; and now he knew they'd never really stopped at all: there had been another one, lying under his cap when he'd picked it up, invisible but very real.

A nurse came in, dreadfully young and with pretty eyes dull from sleeplessness, her hands raw with carbolic.

'You've got to be washed,' she told Vic.

Aubrey smiled to her. 'May I stay just five minutes more?'

'Well yes, sir, but if Matron—'

'Don't worry. I really mean five minutes, by the clock.' He waited until she'd closed the door, noticing vaguely that its handle was loose, like the one on Vic's door at Ashbourne. He didn't know what he could say now; five minutes wasn't long in which to lay the ghosts of twenty years. 'You always wanted to do everything I could do. I suppose that was it.'

'You mind if we don't get out the family album? All that's over now.'

All the things we ever knew.

'Don't you remember the time I bashed the Daimler's mudguard?' It was the only thing he could think of at short notice. Perhaps there weren't any others; he'd never disgraced himself: life had been too smooth, and it needed effort to get into trouble. 'Father was furious and I wasn't allowed to drive it again.'

'It wasn't you,' Vic said mockingly, 'not even that. Freddie told me what happened.' His eyes closed again wearily. 'The only time you ever got it in the neck it was for someone else.' They listened for a moment to a trolly going past the door, its instruments tinkling. 'Have a good dinner at the Savage Club. Sorry your little brother can't join you there, but he's got to be washed.'

Waiting for Father in the hall of the club he read Julian's letter again; it was fairly long and written with obvious enjoyment.

By a bit of luck I'm the Lord High Censor for this batch of mail or I'd get shot at dawn for the scandal I'm going to pass on. I can't vouch for its accuracy because some of it's what the troops would call 'cookhouse official', though the Old Man has dropped a few pointers and they all seem to fit in. I can't resist giving you the juicy bit first, so hold your breath. Brigadier-General Mainwright has actually been sacked! Apparently he'd been ripe for a fall, but no one had had the nerve to strike the first blow until my stout friend Captain Aubrey Talbot pitched in, and then he went down like a house of cards. Colonel Forsyth was of course your militant ally and was absent for three days at Staff soon after you went on sick-leave. He's playing it very regimental and we're obviously expected to behave as if nothing has happened. The troops are delighted with – no, I must be more accurate. Their bitterness has been lightened by the news that the Brigadier has got the sack instead of you, and incidentally – as you'll probably be in command of C Company now – you should be told that those who came out of that ghastly shambles with us are prepared to follow you into the jaws of hell itself. Their loyalty towards you is movingly instanced by something I have overheard several times; when someone among these original hard-core members of the company wants to distinguish himself from the new drafts allocated to us, he refers to himself as 'a Talbot man'. I should imagine you must be the first captain in this war to have commanded his own private army!

Rumours are still rife and I'm taking pains to scotch the most sensational. Both Nigel and I (he's back with us, by the way, displaying an impressive set of stitches) respect your not wanting to tell us what really happened outside the C.C.S. that morning, but the hottest rumour of all is that you 'knocked Mainwright spinning'. The rank and file are satisfied that only this can explain why you were put in close arrest immediately afterwards. I'm spreading it abroad – for the sake of your honour – that even with one arm in a sling and your head full of ether you're not a man to pick on a little squirt like him!

But enough of all this. You'll by now have realized that this protracted epistle is being penned more for my pleasure than yours. Whatever battles there are to be recorded in the annals of our regiment, Talbot v. Mainwright will surely take pride of place, even though it'll have to be written between the lines! Your stout henchman Freddie is in good shape and – I swear – an inch taller. The news from 93rd Field Hospital is that your young protégé Tom Follett is well on the mend and should be rejoining us after sick-leave in a month or so. On the Home Front, Diana mentions in a letter that 'great changes are in view', but whether this is quoted from her astrology chart or she's been made a matron I can't say. If you happen to run into her, please give her my fondest love.

Sir William arrived punctually at the Club, brushing the rain-spots from his jacket and seeing Aubrey the instant he came through the doors; but their meal was delayed a few minutes by a chance exchange with a retired general whose surname Aubrey didn't hear. Dominating a knot of members in the hall, he was delivering his opinions in tones loud enough to attract wider attention, which in fact they shortly did.

'... And I contend we owe it to ourselves to make it clear that the British Empire can manage perfectly well in fulfilling her obligations to Belgium without the help of America – or indeed anyone else.'

Sir William halted sharply on his way past. 'Poppycock!' His rich undertone, Aubrey thought with amusement, could stop any conversation dead at a hundred yards. 'That's the spirit that's got us so far along the road to survival, George, but it's not going to get us to the end.'

'Alarm and despondency! And from a man with the public ear!' The general swung his glance to Aubrey, thinking himself outgunned by two to one, but faced Sir William again without dismay, having noted his companion's lowly rank. 'I suppose it's the old cry, is it? Neuve Chapelle!'

'No. It's the new weapon. Think about it, George. And remember this is an island.'

Going into the dining-room Aubrey asked his father: 'Are the Americans coming in?'

'There's no sign yet. The country's buzzing with rumours but it's mostly wishful thinking. Asquith wants them in, I can tell you that; Wellington House has been piling on the propaganda since the *Lusitania* went down. Now they're making a film for the American picture-houses – *Britain Prepared*. Tell you this, I hope they never come in. God knows we'll need them but there's enough manhood going through the mincing-machine without hunting for further supplies. You've just seen Victor, haven't you? How's he looking?'

'He'll be all right.'

'Try the mutton, Australian, the last we'll get if those bloody submarines keep it up. Of course he'll be all right, got the Talbot constitution. But I asked him about you, before you got your leave, and he didn't seem very communicative.'

Aubrey suddenly found his father's attentive eyes on him and knew he couldn't baulk the issue. He'd hoped to keep silent: Father had Vic and himself enough on his mind and it wouldn't ease his worries if he knew how casual the slaughter was out there.

'You wouldn't expect him to be communicative, would you? He's been through quite a bit.'

His father handed the wine-list back to the *sommelier*.

'Is he jealous, d'you think?'

'What about?'

'Your promotion. Brothers can be jealous, you know.'

'Not Vic, surely.' Where would the next one be, under his napkin? *I hate you.* But perhaps he could do something about it now that he knew.

'I'm not just poking my nose, Aubrey.'

The note in his voice was one of quiet appeal and Aubrey looked up quickly, realizing that for the first time in his life his father needed his help. Vic must have made it pretty clear they were bad friends.

'He just thinks,' Aubrey said carefully, 'that I've done something that should have got me shot, so my promotion hasn't gone down too well with him. Did he tell you how he was wounded? I mean about the action itself?'

'He called it a "mess" and said it had "come unstuck".'

'Quite true.' But Vic meant it had *become* a mess, whereas the whole battalion had seen it was a mess to start with. He was suddenly impatient with the boy, with his desperate need for recognition that forced him into doing stupid things, dangerous things. Was he the only younger brother in the world? Were there many like him, strutting and fretting and butting their heads against obstacles that didn't really exist? Then God help everyone else. 'Is that all he told you about it?'

'He said you'd all been warned about "careless talk".'

There were marigolds on the table, their petals just turning brown at the tips, the water too low in the bowl; but no candle, no cognac in a mug. 'The action,' he said, 'was costly. At the stage where we'd lost three-quarters of our men I asked permission to withdraw the rest and said that if I didn't get it then I'd surrender to the enemy. I got permission. The Brigadier told me I was up for court martial and I said if he did that to me I'd publicly accuse him of wanton killing. He called immediately for two military police and I was put under close arrest.' He looked up. 'Vic tell you anything about this?'

'No.' His father's stillness was absolute, both compact hands lying flat on the white cloth, his eyes possessed by the images that Aubrey's words had evoked. A spoon in the cruet vibrated as he said: 'But what a story . . . Banner headlines . . .'

'Oddly enough,' Aubrey smiled, 'that was exactly what I promised him. I suppose I've heard you say it so often that it came more or less naturally.'

'Is it too late now?'

'A bit, yes. I was sort of called off. My Colonel had me released and sent to a base hospital for convalescence; he said that certain enquiries were being made and in the meantime promised that if I were ready to forget the whole thing there'd be no court martial. Of course I was floored by that.' He said ruefully, 'Sorry about your scoop. You'd really have run it, would you?'

'Oh yes. Yes indeed.' Sir William broke a bread roll like a man's neck. 'It would have smashed the paper and they'd have slung me into prison but by God I'd have done it.'

Aubrey looked appalled. 'I don't understand! Can't you print the—'

'No. We can't print the truth. And that's the blackest crime of all in this infamous war.' He sat very erect, and his hands, flat on the table with their fingers spread, suggested to Aubrey the classical attitude of a lion *couchant*. 'You've heard of the Defence of the Realm Act. I may tell you that over the Press and even the private citizen its powers are unlimited. You see the newspapers for yourself over there; you've seen tragic defeats turned into paper victories. The correspondents have to get their copy from the official intelligence headquarters of the High Command, whose policy is to show the brilliance and sagacity of its own generals, to justify the most hellish losses and indirectly to justify the continuance of the war itself. I have five major correspondents at the battle fronts – highly qualified observers – and if they were allowed to send me their own true version of events in Flanders I wouldn't be allowed to print it, and if I printed it – in one last defiant edition before anyone could stop me – I and my editors would be arrested and our presses commandeered for use by the offices of propaganda.' He reached inside his jacket, brought out a morocco folder, and selected a news-cutting. 'Listen to this. *Brilliant Action by London Regiment. Lightning Attack Captures First System of Enemy's Defence. In a superbly planned operation modestly described here as "a sideshow" a unit of the 3rd Duke of Lancaster's yesterday stormed the German front line on a thousand-yard sector and within a few minutes achieved its objective, sustaining the minimum of casualties despite vigorous resistance.*' He glanced up, expressionless.

'Oh my God . . . What date's that?'

'August the seventh.' He span the cutting for Aubrey to read. 'You know why I kept this? Because you and Vic were in it. One of my reporters told me himself, said he'd had a word with you.' He waited until Aubrey had finished reading. 'And this was "a sideshow". You think there's any more truth in the reports of the big offensives like Neuve Chapelle or the one that's just started at Loos?' He put the cutting away. 'This war has to be kept running. The guns have to be fired. The men have to be killed. Because the whole of Europe is committed to what they call "victory" and they won't stop till they get it.' Suddenly his shoulders sagged in an attitude of hopelessness that shocked Aubrey, seeing it in a man so strong. 'But they can't *all* get it.' The mutton was being served and he eyed it with distaste. 'Don't blame the generals and the politicians.

Not wholly. They're a cut-throat gang of blackguards, yes, but the public shares their blame. The much-vaunted "man in the street", the self-sentimentalized "salt of the earth", he's the one, Aubrey, he's the one who'll bleed this country white of its youth and its future. Because he's got no more wits that this bit of mutton on my plate. The great Franco-British offensive at Loos is now in full swing. Splendid. But don't read the head-lines if you want the news. Look at the casualty lists. Ask your sister Pam how much sleep she'll get in the next few weeks and what nightmares she'll have when she can snatch a few minutes from filling the hospitals with boys like your brother. But don't try to find any sympathy for your misgivings in the streets of this fair city; in the pubs and the clubs and the little front parlours your elders are too busy rejoicing in the splendid victories they hear so much about, their pigeon-chests swelling with patriotic pride under their comfortable waistcoats. And spare your tears for the women: they've got a son at the front so why shouldn't every fit young man in the country go out and help him? It's as far as they can see in front of their noses – wear a civilian suit and you've got a white feather – and never a passing thought about *stopping* the slaughter before the last man's gone from home. "Go! It's your duty, lad!"' His eyes were sombre as he looked at his son. 'You give me great joy in my life, you and your brother; but sometimes I wish you'd never been born, you and your whole generation.'

The maroons had been booming and they stood at the opened windows of the club, the big room dark behind them. Search-lights fingered the sky and people had come into the street to watch. Three children squealed with excitement on a balcony opposite until they were dragged hastily indoors when the shrapnel began pattering across the roofs.

Once Aubrey thought he saw a Zeppelin but it might have been an isolated cloud caught by a slowly-fanning beam. Despite the earlier thudding of the maroons and the fall of the deadly splinters in the darkened street it seemed almost a gala occasion; there were voices everywhere and he felt reassured. Julian particularly had been worried when they'd read news of these raids, suspecting they were worse than the reports made out. His mother wasn't 'terribly good at bangs', apparently, and he dashed off an army postcard after the news of every attack, suggesting that his parents should move out of London.

'Is this a bad one?' asked Aubrey. Somebody was pulling the heavy curtains farther aside and he could see a veil of dust drifting down from the pelmet, dark against the searchlit sky.

'About average. I only wish the submarines were as ineffectual.'

His mood had lightened during the meal: Aubrey had shown him Julian's letter to cheer him up. They had also talked about Vic and himself, though he'd taken pains to make small beer of the situation. Watching the beams of light against the clouds he found himself wondering if he should have failed, sometimes, for his brother's sake, lost a few games to him or picked a girl less pretty than Vic's when they were gadding together. Would it have helped? It was too late now: deliberate failure had a price on it; the war magnified everything you did. It was odd to think that if he'd been court martialled and reduced to the ranks, Vic would probably have 'forgiven' him for all his earlier success and become his truest friend.

The shrapnel fell like intermittent hail, and the people drew back into the doorways. Was Pam out in this somewhere, with only a canvas top to the ambulance? He'd seen crowds forming outside Victoria this evening: the first hospital trains were bringing in the casualties from Loos. Pam had been very upset, the first day of his leave, when she'd told him about Alec. They were boxing apples from the orchard ready for taking to Richmond Hospital, and she'd said it over-casually as if she'd been worrying how best to tell him. 'Alec was killed last month, did you know?'

'Alec Fraser?'

'Yes.' She hit out angrily at a wasp.

'I'll bet he asked for it. Always keen on a dare, wasn't he?'

The wasp had actually settled on her arm and she didn't do anything about it: he had to knock the thing away for her. She was looking at him as if she'd never seen him before. 'But you were good friends, Aubrey.'

'Yes I know. It was damn' bad luck, of course.' Her stare irritated him. He'd been good friends with Noël Lindsay too, and David Waring, and Jack Beckwith and God knew how many others. Didn't she know?

206

She said bitterly: 'I was with his mother when she got the parcel. His "effects". The rain had made a mess of the brown paper and the string was all anyhow – they'd been too busy to take much trouble with it. His uniform was quite nicely folded but it hadn't been cleaned; there was mud on it, and blood-patches. They'd just taken it off him and posted it, you see. Is that the best your people can do out there when someone gets—' Then she broke and he held her while the sobbing shook her for minutes on end; an apple fell from her hand and rolled across the earth floor of the shed, the skin coming away from the bruise and gathering dirt.

Later she said: 'I know you're not callous. Least of all you. And I know you see it actually happening over there, just – an every-day occurrence. Not quite what I want to say, but—'

'I understand.'

'The thing is, Aubrey, I don't want ever to get used to it. I don't want this filthy bloody war to wear my sensibilities away till I'm like a stone. However many of our friends go, I want to grieve for each one of them, not put them into a sort of mass grave in my mind.'

How much, he wondered, was he becoming like a stone? There was no point in worrying about it. Callousness was a weapon of war, defending you against the compassion that would leave you weak and exposed, anaesthetizing the feelings in you that would otherwise send you mad.

The anti-aircraft guns trembled in the ground, their echoes poppling between the buildings; steel fragments dripped from the sky and once a broken tile came boomeranging down. But the people wouldn't go indoors; it was a free show – and more than that: they weren't merely spectators; they were themselves slamming in the shells and firing the guns, valiantly defending London against the airborne barbarians, just as they fought the bigger battles that they only read about, feeling the glow and the pride and thanking God that they were Englishmen, and not troubling to thank that same God that they weren't those particular Englishmen over there whose glow and whose pride were lying mangled where rats ran and where the filth from burst latrines lapped at their unburied bones.

The guns barked at the night.

'That's the stuff, by George!' A shirt-front made a glow

beside the heavy curtains, a diamond stud sparking yellow and blue. 'We'll teach 'em to come sniffing round the capital of the Empire!'

Sir William turned away. 'I think I shall finish my wine.' Aubrey followed him, his thoughts still lingering with Pam. She'd talked about Hugh:

'I got a letter from him last week – the third since I did that appalling thing. And he took me to dinner once at a funny little dump in Chelsea – he's only got his teacher's salary because Louise made Charles cut him off without a shilling when he left home.'

'How is he?'

'Oh, all right. I kissed him in public so that everyone could bloody well see. I don't know if he liked it but it was better than what I did last time.' There was a kind of quiet chime in her voice, he'd noticed, when she was talking of Hugh. 'You know what happened when we left the place? It was a terribly hot night and we were walking along by the river for the cool, and some pert little bitch crossed the road, arm-in-arm with a sergeant, and calmly gave Hugh a white feather. I was just going to slap her face when he thanked her courteously and stuck it carefully in his button-hole – Lord, I wish you'd been there! I mean what could the little cow do then except look a lemon!'

In the gloom of the dining-room Sir William sat with the wine glass cupped in his hands.

'I've not given you a very cheerful evening, Aubrey. We've still not quite got over the news about Victor; the telegram said "seriously wounded" and we imagined the worst, a leg or something. Your mother took it hard, though nobody would have known. These things leave their mark, you know, and . . . I must watch my clichés; none of my editors would get past me with that one.' The undertone murmured away to silence and it occurred to Aubrey that his father was trying to say something important. In the half-light the white of his temples was more prominent and the expression in the dark eyes was lost in shadow. 'But for me the evening has been memorable. Not only the story of that bloody brigadier and the way you trounced him; more than that. Your whole attitude towards these foul and desperate times has given me hope. Most of the young bloods over there are fighting a war they thought they'd love. They went off dizzy with dreams of glory and great deeds. But you're fighting a war you knew you'd hate; and that's more difficult, and immeasurably good. And I wouldn't share this wine more willingly with any man I know.'

The guns beat at the dark, far away over the town, stopping and beginning again like idle fingers sometimes touching a drum.

'That's all, Kitty.'

'Yes, milady?' She saw the surprise on her own face, pale in the mirror. The silver brush wavered in the candlelight.

'We're going to write a letter.' She took the girl's hand, leading her to the escritoire and switching on the electric lamp, so that Kitty felt sudden alarm at this change in their long habit. The fierce light dazzled her. 'You shall sit down and we'll think it out together. It's to Tom.'

'Is it?' said Kitty bleakly. 'But I – I'm not very good at letters, I don't think.'

Lady Eleanor's hand rested on her thin shoulder, making a patch of warmth. 'Writing letters is a way of talking to people, and in a moment you'll be sitting beside brave young Tom and talking to him, as if you'd flown with the wind across the sea to where he's waiting.'

'You make it sound so beautiful!' Her eyes grew brilliant. 'You always make things sound beautiful.'

'No, Kitty. I never cheat. There are ugly things too.' In the photograph beside the lamp he looked a boy again, jaunty in his first uniform; yesterday at the hospital there had seemed reproach in his hollowed eyes, as once she had seen him when Uncle Charles had given him a clockwork engine and he'd caught his fingers in the spring. The war had seemed an even more glittering toy; he'd gone shouting about the house with it to show everyone how it worked. Let him learn, and put them all away. 'Life is the only toy worth keeping.'

'Milady?'

Kitty's face was upturned to her, puzzled.

'You're beginning to be beautiful, child. But that's not enough.' She took the onyx pen and dipped it into the ink for her. 'Do you keep all your letters from Tom?'

209

'Oh, yes!'

'Why?'

'He says nice things.' Her eyes began stinging, as they did sometimes when she thought of Tom, because of the way the letters had stopped so suddenly. Her father had said he'd been 'wounded in action' and she hadn't known what to do; she'd cried all night, not for Tom but because she felt so helpless about it.

'Put at the top, *Dear Tom*.' She watched the movement of the pen, touched by the thought that this was the first letter Kitty had ever written in her life; this was why it simply hadn't occurred to her that she could help Tom so easily. 'Now a comma, and start again lower down.' She reached and switched off the electric lamp. 'Can you see well enough?'

'I think so.'

'I am writing to you by candlelight . . .'

The Annexe to 3rd Nursing, St Mathias Hospital, had its front entrance at the end of a coke-dump, and the smell of greens cooking was the only sign that this soot-bloomed monument of blood-red brick was a human habitation.

'Nurse Lovell? I'll have to see.' Hot little eyes smouldered up and down his uniform while flecks of carrot went on dropping from the grater in her hand. 'Who shall I say?'

'Captain Talbot.'

She turned away with a flick of her bottom that would have put her straight into the front row of the chorus had he been a manager; he felt vaguely glad he was not. Rain began while he waited, the first heavy drops spitting among the coke.

'She's gone.' She tucked a curl seductively under the edge of her soiled linen cap.

'I see. Do you know where?'

'I never asked.'

'Woburn College!' piped a disembodied voice. The passage had the unearthly light of a mine-shaft.

'That's where,' the girl nodded.

'Where is that?' Aubrey asked. It sounded like some dreadful parlour game.

'Where's—'

'South-west One!' A saucepan clanged.

It was half an hour before he found a taxi because the rain was almost solid now, dropping from a sky of gun-metal blue. The streets were awash and the taxi skidded twice on its narrow tyres, once frightening a dray-horse.

'It's time they took them animals off of the roads!' the driver shouted. 'Place is like a farmyard! I got a boy over there. Henry Adams. You know 'im do you?'

'I don't think so!' The rain roared on the roof.

'He says it's not so bad. Says the grub's good!'

'Very good, yes!' He took off a shoe and shook out a chip of coke that had been bothering him, draining the worst of the water out at the same time.

'They say conscription's comin' in! I should 'ope so too – time them sneakin' little Cuthberts was told to do their bit!'

'I'm sure you're right!'

Woburn College was rather cleaner than the Annexe to 3rd Nursing and full of young girls in a state of excitement about something. Two probationers raced off to see who could find the answer first, and he was left standing among an assortment of bags whose handles bore labels, some green and some red. The notice-board told him that *Course IX Foreign Service* had ended yesterday and in sudden alarm he remembered Julian's letter. *Diana says that great changes are in view.* He checked the notice-board again: her name was there all right, under *Drafts in Readiness*.

'You've only just missed her!' They began talking both at once and he listened long enough to get the basic facts before squelching down the steps and looking along the street. The bus-stop was a hundred yards distant and through the rain he saw a huddle of blue-cloaked figures melting into a top-decker. During his sprint he was attacked by the kind of dog that considered a running man was essentially suspect, but managed to kick it by a bit of luck and without breaking his stride. It was surprising, he realized shortly, how fast these motor-buses could go.

'*Taxi!*'

The bow-wave came at him knee-high but he was thankful to have grabbed one so soon and anyway it was more comfortable to be thoroughly soaked than dismally half-damp.

'Catch that bus for me!'

He sat lifting and dropping his feet to watch the water come spurting up from his shoes. There seemed quite a lot.

'Wanter get on it, do you, guv'nor?'

'Of course! Five shillings!'

They managed it in two stops and he found himself swaying among a whole bevy of young women in cloaks, their faces pink and excited and with rain clinging to their cheeks. 'Diana,' he kept saying resolutely, 'Diana Lovell. Nurse Lovell.' The bus lurched through the deluge. 'She's with you, isn't she?'

A man with a ticket-punch was forcing his way along. 'Where to, guv?'

'I don't know. I'm looking for someone.'

'Well there's quite a nice choice, ain't there?' He rang his punch cheerfully. 'Victoria, it'll be.'

'Of *course* we know Diana!' a girl was saying, smiling a mermaid smile through tendrils of wet hair. 'I swop cubicles with her!'

'Oh really?'

'Are you her brother?'

'No—'

'Then you're Bobbie! She often—'

'Not really, no. Look, I—'

'Anyway she'll be at the station by now – she was on the earlier draft—'

'Victoria?'

He was already waving to a taxi from the footboard, absently aware that the muscles of his left arm seemed to be on fire. The taxi had sighted his signals and was slowing, its nearside tyres sending up fountains of water from the gutter with some orange-peel among it.

The station was strangely filled with light when he reached there; the downpour had turned itself off and the edges of the piled clouds were blinding as the sun struck through. He dodged between soldiers and women and railway officials along the outbound platforms, knocking a wad of sodden newspapers off a trolly and jumping a crate of pigeons. A whole lot of V.A.D.s in dark cloaks were standing near a tea-canteen and he asked the first one he came to. She was reading a letter and looked up quickly, surprised.

'Could you please tell me if Nurse Lovell is with your group?'

She just stared at him, an attractive little thing with her face still brown from the summer, and he realized he was out of breath and in rather a mess. Her smile came slowly as if she were watching a conjuring trick she'd decided not to believe in.

'But I was just reading about you,' she said, 'this very minute!' She held up the letter and he saw with a feeling of light-headedness Julian's handwriting.

In a moment he said: 'You're Diana.'

She nodded quickly and the first picture faded, the one he'd carried in his mind since last winter: the pale Dresden fragility, the knot of fair hair in the mauve ribbon, the impatience in the intense blue eyes.

'Remember me now?'

'No. But I will from now on.'

A boy ran past with papers in his arm. *'Great vict'ry at Loos! Vict'ry at Loos!'*

'I feel I've changed,' Diana said. 'I'm glad it shows.'

'You weren't so lovely.'

'I'm not such a prattling little nitwit either. I hope that shows too.'

'When does your train go?'

'Any minute. When does yours?'

'Not till later.'

'Haven't you got a trench-coat?'

'I left it somewhere.'

'You're absolutely drenched.'

'It was raining.'

The light-headedness wouldn't seem to go but he didn't mind. His left arm was throbbing again. They were all climbing into the carriages and she turned her head for a moment. Her eyes were darker when she looked at him again. 'How is your brother Victor? I heard he—'

'Getting on fine. Are you making for France?'

'Yes. We're not meant to know if it's there or the Middle East, officially.'

Someone called – 'Diana!'

'I'm coming!' She said quickly – 'I'm going to join the hospital where Moira is – Nigel's fiancée, you—'

'Yes—'

'She's a sister now and she helped wangle things for me – my parents don't know I'm going – I'm under age and they'd stop me.' She looked suddenly forlorn. 'I've been such a rotten daughter to them. I lied about my age – you've got to be twenty-three. Will you be in it, Aubrey?'

'In it?'

'The big push at Loos.'

'*Diana!*' they called. A guard was moving people back.

She took her service kit and swung it up for them to grab, jumping after it and looking down from the window. 'You're a captain, aren't you? Julian says in his letter you did something magnificent but he couldn't say what. I said you looked invincible, remember?' The heavy couplings banged and she reached down for his hand, saying slowly and clearly, 'Stay invincible.'

'*Great vict'ry at Loos! Vict'ry at Loos!*'

He saw a red cross reflected in the grimy window beside her; a hospital train was pulling in with water still streaming from it and glittering in the shafts of light that struck down blindingly from the station's heights.

Behind him a woman said shrilly: 'If this is a victory then we don't want any more!'

The carriage jerked again.

'Diana. We may see each other over there.'

'Yes. I'll write with my address.'

The iron wheels rolled, parting their hands, and he stood watching until there was only paper blowing across the empty lines.

XI

The sky was a flat grey sheet of steel lying tilted across the iron finger of the church to the east and the black girders of Cordonnier Wood to the west. The land lay under frost, blue-white and over the minutes turning grey as he watched from the dugout entrance, the last light of the day metalling the surface of the shell-holes where the ice was forming again. Everything was metal here, steely and angular; the air smelt of it and the hands felt its chill.

'Captain Talbot, sir?'

The runner's breath steamed; there was frost on his shoulders and knees.

Bn. to all Coy. Commanders. Special attention is called to Order No. 451/A/Loc. Cond. re the use of timber for unauthorized purposes. The most stringent disciplinary action is to be taken in all cases of non-compliance.

He sent the man away with a signature. Above the Reserve parados he could see the group of moving figures, their axe-blades glinting as they rose and fell; the scene was apocalyptic: they were the last men in a dying world, gathered here in the wilderness of winter to smash the artifacts of man for the making of flame, so that in their going they might symbolize all life that had been. In truth of course they were chopping up duckboards to burn and warm themselves. Most reprehensible, and disciplinary action should certainly be taken, since duckboards were vital to properly drained trenches; on the other hand what use were trenches if the men in them were dead with frostbite? The High Command, in its Order No. 451/etc, hadn't thought of that, or they might have sent more coke to the line.

You in your polished boots . . .

This was something young Hayes had been pointing out two days ago when a shell had blown him into pieces. The soiled bits of paper had been among his effects, and Aubrey had just enclosed them with a letter to his parents. Lt Alan Hayes, 3rd

215

Duke of Lancaster's, killed in action 9 November 1916. *It will console you to know that Alan was a highly efficient young officer, and popular among* . . . Not really, no. In three weeks he hadn't had time to prove himself; but they wouldn't be as interested in his few scraps of poetry as in how good he'd been as a soldier, how brave. The boy himself had written more truthfully:

You in your polished boots who talk of glory,
Leave your high horse and walk these earthly shadows:
All you'll find here are the bones of your soldiers,
And in the far streets a gathering of widows.

The bones had impressed young Hayes particularly. Fresh out of training in the calm of English fields, he'd believed that trenches were cut six feet deep and three feet wide with iron revetments and an elbow-rest below the parapet, so that he had crawled in some surprise along the stinking ditches where the living shared their shelter with the dead whose bones rendered their last service in strengthening the banks of clay.

Aubrey had heard Hayes ask someone: 'But don't they bury them?'

'They're buried, aren't they?'

British, French, German – you couldn't tell their nationality, which proud country they'd so gloriously fought for. The battalion had worked this ground two years ago and it was still here, driving forward and driven back, contesting the burial ground of six hundred thousand dead, their bones daily hurled skywards again by the guns as if mere death weren't enough.

The light was fading as he watched, flickering across the hard surfaces of the steel-engraving, its brutal angles growing oblique as the first shadows crept to soften the frost, the only movement a flight of dark birds low on the horizon and the men busy with their chopping. He went back into the dugout and lit the lamp.

Why couldn't somebody help my Jimmy?

The ink was frozen on the nib of his pen and he held it near the lamp for minutes, trying to form in his mind the consoling phrases. Maj. Rokesley had passed him this one to answer, Lord Vivian Rokesley, new to the battalion, a decent enough fellow though burdened by his obligation to acquit himself well in the eyes of the men, to whom a title was the sign of a 'softie'. 'I hear you're good at this sort of letter, old boy – would you have a go at it for me?'

His hand lingered near the lamp for its warmth, reluctant to write; it would take more than this small flame to ease the cold in the poor woman's heart.

Dear Mrs Boscombe ... I more than understand that in your sad loss you must feel that we could somehow have saved your son Jimmy. Let me tell you that the moment we heard he was in trouble, stretcher-parties were sent out, only to be driven back by enemy fire. After several such gallant attempts to reach him in the darkness, a young American, by name Corporal Quincey, went out alone and succeeded in bringing him in, himself being hit by bullets but persisting in his task; for this errand of mercy he was 'Mentioned in Despatches', quite a high honour and one which your son would surely feel to have been well deserved by his rescuer. Jimmy was given immediate medical attention and transferred to the nearest Casualty Clearing Station through the most difficult terrain, where mud reached to the knees of the stretcher-bearers. The Chief Medical Officer, Colonel Dewlake, a brilliant London surgeon before the war, carried out three highly skilled operations, but unfortunately ...

But unfortunately, Mrs Boscombe, your son is dead. Why torture yourself so needlessly? He is dead. He is bones. There are hundreds of thousands of bones round here and hundreds of thousands of mothers like you with their aprons to their eyes, so what gives you the right to ask why nothing was done, sending your stupid hysterical letters to worry us? Don't you know we'll all be bones before long? Doesn't anyone in England know what our life expectancy is when they send us cheering on our way? *Go, lad! It's your duty!* Your son has done his duty and I hope you're satisfied.

... And I hope you will now feel satisfied that everything possible was done to save this gallant life, and that your grief is shared by every man in his battalion.

The flame drew still in the cold air, a dark tendril of smoke thinning upwards through the lamp-glass to the patch of soot above it.

No, old boy, I'm not very good at this sort of letter, I'm bloody awful, because I can't put my heart in it, I just can't care any more, it's routine now, burying bones, composing epitaphs. Callousness is a weapon of war, my friend, as you'll soon learn.

The ashplant leaned against the riven clay of the wall and in a moment he took it and went outside, feeling the coiled copper wire that was now its new handle: it had been split and Freddie had repaired it for him, knowing it was the only possession he valued. The hour was not late but the winter light had left the sky and the men on stand-to, their helmets a black frieze against the glimmer of No Man's Land. This was the hour, in that other world, when you would come in from the rugger-field tingling and famished, to devour small mountains of toast and butter while the first lights were switched on and laughter set the tone for the evening. Alan Hayes had written of this too:

Here is my world, a shell-hole, roofed with the smoke of war;
Yet my heart dwells other-where in the world I knew before:
This is the midnight meadow where I lay beneath wide skies,
Softly drawing the frozen rain of starlight to my eyes.

But the time had gone when he could have lived in one life and dreamed of another, as that boy had done. He was growing old with the growing old of the war, and England had slipped below the horizon of the years at last. This was the one world now: he was born this morning, here among the aching detritus of man's hate for man, and this long day was the measure of his life. He believed he would die here, and in dying would remember only the furnishings of this real and only place: the stark figures of the sentries against the frost, the white glow of a skull embedded in the clay beside him, the snout of a machine-gun poking from its post on the skyline.

It would have helped – oh God, it would have helped – if there'd been a letter from her today, even a postcard to say she was all right; but there'd been no word for a week now, either for him or for Julian, and it was said there'd been a raid by a squadron of Fokkers on 12th Field Hospital near Sartelles. You could never get hold of reliable news however you hungered for it; all you could do was feed your fears on the bitter scraps of rumour.

Walking the silent trench he forced himself not to think of Diana; but the dread remained, a sensation of coldness lying curled inside him, part of the greater cold that lay every-where around; he was a creature of ice, one with the winter here.

Yet a man was singing, slow and quiet. A man daring to accept the unacceptable.

'Sentry!'

'Sir?'

A figure turned, the tune broken.

'What the hell are you thinking of? You know how far we are from the enemy lines?' He felt his anger warming him. 'Report to Sergeant Kilderbee the minute you're relieved. You're on a charge.'

At the turn of the month they were picking at the ice of the shell-holes to use for water, choosing the shallow ones where there wasn't a corpse. Rations came when you were lucky: mules and horses were dying from cold; engines froze, and Jerry's snipers wouldn't let up: too often you'd be sent back to help bring supplies, and come across your supper halfway to the line, the stew spilled from the big rope-handled cans in a frozen brown puddle with the Catering Corps wallahs lying stiff beside it.

They went in little private groups to the ruined village, scrounging timber to burn.

'You know what?' The paper was weeks old and half-shredded by rats, lying among smashed china and a coffee-jug; the people in this house had been at their breakfast when the shells had come. 'The Emperor Franz-Josef of Austria-Hungary's died.' Clarkson knew a bit of French; he was one of the new draft, quite an educated boy, always kept his finger-nails clean, worried over them.

'Has he?' Geoff Tuffnel said. 'That's a shame.' He was bracing a rotten beam with his shoulders while Wiggy and Tom loosened the brickwork with the hafts of their bayonets. 'My chum Oscar died last night but it won't be in the headlines, will it?'

Clarkson said nothing. Tuffnel was like that, he realized: rub him up the wrong way whatever you said. The new chaps had already learned to keep their distance from him – he was a big fellow and you had to be careful. Only a few understood him: Cpl Stokes and Quincey and little Wiggy and that crowd, the ones who called themselves 'Talbot men'.

'We'll miss poor old Oscar.' Wiggy was sunk into his great-coat, the tip of his blue nose poking out; it was too big for him by half, because you always had to take off your coat and leave it aside when you went over the top and if you got back you couldn't always find the right one again. 'I can remember sayin' that once before, about missin' old Oscar, then 'e turned up again, didn't 'e? An' we got 'im to play us a tune.'

'He won't turn up again this time,' said Tom. The bricks were coming away from the beam and Geoff was taking the best part of its weight now, but not showing anything; Geoff could hold a house up.

'I'll miss him, though,' said Wiggy.

'Well that's the best epitaph,' Geoff said, 'any man can have.'

'Epitaph?'

'What you put on tombstones.'

'Oh, them.' He stood back, wondering whether to take some of the weight or run clear. 'You manage, Geoff?'

'Yep. Stand away.'

He was a wonderful man, thought Wiggy, and it was surprising to think he was a friend of his; you could say that: Geoff was his friend. But it was a bit like the lion and the mouse that chummed up in the story: you couldn't help thinking where you'd be if Geoff suddenly wanted something to eat and forgot you were his friend. A lot of the blokes didn't care to come too near him, even when he wasn't balancing a hundredweight beam on his shoulders. They didn't know, though; it wasn't because of that. Only the four of them knew: Sam, Percy, Tom and himself. Nobody else.

'Mind your feet, then.' Geoff lowered the beam as gently as he could because it wouldn't take much to fetch the whole of this ruin down. Then he took one end and Clarkson the other, with Tom and Wiggy in between, and they carried it through what had been the village street. It was rotten with woodworm but that kind of timber burned the best; you could cook a good few hundred bangers on this lot, if you had a few hundred bangers.

'Say the word,' Geoff told them, 'when you want to rest.' But they wouldn't do that till they were near buckling at the knees, for their pride's sake. Their boots kicked through rubble, knocking the frost off it. Christ watched them from the scarred and rusted cross that leaned near the brick-heap that had been the church; a priest came here, they knew, whenever stray shells hit the village, to make sure the cross didn't get knocked over again.

The *estaminet* was somewhere near this part, and Wiggy always looked to see if he could find the big blue signboard among all the mess, because they'd loved that place; everyone in the whole battalion must have passed a bit of time there in the last months before the German batteries wiped it out. The board had said *Chez Michel* in red-and-gold letters, which was the proprietor's name – quite a lot of the people who owned these *estaminets* were called *Chez*, Wiggy had noticed, so perhaps it was the French for Charlie or some such name.

Did Geoff ever think of this place when they passed it scrounging for wood? You couldn't tell – and you wouldn't dare ask him. None of them had talked about it, even out of Geoff's hearing; it was a sort of unwritten law between them.

Wiggy hadn't wanted to go with them that night because he'd saved every shilling of his pay to send home and wasn't going to sponge; but Sam had said, 'Tonight's on General Grant, so let's get goin'!' The *estaminet* was packed when they got there because the battalion had been a month in the line with the shells very bad and the troops had plenty to get off their minds. A lot of them were half-pissed already but their mates were looking after them so they wouldn't try any larks with the girls serving the drinks. Geoff got a table quick as anything although the place was crowded and Sam slapped a fat wad of franc notes on the scrubbed wood – 'Set 'em up, sweetie, a bottle a man!' The girls took to him right off and before long he'd got one of them perched beside him on the bench although they were so busy serving. Sam was due for leave and that was why 'General Grant' was standing them treat tonight; he'd been talking about it for weeks because there'd been no chance for him to see 'li'l ole England' before; he meant other places than London. And he was going to find the grave of one of his 'noble forebears', his great-grandfather who'd been born in Cornwall and was actually an Englishman.

So there were five bottles of 'plonk' on the table, 'plonk'

being really 'vang blonk', a famous French wine; and Sam had his arm round the girl, looking quite handsome and dashing in his silk scarf – he'd undone his dog-collar and tucked the scarf inside, a thing you wouldn't normally dare do of course. Tom was smiling at them, a bit cautious though because the last time he was wounded he'd got it in the face and the worst of the scars – an awful one right down his cheek – hadn't healed properly yet; and Percy was pretending to look shocked because the girl was very young; and Geoff was just sitting quiet drinking his 'plonk' and listening to all the singing that was going on. Then the two military policemen came in.

You could see they were looking for trouble because they started booking people right off; but the noise didn't die down till they got round to Sam, since none of the other blokes had argued the toss – if you hadn't brought your rifle along you couldn't give an excuse because there wasn't one, you were for it and that was that. Sam had his rifle but it was his silk scarf that worried them, like it was bound to.

'You're improperly dressed.' They were big men, as big as Geoff, with heads like boulders, you could have told they were M.P.s even if you'd seen them stark bollock naked under a shower.

'Who, me?' But Sam gave them his pass and pay-book and they wrote down his name and number; and Geoff's face went quietly sort of grim with his jaw sticking forward, though he didn't say anything. 'Am I on the hook?' Sam asked them, still with his arm round the girl.

'How did you guess?' They gave his papers back.

'Look, boys, I just came here to relax. Don't you ever relax? It's good for you!' His big white grin was still showing and they didn't seem to like that. 'C'mon, give a guy a break why don't you, huh?'

'You a Canadian?'

'Say, you need to get your accents right. I'm from the States.'

'A bloody American?'

Sam's grin went off like a light and he was standing up and the girl looked suddenly frightened and the noise had stopped and they all heard Sam say, very calm – 'No. Just an American.'

One of the drunks started singing again and someone shut him up quick. Sam's hands were bunched up and in the quietness Geoff said: 'Don't worry about it, Sam, they're only trying to rile you.'

That was quite true, as Wiggy could see. There was nothing you could ever say to an M.P.; you might just as well talk to the hangman. That was why everyone hated them – you were always wrong, whatever you said. After a month in the deadly rotten stinking line you had to stand in front of these safe-billet bastards as if you were a snotty-nosed school-kid with your hand held out.

'Foreigner, eh?'

'Why sure, if you want it that way. A foreigner.'

They didn't move their heads but they knew everyone else in the place was watching by now and they seemed to like that.

'What's a foreigner doin', then, in the British Army?'

Sam gave them his grin again. 'I guess I just came along to get it organized.'

It wasn't so much the wrong thing to say, he'd said it to the wrong people. Their faces went like bricks.

'You better watch yourself then, Yankee. This army's organized enough to push you in the cooler for the rest o' the war. Take a tip, eh, from a friend.'

They went on their way, knocking against the tables, kicking a man's foot aside, looking for trouble, their khaki smart and clean, not like the others, because they hadn't slept up in a hole in the ground for a month with rat shit for a mattress, like the others.

Sam sat down with his grin still there but sort of rueful. 'Well I guess that's my leave gone sky-high, huh?'

Percy tried to say something funny but no one laughed and Geoff sat so still that Wiggy didn't like to look at him, but couldn't help it; you could feel the anger coming out of him like hot sparks although he didn't move and didn't speak; it was all in his eyes – they stared at nothing, fixed like a cat's eyes, very big and very black in the middle.

'Bastards,' said Percy. 'Right bastards.'

'Oh, they're okay,' Sam said. 'It's their job, ain't it?'

And that was all that happened. They stayed a couple more hours and Percy made some jokes and they joined in with the singing, except for Geoff, and told themselves they were having a very nice time. Chez Michel turned them all out himself at midnight, a huge fat man with little bright eyes and warts down his nose in a row, but ever so funny, waving at them with his big fat arms as if they were a lot of geese on a farm, with the girls helping him and laughing.

Outside Geoff said: 'Don't wait for me.'

Anyone else, you'd have asked him why he wasn't coming, but they didn't ask Geoff; they were glad to get away from him, tell the truth, for he was no company. They went off singing, the four of them, *There's a long long trail a-winding*, that one, a lovely song it was and very popular; and the last mile they had to help Tom over the bumps in the lane because he wasn't used to so much plonk.

Geoff turned up later, just as they were kipping down in the barn, but he didn't say anything and they left him alone, not that he looked nasty or anything, in fact he was whistling under his breath while he unlaced his boots, as if he'd enjoyed the evening after all.

The news got round next morning and a Provost officer went through the camp asking questions, but nobody knew anything and even if they did they wouldn't split – the Provost didn't have a chance, of course. If they could have found the notebooks the M.P.s had been carrying they could have gone down the list of names booked on a charge that night, but the evidence was gone as you might say. It was a cook in B Company that'd found the two M.P.s, lying near a horse-trough he said they were, 'stone-cold bloody unconscious an' with lumps on their 'eads you could've put a bowler-'at on – I scarpered quick, I can tell you, 'fore they woke up an' saw me there!' He went on a lot about it because everyone wanted to know the details – Sam wasn't the only name they'd got in their books that night; it was the best bit of news they'd heard for a long time and it cheered the place up, and when it was dark some bloke chalked some words right across the stores-tent – GREETINGS TO OUR UNKNOWN FRIEND!

Sam went on leave just as he'd planned. When he came back he told them all about the girls he'd clicked with but it wasn't till they were sitting alone together – Geoff, Tom, Percy and Wiggy himself – round a bit of a fire they'd made to nosh their supper by, that Sam spoke the only words that they'd ever said between them about that night at *Chez Michel*. He made sure no one else was anywhere near, then looked at Geoff straight in the eye. 'I want you to know I had me a good leave. It was great, real great.' And Geoff said: 'I'm glad.' Then they went on eating their stew.

Their hands were getting sore, chapped by the cold and rubbed by the heavy beam they carried. They crunched through the ice of puddles.

'I need a rest,' Geoff said. They knew he didn't, but were thankful. They stood getting their breath and watching the dog-fight that had started somewhere over the lines: some Taube recce-planes were nosing in and a flock of Sopwiths were diving on them from much higher, whining and snarling through the grey winter sky.

Wiggy sat down for a minute, looking around him on the ground as he always did; no matter where you were, there was the chance of spotting a bit of business – cap-badge or a Jerry bayonet, worth a bob or two. Last time on home-leave he'd gone up Dock Lane jingling like a horse's harness and squeezed three quid out of the antique-shop man – three quid, more than two months' army pay! – and bought Mum a coat with a fur collar for the winter, she'd be wearing it now, as he sat here. He'd have a shop of his own, this rate, if he came through the war, *Wilfred Bennett – Antique Dealer* in red-and-gold letters on a blue board like *Chez Michel* had been.

Geoff was standing watching the dog-fight with his head up and his arms folded, put you in mind of a statue, a famous person done in stone. His friend, fancy that. Sam's friend too, and no mistake. Not that Geoff had done it just so Sam could have his leave, although that was part of it. No, it was them two fox-eyed bastards calling him a 'bloody American' and a 'foreigner' after all that Sam had done for their own country, that was what Geoff couldn't stand. Nobody liked the Military Police but there was nothing you could do, unless you were Geoff, then they'd be found with their heads bashed together. There was nothing Geoff wouldn't do. They ought to make him a general and tell him we'd got to win the war, it wouldn't last five minutes after that. Maybe that was what had been in their mind when they'd offered him a commission not long ago: Col. Forsyth had wanted to send him for training but Geoff had refused. He'd told them afterwards – 'They need men with a sense of responsibility, do they? Then they've had this one. I'm not sharin' their responsibility for anything that happens in this bloody mess, I'll tell you that.' Wiggy was glad he'd not gone for an officer; he'd have missed him worse than Oscar.

They picked up the beam and went on, talking a bit more now because the halt had restored them.

'Young Talbot's back,' said Percy, 'have you seen him? My God, he's got thin, bloody nigh unrecognizable.'

'It's been a long time,' Tom said. Mr Victor had been home at the Manor still, the last spell of leave he'd had, looking so different that he'd been shocked by it; dreadfully thin, as Percy said, and sort of dried up, 'shut up inside of himself', as Cook had said, grieving. And when he spoke it was the way a dog barked when it was chained up and wanted to go free. 'How's the war getting on without me, Tom?' His eyes darting about and his smile kind of crooked as if he was sneering at himself. 'Don't go and win it before I get back there.' It worried you to hear him go on. Whatever made him want to come back out here when he could stay at a lovely place like the Manor and take a nice long time getting better? Mr Charrington said he was round at the Medical Board every week, not giving them any peace, telling them he was quite fit enough to rejoin his unit. You could see he wasn't.

'Are they brothers,' Jim Clarkson was asking, 'those two? He and the captain?' Jim hadn't been with the battalion long.

'That's right,' Tom said. He was always quick to speak when their name came up because he knew them better than anyone, except of course for Mr Kemp, and it gave him a warm feeling inside.

'The captain's a fine man,' Jim Clarkson said.

'He is,' Geoff answered even quicker than Tom.

'An unusual man,' Jim said. They picked their way across ground where there'd been shelling, nearing the line. The Sopwiths had flown back to the rear now and the sky was quiet. 'You know what happened, a while ago, when he slapped me on a charge?'

'What charge?' asked Percy.

'Then I didn't tell you. I was on night guard and he heard me singing. Not loudly – we weren't far from old Jerry. I was feeling a bit relieved, that was all; I'd only been out here a

226

week and things were so quiet that I thought the war was a push-over.' He gave a short laugh. 'That was before Jerry started on us.'

'Put you on the fizzer for that?' asked Wiggy. It didn't sound like the captain.

'I've not finished.' They skirted the ice of a shell-hole where a skull watched them pass. 'The next day he sent for the three of us – myself and the two chaps who'd been standing guard on each side of me. Caps off and marched in – I thought I'd had it. You know what he said? He said I'd clearly been aware that the enemy was close, as I wasn't singing too loudly, and the charge was "ill founded", so I wouldn't hear any more of it. He added that any man who'd got the heart to sing in the line at this stage of the war was welcome in his company. Dismiss! Now don't you think that was extraordinary?'

'No,' Geoff said.

'You know him better than I do, of course. The thing is, why did he send for the other two chaps as well? They hadn't been—'

'They were with you when he bawled you out, and he wanted them to be there when he apologized.'

Clarkson looked past the others at Geoff's thickset back. 'Do you honestly think that was it?'

'I don't think. I know.'

'But I mean you don't expect that sort of consideration out here.'

'An' you won't often get it. But you'll get it from him.'

They made one more halt before they reached camp.

'The longer you carry somethin',' Wiggy said, 'the 'eavier it gets. Why's that?'

'It's the dew gathering on it,' said Percy and laughed like a pantomime demon.

'What we'll do is,' Wiggy told them, 'when we get back, we'll burn this lot in one piece 'stead of choppin' it all up. Terrific great blaze, eh? An' we'll sit round it toastin' our tootsies an' singin' carols. Chris'mas is comin', we mustn't forget that.'

'And we'll—' began Percy and stopped himself. He'd been going to say they'd hang up some mistletoe and kiss Kilderbee's arse; but there'd been something wistful in Wiggy's tone: they'd

227

only been out of the line a few days and he wanted to make the most of it. There were times when you wouldn't get a laugh, and times when you didn't want one. 'We'll send old Sam down to the cookhouse and see if he can charm us up some bangers.'

'That's right,' Wiggy said in excitement, and they lifted the beam of wood and went on, feeling how much less heavy it seemed to have got.

It was dusk when they came to the tents, and Sgt Kemp called out, 'Where have you men been?'

It sounded official so they left it for Cpl Stokes to answer. 'Firewood party, Sarge.'

'We're warned for action. Report to your section leaders an' put a jerk in it.'

On the eve of the attack the weather broke and a thaw set in and there was rain, but the plans were not changed because the offensive was on a divisional scale in close strategic liaison with the French – 'Vengeance for Verdun' – and along parts of the front there was hard ground still, though not here.

Here at Vauxcourt the 3rd Duke of Lancaster's went over the top already soaked, climbing from flooded trenches to stumble through mud with the rain beating on their backs and the shrill of the whistles desolate in the haze, the smoke of the bombardment clinging and crawling so thickly about them that some feared there was gas and squeezed their masks on to push forward again half blinded, their heads down against the winnowing storm of the bullets.

Towards afternoon the rain eased and the rings spreading across the surfaces of the shell-holes thinned away, though many were churned from time to time by the movement of drowning men. The land was quieter now; the voices of the dying reached more clearly than the hammering of the guns. The attack was over. It had not succeeded; it had not failed; there had been no ground gained nor any lost; there were as many dead in the German lines as lay out here under the last soft easing of the rain; this day's work, then, could be hailed in both London and Berlin as a victory, since there had been no defeat.

The living were constantly on the move, brute thought alone stirring them; sluggishly they turned on their muddied limbs, on their knees or on all fours or on their stomachs, squirming through the pasty softness of the mud to leave their muddy tracks, the mud receiving them and sucking at them, deceiving them and drawing them down into water they had thought was mud because it was mud-coloured and smooth, as smooth as the mud itself, the weight of the mud itself bearing their muddied bodies down upon mud. The mud moved, alive with its sores and parasites, all the brave phrases wallowing, the dignity of man, the mud smothering, the sovereignty of nations, the mud sucking and not letting go, the will to win and glory on the field, here the glory and here the field, say what you will.

Germans were here too, the enemy, differenced by his way of speech in the earlier hours of today but now of a common language as he moaned of his pain. The Germans had launched a local counter-offensive in reply to the enemy offensive, that is to say the British and the French offensives, they being the enemy from the German point of view, clearly differenced by their way of speech; there had been many offensives launched, with victory for all, since there had been no technical defeat. The mud boiled with movement, a bubble bursting to shriek pain out from the mouth beneath; blood surfaced here and there to relieve the monotonous brown of the mud, bringing it brightness till the heartbeat ceased; from a hump of mud a blue eye stared, dulling, at the unseen sky.

Stretcher-bearers!

A shell, unexploded, now burst and the mud spewed up a fountain of inconsequential bones, its filth pattering back. There'd been no point in that.

No point at all. He moved again, surprised at his own strength. There'd been no point in any of it, for Christ's sake. He got to his feet and the mud slipped under them but he cursed and kicked at it, furious. He couldn't find his ashplant and had to grope for it in the ooze where bones were slimy and the flesh – some of it decaying and some still firm, alive or not long dead – repelled his fingers to the point of nausea. He found the ashplant though and felt better with it in his hand, the coil of copper wire where Freddie had mended it, was Freddie alive still and where was Vic?

They cried out everywhere and he stood looking about him. His head still sang from whatever had hit it or nearly hit it and there was cordite on his tongue and mud caking his face. Christ, how they bloody well moaned, as if there were something you could do about it; moaning and screaming and bubbling, damn them, what did they expect, what were they here for? A German was crying out quite near him and an Englishman was telling him to shut up; their shapes heaved under the mud. It was disgusting, all this. Mankind was a sickness, a disease crawling over a clean sphere of rock spinning its unimpassioned way through infinity; man was a sore, a pox on the pure breast of the earth. Look at him.

'*Vic!*' he called.

Filth fell from him as he stood straighter. A few people were trying to reach the wounded on the flank but some wretched Hun was firing at them from what was left of their line.

'I'm dyin',' a voice said near him, 'I'm dyin'.'

Absently he said, 'Never mind.' But this wasn't good enough and something would have to be done. The mud sucked when he moved, then suddenly his foot came up and the shoe was left behind; he noticed he was standing in a mottled pool of blood, beautiful as a dark red rose, but there was nothing he could feel, no pain anywhere. '*Tell that fucking Hun to give over, someone!*'

People in field grey wormed through the mud, trying to drag in the wounded. On the flank an arm with a red cross on it was flung up as the gun rattled again and a stretcher skewed over, the crimson thing on it tipping and hitting the mud with a flat *thuppp*. They were getting nowhere.

'Vic!' he called again, from habit. His hands tore at the field dressing and got out some bandage, a lot of it, all there was; it looked extraordinarily white and pure in a world of mud and he trudged forward towards the shambles of barbed wire and burst sandbags, his other foot sucking free of its shoe. The gun chattered somewhere on the left.

'That's the enemy line, sir!'

'I know it is.' He tried to see what had spoken but there were only humps of mud everywhere; the stuff dripped from his arms as he held the bandages as high as he could. 'Parley!' he shouted angrily, 'Parley! *Sprechen*! *Sprechen*, you bloody fools!' The gun sounded louder as it traversed and he felt a tug at his tunic and waved the bandages and yelled at them and went on yelling and waving, slopping through the mud towards the people in field grey.

One of them shouted, not to him but to someone in his own group, and a big man started signalling-motions and soon the machine-gun stopped firing.

'That's right!' Aubrey called. '*Sprechen!*' He slipped and went splashing into a pool and a half-naked body floated slowly over face-uppermost, its eyes defined by maggots. 'This is difficult going,' he said to no one, perhaps just to hear his own voice as a way of keeping sane.

The envoy should approach the enemy's forward positions at a slow pace, taking with him, if possible and convenient, a trumpeter, bugler or drummer.

He clambered to firmer ground again and held up the bandages. Slime dripped from them on to his face.

'*Kamerad?*' the big man shouted to him.

'No, you clod! *Nein! Parlementaire!* Fetch one of your officers! *Offizier!*' His arms were getting tired and it made him angry.

If signalled or ordered to retire, the envoy must do so at once, or he loses his inviolability and may be fired on or made prisoner.

'*Kamerad!*' the idiot shouted again.

'*Nein Kamerad, nein! Sprechen mit Offizier!*'

They questioned each other. Their faces were haggard and one of them fell down while they were talking, his arm gleaming with crimson from wrist to shoulder. Somebody else was coming towards them and they tried to draw themselves more upright.

'*Was ist los?*'

'*Es ist ein englischer Offizier, Herr Leutnant. Der will uns etwas sagen.*'

They helped the fallen man to his feet and stood swaying with him, ludicrously attempting an attitude of attention in the presence of their officer.

The greatest courtesy should be observed on both sides and the envoy should be accorded the honours due to his rank. Abuse of a flag of truce constitutes gross perfidy and should be reported at once to the enemy command.

'Do you speak English?' Aubrey asked. He let go of the bandages and they floated like garlands across the mud.

'Some, yes.' He was a thin youth, feverish with having had to know and see too much, too young. His eyes were vacant

231

with fatigue and he was squinting to get things in focus. '*Was ist* – what is your trouble, Herr Hauptmann?'

'I want a temporary truce so that we can both get our wounded in.' He braced his legs, feeling them trying to buckle.

'Truce?'

'Armistice.' He held the boy's arm. 'I want to see your commanding officer. We can save a lot of lives, German as well as English. But we must hurry.'

The fighting had been more sustained along the north flank of the salient where the ground was harder, but within the past hour confusion had set in and groups of men wandered there, seeking what cover they could along hedgerows and among the stumps of trees, firing at random as they withdrew; some had lost direction and realized too late that they were advancing again, dropping in their tracks as a gunpost sighted them.

It was one of such groups that Vic came upon, close by a hill where rainwater seeped to the ditches below; he was at this time quite alone, having failed to recruit a useful force from the walking-wounded and take it forward in the hope of doing damage. These nine or ten men were straggling below the crest of the hill and seemed half stunned, though none appeared to be actually wounded.

'Where the hell d'you think you're going?' His revolver was already to hand and he waved it at them. At the sound of his voice they faltered like sheep, their rifles dragging; they turned red eyes on him but made no answer, their faces expressionless under the masks of mud. He'd seen this sort of thing before: in the heat of a battle there were always a few bodies of men who were cut off and left without leaders; still fit for more work they lacked only orders. 'Come on, I'm taking you forward, so get those rifles up!'

One or two lifted their arms to the high port, but several began moving on as if they'd heard nothing, and these he stopped:

'I'm shooting the first man who refuses!'

They faltered again and one of them detached himself, approaching; Vic saw a sergeant's chevrons on the mud-caked sleeve and in a moment recognized him.

'It's no use, Mr Victor.' Kemp's eyes were steady enough,

though immeasurably bitter. 'Number 4 Platoon got cut off near the guns; we're the only survivors.'

'How many are wounded?' He stared along the file of slack figures. They stared him back.

'None, sir, but they're done up—'

'If they're not wounded then they're fit!' He heard a crack in his voice and was warned: the Medical Board had passed him out for France under protest and he'd been told to take things easy for a time; it was his temper that had kept him on his feet today, his rage at the weakness of his body. 'They're fit and they've got weapons and I'm taking them forward.'

'Then you won't live an' nor will they.'

'Listen to me, Sergeant Kemp!' His tone cracked again but he couldn't control it. 'You'll go down there and rally whatever fit men you can find to give us a rearguard.' He wasn't taking the Talbot wet-nurse with him, by God. 'The rest of you smarten up and follow me!'

He stumbled as he turned away from Kemp, the weakness pulling at him, the rage jerking him straight again. He was aware that they hadn't moved and that their faces watched him; he was aware of the silence and in the silence the voice of Kemp addressing them:

'Hold fast. Those are my orders.'

Vic swung back to face him.

Rain fell softly on his neck. He kept still for a minute because the more he moved the worse it was: the mud below the water seemed to get more hold on his boots, and every time he reached upwards his hands slipped and only brought more mud down; the water was icy, numbing him. Somewhere in the same crater there was a bubbling; a man was drowning there. He kept very still, to rest himself before he tried again; he thought of other things. Her letter was in his pocket and he thought of that.

I am writing this in the conservatory. She always began like that, ever since the first one, which had said she was writing by candlelight; she wanted him to know where she was so he could picture her. *The snow on the glass roof makes it strange here, not dark and not light, it is like being in a goldfish bowl. I knew it had snowed in the night, when I woke up this morning, because the ceiling was whiter than usual, and I laid there a long time thinking about the snow I would see when I went to the window, then my father came and pretended to tip the water-jug over me so I would get up. I have been helping Milady with knitting socks for the soldiers. Did you receive some socks last week? I think they are too big for you.*

There was a cry among the bubbling noise, like a dog whimpering, then the bubbling stopped altogether and he reached up fiercely with his fingers closed so the mud wouldn't slip through them but he was only sinking lower in the water all the time and his face was against the mud and he couldn't breathe properly, *Kitty*, he thought, *Kitty*. He stopped moving. The water froze at his throat. *I think of you often during the day and sometimes when I brush Milady's hair we talk about you, she calls you 'my brave Tom', which is a nice way of saying your name.* But even without moving he could feel the water coming higher under his chin; he lifted his head and the rain fell on his closed eyes.

Boots squelched.

'I dunno. We got 'im out but I wouldn't give much for 'is chances.'

A voice called something in German.

'All right Fritz, there's others before you.'

They slithered and the stretcher hit the mud and they cursed and a man moaned.

'Hold on, Bob. There's a bloke in this crater up to his neck, give us a hand.'

Where there had been the flat shining mud with its aching movements and no sound but the cynical bang of the gun there were now figures making their way without fear and taking no heed where they went, looking for the living among the dying, among the dead; and from both lines others had come to join the bearers and the orderlies: cooks and runners and signalmen, khaki and field grey, while the padres knelt beside the limbless and the hopeless, speaking words of comfort in while their blood ran out. Many worked but many waited and everywhere men crawled, those in brown to the west and those in grey to the east, instinctive in their slow migration and unwilling to lie here a companion to indignity while they had life enough to go their way alone; from one of these a ribbon of blood drew out as he dragged his body along, pausing sometimes at the spreadeagled ruin of a man to pick at him, three badges so far

234

and an officer's revolver, beautifully chased at the butt and with German writing on it so you could prove it was genuine, two quid for a model like that, worth twelve badges or thirty buttons, the man in Dock Lane said.

He'd seen the blood and knew what it was about; that was why he was taking this chance of doing a bit of business: he wouldn't be here again. Look at it like that, calm-like, and you wouldn't faint; and you mustn't faint or they'd take you for a stiff and not bother. He dragged his leg after him; he could feel both of them, but they said it often happened, you went on feeling it for a time. Another lapel-badge, three bob, six bob the set, there were pickings here all right; a nice wrist-watch, but he left it, he wasn't a common looter, this was a respectable profession.

'*Hilfe . . . Hilfe.*'

'Eh?' This one was still alive. 'All right, mate, you jus' keep still an' don't worry.' He looked across the mud – '*Oi!* There's a Jerry 'ere, wants 'elp!' It'd been meant for a shout but it only sounded like a croak, sod it. '*Bearers!*' It sent him dizzy trying to holler. The Jerry's eyes were moving, taking notice of him. 'They won't be long, cock, they got a lot to do, see. I'll stay 'ere till someone comes.' It'd mean losing good business but they'd never find him otherwise. He rolled on to his side and waved his arm, trying to holler a bit louder this time. '*Oi!* Come on, I got a customer!'

The rain fell more heavily from the lowering sky and made a shine on everything; the stretchers plied between the lines, their bearers as red as slaughter-house men.

'Sam!'

'Yeah?'

'Tom's all right. Fell in a hole, that's all.'

'Thank Christ.'

The padres moved among the craters, blessing their foul water to render it holy for the drowned.

'It's no good, chum. I'm done for.'

'No you're not.' Geoff Tuffnel went as steadily as he could but it wasn't easy on this ground; it wasn't ground at all, it was bone-soup simmering in the rain and when you didn't slip you tripped, catching your boots on buried things, some soft, some hard. 'We're nearly there,' he told the man on his back.

235

'Chris' sake leave me be. There's others.' Then he screamed as Geoff lurched, a rifle tripping him.

In a minute Geoff said, 'It's not far now,' but there was no answer. He kept going, his back on fire with pain that wasn't his own. Two German bearers passed him, going the other way: some of them had got close to the British line in the counter-attack. One called something to him – it sounded like '*Piccadilly!*' – and he grunted a wordless reply, feeling the anger spreading in his mind again because today he'd learned something that he'd have to think over carefully and then finally do something about. War was a game.

It was a game and it had rules and he'd stood with his mouth open like a fool, listening. The German subaltern had fetched someone higher in rank, an older man with a fat neck and a monocle, a good deal shaken up but with one of those laughs that some people turned on and off while they were talking. Gone up to the captain and banged his heels together and saluted.

'Von Eidrich – Hauptmann.'

'Captain Talbot. How do you do?'

Then they shook hands.

'You are an official *parlementaire*?' The monocle fell out and he screwed it back.

'Yes, I want—'

'On whose authority?'

'My own.'

'I like that!' The laugh came. 'That is very British!'

'Look here, I want a truce organized so that we can pull the wounded in. You're in no better shape than we are, so what about it?'

'I think this is how you British built your empire, yes?' A big laugh. 'You like to bargain – but the other fellow always gets the worst of it!' He looked around him. 'I shall see my commander. At present neither side appears to be firing.'

'That's not good enough; we don't trust the "other fellow" – sorry to be so British.' They both turned their heads and listened for a moment to a lot of noise coming through the rain-haze from a couple of miles away, rifle and machine-gun and the eerie battle-yell of Highlanders. Here in the salient it was quiet except for the cries of the wounded calling for help. 'Look here, Captain, while you're seeing your commander

236

you can order a cease-fire in your own company, can't you? I've already signalled my unit.'

'I may accept your word for that, as an officer?'

'No, as a man. For God's sake let's get a move on and save some of these lives.'

'Very well.' Turning away he said with sudden vigour, 'It was a good battle, yes? Fought to a finish!'

'Quite splendid. We'll have a lot more, but I want to get this one cleared up first.'

Then within a few minutes the survivors were spilling out of the trenches from both sides, talking to each other and swopping fags and helping the Red Cross boys, not a gun firing anywhere, not even a lone sniper; and Geoff stared around him and saw that there was peace.

He'd need to think this over.

The weight on his back felt heavier now.

'All right, chum?' There was no answer. 'We won't be long.' But he knew by the heaviness that they'd been too long already. Keep on, take him in and get him a decent burial somewhere out of all this muck.

Think it over and then do something about it, now that he'd spotted the trick. This muck, this swamp of blood and earth, had been fields once, near the ruined village of Vauxcourt; and in these fields, in the middle of all the maps and the orders and the killing, here where three gigantic armies staggered together bludgeoning each other into the ground, here in the fields of Vauxcourt the war had stopped. Two men had shaken hands and there was peace. They'd done it so they could bring in the wounded and give them a chance to live. Why couldn't they let this peace go on, then, so other men could be saved too, before they got wounded, before they got killed? Because of the rules. You could stop the war for a while but you'd got to start it again; the game had got to be played like the rules said.

He knew what the war was about, now. They weren't fighting for food or a mate like animals did; they were doing it because they'd all agreed to do it. Announcements and declarations, treaties and alliances, then the whistles blew and the game was on. That was what the war was about. The war was about the war.

He knew, like people sometimes did, that something important was happening to him as he carried a dead man through the fields of Vauxcourt.

'Gilmore!'
'Sir?'
'Where's my batman, you seen him?'
'He got killed, sir.'
'Oh. Find me some shoes, will you, or boots'll do, size ten.'

They were trying to hand-pump the water out of the trench. He slopped through it, leaning on his ashplant, realizing suddenly that he mustn't lean on it like this, like an old man; it was for swinging, for companionship, for comfort, a reminder of the strength of the tree he'd cut it from, the strength of Ashbourne.

The wounded were still coming in. All you could hear were voices and the jerking of the pumps, the same sounds, probably, that you heard on a crippled ship when the storm had died. It had been agreed the truce should continue until nightfall.

Julian was all right; he'd seen him helping someone in. Lord Rokesley was here somewhere too, winded and winged and smothered in mud but not too shaken: he'd weathered pretty well and the battalion could do with chaps like him. Nigel they wouldn't see again; he must write to Moira about it, tell her it was clean and quick; out here you could never speak the truth about the dead.

Some people were straggling through a breach in the parapet, one man with someone on his back, an officer. They were nearly past him before he recognized the N.C.O. in their party.

'Freddie! You all right?'

'Yes, sir.' There was despair in his eyes. Reports had been that Four Platoon was wiped out, trapped near the guns.

'Is that my brother you've got there?' He'd been searching for Vic when someone had told him a party was bringing him in with 'slight wounds'.

'He's all right,' Freddie said; and Aubrey caught but couldn't identify an odd note in his voice.

'Leave him here, then.' There'd be some cognac in the company dugout if the dugout was still there.

The man eased Vic off his back and they propped him on the

238

wreckage of the duckboards; his eyes had come open and he
started weakly pushing the man away. Freddie was going on
down the trench, the men with him; and through the numbness
of his fatigue Aubrey sensed something wrong: Freddie should
have stayed for a minute, sharing a cigarette in celebration;
today the three of them had come close to losing Ashbourne
but it was still theirs.

Vic was struggling up and he went to help him but his hand
was jerked aside and he saw the wildness in the sharp young
face and the dark bruise on the jaw as his brother pushed past
him, shouting.

'*Sarn't Kemp!*'

Freddie turned, the men with him; they stood looking back
silently, surrealist figures, muddied and faceless, their reflection
steadying on the scum of the floodwater.

'Sir?'

Vic swayed, hitting out at the clay to support himself; then
his head jerked up and Aubrey heard that his brother's voice
was no longer recognizable.

'Report to Major Rokesley! You know the charge!'

It was a moment before Freddie answered.

'Yes sir.'

He swung about and moved on with his men.

I'm too tired, Aubrey thought, for anything more today; but
something's got to be done; something, quite evidently, has got
to be done.

'What charge?' he asked.

Vic turned to face him. He looked far gone.

Clay from the parapet, loosened by blast and the rain,
tumbled into the water with the soft sound of decay in a
ruined house.

'He knows,' Vic said wearily. The wildness had left his face
and it was drained-looking. 'You'll have to ask him.'

'*Damn* you, what charge?'

Vic brought his head up in defiance. 'There's more than one.
Refusing action, striking an officer and inciting mutiny.' The
silence drew out and he couldn't stand it. 'Well you wanted to
know, didn't you?'

XII

The owl screamed.

Light danced and she turned her head away from it, tip-toeing through the yellow dark and balancing the beds on the upturned palms of her hands; the beds were piled one on another and reached so high that she couldn't see the top, and with every step they wobbled and shifted and the blood seeped down on to her arms; with every step the weight of them pressed her down and down until the floor reached as far as her knees and she couldn't make any more progress.

Diana! Diana!

Her legs were trapped and she was terrified but stood beneath the toppling pile trying to steady it like a conjurer, moving her arms wildly because the beds mustn't come down. Her back was breaking under their weight.

Diana!

I can't! she cried, *I can't!*

The owl screamed in the yellow wind.

Mary was there. The door swung and the draught sent the candle dancing.

'Diana! Convoy in!'

The man screamed again.

She kicked the rugs off her legs and swung down, dragging her shoes on. 'Morphia,' she said. 'Tell someone, Mary!'

The lanterns were lit on the stairs and Sister MacFarlane went flowing past like a ghost and she followed, keeping close to the wall because the banisters had long since gone for firewood and there was only a rope; she tripped where she always did, on the stair where the stone was chipped.

'A big one,' somebody called, 'sixty-three!'

'Oh my God.'

But they'd known it was coming. This morning the instruments had never stopped tinkling.

The hall of the château was already milling with people and the stretchers were coming in side by side through the great

240

doors where rain blew from the dark. It was the American ambulance unit up from the south: she could hear their voices. The sisters were peering at the field-cards and Matron stood calmly on the big iron weapons chest in the archway: she was tiny and had to see above everyone's head to make any sense of this.

'Nineteen in Surgical, the overflow in Ward Six! Nurse Lovell, please—'

The man screamed and the sound flared among the walls.

'Sister Wilson, give that patient – it's all right, there's someone there now.'

'We ran clean outa dope on the way in, ma'am.'

'I see. Nurse Lovell, please help Sister Tomlinson with severe haemorrhages, Ward Four. And somebody fetch a stiff broom.'

Water was puddling on the flagstones as the orderlies and bearers stood waiting with their loads, the first of them going up the staircase with the rear man raising his end of the poles to keep the stretcher level; the rain on their shoulders glinted in lantern-light and their faces had no expression: they were moving-men, coal-men, carrying furniture, carrying coal, and this they had learned to believe themselves to be, so that their strength shouldn't be undermined by concern for the pain they bore with them wherever they went, the pain in the shape of men.

Across the floor the puddles of mud were gradually reddening. A face passed under the lantern-light, the skin ashen and the lips blue, the eyes staring upwards to the shadows. The whisper went on and on.

'Shoot me for God's sake, I can't stand it no more, shoot me, finish me off.'

Sister Tomlinson turned the red-bordered cards to the light, directing the orderlies. 'Ward Two, and keep his arm in.' Their boots scraped on the heavy stones. 'This one's for me, Ward Four.' The smell of gangrene thickened on the air. 'Surgical, quick as you can. Mary, bring some lavender-bags, would you?'

'Shall I go on up, Sister?' Diana asked.

'Yes, I shan't be long.'

Turning from near the doors she saw the staircase filled with stretchers all the way up, as if they were piled on one another, and a sense of *déjà vu* brushed her thoughts as she crossed the hall and made for the back stairs through the kitchens. At the end of the vaulted gallery they'd already opened up the dispensary and nurses were clamouring for eusol and saline, splints, tourniquets and gauze while the first stretcher was eased past them into Ward Four and Diana followed, her big No. 7 scissors ready to cut the canvas away.

Others came, and others, bringing disorder with them: the doors of the château had swung open as if on to a battlefield and its flotsam had floated in, slowly rising from floor to floor and tiding into the wards until they were littered with mud and boots and filthy uniforms, their legs and sleeves blood-clotted and ripped away, their pockets spilling coins and paybooks and pencils, dog-ends, love-letters, crumpled photographs, their seams crawling with lice.

'Which bed, girlie?'

'The nearest.'

Draw back the blanket from the stretcher and face it as best you can, the green gangrenous stump, the smashed limb with its bones poking under the matted bandages, the twisted spine; forget you felt a moment of hate for these men as they came crowding in to fill your eyes with nightmare, to beg without speech for a mercy far beyond your means; forget your heart then broke for them as it always did and must always do until it could break no more; remember that you asked for this with your young eyes shining and your child-mother's hands eager for hurts to heal, your little cap prim on your head and the cross of the crusader secretly ablaze on your chest; now buckle to and do it, do what you said you would, and do it well.

'Hey Nurse, can you—'

'All right.'

Tetanus arching a back like a drawn bow, the mouth agape in a silent scream and the eyes staring.

Sweat on the stretcher-poles, strong hands slipping.

'I guess this one's—'

'Yes. Cover him, please.'

It was difficult to read the field-cards in the flickering light, easy to make a mistake.

Gunshot wound left humerus.

'Quick, Diana, he's trying to tear his bandage off!'

'All right.'

Severe compound fracture right femur.

'No, Mary – he can't be moved.'

Persistent haemorrhage subclavian artery.

With the disorder, noise came, rising from the stairs and passages into the wards and flowing out again until nowhere in the building was there quiet; pain cried out, claiming that it ruled here; delirium called of the unknown and the unknowable; in the shadows of the screens there sounded the murmur of priests. To this ancient shelter, under cover of night, the war had come whining to lick its wounds.

'Nurse Lovell! Morphia here.'

'All right.'

'You hear that, Alf? There's a revolution gone an' broke out in Russia!'

'Christ, I 'ope nobody gets 'urt.'

Today the first sunshine had come to the windows, and across the floor the shadows of branches moved, tugged by the March wind.

'Hey, Dolly!'

'All right, I'm coming.'

'How long do I have to keep this darn boiler-gauge stuck in my kisser?'

'Open, then.'

'You know somethin'? You have the most sensational blue eyes I've ever seen.'

'Yes, Corporal Quincey, you've told me before.'

'Why sure I did, an' I ain't kidd'n'. They must've poured the sky inside of your head when you were born, then they settled a gold cloud on top an' stood back an' said okay, fellers, this time we break the mould. An' anyway what's this "Corporal Quincey" talk? Can't you ever call me Sam?'

'When you stop calling me "Dolly".'

'Okay, sweetheart, you got a deal. How's my steam comin'?'

'It's a point up.'

'Sure it is. It goes up every time you come down the ward. You know you have the most sensational dimples when you smile like that?'

243

'You know you have the most scandalous reputation in the whole of this hospital?'

'Who me? Wha'd I do?'

'Three of the younger V.A.D.s have made complaints in the past week.'

'Gee-whiz! An' I'm lyin' here helpless in splints! What're they gonna do when I'm back on my feet?'

'That's why they're so worried.'

This morning they had opened some of the windows; the air was sharp and the wind smashed one of the jam-jars of paper flowers but the watery sunshine promised that one day it would be spring. This morning too they had put the screens round the fourth bed from the end.

'Don't give me any more.'

'But it'll help you to sleep.'

'I don't want to sleep. I want to face it, not turn my back on it.'

She put the hypodermic on to the tray. It wouldn't have much effect in any case: when they decided to fight death they fought the morphia as well.

One of the lavender-bags had fallen on to the floor and she picked it up and put it with the others.

'I'm sorry I smell,' he said.

'You don't. It's to keep the flies from bothering you, that's all.' She watched the young contemplative face; his eyes moved to look at the screen again. It was a child's face, beautiful and with the calm that comes at the end of the day; in the shaded light of the screens it had the glow of alabaster, so white was it, so still.

'You've not told her, have you?'

'Betty?'

'Yes.'

'We've told her it's going to take a little time before you're well enough to be moved to England.'

'If I can just hang on,' his blue lips murmured, 'till she's had the baby. I don't want her to get the telegram till after that, or it might stop it being born properly. That's important, see.' Then the eyes were squeezed shut and the blue-veined hands caught at the blanket and the face was no longer calm

244

and no longer a child's and she turned quickly for the hypodermic.

'Get your bullet, did you?'
'Eh? Yes. You want to have a look?'
'I've seen 'em, mate, too bloody often.'
'It was fixed on me arm with a bit o' tape when I come to.
They do that for you, Sister says, when they've pulled the
little bleeder out; souvenir, a lot o' the boys ask for them. There
it is then, look. You're my generous little friend, you are, an'
you're goin' home wi' me 'cause you got me Blighty ticket for
me.'

Behind them the casement began again, the loose panes
rattling in the frame.
'By Christ, we're well off 'ere, George.'
'It's their turn now, the on'y way you can look at it.'
'Spare a thought for the poor buggers though.'
The rattling unnerved them. It sounded like the wind doing
it but they knew it wasn't.
'Mary says I can get up tomorrow.'
'About bloody time.'
'She'd better lock 'erself in a cupboard, an' all. Between you
an' me, George, I'm gettin' that stalky I could screw 'ole in a
fence.'
'You'll have to keep your mind on higher things.'
'I've tried that but it ain't no good. Whatever I think about
I end up wishin' I was screwin' it.'
'Well I reckon it's only natural, I mean whatever they say
against it, it's a natural act.'
'Depends on what you're wishin' you was screwin'.' He
picked up the tin again and began scraping. This one was for
Mum, and when he'd finished the regimental crest he was
going to put 'For Mum' at the bottom, inside a banner with a
fold at each end. The enamel flaked away under his penknife.
'What 'appened to Sidney, then?'
'He's gone with the Beautiful Soldier-boy.'
'Poor ole Sid.'
It was the ward corporal who'd told them, though they'd
heard something much like it when they were still in the line.
One of the M.O.s down near the Vauxcourt salient had been

cutting the uniform off a bad casualty they'd thought was still
alive, when he'd stopped as if he'd been shot. 'God Almighty,'
he said to the orderlies, 'this one's a woman!' It had fair
turned them up. Then the rumour got around, you couldn't
stop it, and some of the Irish boys said they'd seen a young
private going up the line with a draft of reserves, 'a face like
an angel, he had, but fey-looking, not in his mind and would
talk to no one', and the rumour had become a soldier's tale, a
legend; and when you missed a chum of yours after a set-to
with Jerry and asked what had happened to him, someone
would say, 'He's gone with the Beautiful Soldier-boy,' meaning
of course he'd been killed.

The blue paint flaked away. Sharp's Toffee tins were best,
with nice colours and not too much advertisement on them,
gave you a bit of room to express yourself.

'You see what Taffy done on one o' these, George? King an'
Queen, with Windsor Castle be'hind them, sky an' clouds an'
everythin', wonderful it is.'

'He's wasted, then, in the Army.'

'We all are, mate.'

I was with him when he died peacefully.
The notepaper seemed to be floating on the table and she
held the pen away until it steadied again. If you didn't write to
them before you turned in it would never get done at all. There
was no obligation to do it but Matron couldn't cope as it was;
besides which it was something you did for yourself in a way, a
kind of catharsis that allowed you to forget them more easily
and make room for the others in what was left of your heart,
before they too, and in this way, must be forgotten.

*I took him a cup of cocoa just after ten in the evening, and he was
perfectly happy, talking a lot about you. When the crisis came we
didn't even realize it for a moment; he just slipped away as if he were
tired of things and content to go. I sat holding his hand . . .*

Oh God, was it wrong to write things like this? The lies
looked so much worse on paper, making you feel hollow and
deceitful. Put this, then: *Major Neave had been working for thirty-
three hours non-stop from the minute the convoy arrived, and unfortunately
fell asleep across the operating-table before we saw what was happening.
Air entered the incision and subsequently proved fatal.*

246

No, you couldn't put that. Not write at all, then, that was the easiest.

... Until I realized that he had passed willingly into the care of a Healer more powerful and even more loving than we here can ever be.

Leave it at that and sign your name. Don't overdo it or they'll suspect.

The night staff was still noisy on the floor below: a convoy had come in without any warning at all this afternoon, without the usual clinking of the instruments the bombardment made beforehand. The war had just given a sort of casual swipe somewhere and here they were, and here you were, just like old times.

'Diana!'

'What?' Couldn't she even open the door?

She found Mary in the passage with her arms full of pillows. 'I can't stop but I had to tell you – your boy-friend's here!'

'My – you mean Captain Talbot? Aubrey?'

'Yes!' Her eyes widened as she saw Diana's face; then she understood. 'He's not *wounded*, darling – just come to see you. I said you'd go down.'

Even though she was higher, on the stairs, he looked taller than she'd remembered, taller and still invincible, standing quietly against the big doors that had opened to receive so many of the defeated.

'Aubrey?'

They were alone in the shadowy hall and when they came together she just leaned against him and shut her eyes while his arms went round her; there was rain on his trench-coat and she felt how cool it was against her cheek.

'There wasn't time,' he said, shocked by the look of strain he'd glimpsed on her small white face, 'to tell you I was coming.'

'That doesn't matter.' She couldn't move; she wanted to rest for ever in his strength, sleep here, die here. It was over six months since they'd snatched a few hours together at the Field Hospital near Sartelles, and even then it had been more frustrating than anything else: it was a 'mingling' arranged by the authorities, worse than a garden-party. Now her heart raced freely, thumping away. 'Aubrey, how long can you stay?'

'All tomorrow.'

247

She stirred and looked up at him. 'One day?'

'One whole day, right up to midnight.'

'That's wonderful,' she said as gladly as she could. A minute ago he hadn't been here at all and now her hands were in his: wasn't she satisfied? She wanted too much in a war where many didn't even have enough. 'How did you manage it?'

'The Colonel said he'd look the other way.'

She saw now the lines that had come to his face in their absence from each other, and knew that invincibility wasn't offered *gratis* by the gods.

'We'll go in here,' she said, and led him into a dim-lit room that had been a *salle-à-manger* and was now a repository for the furnishings rescued when the Red Cross had taken over. 'The Games Room,' she told him wryly. A space had been cleared in the middle but the ping-pong table stood thick with dust and the dart-boards piled in the hearth were still in their brown-paper wrappings. 'We're well supplied with recreational facilities – if only our feet would stand it.'

'They're driving you too hard.' He was touched to anger by her wan face and the shadows under her eyes.

'No. We drive ourselves, because it's no good stopping; the cart's run away with itself and all we can do is keep ahead of it.' She tugged the yellowing sheets of newspaper from a sofa so that they could sit down. 'Is Julian all right?'

'Fit as anything and sends you his fondest love.'

Dust from the newspapers floated silver below the one lamp that had a bulb in it. A bronze statue stared idly at the pile of dart-boards.

'I couldn't write to you earlier,' she said with sudden urgency, 'I mean when they raided the—'

'Don't worry.'

'But you must have thought I'd forgotten you.'

'No. I thought you'd been killed.'

'Well, that was worse.'

'Only a little.'

'We were handling five hundred patients when the planes came.' She felt for his hand again.

'It must have been hell on earth.'

'Yes.' She began shivering and sat very still so that the feeling would go. She had written to Lady Eleanor a week later: *It was the first time I have ever been made to know that sanity is something you can lose if you don't hang on to it with all your might. The danger itself was nothing; while the bombs were falling we felt totally immune, divinely protected from the sky, but knowing how vulnerable our patients were. This made the explosions seem nothing to do with us – the staff – since they couldn't harm us, so they became a series of sudden crises developing like a fever through the camp, killing men we thought we'd saved and wounding men we thought we'd healed. It was an extension of despair, the madness I came close to experiencing at first hand on that day. I thought – but not in so many words – 'Bring these men to us and we'll try to make them whole or at least see that they die in relative decency, but oh God, don't bring the war here to hound them down as if butchery in battle wasn't enough for them to deal with.'*

Later she had thought it strange that it had been her attitude – mere moral indignation, a sense of injustice – that had nearly unhinged her mind, rather than the horror that had assaulted her senses wherever she turned, the crowding host of images that even Dante had never dared imagine: a boy threshing as his bed burned around him; a dressing-pail hurled into the air and scattering amputated hands; a man swaying on his feet against the screens they had put round him an hour before when he had died in peace.

'You mustn't think about it,' Aubrey said.

'No.' The sound of his calm voice made the fit of shivering die away. 'I wrote to your mother soon afterwards. I had to tell someone.'

'You write to her quite often. She loves having your letters.'

'I send cheerful ones too.' She managed to smile. 'I've adopted her, you see. Or it's the other way round.'

'Julian's told me your own people still seem to think you should have stayed at home.' 'Damn it all,' Julian had said once, as near to anger as Aubrey had ever seen him, 'anyone would think she'd run off with the butcher's boy! The trouble is, she never tells them how uncomfortable things are out here – from what I can gather she only writes to them about the cathedrals she's seen on her day off!'

'I don't expect them to understand,' she said with a forced shrug. 'There's no war, in England.'

'Then we'll just thank the Lord for that.'

'Oh, I do! I'm glad for them, truly. But it's odd to find

249

yourself writing dutiful letters to a couple of strangers who once meant everything to you. But I don't want to talk about that; I don't want to talk about anything.' She was trying to see his face, to accept the little changes in it and commit them to memory; but the dim bulb threw shadow and the outline of his tilted head was uncertain, beginning to float like the writing pad had floated up in her room not long ago; and as his arm drew her against him she closed her eyes and curled her feet up on the sofa. 'I don't quite believe you're here, Aubrey,' she murmured, 'not quite yet.'

'I've always been here.'

'And you'll never go.'

He answered but she didn't hear the words, only his quiet voice among the shadows as sleep came drifting over her.

In the last three years the township of Mauraine had been shelled a dozen times and troops were no longer billeted there; after each bombardment more people had left for good, and now the half-ruined streets served only the few hundred who were too old or too obstinate to move away, or who still believed that at some time before the last building slid to swell the rubble this war would end.

Meat was scarce, the *patron* said, his shoulders lifting to his ears; but there was wine, and if they would have a little patience ...

They sat alone the whole of the evening, assuring him they didn't in the least miss the *ambience*, the *gaieté*, that must certainly have brought fame to the Auberge de la Poste in the golden days before the *catastrophe*. Also they were delighted there was no electricity, since candlelight was more kindly and had an *ambience* all its own, he must agree.

They'd walked in the bleak March wind during the afternoon, exploring the grounds of the château and finding a lake with fish in it, so there was colour in her face and a light in her eyes that she could feel was there after so long an absence. They were both hungry, but didn't really know what they were eating.

'They were wonderful to me, Aubrey – I just turned up without even telephoning and your mother sat me straight down to dine with them as if I'd been expected for weeks.

There'd been a bust-up at home and I couldn't face the rest of my leave in that sort of atmosphere, and then I was suddenly walking through the gates at Ashbourne as if there were nowhere else to go.' In a moment she said: 'There wasn't, really. I went because part of you was there. We talked about you and Pam showed me the cups you got for tennis and fencing, and the sailor-doll she keeps in her room – you won it for her at a coconut-shy—'

'Good Lord', he smiled wistfully, 'I'd forgotten that. It was her tenth birthday and we all went to Richmond Fair, and Vic got into trouble because – well it doesn't matter. Tell me about your—'

'We didn't talk very much,' she said, 'about Vic.'

He looked down. 'He's rather a lone wolf.'

'Yes?' She had seen the hardness in his eyes. 'Julian used a different metaphor, once; he said Vic was a thorn in your side.'

'Rather the reverse.'

'I can't believe that.'

Tersely he said: 'My brother can.'

'I know I'm trespassing, Aubrey—'

'No—'

'But there's so little time and so much I want to know about you and – and the things important to you, so that they can be important to me.'

He took the wine and poured a little into her glass though it wasn't empty, circumspectly turning the bottle so that a drip shouldn't form; watching him she realized that it wasn't the war alone that had brought these lines to his face: in some of Julian's letters there'd been hints of trouble between the Talbot brothers.

'Vic would be better off without me.' He'd never talked to anyone about this, not even Pam. 'But he needs my help, just as all those in my command need it, just as I need theirs. But the more I try to help him the more it saps his independence. So he's driven to do wild things, the result of which is that he needs my help more than ever. It's a vicious circle. The thing is, I've always been a bit more successful than he has.' His eyebrow was lifted cynically. 'Too many cups for tennis ... But that's only because I've never made an effort to do well, whereas he goes bashing his head at things the whole time.

251

That's why he's still a junior sub – the people higher up can't trust him with command, with responsibility; and that bedevils him too, so off he goes again trying to win the war all on his own.' He picked up his glass and drank. 'Well it can't go on for ever.'

'And if you left him to his own devices,' she said helplessly 'you think he'd find more stability?'

'Yes. But how can I take the risk?'

'You'd be watching a child crawling towards a fire, and not lifting a finger to stop it.'

'That's it. On two occasions he'd have got killed if I hadn't been there. The trouble is, he's involving other people now. Becoming a danger to everyone.'

To people like Freddie, a man whose excellence was higher than his rank and whose rank exposed him to the stupidity of a headstrong subaltern.

He'd talked to Freddie first, and to the men who'd been with him, so as to get hold of the facts. Then he went back to Vic, asking him outright:

'You mean to go through with these charges against Sergeant Kemp?'

'They're true, aren't they?' He'd gone alone to the platoon dugout, finding the dregs in a bottle of cheap wine and sitting with it, hunched near a candle that he must have lit for company, because it wasn't yet dark. 'Since when does an N.C.O. strike an officer and get off scot-free?'

'You know damned well he did it to save your skin – and for that you're going to break him. Haven't you—'

'Christ, it's my own skin and I can—'

'*Don't interrupt.*' The note of icy contempt brought Vic's head up and the hate leapt to his dark eyes and burned like sudden fever. 'Get up,' Aubrey told him. 'Get on your feet.' Their shadows moved against the fissured wall as they stood facing each other. 'D'you know why Freddie joined the Army, long before he needed to, a married man with a decent home and a secure position and no fears for the future? A man who'd served our family since he was no older than you are now? It was to look after us. To take whatever chance he could of seeing that you and I got through this war in one piece, because he felt he owed that much to the people who'd looked after him in

252

their turn. By God that's service for you! And you want to throw him into a court martial because he did precisely what he'd set his mind on doing – and saved your stupid little neck when there was no one else around who could help you. He saved your *life*. You know you'd have been dead by now if it weren't for him? Lying out there riddled with bullets?'

The flood-water from the trench was chill round his ankles and something moved against them, bumping; a rat, drowned or still drowning. He was absurdly reminded that he had no shoes on still.

'There was a chance—'

'There was *no* chance! I believe Freddie and I believe his men. Courageous men, the lot of them, with enough sense to make their way back and re-equip and fight again instead of uselessly throwing their lives away in front of the guns, as you wanted them to do, as you *ordered* them to do.'

'It was an order, wasn't it?' Vic began shivering as if the fever in his eyes were spreading to the whole of his body. 'Or have you drawn up some new rules since you got your captaincy? The lower ranks can choose what they'll do when they get an order – that right?'

'Yes,' said Aubrey, 'yes. When the order's from someone like you. You're not fit mentally or physically to take men into action. You pestered the medical board till they sent you out here just to get rid of you and the minute you're back in the battalion you're playing the death-or-glory game harder than ever to make up for lost time. If you're trying to kill yourself that's your own affair but you're not going to take the men in my company with you. And you're not going to press this charge against Sergeant Kemp because apart from anything else you won't make it stick.'

'There were witnesses!'

'Witnesses? Those men? You think they'll speak up for a bloody little subaltern against the man who saved their lives by knocking him down? You've got no witnesses.'

'There's my word, then.' He was backing away as if physically trapped, his head lowered and his eyes restless for escape; and Aubrey knew that nothing of what he'd been saying had made any impression; the bruise on this boy's face, already swelling and darkening under the skin, was slight compared with the hurt done to his pride. If he were allowed to bring Freddie to a court martial it would be for vengeance, not justice. 'There's my word as an officer. It was true, what happened! I don't have to lie!'

'Then there'll be my word too.' He spoke so quietly that his brother lifted his head to listen, his back pressed to the clay where the rainwater seeped in the candlelight. 'And since you set such store by the sanctity of rank, I'll remind you that my word will carry more weight than yours. I shall report that the least competent and the least reliable of my officers, his judgement grievously impaired as a result of serious wounds from which he is not yet recovered, has for personal reasons accused an experienced N.C.O. of an act directly responsible for the saving of men in my command whose lives I value highly.'

It was a moment before Vic answered, his face loose with surprise.

'You'd say that? You'd give evidence against me?'

'Oh yes.' He couldn't quite understand the slow bewilderment in his brother's eyes; perhaps Vic was aware that something he'd always rejected was being taken away, and that it was too late now to consider that it might have been of value. 'I would make it my duty to see that you were thrown out of the battalion and out of the Army.' He said as he turned away: 'You've never wanted me as a friend, Vic. If you want me as an enemy then God help you.'

Lord Rokesley had shown good sense, limping with him along the communication-trench stinking of ether: his leg had caught some shrapnel but he'd declined to count himself a casualty. 'There's nothing in writing yet, old boy, but what d'you expect me to do when an N.C.O. reports to me on a list of charges like that?'

'Turn a deaf ear.'

With a short laugh – 'My word, I must say I like your style of running things. Saves a frightful lot of effort for everyone. But what happens if your young brother decides to insist?'

'Boot him out.'

'Fair enough, I'll boot him back to you. Your own responsibility. Sort of personal thing, this, is it?'

'Yes. Nothing to do with the Army.'

'Then thank the Lord there's something going on out here

254

that's nothing to do with the Army. Incidentally you're going to look rather well in despatches for this truce you organized – inspired act of humanity and all that; the Colonel's quite pleased; I heard him telling the Adj – "Whenever there's only one thing to do in a situation, Talbot's the only man who can see what it bloody well is."'

'Or whenever there's a mess to clear up, there's me with the dustpan and brush. You can't put that in despatches.'

The three candles were burning low and on the table Diana put her hand over his.

'I wish I could help,' she said.

'It'll work itself out.'

'Families are odd, aren't they? People you love can grow into strangers. You don't know your own brother any more, and I don't know my parents. Is it the war?'

'I don't think so. I think the war only speeds things up, things that would have happened anyway, given time.' Along the shelves of the dresser the Sèvres dishes had begun vibrating; somewhere east, where he'd be going back tomorrow, the 'evening hate' had started up. 'There's the other side too, Diana.' He turned his hand so that hers was in his own. 'Strangers can grow into people you love. We haven't said it yet, but we know it's true for both of us.' Time was passing and their 'one whole day' was almost over, and they'd talked about so many things that hadn't been important. 'I want to say it now, that I love you.'

She was very still and the blue of her eyes clouded swiftly, becoming dark; and suddenly time had come to a stop and he knew he could be wrong and that it needn't be true for both of them just because it was true for him.

'I love you,' she said; and he felt the tremor in her hand as the first chime of nine sounded from the clock near the doors. Her face had paled and he said:

'Time doesn't matter any more.'

'No. From now on.'

They lay watching the glow of light cross and recross the ceiling; from the other side of the street French voices called to each other. It sounded as if they were loading a cart; their lanterns moved about.

The big white jug vibrated again on the wash-stand.

'Did you tell him the room was for the night?'

'Yes.'

'What will he think when we leave so soon?'

'He's a Frenchman. *C'est la guerre, c'est la vie, c'est l'amour.*'

The ceiling was ringed with plaster-relief, a rondel of roses; a huge crack zig-zagged across it like the one in the dining-room below. While they had been making love they'd heard the white jug vibrating to the distant guns, so that there'd seemed something defiant in their passion as if this was their answer to the dark out there where men were dying; but she didn't want to think of it in those terms. They had made love not as two unimportant members of a mad species whose lusts killed and created with the same brute indifference but purely as lovers, each of supreme importance to the other and together more important than the whole wide world that would have to wait for them while they played here naked for the sake of love itself, drowning in the depths of an intimacy she'd never believed possible.

'I was a clothes-horse,' she murmured.

'A what?' She heard laughter in his voice.

'Before tonight my body was just something to carry my mind about with from place to place, a thing to hang clothes on according to the weather.' She stretched her length against his fine lean nakedness, luxuriating. 'Now it's burning with a heat I can hardly bear. I shall feel things, from now on, when I touch them; my fingers were blind before. I'm burning and streaming and flowing and alive at last and in love, and even the wine's bemusing me now, I can feel its dreaminess – we had quite a lot, didn't we, or it was quite a lot for me, but it was you I was drinking, and if you hadn't brought me up here to this paradise with a cracked ceiling I'd have gone away stone-cold sober. Don't mind what I'm saying, and don't laugh, or only tenderly because you love me; I'm not perfectly sure what I'm saying but I know I mean it, every word, is that possible?'

'Glorious little Diana.'

'Yes, that's me now, full of the glory you gave me. Don't ever ask for it back, or I'd die.'

'You'll never die.'

256

She raised herself with a sudden fierce movement and leaned over him, her small breasts jutting and her head thrown back, her eyes brilliant in the glow of the lanterns outside as she stared at him for a moment in silence; and in the silence the waterjug trembled on the other side of the room.

'Nor you, Aubrey. Neither of us. We refuse that. We refuse.'

They had been here only a few minutes, standing in the entrance of the Auberge de la Poste watching the work going on across the street. The house over there, the *patron* had told them, was about to collapse, and the people were saving what they could of the furniture.

The lights of the Ford ambulance came dipping over the cobbles; it was different from the one that had brought them here. The driver called down from the cab:

'Luke said to pick y'up around eleven, that right?'

He put them into the back and sometimes shouted to them as they bumped across flooded potholes, taking the minor road to the château; the only light was from the backwash of the headlamps. Neither felt like talking: in the room at the Auberge everything had been said; but to sit in silence would make it seem they were waiting only for time to pass, hurrying them to their leave-taking.

'Are you still near Vauxcourt?'

'North of there now. We've been holding for the Canadians.'

She sat with her head on his shoulder. Through the open hatch and the windscreen they could see the headlamps flooding whitely across the trees.

'What's your matron like? A fire-eater?' She never said much in her letters about the hospital.

'Oh no. A wonderful little Scotswoman. It was she who turned the light off for us last night, I think. This morning she asked me if I'd slept well, and I said yes thank you – without batting an eyelid – and then she said was I sure I hadn't got a stiff neck . . .'

The Ford bounced over flooded ruts.

'You ever bin bareback ridin'?' the driver called through the hatch. 'Guess this ain't much diff'rent!'

Aubrey held her more tightly.

'How did Moira take it?' he asked.

'Moira?'

'When she heard about Nigel.'

She twisted to look at him. 'Was Nigel killed?'

'Surely she must have told you? I wrote to her the same night.'

Diana was silent for a moment and he could feel the tenseness in her hand. 'It can't be true,' she said slowly.

He watched her face, puzzled. She'd only met Nigel twice in her life, to his knowledge: at Ashbourne on his first leave, and at one of the 'minglings' at the field hospital when Nigel had been to see Moira.

'When did it happen?' she asked.

'Months ago. Not long before Christmas.'

She was quiet again and he didn't disturb her thoughts. At last she said: 'Aubrey, have you ever heard of the "Beautiful Soldier-boy"?'

'Yes, I have.' The legend was cherished especially by his own battalion, since reports from the men of neighbouring units – particularly the Irish Guards – had said that on his way to the line the 'Soldier-boy' had been asking how to reach the 3rd Duke of Lancaster's position; and it was Maj. Westlake, one of their own M.O.s, who had made his incredible discovery a few days later, and although it was hushed up immediately the rumours had taken hold. Diana said gravely:

'Moira didn't tell me Nigel had died. But I think now that she got your letter. It was just after the raid on our camp, and most of us were still feeling the shock; I thought that was all that was wrong with Moira – she couldn't speak to anyone, and sometimes left her room at night to wander about. I can't quite describe it – you know how terribly intense she used to be when she was with Nigel—'

'Yes—'

'Well she went sort of fey, at this time, as if she didn't know us any more. Matron offered her leave, but she said she didn't want any, so it was made an order: two weeks' home leave on special grounds. I tried to help her to pack, that night, but she wouldn't let me. The next day she was missing.' She stared at him in the restless light.

'Oh, my God . . .'

She was holding his hand very tightly. 'We never saw her

again. She was posted as missing on active service. But how can a thing like that be true, Aubrey?'

With a feeling of awe he said: 'It could be true of someone like Moira.' He remembered her that night at Ashbourne, not beautiful but flamboyant, smouldering with an almost blatant sensuality and totally absorbed in Nigel, her heavy-lidded eyes consuming him.

'Yes,' Diana said in a moment, 'I could believe it of Moira.'

They sat without speaking again until the heights of the château reared above the skyline. Beyond them the cloud-layers were lit by the curdled colours of explosions, and even here in the bumping confines of the ambulance they could feel the pulsing of the guns.

I don't understand, Diana thought. Day after day when they heard the guns they knew there were legs being blown off and eyes blinded, not far away across the tender green of the corn, and knew that men and half-men would soon be brought to them for the little that could be done to mend what the war had smashed. The inevitability of it sometimes frightened her: you knew that when you set up another bed, the clean white sheets ironed and smelling of soap, there would soon be a man in it or the still-living remains of a man; and this was accepted as normal: fit young males of the most intelligent species on earth, their loins rich with the seed of immortality, were being thrown like vermin on to a burning rubbish heap a hundred thousand at a time. Maj. Neave, a gifted man and dedicated to his vocation, had once betrayed the sense of hopelessness that had come to undermine the very spirit of his work. 'Best we can do,' he'd said as a boy was lifted from the theatre-table. 'It won't be a pretty scar but who cares? As long as he can carry a rifle again, that's all they want.' Sometimes she'd lain awake too weary for sleep, asking herself why someone didn't do any-thing about this never-ending war; then she'd realized that only those in high position and with great power could bring an end, and that they were using all their force to keep it going.

This was the norm, the accepted way of life on earth. Don't question it or you'll be taken for an idiot.

The château was quiet and few windows were lit; tonight there had been no convoy in. Aubrey fetched his overnight kit from the 'Games Room' and came out to the crumbling steps where she was waiting. He was to pick up a Signals transport at the crossroads a mile away. They kissed and she felt the courage surging back into her just for this long moment; then he looked at her steadily, trying to think of something he could say that would be lasting; but there was no time left.

The clouds flickered in the east.

'Till soon,' he said and went quickly away.

XIII

'I need a hundred thousand men,' said the General.

He turned and stood with his back to them, his glassy blue eyes gazing from the window across Whitehall utterly without expression. He was well known for this tactic: the blunt presentation of his back, indicating that there was no argument to which he was prepared to listen, had so often been successful in persuading his antagonists that their guns were hopelessly spiked.

'You've already made that clear,' said the Minister. Thin, urbane, quietly spoken, he sat at the polished desk studying his perfect finger-nails. It was said of him that his sole function, under the personal eye of Lloyd-George, was to keep the military in its place; and his long acquaintance with the General had taught him that simple provocation was all that was necessary to make him turn round again. 'The only question is whether you should have them.'

The strained atmosphere made the silence seem longer than in fact it was. One could almost feel a quiver in the air, and Charles Sadler was reminded of a fight he had once seen in India between a mongoose and a cobra.

The General was facing them.

'Do you want victory?'

'We do. We question only your means of getting it.'

Charles passed a hand over the back of his head uneasily. He wasn't used to hearing major decisions – terrible and far-reaching decisions like this one – in their making. He had been brought in to attend this conference merely as a bystander, the representative of the Bureau of Propaganda sent here not to confer but to 'explore new areas in which the public may be informed without needless loss to morale'. In other words, as William had said over their brandy last night, 'to find out how to tell them even bigger bloody lies so that they won't believe the casualty-lists when they see them'. Charles never denied the truth in much of what William said about his work for the

Bureau, and their friendship was old enough to withstand their differences; but he went less often through the wicket-gate in the orchard to talk to William, and told himself that it was because his work kept him late – which was true enough.

'The Americans . . .' murmured the First Secretary, sensing a way of supporting the Minister but not quite sure how best to pursue it.

'The Americans,' said the General icily, 'have less than eighty thousand men in France at this moment – nine months after their entry into the war; and their contribution in battle has so far been precisely nil, which puts in its rightful place the hysterical relief that greeted the arrival of their First Division under arms. If I am obliged to wait for action on the part of reinforcements such as these I see no point in the continuance of hostilities at all!'

The Minister looked about him, deliberately avoiding the immaculately uniformed figure with its display of ribbons. 'Gentlemen,' he said calmly, 'we should get certain facts into perspective, I think. After the crippling and – it is claimed by some – the unjustified losses of last year, the Allied fortunes reached their lowest extreme at the beginning of this one. Since the start of the German submarine blockade we have lost over four million tons of merchant shipping and comparable vital supplies. The military collapse of Russia will shortly release approximately a million German troops for the Western Front. The French offensives have been crushed with such effect that mutiny has broken out on a substantial scale. The whole of what we call the civilized world is horrified by the futile loss of manhood at this moment taking place in that hellish *abattoir* across the Channel.' He moved a pencil on the desk, aligning it carefully with the grain of the veneer. 'I don't seek to dramatize. The drama is only too manifest. There is of course a ray of light in all this darkness, and a very bright one. My personal relief at the entry of America into this war is rather more practical than hysterical, and my patience is more durable than the General's, since he is a man of action and I am not. The United States army was a small one at the time when they broke off diplomatic relations with Germany, and they were not prepared for war. Their country is so large that they are faced with a problem even in assembling their forces at their own ports of embarkation, and the battle-ground is three thousand miles distant across an ocean infested with enemy submarines. Further, I consider General Pershing not unreasonable in his wish to form an independent American army for deployment in the field, rather than to place his troops under foreign leadership—' his eyes flicked upwards and down again – 'that has squandered millions of lives for the possession of a few miles of uninhabitable mud.'

His urbanity remained intact on the surface but he reached rather quickly for the file of papers and his tone was suddenly chill. 'The casualty figures for the battle of Passchendaele are still coming in and to date they stand at two hundred and forty thousand for a period of three weeks. In short I would support with all my powers the proposal of a holding action designed to safeguard our troops until the Americans are ready for their offensive, so that we can offer them the assistance of men still fit to fight instead of the bloodied remnant of an army slaughtered out of hand.' He dropped the file back and looked up. 'If you need a further hundred thousand men, General, in order to furnish the launching of what I would consider to be a precipitate campaign, please know that I shall hope to persuade the Prime Minister that every useful barrier should be placed in your path.'

Air must have got into the central-heating pipes. They all sat and listened to it bubbling, and no one looked at the General.

'I doubt,' he said with the air of a man flicking down the trump, 'if the King would support your views.'

That he was *persona grata* at the Palace was common knowledge, and his campaigns in their planning-stage on the sand-table were probably impressive.

'My admiration for His Majesty,' the Minister said, glancing across his finger-nails, 'is in great part due to his high regard for the constitution of the monarchy, by whose terms he is obliged to choose ministers to advise him.'

It was at this moment that there came down on Charles Sadler, propped on his chair in a quiet corner of the room, a sense of depression so overwhelming that he thought he was going to faint. It was nothing to do with his malaria, he knew at once. It was as if an attack, long-expected but so sudden as to find him unprepared, had been made on him by all the uncertainties and miseries and self-recrimination that had been steadily gathering their forces against him during more than three years of war: the disloyalty of his son in refusing to honour the family name and take up arms; the bitter hostility of his wife whose pride was as deeply injured and who blamed him for his weakness in 'condoning cowardice'; the stigma of his own inadequacy, 'physically unfit for military service of an active nature'; and the hypocrisy of his work, for which his most valued friend showed unconcealed contempt.

'. . . An undertaking by the High Command . . .' the First Secretary was saying; then they were all turning their heads as his chair scraped back and he tried to find the door – 'I do apologize . . .' It was suddenly opened for him – 'Some fresh air,' somebody said, and another voice murmured in solicitous explanation, 'Malaria, you know . . .' Then he was in the damp November street, walking nowhere but letting his feet take him on while his demons jostled in his head for the privilege of being the first to damn him now that they had him alone.

Is it the only work you can do? Louise asked him for the hundredth time. *Don't you see how it leaves you open to ridicule?*

They wouldn't let him go. *We realize your difficulty*, said the Bureau *but it's purely personal and therefore – if you'll forgive me – unimportant. Is your country to lose the services of someone with your high qualifications just because your pride is indirectly hurt? People are making bigger sacrifices than that, you know!*

A colonelcy to keep him content. His task ennobled by self-sacrifice.

A darting news-boy spun him half-round and he nearly fell. *'Bolsheviks seize power in Russia!'*

In Trafalgar Square where the Column leaned upwards against the fog the people who passed him loomed and faded through the gloom, their faces winter-pinched and their dark clothes merging with the coming of the night. These streets, once bright with lamps, were now black with widows.

'Brandy,' he said. His elbow was throbbing: he must have bumped against the door, coming in. But his head was already clearing before he cupped the fuming glass in his hands and lifted it. If the need was for a hundred thousand men to be herded into those darkly-riding ships for the slaughter-house, each man with a name and a home and the hope of life still burning strongly in him, how could the decision of life or death on such a scale be argued at a polished table by so few of their fellows, in a room where the dust was daily flicked away so as not to offend, in a place so removed from the reeking wastes where those hundred thousand must carry their hope of life like a candle in a gale, their trust still high in those who had sent them there?

Because, simply enough, the decision had to be made; therefore someone must make it. The war must be furnished with its unending needs, its survival taking precedence over all other things; dragging its bloodied limbs in circles, a creature whose vastness alone made it sacred to man, it must be fed or it would die; and that would be unthinkable.

'Hear the news did you, Colonel? The Bolshies are on top in Russia. What's that goin' to mean?'

'It means the war won't stop.' He pushed his empty glass across the bar.

'Same again, sir? I reckon you're right; nothin' won't stop it now. It's got a hold, as you might say.'

'We don't want it to stop. We don't think enough.'

'Well I don't know as I'd go as far as to say that.' The bubbles winked in the measure. 'Suit me all right if they called it off tomorrow, got no 'opes of any coal for the fire in 'ere this Christmas an' 'ow long is it since we tasted a bit o' butter, eh?' His small bright eyes passed across the face of his customer and turned quickly away. 'O' course that's not the important thing, I realize, but if I can't provide what—'

'No. That's not important.'

Nothing was, now. Importance of any kind had lost its meaning at last. Even the decision they were making up there in that dustless and polished room would be wrong whichever way it went: the argument behind those careful words had not been why a hundred thousand men should go to war, but when. It was asked only whether they should die in vain, not whether they should die at all.

There was only tea at the mobile canteen and the buffet was on the east-bound platform, otherwise she wouldn't have seen him.

'Hugh!'

As he turned she thought for an instant that she'd made a mistake: his eyes seemed not to know her. Steam gushed suddenly from an engine, deafening them, and she could see only his lips moving. When the roaring stopped he smiled and said again:

'Hello, Pam.'

'Where are you going?'

'Dover.'

'What's happened?'

'Nothing.'

The line of coaches began crawling and she asked: 'Is this your train?'

'No.' The wind tunnelling through the station blew his fair hair about and his fingers raked at it as if the attempt at neatness might please her, taking some of the hurt away. 'I would have tried to see you,' he said, 'but I didn't know—'

'It doesn't matter.' She took his arm. 'For God's sake come and eat some buns while I'm swallowing hot Bovril.' The whole convoy had been waiting nearly three hours and she was frozen but at least that was better than being half starved; she could have wept at the thinness of his arm as she pulled him towards the buffet. He'd never had much flesh on him but in the month since she'd last seen him his face had become actually gaunt and she was already terrified that he was TB, knowing that one of his uncles had died that way. 'Do you ever have mealtimes at that school or is it nothing but bloody lessons?'

He asked for coffee and for her sake took a sandwich: two slices of unbuttered government bread peeling away from a scrap of tinned meat.

'Well, look at this!' he said. The waitress had left a lump of sugar in his saucer.

'She likes your blue eyes – they're more effective than a uniform.' He looked down, dropping the sugar into the coffee. He never responded when she said things like that; of course a young lady ought not to say them but in actual fact she wasn't a young lady but a sweaty old ambulance driver and if Hugh wanted to feel embarrassed that was his look-out.

'I would have tried to see you,' he said, 'but—'

'I told you it doesn't matter.' She shoved her nose into the mug of Bovril.

'It matters to me. I didn't know I'd be going back so soon, and this time I wouldn't have been much company – you can see that for yourself.'

'Was there a shindy?' She knew that Louise vented her spite on him whenever he spent a week-end at Carisbrooke: she'd seen him like this before, quiet and bruised and withdrawn, and it broke her heart but there wasn't anything she could do about it because he'd run a mile from any show of sympathy.

'More than a shindy,' he smiled, 'this time.'

'Why do you make yourself go there, Hugh? You don't get much fun out of it.'

He stirred his coffee, his mouth pensive. 'It's not been easy for them since I blotted my copybook, and I decided it might help them if they could lash out at somebody else instead of each other; and my qualifications as kicking-boy are quite impressive.'

'Hasn't it struck you that you could be just making things worse? If you stopped seeing them, they'd have a chance of—' She broke off but it was too late.

'Forgetting me, yes. I wouldn't mind that.' He pushed the cracked plate carefully away, the sandwich half eaten. 'It's only the house where I happened to be born and I didn't bring it much joy.' His smile was hesitant – 'Ashbourne was where I really lived, you know that.'

She nodded, unable to speak for a moment. There was a limit to the things she could say to Hugh, a line that she most wanted to cross when it was least safe, when a word of affection would come out dolled up like an unsolicited gift that he'd accept from kindness but want to refuse; and that would be the end. The little she had of Hugh she wanted to keep, if it was only the privilege of dragging him into a station buffet and talking to him while he picked at a fly-blown sandwich just to please her.

'But you never go there now,' she said. He had a way of not answering that never seemed boorish: a sudden direct glance that respected you for knowing the answer already and for not wanting to hear it made clumsy by words. Aubrey had told her: 'He says he'd rather lose friends than embarrass them.' That was why he didn't go to Ashbourne any more, even when her brothers came home on leave.

He was looking up at the clock and she asked:

'What time's your train?'

'I don't know.'

'You don't—'

'I just had to get away, and Dover's the only place I know.'

'Will you ever go home again? I mean to Carisbrooke.'

'I shouldn't think so.'

Which meant, she thought dully, that she wouldn't see him again. He only came to London to 'help' Charles and Louise, sometimes meeting her for a meal before he caught the night train to the coast. As a duty, probably, to 'keep in touch' since they'd known each other nearly all their lives; or she reminded him of Ashbourne, the place where he'd 'really lived'. One had one's uses.

'It must have been a bad shindy, then.'

'Not quite that. No one did much shouting this time.' There was never of course any shouting at Carisbrooke: 'shindy' was a typical Pam expression and he assumed she knew his parents well enough to picture the kind of scene they staged when they couldn't any longer stand the silences and the over-polite closing of doors. He was used to them by now but they still left him with his nerves on edge for a week afterwards.

Perhaps this time he really wouldn't go to see them again, though he'd made this decision – and revoked it – once before, when he'd been to tell them the result of the Tribunal and been shocked to see how desperately they'd counted on his being pushed into the army. The Tribunals were assembled from a hotchpotch of local dignitaries as willing as anyone else to enjoy the abuse of minor power, and a conscript had to make his case against blind prejudice; the few who followed right through in their refusal to support the war found themselves stone-breaking on Dartmoor, and cases of death by privation and brutality in His Majesty's prisons had been the subject of official enquiry.

'You don't ask for total exemption, Sadler?'

'No, sir.'

The place had once been a gymnasium; the panel sat below a filthy skylight where dead leaves shut out the afterglow of the sun. A few of the people along the public benches seemed to be reporters, their notepads self-consciously in evidence.

'Is that because you've heard that partial exemption is relatively easier to obtain?' He had the unhappy look of a man convinced that he alone lived honestly in a wicked world.

'Am I to state my own case, or is it to be made from random assumptions?'

There was a distinct 'Coo!' from one of the reporters and his pencil began jigging over the pad. At the Tribunal bench a greying parson rubbed his glasses and took another look at the appellant.

'I would strongly advise you to watch your words. You appreciate, do you, that if this case goes against you there are those empowered to have you shot?'

'Illegally, yes, but not empowered by Parliament.' It was too obvious a threat in any case. Asquith had come down heavily on the report earlier this year that seventeen conscientious objectors had been forced into non-combatant service and handed to the army in France 'for shooting in the event of refusing military orders'.

'Why is your arm in a sling, young man?' This was a woman, plump and with small restless hands constantly straying over papers that were probably irrelevant. Hugh thought she'd spoken up to remind the other members – all of them men – that minority had its voice.

'I was in a burning house, madam, two days ago.'

'You were rescued by the firemen?'

'No. I went inside some time before they came.'

'For what reason?'

'There were children in there and we wanted to get them out.'

'Whom do you mean by "we"?'

'Two soldiers and myself. We were passing in the street, during a Zeppelin raid.'

The parson asked quickly: 'Was this in Westmore Road?'

'Yes.'

'I saw the report,' said the chairman. 'The two soldiers did valiant work before the firemen arrived on the scene. There was no mention of a civilian, in my own paper.'

'There wouldn't be, of course,' Hugh said.

'So we are to take your word for it that you were there, and displayed the courage of a soldier? You hope to persuade us that your case merits our sympathy?'

'It can't affect my case in the least. The lady asked me why I'm wearing a sling and I answered her.'

The captain with Provost badges leaned forward.

'Would you in any event claim that you possess the courage of a soldier in uniform?'

'With respect, Captain, the military representative isn't entitled to question me.' It wouldn't make him any more popular but it was worth reminding them that civilians took precedence over the military. The reporters were scribbling again.

No one seemed to know what to say next. The authority vested in them didn't magically endow them with any ability in cross-examination; these were just ordinary people thrust into a situation that really required trained minds if there were any justice to be done.

The plump little woman had been watching him beadily from under her feathered hat, and now braved the silence.

'What exactly *is* your case?'

It was the first intelligent question and Hugh was almost taken by surprise. 'Thank you, madam. My case is that I hold a teaching degree, that I am in fact occupied in teaching children at a state-recognized school and that I should be allowed to continue my work, which is ruled by the Pelham Committee as being of national importance.'

'Oh, come now!' The chairman's sculpted and rather patriarchal head was lifted impatiently. 'The children of this country are doing work of national importance themselves! In the fields, on the farms, in the shell-factories – I can assure you they're far too busy helping us to win this war to let you try teaching them arithmetic!' He held himself a little to his left, in the direction of the public benches. They were mostly women who sat there, nearly half of them in mourning; they had come here to console themselves that there was still justice in the land, that these smarmy little artful dodgers had another think coming if they thought they could stay safe at home while their own menfolk were out there across the sea giving their lives. But the chairman was aware more of the reporters as he said with slow solemnity: 'We must never forget that in the hour of this nation's greatest need, when our very lives depended upon the constant supply of guns for our gallant army and food for those at home, our children came forward, their small hands eager to share our heavy burden and to safeguard their precious heritage.' His noble head swung towards Hugh and the tone sharpened. 'And this feeble youth would sit them at a desk and teach them arithmetic – if we let him! Whose is the work of "national importance"? His, or theirs?'

'*Theirs!*' called a woman in black and the public benches were at once astir. 'Put 'im in the Army an' make 'im fight!'

A man beside her pulled her down. The chairman hit the desk with a ruler and the constable at the doors lumbered forward.

Hugh put his hand on the back of the chair that was placed to show where the appellant should stand. His stomach was turning and he could feel the blood leaving his face; the feeling wasn't unfamiliar and he tried to overcome it, as he always tried. He had felt it throughout his childhood in moments of despair, and in the crowds near Parliament that night when the people had cried out for a war. It was fear but not – here and now – the fear of losing his case; he knew quite well that he would probably be forced into military service and become the butt of the N.C.O.s in charge of him: if only a tenth of the stories were true – the reports, some of them official and the subject of enquiry, of brutality used against 'pressed conscripts' with the excuse of 'bringing them into line' – he was in for a bad time; but that would affect only himself and he would cope with it as it came. His fear was more abstract than that, more instinctive; no one in the crowds on that August night had wished him any harm yet he'd felt it then. It was the fear of his own kind, the blind unreasoning power of the herd to kill what it couldn't understand.

The poor woman who had shouted didn't wish him harm. If he could ask her, over a quiet cup of tea in her parlour, whether some unknown corporal had the right to bait and maltreat him in punishment for holding views different from his own, she would probably say no, that wasn't right. All she could see now was a young man alive and safe in the place of the son who would never come home to her again.

The sickness was passing but he kept a grip on the chair-back: he didn't want this 'feeble youth' to faint in front of all these worthy people. He was watching the well-groomed head of the chairman, surprised that any man could go so far in life and understand so little of it. And suddenly Hugh was angry with him, with all of them.

'*Precious heritage?*' The chair rocked as he pushed it away from him. 'Is that what you call it? A world war with the guns shaking the streets of London and the fathers of these children packed overseas for slaughtering like cattle? Is *that* the 'precious heritage' they're so 'eager to safeguard' with their 'small hands'? Then God help them!'

'Silence! Your case is dismissed!'

'My case hasn't been heard!' But they were going to hear it; in the unruly classes of the early days he'd learned how to speak effectively, how to use pauses. 'And my case is that I can do more for the children of this country than those who say we need their help.' He waited, counting three seconds and cutting in again before the chairman could speak. 'Has the older generation blundered so far into this tragic impasse that we need *children* to get us out of it? If that isn't "feeble", what is?'

'*Constable!*'

Hugh turned and saw the policeman coming across reluctantly from his comfortable pitch near the doors, a young fellow reddening with embarrassment, his boots alone disturbing the hush. In a moment whispering broke out on the Tribunal bench: the plump woman was pulling at the chairman's sleeve and the parson leaned towards them, half out of his seat and giving quick little nods like a bird pecking. The public benches were astir and one of the cub reporters was in argument with a man behind him. Hugh could hear the constable sidling back to his post, hoping no one would notice.

The chairman had turned one shoulder to his colleagues and sat sulking, his proud head held aloof; it was the woman who spoke to Hugh.

'Now you mustn't cause any more trouble,' she said with a nervous smile. 'We are ready to hear your plea but your remarks must be relevant and you must be as brief as you can – there are others waiting.' The bob of her feathered hat was quite gracious.

'Thank you, madam.' Hugh realized that he was damp with sweat and had a sudden fierce thirst; he could feel, still, the impression of the back of the chair across the palm of his hand: he must have been gripping it rather hard before he'd pushed it away. There was no further need for calculated pauses – the chairman had obviously washed his hands of the affair and wouldn't try again to shout him down. 'But I won't speak for myself; I'll speak for the children – their case is more urgent than mine. Our Government lets them work thirty-three hours a week in the heavy industries at the age of twelve; at thirteen they can leave school altogether for the factories and work full-time; and at fourteen they can go into the coal-mines and work in the dark, shut away from the fresh air and the sunshine that even a pig in a field can enjoy – and these are *children*, their young bodies not yet formed and their young minds closed to every thought but the assembly-belt and the coal-pick and the wage-packet. And while we're worrying about the appalling rise in juvenile delinquency, asking ourselves what's "becoming" of our children today, we're busy teaching them how to make guns and shells for the killing of their own kind, and rewarding them with money they can squander in the picture-palaces because we've shown them that the only "fun" they can have is the kind they've got to buy. Who's to control them, or even talk to them? Their fathers are at the war and their mothers working the clock round in the factories and hospitals and no one else cares a farthing for them.' He looked deliberately at the blockish head of the chairman. 'The true "precious heritage" of children is childhood. And we've taken that away.'

It was all he wanted to tell them. He didn't know if they'd understood; the women in black and the few men among them sat very still, watching him with a rather bovine gaze that disconcerted him: these weren't the receptive minds he'd debated with at Cambridge and the school at Dover. Nobody on the Tribunal bench seemed prepared to question him: except for the chairman they sat watching him with an air of slight shock, as if he'd been telling them a risky joke that hadn't quite come off. His thirst kept nagging and his eyes were drawn to the glass beaker on the Tribunal bench; and the plump women apparently noticed this.

'Would you like a drink of water?'

He looked at her in surprise. 'I would, rather.'

She poured some for him and he drank, the relief to his parched mouth evoking a rush of gratitude, which he tried to put out of his mind; small mercies took on inflated values when you were powerless.

'Do you want to say anything more?'

'No. That's all.' The talk was growing louder at the side of the gymnasium and he noticed for the first time a soldier among the people there, grey-headed and hollow-faced, the long war dull in his eyes; he'd come here like the widows, wanting to see justice done and this cocky little whipper-snapper thrown to the guns, as every fit man should be. 'Well yes,' he said, 'there is just one other thing. We think a lot of our "gallant soldiers"; we send them comforts and when they come home on leave we put the flags out for them – we stand them a drink and slap them on the back and tell them what heroes they are; but it's easy enough to praise a hero when he's with us, and as easy to forget him when he's gone. A lot of these men are fathers – especially since conscription came in – and while they're fighting out there we're supposed to be looking after things at home so they'll have a decent place to come back to when the war's over. But when they do come back, what sort of children are they going to find – the same ones they left in our care or a bunch of semi-illiterate little guttersnipes they won't even recognize? All that these men will have known of their own children will be the snapshots they took away with them, as a keepsake and a comfort, to remind them what they were fighting for; but when they come home that's all they'll find left of the bright future they risked so much to keep safe – the snapshots that we've been quietly tearing up while their backs were turned.'

Suddenly the chairman moved his head, as if his patience were exhausted; and some of Hugh's anger came back because here was the real enemy: ignorance. 'So that's my case and those are my opinions and you can have me shot for them or sent to Dartmoor with the hardened criminals. All right – but if that's your answer, don't ever sing the praises of "our gallant soldiers" again, because you'll have shown that you don't care a damn for them or their children either.'

274

No one, in the end, said a word to him; he was told to leave while they considered. Two days later there was just the drab-looking government form in the post and a clerk's scrawl in the space allotted: *Exempt from military service.* One of the newspapers said there'd been cheering after he'd left but he'd not heard any; the press always sensationalized.

There'd been no cheering at Carisbrooke. His mother just walked out of the room when she heard, and his father had nothing to say, not a word. He knew he'd lost them, then, just as if a bomb had hit the house while he was away. He'd made up his mind not to see them again, but thought later it might be from lack of courage; so he'd had another go at it because he'd rather they 'shouted' at him than each other.

But this time looked like being the last. He'd never had to come away on Saturday afternoon instead of Sunday night because none of them could stand it any longer. Pam was probably right: he ought to let them forget him now. Pam was right so often, but never reminded him of it. Perhaps it wasn't wisdom – she'd have laughed at that thought – but a flair for looking straight into the heart of things with her dark level eyes. It was quite possible that he could never have stood these week-ends if he'd not been able to see her afterwards; but this one had been so wearing that he wouldn't have wished his company on anyone, least of all Pam.

'My father's leaving Propaganda,' he said.

'Leaving?' She stared at him. 'But it was the only thing that gave him any – any sense of direction!'

'I know.' His smile was faintly cynical. 'He now seems to think it was the wrong direction.'

'Was it something you said?'

'My God no – I never talk about my views. He'd been to some conference or other and finished up in a pub.' He noticed Pam glance down quickly. 'He said things had "got out of hand" and that "life was no longer sacred" – apart from several other fairly obvious remarks. He even said I'd been right, all along.'

'*Right?*'

He looked at her sharply. 'About keeping out.'

'Then – then you've won your battle!' Her dark eyes were brilliant. 'After all this time!'

'No,' he said with a shrug. 'He's lost, that's all. It wasn't a battle: what he's lost are the illusions that made his generation so cock-sure of themselves when they ran out to play soldiers. Anyway it was the last straw for my mother, and that's why I had to get away.' He glanced across her shoulder as the door swung open and a girl hurried in, a girl like Pam with bobbed hair and a peaked cap and greatcoat.

'But now that he's on your side . . .' she said helplessly.

'I don't need anyone on my side.'

She stared at him levelly for a moment, then looked away. 'That's true. You never have.'

The girl in uniform had seen her. '*Pam!* Train in!'

She swung round and called back that she was coming. Hugh was getting up, leaving a tip, and she looked at him steadily, at the hungry poet's face with the mouth still young and the light blue eyes already old with mistrust; she wouldn't see much of Hugh again.

She got her driving-gloves. 'You're in luck, old boy – I've got to dash.' He came with her to the doors. 'Aubrey's coming home on leave in a few days, did you know?' They pushed through a group of lost-looking soldiers; across the station the hospital train was shutting off steam and she believed she could smell the gangrene even from here.

'He's what?'

'Coming home.' They dodged past milk-churns towards the subway. Maybe Hugh might make the trip up to London next week-end, to see him.

'That's magnificent,' he said and took both her hands. 'Give him my good wishes.'

She turned once before going down the steps and saw him wave.

Mum had her blue art-silk frock on and the big cameo brooch, and Dad was in his grey double-breasted. They didn't go down to the King's Arms because they knew by now that he couldn't stand all the back-slapping, and anyway no one could beat Mum's cooking.

'A little bit more, Geoff?'

'Too true.' There was butter on the potatoes, even. 'This is pre-war style, this is.'

276

'They put a few little things by, down at Hobson's, when they know you're coming home.'

The thing was to take enough to let her know he appreciated it without leaving them short when he'd gone back; they'd not eaten like this for months, he knew that. He wished they wouldn't put on their best, the day he came home; it was as if he was 'company' and it made him feel like a stranger, but what could he say? They did it from kindness.

'How's the darts then, Dad?'

'Oh, all right. I don't play much.'

It was harder to talk, this leave. All he wanted to talk about was what he'd seen out there but it'd only worry them and he hadn't come home for that; and they couldn't seem to think of much they wanted to say. What was there to tell him anyway?

'You must be getting sick of this war,' he said. He'd taken the Tube from the main-line station and wondered what could have happened: there were people sleeping down there, whole families, because the raids had been getting worse; little kids trying to get off to sleep while the trains came in and out and people walked past nearly tripping over them. And not a smile out of anyone; all you saw was grey faces and shabby clothes.

'*We* must be gettin' sick of it?' said Dad sharply. 'Picnic for you boys, is it?'

'It's easier on us, you know. There's no food or clothes to find an' no rent to pay – you just obey the orders and that's it, there's no time for any thinkin'. Little Eth all right now, is she?'

'She's better for seeing you, Geoff,' his mother said, 'you've no idea how she perked up when she knew you were coming – there's no bottle of medicine that could make such a difference.' She took her fork again, pretending to eat some more. Doctor Leckie had given her something for her appetite when he'd come to look at Eth. 'You're not eating enough, Mrs Tuffnel. The rations aren't *that* short, you know!' But she couldn't force herself and wasn't going to try. Last Tuesday she'd not touched her supper and Dad was quite cross, not knowing what to do for her. She hadn't told him what had happened. There'd been a long queue at the butcher's and she'd seen the telegraph-boy on his bicycle turning down their street; she'd run all the way home but he'd gone on past for someone else, and she didn't remember how she'd got back to the queue again; the butcher went and fetched her a glass of water and she said she'd left the gas on, that was all, and running took it out of her.

She saw Dad watching Geoff when he wasn't looking, and knew what was in his mind. This was Geoff's seventh leave and the news got no better; you were frightened to go in the queues these days, knowing there'd be someone else in new black clothes with their eyes still red from crying. You couldn't even tell them, like you could once, 'My Geoff's coming home next week!' There were some who didn't want to hear. And you began feeling how lucky you were, up to now.

'We'll go down the King's tomorrow.'

'All right, son.'

'Have a go at the board – you don't want to lose your form. Once a champ, you've got obligations – that's right isn't it, Mum?'

'That's right, Geoff.'

Their knives and forks scraped in the silence.

'You'll be seein' Judith, won't you though?'

'I'd like to pop in.'

'Of course you must. She's a lovely girl, she is.' She caught a glance from Dad. 'You get letters from her, I'm sure.'

Something in her voice made Geoff look up. 'She writes a lot, yes. Why?'

'Well, I just mean—' She moved the gristle to the side of her plate.

'She's delicate,' his father said, 'that's all. She's what you call a delicate young girl. Her mother says—'

Geoff asked quietly: 'Is Judith ill?' His big hands lay flat on the table suddenly.

'It's just the winter comin' on.'

'Do you mind,' Geoff asked them, 'if I go round there tonight?'

His Mother fingered her brooch. 'We told them you probably would.'

The house was dark when he went up the path and knocked. The street-lamp made a sick greenish light on the leaves of the ragged privet: the gas was turned down low – they called it a 'dim-out'. He knocked again and heard something behind him and turned quickly.

'Geoffrey, is that you?'

She was struggling with the gate and he went to help her; she was carrying a parcel and her electric torch flashed once across his face. It wasn't till they were in the front room that he could see her properly.

'I popped out for some beer,' she laughed, still out of breath and too shy to come close to him, using both hands to comb at her ginger hair. 'I've had it cropped short – we all got told to do it, so it doesn't get caught in the machines.' Her green eyes went on smiling because he was here but she couldn't think of anything more to say, and he was so quiet, just watching her. The light in the ceiling threw down a flat hard glare and he went across and put his big arms round her as if to shield her from it.

'Hello Judith.' They didn't move; he could feel her heart beating; she murmured his name, her face snuggled against him; he stared at the row of Coronation mugs along the mantelpiece, where there was a photograph of himself in a gilded tin frame. Someone had written on it in ink, going over the letters twice to make them stand out: *Geoffrey Tuffnel, Military Medal*. They stood like this for a long time, not talking.

She lit the gas fire and got some milk from the kitchen while he opened the beer. 'I drink a lot of milk, because I'm meant to. I get extra rations.'

'It'll do you good,' he said. 'Where's Dad, then?' He'd have to talk to him.

'He's on late work.' She took small sips, holding the glass away while she swallowed, like a bird drinking; the yellowness hadn't gone from her skin; her eyes were very large in her thin shadowed face and he thought that if she shut her eyes he'd see all the life go out of her, all there was left. 'Mum will be home soon. She's on the buses now, a conductress.'

'Is she?' He took his beer from the table again and drank some, because she'd been out for it specially. 'You're not with the chemicals any more, are you?'

'Oh no, I've been off that over a year now, Geoffrey.' She'd never called him Geoff. 'I'm making machine-guns now, parts for them.'

'Are you?' He smiled for her. It must be exciting, making machine-guns. He said, 'You don't want my picture there, Judith, on the mantelpiece.'

279

She swung her head to look up at it and he saw the thinness of her neck. 'But why ever not?' There was fright, almost, in her eyes, as if he was going to make her take it down.

'It was better when Harry's was there.'

Her eyes lost their light and she said in not much more than a whisper: 'Dad took it down. They've got it in their bedroom. He knew Mum wanted to take it down but she couldn't. People used to say, "Is that your boy, then?" People that didn't know.' She finished her milk. 'Your picture's nice there. Dad said we ought to have it there. They think the world of you, Geoffrey.'

'Then that's a lot too much.' He got up and shut the top of the window because there was a draught. 'We've got to look after you, Judith. You'd manage all right, wouldn't you, in this house, if you didn't go out to work? I know I shouldn't ask things like—'

'Of course we would.' She went to the table and began pouring some more beer for him. 'Dad's an under-manager now and—'

'I won't have any more. But it was very nice.'

'All right. And with Mum on the buses we're almost rich. I don't do it so much for the money; I just want to feel I'm doing something for the war.'

His jaw came forward and he spoke low in his throat. 'I see. An' what's the war done for you?'

It wasn't till near the end of his leave that he had a chance of talking to Mr and Mrs Ross, without Judith there; and it wasn't any use. They'd have had her out of that factory double-quick, Mr Ross told him, long before now; but she wouldn't listen. She felt that after all that Harry had done, and all he'd given, in the end, she'd got to do something too – 'for the boys themselves,' he said, 'boys like him, and like you, come to that. Put something in their hands to fight with, that's the idea she's got into her head and we can't talk her out of it. All we can do is feed her up and see she's got warm things to put on and hope she'll see reason one fine day. We got her out of chemical work and stopped her doing night-shifts – I went to the manager without her knowing.' He looked hard at Geoff from under his ginger brows. 'Like a butterfly, isn't she, you could blow her over in one puff; and gentle as can be, just like her mother; but when Judith's made up her mind about something, that's it. So when you go back out there, Geoff, don't ever think she's being neglected; we're doing all we can.'

He left them early that night. Judith had agreed to go up to bed with a hot milky drink and he didn't stay on to talk about her, or they'd think he didn't trust her own mother and father to see the danger. It wasn't consumption, he knew that much – they'd had tests made at the Greenwich Free.

The only bus that came past the bottom of the road had a strap across the footboard and they wouldn't let him on, although it was empty. The driver got out to help his mate change the name-boards to 'Private'.

'When's the next one?' Geoff asked them.

'You've had it, chum!' The conductor took out his watch with a kind of flourish. 'We been on strike five minutes!'

The driver waddled comfortably back to his cab, heavy in his thick leather coat. 'An' nobody can't say we never warned 'em this time!'

The conductor swung up on to the step and started fixing the strap across when Geoff reached out with one hand and dragged him down again, spinning him round and throwing him on the pavement; then he unslung his rifle and leaned it against the side of the bus and went up to the driving-cab. 'Come on out of there. I want to talk to you.'

'Eh? What's the game, then?' He twisted his fat neck round to see what was going on. His mate was trying to holler for the police, getting on to his knees.

'Want me to fetch you out?' Geoff asked the driver.

He came down like a ton weight, perhaps with the idea of knocking the soldier flying. Geoff stepped aside and let him go sprawling and took the conductor by the collar and pitched him down again across his mate; then he stood over them with his big hands by his sides.

'On strike, are you?' He wasn't shouting, they were quite close enough to hear. 'More pay? Better conditions, that it? You know what I get paid for the job I do? You know the conditions I work in? Eleven bob a week and the grub thrown in if the rats don't get at it first. We sleep in the mud, out there, an' we wake up in it. We live in it and fight in it and a lot of us die in it, but when we're lucky we get a bit of leave so we can come home an' remind ourselves it's worth it all, because the people we're doing it for are keepin' the place decent for us.' The conductor was trying to get up and his leather bag tilted, spilling a few coins; as he reached out to stop them rolling away Geoff's boot came down across his wrist. 'That's all you think about.' He looked at the driver. 'How big's this strike? How many of you?'

'If you'll let me get on me feet, I'll—'

'How many?'

'I dunno, off-'and, honest! Three or four 'undred, p'r'aps, south o' the Thames—'

'Three or four hundred,' Geoff nodded. 'Half a battalion.' He turned slowly away to fetch his rifle, coming back to stand over them again, the heavy brass butt on the paving-stones and the barrel gripped in his hands. 'Half a battalion of useless poxy little layabouts not fit to wipe the boots of the lowest private soldier in the British Army.' The rifle came up and the conductor whimpered, shielding his face; but Geoff was only slinging it by the strap. 'When I'm back out there with my mates they're goin' to ask the same old question – "How's England gettin' on, then?" And I'm goin' to tell 'em it stinks.' He stepped over them and walked away. 'England stinks. Even the pavements are choked with rubbish.'

Towards the end of the month the sun came out for a few days, its pale blob hanging above the smoke of the city. Halfway through his leave Aubrey actually spent an hour in a deck-chair behind the conservatory, reading for the third time a letter from Diana. It was very short. *I'm miserable,* she explained, *because I was so longing to see you again at Ashbourne, in your own background.* She had been trying to get some leave to coincide with his, but Passchendaele had put a stop to that. *We've only ever met there once in all those years, and we weren't the same people, were we, then? Never mind. Julian has wangled some local leave and he's coming to see me, which is going to be wonderful because it's nearly six months since I saw him last, and anyway I'm going to make him talk the whole time about you.*

Voices, somewhere in the grounds, distracted him; and after

a while he got up and wandered through the rhododendron paths to see what was going on.

'I dunno. Jus' give it a good slosh, Alf.'

'Thing is to get it over the net, I know that much!'

They were still dashing about when Aubrey reached the court: four army privates in their P.T. kit, their khaki hanging over the little slatted chairs. They stopped when they saw him, coming across rather sheepishly, their faces pink from the exercise.

'I'm Talbot,' he smiled and shook hands with them in turn. 'It's good to see you here.' They were from the Oxford and Bucks on home leave; his mother had told him that Ashbourne was 'open house' to anyone at the Y.M.C.A., and he'd heard that Cook spent half her days baking cakes.

'Makin' too much noise are we, sir?'

'Not a bit. You're not hitting enough balls, that's the only trouble!'

He took one of their rackets and the instant it was in his hand he knew it was his own, the long-handled sixteen-ounce with the green rubber grip: and suddenly the whole scene changed as if a forgotten dream had started rushing through his head, dazzling him with its colours – the sun was hot and Vic was there in his white slacks beside him, with Pam and Hugh across the net and Mother watching from under her pink lace parasol, the scent of mown grass on the air and the piping of thrushes from the orchard, the hum of the strings to a ball perfectly hit . . .

They were waiting respectfully, the four young men, pretending they were eager to learn; but he knew he shouldn't have come to bother them: they'd been having a lot of fun, laughing about their clumsiness. It was too late to back out now.

'The thing is to keep your eye on it. Lob it up nice and slowly, then catch it full and square just as it starts falling.' He threw up the ball; it was an old one, bald and puddeny and stained with green, and he wondered suddenly if he could hit it at all, let alone 'full and square' as he should. Rising from his left hand it turned black against the watery sun, slowing and becoming almost still; and the racket swung hard.

'Ber-*limey!*' One of them laughed, and his friends joined in. It had been all right: the poor old grass-stained warrior had gone scorching down and was still bouncing as he sent the next one after it and then a third in a series of easy swings that brought back the dream again of those young summers for a minute more.

'Let's see you do better.' He didn't stay long. One of them, a stocky boy with his face set in an alarming grimace of determination, sent a ball sailing well over the trees and they all waited nervously until they heard it rattling among the tiles of Mr Willis's potting-sheds. 'Very well hit,' said Aubrey, 'but direction's a bit important too.' It got an easy laugh and he left them to it.

His mood was quiet for the rest of the day, and Pom-Pom, dashing home 'between trains' to talk to him, asked if he felt all right. It was quite beyond him to explain the sense of awe and humility that overlaid his every thought: the awareness of the immeasurable luck that had led him through so many perilous roads to the haven of Ashbourne again, where today he had done so trivial and miraculous a thing as to hit a tennis ball across the net, as he had once used to do.

He was at the piano the next morning when the telephone rang. The roses in the silver bowl were ivory-white, not scarlet as they'd been when Diana had stood here, turning and laughing to him – *I saw your reflection in the bowl* ... Two or three petals had fallen while he played, and lay curved and quiet on the satinwood while the telephone went on ringing in the hall. Charrington didn't seem to be about so he got up to answer it himself.

A woman's voice asked him who was speaking; its tone was oddly flat.

'This is Aubrey Talbot.'

For a moment there was no answer. He could hear the faint buzzing of the line, and Cook's voice calling to someone below in the house. He felt uneasy, as if the flat colourless tone of the unknown woman were on a wave-length that affected his nerves.

'This is Mrs Stuart Lovell.'

He wouldn't have caught the name if it hadn't been well known to him: the line seemed to be fading and coming back; or it was her voice.

'Oh yes – good-morning, Mrs Lovell. How are you?'

It was so quiet in the house; the only sounds came from a long way off: the knock of a broom against a wainscoting where Elsie was cleaning; Mother's voice, talking perhaps to Kitty; the running of a tap in the kitchen. There was the smell of polish here in the hall, and a faint draught came from under the door because this morning the wind was in the east. Perhaps he noted these things so that he should have his mind occupied while he waited, so that the dread shouldn't come flowing into it like chill black water into a ship. But there was nothing to go on; it was just that these days anything could happen. She'd ask him if Lady Eleanor were there, and he'd go and fetch her.

'I heard that you were at home, on leave.'

'That's right, yes.'

'That is why I am telephoning.' The fading made it difficult to hear what she was saying; either she was holding the mouthpiece too far away or was unwell. Then he heard her say: 'Julian . . .' in a tone that meant she hadn't finished but must wait before she went on.

The light striking upwards from the polished surfaces suddenly blinded him and the draught from the east wind became icy.

'Mrs Lovell, could you speak a little louder? Did you say "Julian"?' But he knew she had. Nothing lasts for ever. You're playing the piano at peace with the world and a bullet comes flashing into the house from the war outside because you've got to be reminded that there's no shelter for you anywhere, even here.

A different voice was speaking suddenly, a girl's, hesitant and sniffling. 'The Mistress wanted to tell you that Mr Julian has got killed. There was a telegram just now.' A sound had started in the background, high and faint and moaning, strangely unhuman. 'Can you hear me all right, sir?'

'Yes. Please thank your mistress for telephoning, and say that I am coming over at once to see her.'

Cutting his leave short by three days he caught the night train from Charing Cross. Mrs Lovell had agreed not to send a cable to Diana, since she might not have heard yet and he might be in time to break the news himself.

XIV

But for the earlier coming of the September mist it still seemed summer; most of the men were in the open air, their voices carrying clearly among the massed camouflaged tents; from the transport park the murmur of engines and harness never stopped. A week ago it had been quiet here, more like Rest than Divisional Reserve, but over the days the noise and movement had swelled in a slow wave from the rail-heads south of Verdun, to break over the camp and leave confusion boiling.

'We're for it this time.'

Nobody answered Clarkson. He sat looking at his nails, thinking he shouldn't have said it; his nails were ingrained with black, an amalgam of gun-oil, boot polish and the soot of explosion; he couldn't do anything about it now and had given up trying. The only thing that mattered was staying alive.

Barclay-Smith was monkeying with his slide-rule, checking some figures in a half-torn newspaper. Sam Quincey was cleaning his rifle, frowning over it in concentration. Tom was writing a letter, using the red bitten pencil they shared among them. Geoff sat with his big arms folded, watching the R.E.s at work across the churned grass of the camp; in the field alongside they were making a compound, and their mailed gloves flashed as they paid out the rolls of barbed wire. Percy was not here with them; a week ago he'd been made up to sergeant, replacing Lee, though he was never far away from this little group. These were the 'Talbot men', all except Jim Clarkson whom they had accepted, long ago and with nothing said, as being of their kind.

'I've been working a few figures out,' said Smithy, and put his slide-rule away in its special bag. 'The average life expectancy of a rifleman in battle is thirty minutes, because he moves about. A machine-gunner lives twenty, because he offers a fixed target. Junior officers and captains, taken as a group, can count on ten. Senior N.C.O.s of more than—'

'Shut up.' Geoff turned his head once and looked away again.

Smithy shrugged. Facts were facts, good or bad, and so long as you could figure them out you could keep a sort of control over them. He stared past his long sharp nose at the people making the compound; it was for a thousand prisoners, so someone obviously felt hopeful. Farther away some Labour Corps wallahs were digging a mass grave; Tom and Sam had been on a fatigue-party most of today, helping with it, and he'd spared them the figures he'd worked out: the chances were that thirteen per cent of the fighting-troops helping the Labour Corps on that job were doing it for themselves.

There are so many roses where you are, Tom wrote with the red bitten pencil, *but you are the only one I think about, because you are the loveliest of them all.*

Perhaps he shouldn't put such things in his letters but he might never see her again and he wanted her to know how he thought of her. He'd not been to the Manor for nearly a year after he'd left the hospital; then Mr Kemp had spoken to him soon after he'd come back from leave, saying it wasn't right he should keep away from Kitty, she was quite upset at not seeing him; and this was true, as he knew from her letters. *If I didn't know you, Tom, I would think you to be a vain person, worrying about your face like this. Mr Kemp has just been here with us, and he said you look more of a man than you did before, a 'real little warrior' he told us. And it wouldn't make any difference whatever you looked like because I know what you are, and I miss you so very much.*

He'd braved it the next time home on leave, walking up to the house feeling like some awful monster that had crawled out of the sea, and it seemed as if all the windows were wide open with everyone watching him. Kitty and Lady Eleanor were in the cabbage-plot – the place where there'd always been delphiniums before – with galoshes on and muddy gardening-gloves, and Milady had said straight out how 'very handsome' he was looking after all this time. In fact he had to mention it himself, about his face, saying he was sorry it wouldn't ever be any different now; and Milady smiled and said if it worried him then Kitty must 'make haste and kiss it better'. He was shocked at this and tried to turn away but Kitty was quicker and her face was suddenly touching his, cool and soft like a flower pressed against his scarred cheek, and he shut his eyes and felt sick because she was so pretty and doing something so horrible; then they were both laughing softly when he opened his eyes, and a strange thing happened – the stiffness on that side of his face had gone away, and he knew it was true that people could be 'kissed better' from whatever they were suffering from.

He brushed a midge from the note-paper and left a smear, licking the tip of his finger and washing the worst of it away. *I might not be able to write again for a little while, but I will be thinking about you, like I always do.*

A staff car with a general's pennant went swerving on to the perimeter road and left dust floating behind, and Geoff saw Maj. Talbot in the back with Col. Rokesley. It happened every day – conferences at Staff H.Q. – and he wondered how it felt for those two, having to go and listen to a lot of gas from a mob of brasshats who'd never seen the front line for themselves. They were getting very excited of course in the High Command these days; the Hindenburg Line was getting hammered and there'd been victories at Amiens and Bapaume and the Scarpe – it must look all very fine on the map-tables. The man they ought to send for was Smithy, if they wanted some facts to help them plan their campaigns. Thirty minutes for a rifleman, twenty for a gunner. Out here where the fighting was done you knew that a victory was just something that'd kill you if you stayed too long. Harry Ross. Bill Jones. Oscar. Pop Jarvis. Frank Adams. Dicky Gilmore. And Wiggy gone home with one leg. Just in their own small circle of chums. That was victory. Put out the flags for that.

'Hey, watch it!' said Sam, looking up.

Percy Stokes was here, mincing towards them with his arm hanging down as if the weight of his brand-new sergeant's stripes was trying to overbalance him.

'Now come along, you lazy good-for-nothing fellows!' He'd never dropped his act of guying the officers since he'd first got his lance-jack's chevron, but he only did it for these – the Talbot men.

'Piss off,' Geoff told him. This too was their tradition. They knew what Percy had got for them: a list of fatigues as long as your arm.

'Oh you really are *such* a common person!' He stood in front of them flicking his imaginary cane. They were dead-beat and he knew that. They all were, every man in the camp. Yesterday he'd heard the Colonel telling a staff officer, 'All I shall ask of the Brigadier is that he doesn't allow my troops to get beaten into the damned ground with fatigues before they're sent into battle.' But he asked it every time and the answer was always the same; and in the end it was for the N.C.O.s to put the men to work and they hated it. They knew that the death of many a man in the field began long before the whistles blew, by the taking away of his strength.

'You come to tell us the tea's ready, Percy?'

'Well yes and no, my good man, yes and no. Mostly – er – no. As a matter of fact we're all frightfully excited because there's a new consignment of shells arrived down at Transport—'

'Shit,' breathed Barclay-Smith. Shell-humping was the worst.

'Well yes,' Percy nodded, giving a genteel little cough, 'of course there's a certain amount of it about – I mean to say, we know what horses are!' A shrill giggle. 'But the thing is, the Brigadier-General and I feel that you chaps might find it simply ripping sport to help those gunner fellahs with the good work, what? Now do tell me how the giddy idea strikes you.' He put his fingers carefully into his ears.

Geoff was the first to get up, and Tom put his pencil away. Smithy didn't move. 'For Christ's sake, Percy, tell 'em you couldn't find us.'

Percy turned away, flicking his buttocks. 'Of course if you don't *want* to . . .'

Smithy still didn't move, and Geoff said: 'Come on.'

'Listen, I was humping bloody shells all morning, and so were you.'

'An' we're goin' to hump a few more.' Sam and Tom were joining Percy along the row of tents and Geoff said in a low voice: 'He didn't make it an order, did he? That's why we've got to go.'

The sky was noisy the next day. A few enemy recce-planes began coming over again in the afternoon to plot the movements of troops and guns west of the line, and a barrage-balloon was hit by tracers and threw out orange flames, heeling over and wallowing lower and lower like a fabled beast in its death-throes, the flamboyant prelude to a dog-fight that milled for almost an hour above the lines as a whole squadron of Martinsydes took on a group of black-crossed escort units trying to bring in a lumbering C.III to the ammunition dumps, with a flock of French Spads circling for the kill.

In the evening the shelling began again but the eastward movement along the roads from the rail-heads never stopped. The land was alive with men, horses and machines flowing sluggishly through the hills and branching off to unlimber the guns, flowing again and eddying among the coppices where the camps emptied and filled as the spearhead companies were moved forward and the reserves moved in, while along the lanes and through the valley folds the signals trucks spun out their wire threads from post to post, busy as spiders.

Night fell and the dark sky blossomed with flares and the earth shivered to the guns but the movement went on, its ramifications so vast that the storm of shells could check only a few of its tributaries where the ground was more exposed. Lights winked at the crossroads where the military police manned permanent posts.

'Keep going for six miles and watch for the signs!'

Boots tramped, their rhythm measuring the hour.

The signals were going back.

19th Battery emplaced.

A convoy shunted to a halt and figures came forward, their shadows thrown ahead by the lamps.

'Who are you?'

'West Kents!'

'You're off your route! Back a mile and turn south before the village, and for God's sake don't block the road while you're turning, we've got half the Third Army coming through!'

Dawn, Monday.

Blue Area manned.

The trees of orchards, heavy under the fruit that no one had time to harvest, lay half flattened by the spread of camouflaged tarpaulins as the guns came in, the iron-bound wheels of the limbers crushing apples shaken from the boughs. The birds had gone long ago.

4th and 5th London Batteries emplaced.

Mules lay dead near the crossroads and a ration-cart sprawled upside down across a shell-hole. 'Salvage what you can but get a move on, you're behind schedule!'

A thousand men reached Bronville, marching seven hours and dropping where they halted. 'Get them on their feet, we've got billets near the farm!'

'I can't, sir. It's more than they can do.'

'Christ, what a shambles. Well I suppose we can say you've arrived. Signaller!'

7th Wessex encamped.

The cavalry moved by daylight in squadrons extended abreast where open land gave passage, closing their formations where soft ground forced them to the already crowded roads; hooves ringing and pennants flying they drove their way past the never-ending lines of marching men, leaving them smothered in dust. But the motorized columns refused to give way; after four years of war it had been shown that the cavalry could do precious little to win it.

Dawn, Thursday.

Red Area manned.

Westwards, mile by mile, the roads were growing quiet, their macadam rutted and bruised by the marks of wheels and their borders littered in many places by the wreckage of transports. Dust was settling at last across the hedgerows of the lanes, and leaves torn from their stems fluttered to the first winds of autumn. At a crossroads a dog sat scratching and for a moment was still, its ears cocked to catch the last of the echoes among the hills. Moles stirred in the ditches, and owls were about.

The skeins of bright copper wire spanned the evening sky.

All forces deployed.

Halfway from the forward assembly area to the line the 3rd Duke of Lancaster's halted for a rest not far from the Clisson-Montfaucon road. Its officers gathered in the shade of poplars, and here Aubrey made a point of approaching his brother, as was his habit of late. He knew by now that Vic would never come to him except when duty demanded and he was determined that they shouldn't spend the rest of the war as strangers. On home leave they saw nothing of each other: Vic always contrived to delay his leave until Aubrey was back in the line,

and it was getting more and more difficult to pretend at Ashbourne that this was a matter of bad luck. Father knew the truth, of course, but said nothing.

'Smoke?' he asked Vic.

'Thanks.' The heavy chased silver glinted in the afternoon light. 'Julian's, wasn't it?' He asked only to make civil conversation.

'Yes. My proudest possession.' Lord Rokesley had come to him with it when he'd reported back from leave last year: 'Young Lovell said he wanted you to have this, if anything happened.' There'd been a note with it: *Just a keepsake, and a bit battered, but you might want to have it straightened out. If I'm allowed any time for a last thought, it will be that Diana now has you in her life, for which I thank God with all my heart.*

From along the road they heard troops on the march and a song they didn't recognize. Possibly they were Canadians.

'Feeling fit?'

'Perfectly.'

The answer had the tone of a rebuke. The summer 'flu epidemic, sweeping through France and England alike, had left Vic untouched, but he'd gone down recently with trench-fever and spent two weeks at the base hospital near Beaupréau, a sign of weakness he resented the more since the cause was 'non-combatant'.

'How's Freddie today?'

'I've no idea.'

Aubrey drew on his cigarette; the curt response was expected but he didn't let it worry him. He meant to remind Vic at every opportunity that any bad feeling was entirely his. Freddie himself had said, soon after that appalling scene when Vic had threatened to put him on a charge, 'He's young still, Mr Aubrey, an' he's not got himself sorted out, an' if you an' me can help him do it then it's all I ask.'

It was hard going but they didn't intend to give up. Vic, leaving home and his boyhood to play with a war, had grown not into a man but a savage, and they'd have to tame him as you tamed any wild creature: by showing him there was nothing to fear.

'We've got to look after Freddie. We're responsible for him just as he's responsible for us.'

The sharp young face was turned suddenly. 'What d'you expect me to do? I think we've proved that I've got no authority over Sergeant Kemp.'

Aubrey flicked away his cigarette. 'It's not a question of authority. He's one of us and what I'm talking about is a sense of loyalty.' He strolled away to squat over the maps with Rokesley.

The body of troops were coming abreast, still singing, and from the roadside ditches where there was a little shade the men of the 3rd Dukes watched them.

'What's this lot, then?'

'Aussies, ain't they?'

'Course they're not, Aussies don't wear hats like them.'

Some of the men were getting to their feet; worn out by constant fatigues and the morning's march it was still in them to be roused by the steady rhythm of these troops as they came swinging by with a confidence that had not been seen for years now across this ruined land.

'Cripes, they're big enough blokes, look at 'em!'

'I've got it,' Smithy said, 'they're the—'

'Ho-ly *Jee-sus*!' Sam was on his feet and scrambling up the bank whooping like a Red Indian, running alongside and falling in step with them – 'Hey where you from, goddarn it?'

'Milwaukee!' a man called, grinning, 'how's about you?'

'Green River, Wyoming – Sam Quincey!' He thrust his hand out, hopping in delight. They reached across each other to shake with him.

'Jake Southern! This is Barty Woods!'

'Holy cow – it's good to see you boys!'

'How come you're got up like a Limey, Sam?'

'Hell, I was the whole o' the U.S. Army till you guys showed up! What kept you so long?' He broke step and let them go by, calling and waving to them, the dust from their boots gathering on him until he stood alone in the middle of the road. The sound of their lusty singing floated back.

'Y' know somethin'? We just won this damn' war, as good as! Look at them boys go!'

'God help them.'

'Huh?'

Geoff leaned on his rifle staring along the road, along all the roads that had seemed as straight as this one, and as promising. 'There was a time once,' he said bitterly, 'when we used to march like that.'

Towards the lines they met ambulances bringing back wounded from the night raids that had been mounted to test the enemy strength; the reports spoke of fifty per cent casualties. On the last mile of the march they passed a camp where carpenters were working in the open, steadily hammering. Many of the troops looked the other way but a few called out, venting their anger.

'Mind you don't fall in, mate, or I'll come an' screw the bloody lid on!'

'You leave any splinters inside an' I'll come back an' haunt you!'

Colonel Rokesley sent an immediate signal to Brigade:

Respectfully suggest that the construction of coffins in the proximity of roads where fighting-troops are being marched to the line can only undermine their morale.

The next day was the last for the delivery of mail and newspapers, and the postmen's bags were heavier than usual.

BIG PUSH IMMINENT IN YPRES SECTOR.
'SUPREME CONFIDENCE IN SUCCESS' SAYS MILITARY SPOKESMAN.

To the troops in the line there was nothing new in this but it still left them angry. 'Christ, they censor our letters so no one at home knows where we are or what we're doing! What's the point in that when all they got to do is pick up a fuckin' newspaper? You know, I'm coming to the conclusion that this bloody war's being run by a bunch of mental fuckin' defectives!' In the last days before an attack they were sensitive to everything but most of all to the suspicion that those in whose hands they must put their lives were incompetent – or worse, careless.

The letters were longer today and they read them more than once, lingering over the phrases telling them they were loved, reassuring themselves that if they were to go they wouldn't go unmourned. But how could those at home give comfort without underlining the need for it?

We shall think of you and pray for you, as we always do and always will.

Keep your chin up, son, and don't forget we'll all be cheering you on from over here.

If there's ever been anything in my letters you didn't quite understand, don't let it worry you now. All you need to know is that I've never stopped loving you.

They sat near their rifles, their boots unlaced and a fag going, half their minds far from here. Geoff Tuffnel leaned with his back to an ammo-box, thumbing open an envelope and letting it fall as he read. Sometimes a voice came.

'Blimey, there's a bomb come down on the Star an' Garter near where I live! They were all in the cellar, though – an' pissed as a fart, I don't mind bettin'.'

A squad of R.E.s went dodging through to the line carrying direction-signs and rolls of white tape. A recce-plane was buzzing somewhere above them in the scattered cloud.

'My Dad's got first prize again for his chrysaneth – chrysan – for 'is daisies at the Croydon Horticut – Horticuli – flower show las' week, what you think of that!'

The ack-ack batteries had got a bearing on the plane and were pooping off at it.

'There you are, Geoff, this is my youngest, look. The other two are girls. See anything of me in him, do you?' He held out the sepia photograph. 'He's going to do great things, this boy, or better than what I've done, any rate. Geoff?'

The big hands beside him held the letter steady, creasing its edges, gripping too hard. His eyes weren't moving over the lines any more.

'Geoff! Take a look at my youngest. He remind you of anyone, eh?'

In a moment Geoff turned his head. 'What was that?'

'Look – my kiddo, first picture I've seen! Put you in mind of someone does he?'

Geoff nodded dully. 'He's like you, Ted. Like his father.' He turned away.

'Think so?' He held the photograph at arm's length, chuckling. 'Well I never! Image of me already, is he, well fancy that!'

•   •   •

295

The battalion was paraded in the afternoon, lower ranks only. No reason was given but the reason was known. The N.C.O.s stood stiffly with their rosters.

'Wallace. 438 Smith. Maddox.'

The ranks were unusually quiet.

'Barclay-Smith. Jacobs. 293 Brown.'

The officers and N.C.O.s had already gone down to the transport lines: Maj. Simms, second-in-command of the battalion, two captains, five subalterns, two company sergeant-majors and ten sergeants. They were to form the cadre in Minimum Reserve, withdrawn from the attack so that in the event of heavy losses they could reorganize the survivors.

'Sarn't Bruce!'

'Sir?'

The men of No. 4 Platoon, C Company, stood waiting while Bruce and the Adjutant consulted their lists.

A man in the ranks said under his breath: 'Get on with it . . .'

A murmur came from beside him. 'Your name's on it, Mac, or it isn't, so there's nothin' you can do.'

But you thought of it both ways. Give a year's pay to hear your name called on this parade, on the other hand you'd feel you were letting your mates down, slinking off to the transport lines while they went over the top.

The adjutant passed on to No. 3 Platoon and Sgt Bruce faced the men again.

'Right, stop that talking! Tremayne. 292 Rawlings. Reeves. 187 Jones. Clarkson.'

The names were always picked at random except where there were brothers, in which case one of them was sent into Minimum Reserve.

'Fowler. Coppins. That's the lot. Right, all those I've called out, report to Corp'l Baily!'

Parade dismiss.

'Cheero, Tom, take care of yourself, lad.'

'Good luck, mate.'

'See you when you get back, eh?'

Some of them shook hands.

'Look after this for me, Jim.' A knife with a carved bone hilt. Jim had often admired it.

'Keep it with you, chum, it'll bring you luck.'

'Take it, come on. 'Case I lose it, see.'

'Well – all right.'

Corporal Baily led his party away and only when they were out of sight did they lighten their step.

In the transport lines 1st-Lt Talbot had put in a request to see Maj. Simms. 'I didn't want to miss this one, sir.'

'Why not?'

'Well it looks like a big show and I'd like to do something useful. Couldn't someone with less battle experience take my place here?'

'Sorry, but it can't be done. I think we can rely on your brother to "do something useful" for both of you.'

'But surely—'

'I said it can't be done.'

Vic said with his mouth tight: 'Very well, sir.' He turned away.

'Talbot!'

'Sir?'

'Get that salute a lot smarter.'

In the evening the battalion was paraded in close column of companies, all ranks present. Cloud was still drawing in from the north and there seemed promise of rain. Along the west horizon lay a streak of late sunlight, thinning and yellowing as the minutes passed; against it the figure of Col. Lord Rokesley sat erect on his black charger.

'Stand the men easy, 'Major.'

Regimental Sergeant-Major Blossom swung to face the companies.

'Battalion . . . Stand at – *haice*! Stand – *haisy*!'

The murmur of gunfire, never ceasing during the long afternoon, echoed from the hills south of the salient; the cloud-base was already flickering overhead, brighter than the day's last light.

Rokesley shifted in his saddle, doubtful of his chances here: he was speaking to jaded and disillusioned men, their bodies aching and their minds embittered by the labour they should not have been called upon to do in their last few days before battle. The veterans among them – and there weren't many – had gone storming into the field four years ago with the courage of crusaders and a whole new world to win, only to see their comrades slaughtered in the mud, thrown wholesale against the guns as if the policy of their generals were to exhaust the enemy of his ammunition and nothing more. The greater part of these men were conscripts, young men fighting an old war, and they wanted none of it. It was no good telling them the tide was on the turn or that tomorrow would see a glorious victory. They'd seen the coffins being made for them behind the lines and that was all they knew.

He swung his horse broadside and so close to them that he looked into the very eyes of the front rankers.

'There's been a lot to do in the past few weeks – a hell of a lot! But you can't work miracles without a bit of effort, and that's what you've done – you've brought off a miracle. You've seen to it – you, every one of you, every single man – that in the face of all the obstacles God ever made, an army has been put into the field under the very nose of a watchful enemy. And now you're going to rest, as you more than deserve, for nearly twelve hours. That's not long but it's all the time we can spare because we're going to help finish off this war and go home and nobody's going to stop us – certainly not the German Army, what's left of it!'

With the lightest touch of his spurs he moved the charger into a rhythmic stride along the ranks, making it seem that impatience itself had stirred both horse and rider with a sense of great events. Wheeling with a deliberate degree of flourish he reined in and faced them again.

'Tomorrow we're going to start a damned great battle! The noise we're going to make will be heard as far away as England and they'll say – "By God, that must be the 3rd Dukes with their blood up again!" Will they be right?'

The murmur began fitfully, then rose to a roar so suddenly that his mount tossed its mane and would have shied if he hadn't been ready to hold it close-reined. He'd hoped for a response; this was an ovation and he was moved by it. There'd been other things he'd planned to tell them but the moment had passed: he was listening to a battle-cry and that was enough. Coming to the salute he took heart from it, then wheeled away.

.   .   .

Dew lay along the sandbags, soft grey satin touched by the first coming of the light; the scent of autumn breathed from the crumbled earth.

A match flared in a cupped hand.

'Got one for me, Bert?'

'Me last one. 'Ave a puff.'

They stood packed in the trench with their shoulders nearly touching. The battle police were deployed at close intervals, covertly watching the troops for signs of panic: a boy near a traverse had gone white about the face in the last few minutes and kept looking round, licking his lips; an M.P. stared straight into the young desperate eyes. *You'll have to go, son, you'll have to go.*

The morning was unnervingly quiet. Perhaps it was like this most mornings, they couldn't remember; it was the waiting that made you notice things. Pee-wits called from the valley and a dog barked a long way off with a constant *yap - yap - yap* that got on your nerves till you hoped to Christ someone'd shoot the bloody thing.

'Geoff?'

The rain that was promised last night had never come; the wind had shifted soon after midnight and they felt its cool brushing their cheeks; there was the taint of putrefaction in it, and chemicals.

'Geoff?'

The dark head turned.

'You all right?'

'Yes.'

'I just wondered.' Geoff had been quiet, even for him, since yesterday afternoon. As long as he was all right.

A young subaltern leaned near the M.G. post, watching the faces of the men. If any were scared – just one would do – it was all right, he'd feel he'd got company. Someone moved beside him and he turned his head.

'Hello Talbot. I thought you were out of this show.'

'Change of plans.' He'd come up with the ration-party and all he had to do now was keep out of Aubrey's sight.

A man coughed and the sound was trapped, muffled by the close-packed bodies; he felt embarrassed: it was like when you coughed in church.

Sergeant Bruce stepped neatly between the troops and the line of battle police, checking each man. Haversack in rearward position, water-bottle on right hip, bandolier over the right shoulder and under the left arm, bombs in each side-pocket, coloured tabs in place.

A kid stood shaking, clinging to his rifle, his head lowered and his breath coming in slow shudders. Bruce heard him and turned back.

'Had your breakfast, boy?'

'Yes.' A whisper from the drained white face. The man next to him said:

'I'll look after 'im, Sarge.'

'We all will.' He poured a tot into the metal cup of his flask. 'Come on, this one's on the King.' He watched the strained smile touch the boy's face and looked away while he drank, choking over the spirit. What had happened, then, to England? It was meant to be a strong nation, the head of a great empire, proud of its flag. What kind of men had dragged this kid from his home to stand him here at dawn today, a razor in his kit he was still too young to need, a rifle in his hand too heavy to run with, a knot of fear in his stomach that would cripple him when the whistles blew and the M.P.s came to push him over the sandbags to his death? Didn't that bloody country want its children any more, that they had to be got rid of like you drowned kittens in a sack?

'All right now, lad?'

'Yes. Yes thank you.'

'We'll look after you, don't worry. We're just going to finish this bit of business, then we'll be off home, like the Colonel said.' He screwed the cup back on the flask and passed on, bitter with shame.

A man eased his tin hat but it slid forward again because of the sweat under the band. 'What's the time, Paddy?'

'Time it started, boy-o, that's all I know.'

The light was strengthening. Dew spangled the spiders' webs across the broken ground.

Company Sergeant-Major Kilderbee was passing the flank redoubt when the barrage opened up. He was an experienced soldier but the first shock of the guns stopped him dead in his tracks and he put a hand to the sandbags to steady himself.

Some of the men had cried out, thinking a shell was coming at them out of nowhere; then they looked at each other with their mouths open in a silent laugh as the sky bellowed above their heads and the duckboards lurched underfoot.

Near C Company dugout the earth began trickling from the parapet, some of it lodging among the telephone cables. Capt. Barnett, liaison officer to the forward assault companies, flicked them delicately with his cane to clear them. Noticing Maj. Talbot consulting his watch he made his expression a questionmark – it was impossible to speak – and the major nodded. The barrage was on time.

Aubrey looked at the sky. The low cloud was flushed with acid colours, a false sunrise that spread from hill to hill to pour a nervous light across their slopes. The forward batteries were too near the line for their shells to be seen as objects but the sky had the look of a sea disturbed by sudden gusts of wind, rushing and whirling into spirals of freak turbulence that shifted massively eastwards as the minutes passed.

Captain Barnett had his lips pursed in a whistle, and Aubrey nodded again, standing with hands on hips. At their final briefing Rokesley had said: 'There'll be fourteen divisions going in – British, French and American – in support of the New Zealanders and Australians already holding the salient. We've been promised a two-hour barrage from close on three thousand guns, which ought to make a noise worth hearing.'

It was more than a noise: it came from no particular direction, filling the sky and spilling over the earth. When you opened your mouth the air pulsed on your tongue and when you shut your eyes you could feel the lids quivering. Whatever you touched was trembling; your body itself trembled. Nothing was still.

Counter-battery fire had started up in the first half-hour and some of the shells dropped short.

'*Stretcher-bearers!*'

Part of the C Company trench vanished in a shock of orange flame and then sent sandbags hurling aloft; the explosion was barely heard, being merely an extension of the tumult that had come to dominate earth and sky. A thunderstorm had fallen to the ground and raged there.

Somewhere between Geoff and Sam, Tom Follett slid to the

duckboards and sat with his head on his knees. It was all right, you didn't have to mind this noise because it was helping you, smashing the enemy trenches and wire so you wouldn't have so much to do when you went in. You had to go on thinking about this, inside your head where there was a little bit of silence left.

At the end of the first hour there were men leaning against the parapet, their bodies angled forward as if a gale pressed them there. They'd forgotten what the noise was for; they only knew it was too big for them and wouldn't let them alone. Their hands pressed at the shivering clay as if they could hold it still.

Daylight had come, bringing the nightmare out of the dark and hanging it across the sky in streaks of smoke that floated up from the guns and spread in a man-made cloud reeking of chemicals.

Someone turned away from the fire-step and wandered blindly with his hands to his face as if he believed there was somewhere he could go where the noise couldn't reach him any more. One of the battle police grabbed him and led him back to where he'd left his rifle. He stood with it shaking, the tears bright on his face.

At 0845 hours the senior N.C.O.s began threading along the trench to take up their positions.

A boy swayed from the parapet and fell stiffly, toppling like a doll, and his rifle crashed down across his back. Nothing had touched him but the sound-waves that had built against his senses minute by minute until they were overwhelmed.

The noise wasn't all they had to deal with. Somewhere across the parapet lay the jumping-off tapes.

Tomorrow we're going to start a damned great battle!

They'd all cheered. It had seemed very grand.

Tomorrow was now.

The sergeants were shouting. *'Fix bayonets!'*

Many couldn't hear them above the beat of the guns. Their friends nudged them. The blades made a glinting frieze along the sandbags.

By the machine-gun post Vic saw the young subaltern draw his revolver and slip the catch and put the muzzle into his mouth and pull the trigger.

302

Just before the guns lifted at 0900 hours Capt. Barnett saw a short neat sergeant approach Maj. Talbot near the C Company dugout and shake hands with him.

As the barrage began creeping forward there sounded the faint shrilling of whistles.

XV

The ground shook as they went forward. Their own barrage had lifted to creep a hundred yards ahead of them but the enemy batteries were feeling their way across the area and they ran with their heads down, their helmets angled against the mortal gale that swept the land; and the land heaved under them.

The leading assault-wave pitched into craters still thick with the gas of the explosion, clambering to the far rim and running on.

'*Come on the Dukes!*'

Three men ran together. They had always been friends, growing up as neighbours in Bromley Villas, getting their comics at Lawson's the newspaper-shop and chalking rude things on Ma Cooper's gate because she was an old cat. They had been called up together and they were neighbours now as they ran side by side across the shuddering earth and into the shell that tossed their fragments high above where they had just been running side by side.

'*Keep spread out – don't bunch!*'

There was no machine-gun fire. The remnant of the leading platoon had reached their first objective: the front-line trench. But it had gone; the barrage had levelled it and strewn the wire in great loose skeins that writhed on the ground as the shelling vibrated them. Men tripped there, the barbs hooking at their clothes and trapping them; and some of them screamed the moment they felt themselves caught: whether they ran or kept still the chances of being hit were about the same but they had to be free to run; they couldn't hang quivering here on the wire waiting for death.

The light was metallic, a bronze haze drifting across the craters. Men moved through it doggedly, their shadows thrown against the smoke of the last shell by the flare of the next.

'*Stretcher-bearers!*'

Tom ran as hard as he could, keeping his eyes on the ridge that was C Company's second objective, sometimes seeing the flicker that meant a machine-gun: the Devons were going forward on the flank ahead of them and meeting resistance. Tom noted things like this, watching out for the wire and keeping in line with his section-leader, but his real mind floated somewhere above him, nothing to do with his body; it thought about other things while his clockwork legs ran on. Would they call everyone together one day and say stop the war, or did they mean to get everyone killed first, so there wouldn't be any argument as to who'd won? It would be nice to see inside the minds of those people, just once, the people who managed everything for you. You'd got to trust in them but it would make you feel better if you could just see what they were thinking, so that you knew they weren't making mistakes. His legs ran mindlessly under him for a minute more and then the air rushed and he threw his body down and lay still while the sun burst and mountains collided and the earth rocked beneath his chest. The hot wind tugged at him and he bit at the clay with his eyes shut tight and heard voices calling faintly from outside his head. Your head was where you had to live, sometimes, all of you, curled up where nothing could get at you.

Bits hit his neck and hands and something rang against his helmet. He lay choking in the fumes, listening to someone screaming. A long time after this he got up and started forward again, but it wasn't a long time really because Cpl Sykes was only a little distance ahead, and he caught up slowly. Mr Kemp was on the other side and farther away, shouting something, perhaps meaning they must all keep in line.

A pigeon went winging through the smoke.

Someone yelled: 'They're through! The Devons are through!' He stopped and for a second or two stood stiffly, then fell on his back, the way a child would do, playing soldiers.

The first prisoners began going back soon after noon. They were mostly from the reserve trenches, survivors of the preliminary barrage, and staggered blindly across the churned wastes, bumping together and falling, helping one another up, their bloodless faces swinging like the heads of oxen under the yoke. One of them seemed mad, walking with his head thrown back to laugh at the sky; another man hit out at him to make him stop but the blow caught someone else and he reeled away, falling.

The bearers made their way among the craters, bloodied from the waist down as if they carried knives, not stretchers.

'*Don't touch me!*'

'All right, chum. Let's get you out o' this, then.'

'*Christ sake leave me be, I can't—*'

'Get his feet, Bob. Easy now.'

'*No! No! Don't—*'

'Easy does it.'

The thing writhed on the wet shining canvas and the scream died away to choking. Their boots slithered and then they steadied, finding their rhythm.

A padre crouched among the wire, looking down into the dulling eyes of a boy whose left hand clutched a lucky mascot of some kind, a small animal made of grey felt with some of the stitches pulled away. 'And may God in His infinite mercy receive you unto His house . . .'

'*Bearers this way!*'

The smoke drew low, creeping into the craters. A faint drizzle had started, darkening the earth. Farther to the east the popple of gunfire echoed from the ridge.

Geoff knew that he'd lost touch with his platoon but made no attempt to catch up. There were stragglers near him still going forward as he was, some of them foraging for ammunition among the dead. He spoke to none of them. Blood seeped from his arm, covering his hand. He walked slowly but with his feet quite steady, knowing that in this way he would get there faster than if he ran. He didn't know yet where 'there' would be. Not the ridge, the second objective. He knew that 'there' existed.

He'd torn it up and thrown it away because he wouldn't need to read it again. *You will not want news of this kind, Geoffrey, when you are so far away, and I will not burden you with a long letter. Our little Judith passed on during last night, just after her mother and I went to the hospital to see her. This would be on 12 September, a week before her birthday. We talked about you, of course, and she was quite cheerful, though very weak. That is all, then. We know that you are with us in our grief.*

Wire caught at his legs and he pulled it away. There was some shouting over to his left where a pocket of Jerry reserves was trying to fight a rearguard action. The trench was bad

306

here; you could only see where parts of it were by the bodies lying about. He clambered through it and made his way to the right, where an explosion of some sort had wrecked the traverse; it looked as if it might have been one of their own ammo-stores going up. Smoke was coming from some timbers that had caught, and his eyes were smarting from it.

Then there were the two Germans. He got his rifle up but they'd not seen him yet. One was quite an old chap with scars on his doughy face and his grey hair cropped close to the scalp; the other was a thin boy, his cheeks hollow and blue-white under the dirt, his eyes watching the man with trust in them. It looked as if he'd been buried alive and his friend had pulled him out. The two of them were crawling over the rubble, the old one helping the kid to move because he'd lost the use of his legs.

Geoff stood looking down at them for what seemed a long time, the rifle in his hands. Where are they going? he thought. There wasn't anywhere to go. The man rested for a bit, holding the boy across his knees and talking to him; Geoff didn't understand the words, only the tone of them, the hope in them. The smoke crept through the trench, making them cough.

The man moved again, getting to his feet by sliding his back up the earth wall inch by inch, bringing the boy with him. Then he saw Geoff standing over them and the hope went out of his face; he looked down at the rifle and up again into Geoff's eyes. The boy had seen him now and a spasm of terror jerked through his frail body. He lay hooked over the man's arms, the dirt still falling from him. They didn't move any more.

Geoff looked at them in silence for a while, as if one day he might want to remember their faces, the old man's and the boy's; then he swung the rifle high and lunged downwards, driving the bayonet into the earth, and walked away. Behind him the butt quivered and then was still.

He walked for a long time, all through the rest of the day.

Sergeant Stokes took another pace and the ground lifted under him and threw him against the wall of the dugout and a man yelled —

'*Sam!*'

'What'n the hell?'

'The sergeant's gone!'

The rest of them stopped. Earth from the explosion pattered on their helmets. They gathered by the dugout, fifteen of them, the remnant of No. 4 Platoon. There had been fifty-six. They had kept together most of the time, making their own way on the left flank of C Company through the enemy lines and across the stream that ran below the ridge. Lt Robinson had led them as far as the stream and then a shell had come, smashing the footbridge; it was one of the metal supports that had caught him, whirling like a crowbar. The sergeant had brought them on to the trenches here, or what was left of them: it had been the old defence-line of a year ago, full of skeletons with their spiked helmets still on, an eerie place.

Sam came across to the dugout.

'Percy?'

There wasn't much to show because his legs were buried in the earth, but the blood was draining from his face and his eyes were screwed up tight. 'Oh Jesus,' Sam said low, 'oh Jesus.'

'Don't come near me, Sam!' His breath hissed as earth tumbled from the wrecked wall. 'There might be some more of them. Keep the boys away, Sam.'

'Okay. Okay.' He began sifting the earth with his fingers, scooping it away on the surface. 'But we have to get y'out of here, see.'

'No.' Percy's face was ashen, and crimson was seeping through the soil around him. 'I'm all right as I am.' He turned his head in little jerks until he was looking at Sam. His eyes were bright; the rest of his face was losing the look of life as his heart went on pumping it away. 'Take the platoon, Sam. I'm handin' over.'

'Sure I'll take 'em.' His fingers turned the earth, sifting it as if for gold. 'We just have to pull y'out of here first, see.'

Percy didn't say anything and Sam went on working for a while and then looked up and saw his face, and his hands stopped moving. The drizzle fell cobweb-fine, borne on a small wind from the south.

The redoubt was on the right flank of C Company's assault-sector, half a mile from the foot of the ridge and a mile from their second objective: the fold in the ridge itself where the enemy was entrenched. The redoubt had been designed to take advantage of a natural basin, perhaps a dew-pond where cattle had come to drink in earlier times.

The pigeon was warm in Freddie's hand; he could feel the beat of its heart.

Corporal Sykes was quiet now; they had made box-splints from the thigh-bones of a skeleton: the redoubt had been abandoned long before today and there obviously hadn't been time to bury the dead. They'd found three spiked helmets and set them upside down to catch the rainwater, though they couldn't hope for much.

Aubrey wrote: *15.42 Defending German redoubt A-13-27* with *22 men. 5 rounds left. No water. Assistance required.*

Two runners had been sent back an hour ago, volunteers who'd been told what their chances were, though they hadn't needed telling. The machine-guns on the slope had started up within seconds of their reaching the rising ground behind the redoubt but no one had actually seen what happened to them.

Aubrey slipped the message into the cartridge and Freddie opened his hand; the bird rose and wheeled towards the north-west, dipping low through the rain-haze.

From below the wall of the redoubt Tom watched it, marvelling. Even Mr Willis didn't know about pigeons. 'I dunno how they manage it, Tom, it's beyond the likes o' me. But then, how can you fit all of a big oak inside of a tiddy acorn? It's His works, is all I knows.'

Archie Dowson lay beside him, very still. Tom felt he ought to go on sitting here as long as he could, to give him company while he was going on his way like the bird had gone. There were four others but they couldn't bury them because Maj. Aubrey had said nobody had got to stand up any more: 'You know what our situation is. The attack has been pivoted on this flank and their reserves are commanding the area immediately south of us. They know we're here but they don't know how many. I'm not going to tell you we shan't be discovered before dark – if they keep on going they'll find us right in their path. But if we lie low there's a chance of calling up some covering-fire that'll help to get us out. It's not a big chance. I want you to know the worst because then we'll try all the harder to do something about it.'

Tom saw a beetle crawling over Archie Dowson's hand, and brushed it away. Archie had said: 'Jim's goin' to like havin' my knife.' It was the last thing he'd ever said; he meant the one with the carved bone hilt, and Tom wondered that it could have been so important to him, talking about it when he knew he was dying. Perhaps it was like Oscar's mouth-organ and Smithy's compass and slide-rule and all that: you needed something to keep with you, making you safe. But Archie must have known he was going to die this afternoon, giving his knife to Jim. How had he known? It was the way the pigeons flew, perhaps, the way the acorn grew. What old Mr Willis called 'His works'.

Someone said: 'Christ, I've got a thirst.'

'Keep it to yourself, then.' The voice was savage. They'd all got a thirst on them; it was another thing the bloody High Command had never got round to finding out: in battle you burned up your moisture quicker than ammunition and all you'd got was a tin flask and lucky if it wasn't full of bloody holes inside five minutes.

They all watched the major.

Freddie crouched on his haunches, sorting out his shell-dressing. His eyes were bloodshot and there was a dent in his helmet as if someone had hit it with a meat-axe; he'd caught some of the blast from the five-nine that had finished Kilderbee. He spoke quietly so that no one else could hear.

'What do we do when they come, Mr Aubrey?'

'It depends.' His throat was sore from the lyddite fumes and his head throbbed whenever he moved; he didn't think he was wounded anywhere and he didn't intend to look; his whole body was a vast bruise: they'd been an hour clearing the Hun out of the reserve trenches and two hours running the gauntlet of shells from the batteries south of the ridge. 'It depends on when they come and how many there are. If there looks like a fighting chance we'll fix bayonets.'

He had walked alone through the day, going south all the time; and now he stood on the hill facing the way he had come. Smoke filled half the valley and was lit by flashes; it was like a slow fire burning. That was the war down there. The game.

He'd seen a lot of Judith on the way here, combing her red

hair and smiling to him. *I've had it cropped short, so it doesn't get caught in the machines.* But he wasn't here because of Judith.

There were trees on the hill and he went into them, turning to sit and watch the valley. On his way through the day he'd felt strange sometimes and had wondered what he could be doing, walking alone; but that had only been because his hands were empty. He'd carried a rifle across land like that for four years and it took some getting used to, walking like a man, alone. There'd been shelling and some bearers had yelled at him to get down but he'd walked on. *He's off his nut, Arthur, we'd best clobber 'im an' take 'im in!* But he'd shaken them off.

The leaves made a light rushing above his head and he looked up at the wealth of their greenness spread across the sky; the earth smelt sweet and he dug his fingers in to feel how rich it was. The war had never been here; this was the past and he remembered it and could have wept for love of it. He'd known for a long time he'd be here one day, ever since he'd found out what the war was, in the fields of Vauxcourt. A game.

God alive, he'd been slow about it but never mind. It had needed something to get inside his head and blow up there; so maybe it was because of Judith after all. Her and the two Jerries down there.

It was raining in the valley; the smoke of the guns made a grey sea stained with the flashes they were sending out. Some were firing east and some west; he could see plainer from up here what they were doing. They were smashing up the earth to make a grave of it.

He heard movement in the trees behind him but didn't turn round; there'd be living things here. The blood had long since clotted on his arm; whatever it was would heal; everything would from now on; one day he'd be able to think of Judith as nothing more than a girl he'd loved, instead of half his life torn away from him, caught in the machines.

The smoke swirled in the valley, daubed with the feverish light of the guns. They weren't tired of the game yet; there were too many people enjoying it, strutting up and down Whitehall, in and out of Parliament, silk hats and taxis and important documents, *in the interests of the nation,* ministers and generals and officers of the state, *the needs of the armed forces,* wing collars and spats to keep the wet off their shoes and not one of them, not one of them with sense enough or guts enough to stand up and shout *for Christ's sake, England's bleeding to death!*

Wouldn't go down at all well, that. Policies to pursue, faces to save, reputations to make; besides, the theatres would lose money and the black market would have to close, no victories in the papers and not a flag in sight, no brave boys to cheer on their way and no heroes to welcome home. Stop the war and you'd shut down the biggest circus the world had ever seen.

Well I'm not in it any more.

I know your sort, Tuffnel: you want a moustache and you get one; you want a prisoner and you get one.

Now I want peace.

In a minute he got up and turned away and saw them standing there watching him, three of them in torn field grey, bare-headed and with no equipment. They were old campaigners, men of twenty-four or twenty-five, their faces pocked, scarred and sallow from the trenches, their bodies held in a permanent stoop for fear of snipers, their eyes nervy and watchful. One held a sheath-knife and looked ready to use it, untrusting of strangers. Geoff saw this and was angry and reached for the man, locking his wrist and catching the knife as it fell, flinging it a long way off.

'Won't you ever learn?

There were still two hours of daylight left but the drizzle held the smoke to the ground and they wandered through a fog that stank of explosives, their throats raw and their eyes running.

'What 'appened to Joe?'

'Joe who?'

'Joe Green.'

'Saw him on the wire.'

'Bugger owed me 'alf a dollar.'

'Better ask his missus.'

Prisoners were still coming in by the hundred. A group of them under Cpl Stevens had taken a dozen red-soaked stretchers from their exhausted bearers and were scouting among the craters. The flash of field artillery still pulsed from the southern end of the ridge and the ruins of the village below; the rumour was that Jerry had rushed up reserves and was going to turn his defence into a counter-attack. He could do as he pleased; they'd had enough for today.

The fine rain brought quiet of a kind, muffling all but the sharpest sounds: the clink of equipment and the rattle of the Salvage Corps wallahs gathering the rifles in. Voices were muted.

'They say young Chisholme got it, eh?'

'Yus, stupid little sod. "Forward!" 'e yells at us, wavin' 'is bleedin' stick, jus' as if there wasn' a machine-gun almos' pokin' up 'is arse. We tried to get 'im to take cover but no, 'e wouldn' 'ave it. "Forward!" All 'e could fuckin' think about.'

'Well he was brave enough, you can't deny that.'

'*Brave?* What's brave about stickin' yer neck out an' askin' for it, I'd like to know? What good did 'e do? Oh, there's a tidy few young officers like 'im, make no mistake. They get theirselves worked up over it all like what natives do at a war-dance. 'E thought 'e made a fine sight, see, standin' in the open wavin' us all on. Where would we 'ave been if we'd took notice? It's the glory they think about, see, an' what do they get for it? One up the arse.'

A huge German overtook them, a British corporal on his back and far gone.

'I can't fuckin' figure it out you know, Ernie. One minute we're tryin' to kill each other an' the next minute we're tryin' to save each other. Who's barmy?'

Two medical officers were searching among the craters with their orderlies, pumping morphine into the bloodied bundles that still moaned.

'You all right, Talbot?'

'What? Oh, hello.' Vic looked down from the edge of the shell-hole. The M.O. was a doctor from Richmond, drafted out here a week ago. 'Can't bloody well walk, that's all.'

'Want me to have a look?'

'Christ, I'm well off.' He turned away. 'Thanks all the same.' He'd passed beyond anger because it was a sprain, nothing more; fortunately it hurt like hell, giving him a kind of relief. A non-combatant indisposition, like that time he'd been stuck up at Base with trench fever. He ought to be on the ridge by now enjoying the fruits of victory with Three Platoon instead of limping through this messy field to a dressing-station.

There were stragglers still coming back, a lot of them no more than fatigued, putting it on as if they were wounded. You wouldn't have seen this in the early part of the war, by God; there'd been a thing called morale in those days.

Two of them were bent over something in the mud.

'Better let the Colonel see it, not as there's much hope.'

Vic dragged his leg, pulling the damned thing after him. He'd tried to keep up with his platoon but had fainted clean out twice and that was more humiliating than walking about like a drunken cripple.

'Where's H.Q., then?'

'In a shell-'ole, last I saw of it.'

They straightened up. One held a dead pigeon.

'That a message?' Vic asked them.

'Yes, sir.'

'Come on then.'

They gave it to him. The writing was familiar and he looked quickly at the name of the sender, then read it through twice. The dizziness came back and everything went dark for a bit and he felt one of them grab at his arm. His whole head was singing. 'I'm all right, damn you!' He shook the man off. *'So he's come a cropper at last, has he?'*

'Sir?'

'Christ, I don't believe it!' Shouting or laughing, he didn't know which. They were staring at him. 'I don't believe it!'

The rain was too fine. It filled the air and fell on their hands and faces: it was everywhere but not enough to drink. A few minutes ago they'd emptied the three Pickelhauber helmets into a tin mug but it was less than a quarter full and they'd given it to Cpl Sykes, who was still conscious. Some of them sat with their faces to the sky, their mouths open to feel the rain on their tongues; one man licked his bayonet and held it flat to the rain and licked it again; the steel tasted bitter and cool.

'I 'ave no pain, dear mother, now; but oh! I am so dry. Connect me to a brewery, an' leave me there to die.'

'Shuddup, sod you. We're not goin' to die.'

But they were less afraid of dying than of having to sit here waiting for it.

314

Aubrey had scraped earth away from the top of the redoubt and was keeping observation. There was still sporadic firing from the south-east where a German unit was well dug in and determined to hold out; it was from there that machine-gun fire came whenever they thought they saw movement in the redoubt.

Freddie watched the men, his glance moving from one to the next. Only one or two were trying to make a joke of it and the rest weren't willing to listen. They should have had Percy Stokes here with them.

'How long can we hold out, Sarge?'

'As long as we've got to. Till there's some reinforcements.'

He didn't say where he thought they'd be coming from. Half the battalion were casualties and the other half were consolidating the ridge position. In a couple of hours it'd be dark but there wasn't much hope in that: one parachute-flare and they'd be mown down as they ran.

'The thought that worries me most,' Aubrey said, coming to squat beside him, 'is that they might decide it's worth sending in shells to finish us off.'

Freddie moved his eyes. 'Keep your head down, Taylor, I'm not warnin' you again!' They were beginning to feel trapped, to want the relief of just a quick look above the crumbling wall of the redoubt. He said quietly: 'If they send shells in it'll make a bit of smoke.'

'If we're still here to use it.'

'They'll want some luck to get a direct hit first time.'

He knew Mr Aubrey's mind: he wasn't losing hope so much as blaming himself, yet there wasn't anything he could have done different. This redoubt had been a valuable forward position and they'd got here before anyone else; it was only that the flank had been turned, costing them the last of their ammunition.

'We'll have to get them cabbages up, Mr Aubrey.'

'Cabbages?'

'Soon as we go back. Where all them lovely delphiniums were. I don't know how Mr Willis ever allowed such a thing.'

Aubrey felt the ashplant under his hand, scarred and split and mended with copper wire. For a long time now he hadn't thought of it as anything but the stick he'd carried with him

315

through desolation for as long as he could remember; but that was wrong. However unlikely it seemed that he'd ever see again the tree from which he'd cut this branch, he mustn't forget it was still there. Ashbourne would in any case survive him, but inasmuch as this was in his hand he still survived in Ashbourne.

The shots traced the air directly above the redoubt but sounded higher than before, a faint *wheep-wheep-wheep* that blended now with the sharper percussion of the gun itself towards the east.

None of the men had moved. Freddie swung his head in little jerks like a terrier.

'What was that for,' asked Aubrey, 'precisely?'

'It wasn't meant for us, I know that much.'

They dodged low to the west rampart and dragged sandbags away to make a lookout. The terrain was desolate under the drizzle, the light sheening across the rising ground that kept them captive. The shots hummed again through the haze above them, fanning in a wide traverse as if uncertain of the target; then their sound was doubled in a sudden crackle of counter-fire.

A tremor ran through the earth.

'Trench-mortar, sir!'

'Yes.'

They turned instinctively and saw the flash burst seconds later on the south fold of the ridge. The target was the machine-gun post that had trapped them here for the past three hours. Aubrey took a deep breath.

'Tell them, Freddie.'

The men were on their feet, grabbing their empty rifles from habit. '*Keep down!*' Freddie called sharply. 'Keep down an' hold yourselves ready. We're gettin' out of here but wait for the orders!'

There was no cheering; perhaps they were in awe of what was being offered them: life. In one man the tension broke and he lowered his head to his knees, sobbing. The air was alive now with the ripple of high-velocity shots and the brute thump of the mortar shook the ground at intervals; a second gun had started up west of the redoubt, its sound-waves steady and not traversing. Vic came over the sandbags.

He came over feet first, scattering earth and pitching across

316

one of the dead men below the north rampart, lying still for a moment, his breath hissing in pain. A Very pistol had dropped from his hand. He was not recognized immediately: they were cut off from their own battalion and someone brought his rifle up, thinking he was a German. Aubrey didn't see who it was until his brother raised himself on to one arm, his face white under its spattering of mud.

'*Vic*. Are you hit?'

'No.' He groped for the Very pistol.

Aubrey crouched over him. 'Have they brought in the Minimum Reserve?'

'No.' He was loading the pistol. Sweat ran from his face and his eyes were screwed up in pain.

'Then what are you doing here?'

'Someone had to tell you what's going on. Listen, we're short of ammo for that mortar but the M.G.s can keep it up for two or three minutes. Main thing is we can put smoke out as soon as you're ready.'

'We're ready,' Aubrey said.

The thump of the mortar had stopped.

'*Right!*' called Freddie. 'Two of you take Corp'l Sykes, two more look after their rifles, the rest of you stay close to the walkin' wounded!' He heard the grunt of the Very pistol behind him as Vic fired. 'Once you're on open ground spread out but keep in front of the smoke!' The green flare stained the rain-haze above them, touching their faces with its light.

'Which way over, Sarge?'

'You'll follow me.'

Sykes screamed as they lifted him.

Tom took one of their rifles.

'Vic, where are you hit?'

'I'm not bloody well hit!' He knocked Aubrey's hand away and staggered up and passed out cold and his brother caught him.

'Bomb's down, sir!'

Smoke was billowing a hundred yards south-east of the redoubt, low but spreading. The dull flame of a second bomb glowed and was smothered.

Freddie stood close. 'Smoke high enough, sir?'

'It'll have to be.' He cocked an ear. 'The guns are still

engaged – last chance we'll have.' Vic was still a dead weight and he got him into a fireman's lift across the shoulder.

'Give a hand, sir?'

'No, get the men away.'

'*Right – over the top!*'

Some of the shots came lower as they breasted the slope: the smoke-screen covered them well enough but it was a clear signal to the enemy gun positions that they were making a run for it; the air whined as they topped the rise.

'*Keep low but keep runnin' – don't go down!*'

If they went down and started crawling they'd go no more than a hundred yards before the smoke cleared and left them exposed.

Aubrey had swung Vic round and ran with him cradled in his arms, his own body a shield; the head lolled and the bloodless face was at peace, for a little time released from the bitterness that had aged it over the years; it was the young and barely remembered brother Aubrey carried across this hazardous ground. From behind him came the unhurried whickering of the machine-gun on the ridge as it fired blind through the screen hoping to kill by luck. Two other guns were still engaged in counter-fire; their shots passed more faintly overhead.

A rifle fell and lay abandoned.

'*Keep goin', lads! Keep goin'!*'

Someone went down on the left wing, tripping as the shots found him, their force pushing him over on to his face as if there were no time to spare for his dying.

'*Keep up the pace!*'

Freddie was in the rearguard with Tom abreast of him at twenty yards and directly behind the major; they followed the wounded who lagged near the centre, their gait unbalanced by a useless arm or weakened by loss of blood.

'*Keep goin'!*'

The gun traversed and one of the men carrying Cpl Sykes pitched forward across him; the other staggered, their weight dragging at him. Freddie was there.

'Right, I'm with you!'

Their boots slithered and steadied; they ran together, picking up the pace.

318

The gun traversed.

A man cried in lament as he kept up with the others, the words gusting softly out on his breath: 'Billy's gone ... oh my God, poor Billy's gone.'

The rain's cool touched their faces tenderly.

'*Keep goin'*, *lads, keep it up!*'

Pain stitched across a man's legs and he fell and began crawling.

Aubrey heard the windrush of bullets fluting close; two paces and a blaze of light burst in his head. Somewhere behind him Tom's voice, thin and desperate and dying away – '*Mr Kemp! It's the major ... Mr Kemp ...*'

XVI

The dining-hall of the château rang with voices.

'Coming up for seconds, Diana?'

She shook her head, munching a crust. The first helping had been quite bad enough but there was a queue forming at the trestle-tables where steam rose from the stew.

Babs chattered endlessly. 'Only English cooking could turn French food into English food!' But Diana noticed she was making short work of her 'seconds', actually choking over it at one stage because she had to keep on talking at the same time. 'What a performance, I'm so sorry!' Tears trickled down her red face. 'I think the Lord had a fit of economy on when He gave us the same orifice for eating and talking with!'

Diana drank her cocoa before any more skin formed on it. You could tell there was a convoy due in: the instruments had been rattling all day long and the excitement had been rising slowly until supper-time and now the messing-hall sounded worse than a monkeyhouse. It was nerves, that was all: however long you'd been at the game you were always frightened that *this* time you were going to cut too deeply with the scissors or drop a trephine or mistake the *methyl sal* for the *mist alba* because of the need to hurry. That was the worst nightmare: the fear that when they came in, desperate with the pain you were meant to ease, you'd make it worse.

'Di, is that all you're having?'

'I'm not hungry.'

But they were right, of course: you didn't know when you'd get time to eat again and even if you ate enough for ten people you'd still be famished again before the wards were quiet and you crawled to bed.

'I say, isn't it thrilling!'

Their voices were higher tonight for this reason too: the newspapers had come in for the first time in four days and victories were piling up. The Third and Fourth Armies had broken through at Havrincourt; the Americans had smashed a

320

breach through Ludendorff's defences farther south; the French were hounding across the Vesle and the South Africans pushing as far as the Canal du Nord after pitched battles; and *The Times* reported soberly that the Royal Navy, not content with having broken the stranglehold of the U-boats 'in the sovereign waters of this fortress isle', had brought its blockade of the Continent to the point where famine was widespread and most of the German Army weakened by lack of supplies.

'Take it all with a pinch of salt,' said Babs as she forked her suet pudding, 'but you can't tell me we're not going to win after all! I give it another six months at the most – you want to bet me?'

Diana finished her cocoa. Six months ought to seem nothing after all those years, but it was a life sentence, a death sentence. Six months more of the convoys . . . it wasn't even thinkable.

There'd been no actual fight with Matron. Perhaps there was none left in her now.

'Home posting, Lovell. You leave on the second of next month.'

'But there's so much to do here, Matron!'

'Of course there is, but do you think you're the only one who can do it?'

'I don't mean—'

'I know you don't. It's just that you've done too much already.'

'Can't I put in for leave instead?' The very thought was like an anaesthetic: what would you do with ten days' leave? You'd sleep.

'You're down for leave in any case, then it's Uxbridge Convalescent. You think the convalescent hospitals run themselves over there? They need people like you. Besides, it'll give you a chance to see some of the results of the work you've done out here; haven't you at least earned that much?'

'I don't think of it as earning anything—'

'Then you're lucky I've thought of it for you.' Matron had clasped her hands and leaned over them in the way she did when she was going to say something she meant you to listen to, and her brogue became richer. 'Of all my V.A.D.s you're the one I can spare the least and shall miss the most and that's why you're going. It's too easy, you see, for me to work my best people to breaking-point – because it's only the best who'll let me do it.'

That was yesterday. The notice was quite long enough for her to get used to the idea and she suspected that it was Matron's intention. But this was why she wasn't hungry tonight and why the war news meant nothing. She was giving up before she'd finished. Of course there was work to do in England but the stimulus wouldn't be in it; only here within an average of ten miles of the shifting battle-front could you feel close to the men you tried to help; the war was here and you were almost fighting it with them.

Julian hadn't given up before he'd finished. He'd gone on right to the end.

Watching them she envied them, the excitement in their faces as they leaned over each other's shoulders at the long scrubbed tables, the newspapers passing from hand to hand: Betty Denning, who'd fainted the first time she'd seen a convoy come in; Clare Shipley, gauche, gangling and with unbreakable nerves; the Honourable Rowena, a wad of bread and jam waving about as she held forth on the headlines; Kate – Ursula – Helen . . . She envied them their right to be here still, in three weeks' time. She left the table and was on her way out when it happened.

Sister MacFarlane stood there, slapping the open door with her big raw-boned hand: '*Convoy in! Con – voy!*'

The wave of silence passed through the hall like water through flames. Someone dropped a fork and didn't pick it up; a girl with wide young eyes, new here since the last convoy was in, put her hand to the edge of the table, her face slowly paling: she'd been told what it was like. Lights began fanning across the wall as the leading ambulance swung into the drive.

A newspaper was thrown down. 'Come on, then.'

They swarmed to the door and Diana – seeing them for the first time as if she weren't a part of them – realized they were suddenly different people; voices rose again but they were different voices, as calm now as they'd been excited a minute ago.

'Rosie, which ward are you tonight?'

'Anne, will you take dressings for me? I'm in theatre.'

322

'These your scissors, Betty?'

'Where's Sister Wilson? We're injecting with her.'

In the main hall the great doors came open and exhaust-gas tainted the air.

Matron stood on the iron weapons-chest, hands clasped in front of her.

'Ward Nine. Nurse Denning, cover him again.'

The stretchers filled the staircase, the bearers keeping close to the wall because there were still no banisters.

Exhaust-gas and now the gangrene smell.

'Morphia, please – quickly!'

A boy crooned over his pain, the fair hair soaked with sweat, the dull eyes losing their focus as he was lifted again, the lamps swinging and dimming at the edge of consciousness.

Diana crouched near one of the doors; someone had thrown a shawl round her shoulders because the night was chill. She turned the red-bordered field-cards, calling to Matron.

Sgt E. H. Coleman, R.E. Penet G.S.W. chest.

'Ward Ten!'

Pte B. Hotchkiss, U.S. Army. Frac rt femur.

'American Ward!'

There was no rain tonight but the air came damply in from the dark where stars showed above the humped shapes of the ambulances. Their doors were banging shut, and engines throbbed.

Blanket stiff with blood. Unconscious.

Pte. F. K. Crockersleigh, Artists' Rifles. Sev G.S.W. abdom.

'Theatre Emergency!'

The card was loose and she re-tied the string.

Cpl G. Grant, 4th Arm Adv shell-shock. Neph.

'Ward two!'

Blood was on the stairs and someone mopped at it. One of the lamps had sputtered out: they were always fusing.

A scream shrilled and was smothered; a needle went in.

Maj A. J. Talbot, 1st Inf – the field-card went dark and sounds grew faint around her. *No. He's invincible.*

The head thick with bandages, the face white, unrecognizable.

'Nurse Lovell! Are you all right?'

Quick.

'Yes.' Quick. *Non-penet G.S.W. cran.* 'Theatre Emergency!'

Their faces floated, coming and going.

Voices a long way off.

Where is my leg.

Light and dark and breathing, in and out, slowly in and out. Moments of clarity.

'Where's my leg?'

'There's nothing wrong with your legs.'

'I can't move them.'

'You're not quite strong enough yet.'

One face. Diana's.

'Diana.'

'Hello, dearest.' Floating away.

But sometimes you could listen without their knowing.

'No contusions, no spicules, sinuses undamaged, no abscess anywhere – it looks perfectly all right. You can start easing off the doses but keep him absolutely quiet and absolutely still. Can't you do something about that bloody gramophone?'

The tube again. Glucose. Sick of it.

Later, a lot more sense. 'Diana?'

'Yes?'

'What was it, exactly?'

'What was what?'

'Where was I hit?'

Her hand was warm. 'You had a bullet in the skull. Non-penetrating.' She said it deliberately, perhaps because it could no longer harm him and this had to be pointed out.

'I was lucky.'

'We were lucky, yes.'

Periods of black roaring nightmare.

They left him weak but mentally alert. 'Vic. Please find out if – what happened to him.'

'Who is Vic?' It was a new girl, painfully young and already with haunted eyes: from every cupboard she expected an amputation case to topple out.

'Brother. My brother. Lieutenant V. R. Tal—' Hammer smashing down roaring and black and sickening.

'He mustn't *talk*, Nurse!'

324

But they said later, yes, Lieutenant Talbot was well and had written a note. Here it was.

Apparently you're going to pull through, so now I can sleep. Coming to see you soon. Highest admiration and profound thanks. Vic.

'What? That's wrong. That's not my brother.'

One morning raindrops on his face, warm and quite heavy. A hand squeezing his fingers.

'Hello? Who—'

'Hello darling. I just came to see you. Major Neave says you're through the crisis and there's nothing to stop you getting better now.' Her voice was unsteady. 'Do you understand what I'm saying, Aubrey?'

'Yes. I love you.'

'Oh, God.'

They weren't raindrops.

A day when suddenly all life came back, totally and overwhelmingly. 'Can't I have something with more guts to it than this damned glucose?'

He could think clearly now about the two notes, the one that he'd found waiting for him under his 'favourite' tree: *I hate you.* And the one here beside him. *Highest admiration.* It was going to take some working out and his head tended to split if he thought too seriously about anything. But it was nothing to do with his being wounded, he knew that.

September, the calendar said, 21 September.

'Your calendar's wrong.'

'No, Major.'

'How long have I been here, then?'

'Ten days.'

'I don't believe it. Listen, will you please find out what happened to a couple of friends of mine? One of them is Sergeant F. H. Kemp, No. 4 Platoon, C—'

'There's a letter from him. There are quite a few letters.'

'My head hurts when I try to read.'

'Shall I read it for you?'

'Yes. Please.'

It is really wonderful news that you are making such good progress. You may not have heard what happened when we got out of the redoubt that time. Well, twenty of us arrived at the lines without a scratch, five were lost and two died of wounds the next day. The other three are

325

*reported to be on the mend, including Cpl Sykes. The main thing is that
our young Tom is not nearly so bad as we thought, but it was a 'Blighty
one' and he will be in England by now. What with the way the war is
going, I would say Tom has gone and 'stolen a march' on us. The main
action that day went well and all objectives were carried successfully, and
as the Colonel says, it was a day for Battle Honours. Mr Victor is well
and his ankle is improving. Of course you will have heard from him
long before this. Last night he called me along to the dugout and we
'split a bottle' and talked about what it must be like at the Manor. The
rest of the battalion is due for—*

'Don't read any more.'

A lightness was filling his head, as if he were going to pass
out again; but there wasn't the usual muzziness.

'Do you feel all right, Major Talbot?'

'Yes. Perfectly.' He looked up into the girl's uncompre-
hending eyes. 'That's my young brother he was talking about.'

'I see. Who was the other friend you wanted me to make
enquiries—'

'It doesn't matter. That was Tom, in the letter.'

'I see.' She smiled for him, pretending an interest in Tom.
Her face was small and pinched, with lines under the eyes that
couldn't have been there long.

'How old are you?'

'Twenty-three.'

Last night he'd heard a convoy of ambulances arrive.

He said, 'My God, and you're not allowed to vote until
you're thirty. Who's running that country?'

Sometimes he wandered into the Games Room. The dust
seemed thicker across the ping-pong table and the bronze
statue leaned more wearily from the corner. The dartboards
were still in their pile, still with the brown paper on. The sofa
had gone, the one where they'd sat together all that night. An
ancient calendar hung at an angle: 4 March 1916. A sudden
shiver took him and he left the place. 1916 had gone too. Thank
God, thank God in high heaven, that year would never come
again.

A letter from Pom-Pom: she had written often, even if it
were only a hurried note scrawled 'between trains'. This one
carried unnerving news.

Brace up, Aubrey, you won't like this. They found Uncle Charles in his study this morning. His service revolver, notes left and everything in order. That's all we know at present, although Louise has told Mother a lot and I don't want to ask about it. I don't want to know, ever, do you? He'd given up work in Propaganda, of course, and it could have been just that he'd lost direction, like a lot of people do when they retire – you've got to go on pedalling or the bike won't keep upright any more. And I suppose he hadn't the heart to go on writing his war books – those old battles must have seemed pretty piddling compared with this monster. But it wasn't anything to do with Hugh. (It'll be better to correct that bit than cross it out) It was very much to do with Hugh, but you know what Louise will say – it was because Hugh let him down. I think it was because Charles realized in the end that he'd let *Hugh down, by being so bloody hurt about the whole thing, and not telling Louise where to get off. He didn't know what kind of a son he'd got, and suddenly it was too late to recognize him, or accept him – I can't quite find the word. Love him, then. Louise could have shown him the way. If I had any charity in my soul I'd feel sorry for her, but all I know is that she's been a thorough-going bitch all along. She didn't deserve a son like Hugh, and nor did Charles, and when he finally faced it – he was at least man enough to do that – it killed him. I wish I could blub as I used to, but somewhere between Platforms 3 and 4 I've dried up, for ever. I think it's because I found out I never blubbed for anyone else, only for me.*

Aubrey read the letter twice and tore it up, as Pam would expect him to do. Staring across the crumbling terrace of the château where the wind drove the first leaves from the poplars he saw Uncle Charles wandering past the summer-house in his Norfolk jacket, the short black pipe jutting from beneath the ginger moustache; a man he had never known, whom nobody had ever known. 'Hello, hello! Your folk about, are they?' Liquorice Allsorts for Pam, loose in a bag because too many would make her sick. You never thought of the recently dead as you last saw them, but as when you'd been the most touched by their company. Charles, an unknown man with a service revolver, would forever come wandering past the summer-house.

A son like Hugh. He dropped the pieces into the waste-paper basket – a battered shell-case near the fire-extinguisher. There hadn't, come to think of it, been a letter from Pam that didn't mention Hugh, though they didn't see anything of each other, apparently.

A note from Hugh himself: *Glad you're all right. I don't know any man less suitable for shooting bullets at; it must have been in error.*

'The day after tomorrow.'

'Straight to Uxbridge?'

'Some leave, first.'

He didn't ask her what the devil they'd been thinking of, working her like a slave for so long out here; maybe she'd dug her heels in, refusing to go before now: she'd talked to him about 'letting Julian down' and he'd asked her if she thought Julian would have wanted to see her as exhausted as this.

He said: 'I'll see if I can wangle getting sent to Uxbridge too.'

She smiled and the amethyst blue of her eyes darkened. 'I don't hope for miracles twice in a month.'

They were by the windows of the Rest Room, a gloomy-ceilinged ante-chamber with its quota of antique furnishings spilled over from the Games Room; the nurses never rested here, any more than they played ping-pong.

The poplars were bare of leaves now, across the terrace and the rusted railings of the park. An ambulance was coming in from the town, on the 'ration run'.

'You'll be able to see your people,' Aubrey said.

She looked away. 'I expect it's too late now. I mean, to bridge any kind of gap.'

'You've not had a chance to try.'

'Oh, I'll try all right. But this is just a thing between the generations.' She looked up at him again. 'All families aren't like yours, Aubrey.'

'I probably take it for granted.'

'No,' she said quickly, 'you don't. None of you do, at Ashbourne. I could cry, sometimes, about the love that's there; I've thought of it a lot when I've been in the dumps. It's a love bigger than the house, bigger than anything, sky-high and with clouds on its shoulders. I think most of it comes from your Mother, doesn't it? She seems to – to sort of wander about the place, not doing anything in particular except put a few plants in upside down – Pam told me about that – but really she's rubbing a kind of lamp, keeping the shine on it, recreating everything and everyone there.'

He wanted to laugh, but it was too easy to do that when Mother was mentioned; however cherished, she was almost a family joke. Father was the only one who knew her true value, which was natural enough.

'You're not the first to fall under Mother's spell.'

'I know. Surely everyone does. That's why—'

He was watching her eyes, not listening really, just delighting in seeing her thoughts come and go, altering their colour and their light.

'That's why – ?' he asked.

'I've never understood. About Vic. It must be a kind of exile for him.'

Draught came, rustling some paper in the hearth where vases lay in a grocery-box, half-wrapped. The big doors of the hall had opened and someone stood there, looking around uncertainly. The ambulance had gone past the terrace to the kitchens.

'I think something's happened,' he said, 'to Vic. I'm not sure what, because my head's not been too clear—'

'Happened? He's all right—'

'Oh yes, he's written a couple of times.' The fellow in the hall was an officer, looking lost; the days had gone when a visitor to the Château de Thiéry was accorded a reception. Aubrey called through the doorway of the ante-room – 'Can we help you?'

The figure turned and Aubrey knew him the moment he began walking towards them; the light was dim in the hall. 'This is absurd,' he murmured to Diana.

'Why?'

'It's my brother.'

Diana watched him as he came towards them hesitantly, taking his cap off and tucking it under his arm. All she had ever seen of Victor Talbot was a photograph at Ashbourne, a youthful and slightly devilish face held proudly above a spanking-new uniform and with nothing of Aubrey in it. Nearing her now, wiry and a little tense and less tall than she'd believed, he was Aubrey's brother only in the way he didn't speak immediately, and didn't smile; his dark eyes were enquiring, as if he liked to see who people were before he committed himself even to a word. A glance for her, of passing interest, then he was looking steadily at Aubrey; and she felt at once shut out from them both.

Someone crossed the hall, pushing the big doors against the wind; the rustling in the hearth died away.

'Hello Aubrey.' It sounded a kind of question, a password that must be answered. His eyes flicked up, noting the bandages, and down again to study his brother's face.

'Hello Vic.'

They shook hands rather formally and Diana said:

'Will you excuse me?' She turned aside.

Vic moved his head. 'Am I butting in?'

Aubrey said quietly, 'Diana, this is my brother Victor. Miss Diana Lovell, my fiancée.'

Vic's face went blank for a moment; then sensibility lit his eyes and she was aware of an intense scrutiny.

Slowly he said: 'I didn't know.' And without any change of expression: 'My God, what a glorious girl.' A smile came now and he looked at Aubrey. 'That can only mean congratulations, can't it?' Then suddenly he was out of his depth, looking at neither of them, resettling his cap beneath his arm – 'I got a lift here, from the crossroads. Ambulance full of vegetables.'

'I must go,' Diana said.

Vic turned, watching her pass through into the hall.

'I always knew you'd get a girl like that.' Turning back he said, 'Nobody told me. Oh, I think Pam did, but I suppose—' He shrugged. 'There's quite a lot I need telling. We sort of lost touch, didn't we? Still sing in your bath?' He slung his cap on to one of the stacked dining-chairs and by chance it caught across the knurled pilaster and spun there for a moment, raising dust. 'I see I've kept my hand in, anyhow.' His laugh was forced.

Watching him, Aubrey realized he'd never seen him before, this exact person, his brother. There'd been the over-gay and noisy gadabout, the endearing nuisance eager for escapade; and later the still-feverish but embittered subaltern burning for the honours that despite his calculated courage had never come his way; and now a young man untouched by the war but

330

fatigued by the greater battles he had made his own. And, over all, unsure of himself: that much remained.

'I'll see if I can rustle up some coffee, shall I?'

'What? Oh, I don't mind.' He found a packet of cigarettes and offered it. 'You're nearly fit again, aren't you, I mean apart from the plum-pudding hat?'

'Thanks to you.'

'Oh, that. Did I bring you in or did you bring me in? Bit of both I suppose.' He struck a match.

Watching his brother across the flame Aubrey had a recurrence of the lightheadedness that had come over him when he'd heard that Vic and Freddie had 'split a bottle' together in the dugout. He'd never been able to talk to Vic like this before, speaking easily and freely without listening for the sudden bitter retort that had ended nearly every conversation. His brother's fever had passed and the relief was as heady as if it had been his own.

'What happened about it, Vic?'

'About what?'

'Your little show.'

'I don't quite—'

'Well I mean you pulled thirty men out of a bad spot and twenty got back alive—'

'Oh I see, yes.' He moved to the window, saying nothing more for a few seconds, his fingers fretting at the cigarette. 'Rokesley was pleased, of course. He told me it was a certain Military Cross.'

Aubrey took a slow breath.

'That's magnificent,' he said.

'Well I don't know. Thing is, I've refused it.'

He was bothered about his ash and looked for somewhere to put it, finally using the hearth.

'Did you?'

'Well, yes.'

'Why?'

'I didn't want it.' He gave a short laugh. 'That's simple enough, isn't it? Rokesley said I ought to have the good grace to accept it, if only for the sake of the battalion – you know these C.O.s, they collect medals like milk-bottle stoppers. Anyway I said I wasn't bloody well going to have it and the battalion could go and stuff itself. Not quite those words but I didn't leave him in any doubt.' Suddenly he said – 'You don't mind, do you? I mean the family name can get on perfectly well without that kind of thing—'

'Oh yes. Perfectly well.' He stared pensively at the young head silhouetted against the window. How many times had the boy risked death for that medal? 'But you'll never live it down in any case, Vic.'

'How d'you mean?'

'Effectively, the next one up from the M.C. isn't the D.S.O. It's the M.C. Refused. It's got a unique *cachet* to it, don't you think?'

Vic took a step towards him. 'I want your word, here and now, that you'll never tell anyone.'

In a moment Aubrey asked: 'Is it so important?'

'Yes.' Clearly and slowly so that his brother should understand he said: 'It's the only way I can forget that I once wanted that little tin gong, and very badly.'

'What's wrong with that? A lot of people do.'

'Christ, don't you see? It was *all* I wanted! That's probably why I never got it; there's a kind of natural law about it, I suppose, a kind of self-defeating mechanism at work somewhere.'

Aubrey drew on his cigarette and flicked it into the hearth and in the next instant Vic did the same, as if instinctively to prove that even in the most trivial things they were in accord.

'So that wasn't why you decided to get us out?' He watched Vic's eyes intently. It had been a hell of a thing to ask but it seemed the time for questions like that.

For a moment his brother didn't appear to understand; then he laughed sharply. 'Good God, there was something better than a tin gong for the taking!'

Aubrey closed his eyes. There was something almost physically blinding in the thought that had leapt to his mind, though it was obvious enough and he would have seen it before now if he'd not been so groggy after the operation. What had happened, out there in the shifting fortunes of the battlefield, was that he had failed. It had been a neat enough action, technically: he'd led half a platoon to an abandoned redoubt, a valuable forward position worth holding; but the flank was turned and they were cut off, disarmed and helpless. And Vic had learned of it.

He opened his eyes. 'Yes of course.' Wryly he said, 'There was a peacock in my path.'

Vic looked away. His hands were trembling and he quickly folded his arms to hide them but he couldn't do anything about his eyes, the despair in them, the vulnerability.

'That's right.' His voice was shaking but he over-controlled it, speaking with a force he didn't feel. 'There's a lot of luck in a war. Thirty men without a hope in hell and one of them my brother. It took some doing, you know, there weren't any fit reserves on hand and Rokesley was busy on the ridge by that time and I had to scream blue murder before I could rope in a few crocks to bring up the guns and the mortar. Christ knows how I did it.' Then his voice broke to a whisper and his breath fluttered painfully over the words that had got to be said. 'I just want you to know *why* I did it. That—'

'Vic, you don't have to—'

'Oh yes I do, and you'll bloody well listen. That gallant young sub who risked his neck for his thirty beloved comrades was in point of fact a snivelling little bastard trying to get even with his brother.' He turned away. 'And then they had to go and offer him a *medal* . . .'

Aubrey didn't move. He wanted to go and hold the boy, protect him somehow; but Vic didn't need his comfort.

'Vic.'

'Yes?' He turned and leaned against the window-sill, his arms still folded in a gesture of defence.

'That wasn't you.'

'Wasn't me?'

'That "little bastard" you hated so much. You used to leave notes for him, remember? In my name. All he is now is a –' he threw out his hand – 'a poor little ghost.'

Vic looked away, his restless eyes seeing nothing of the stacked chairs, the Empire sofa under its dusty shroud, the Limoges china in the grocery-crates by the hearth; then he was staring at Aubrey again.

'I'd give a lot to think so. I feel I'm different now, but why? What changed me?'

'The redoubt. I failed there and you succeeded; you got even with me, showed you were stronger. You'd been wanting to do that ever since you learned that an elder brother could be a damned nuisance, pinching all the limelight. Now you'd done it. How could you *not* have become changed, achieving a life-long ambition? The pressure was off and you could see straight for the first time; that's what worries you now: looking back at yourself you don't like what you see.' He gave a shrug. 'Most of us are like that; our past selves don't give us much pride. So forget it, Vic. Yours died in that redoubt; that's where his ghost is, and all we've got to do is leave it in peace.'

One of their cigarettes still smouldered in the hearth and he crossed and put his foot on it; the spiral of smoke climbed and vanished.

'You make it easy for me,' Vic said.

'You've made it too hard for yourself, that's why. Don't forget this: I'd failed and that was all you needed. You didn't have to get us out of there; you could have left us to rot.' He turned to the doorway: 'I'm going to charm some coffee out of the cooks, and we'll have some cognac with it, celebrate.'

Vic stood away from the window-sill, his arms unfolding; hesitantly, as if remembering an old habit, he thrust his hands into his pockets.

'All right. But is that quite the word?'

Aubrey looked back from the doorway at the boy who'd been so long a stranger, keeping his tone light, though it was difficult.

'Celebrate? Yes. For me this is a great day. I've always wanted a brother like you.'

334

XVII

In the morning a light wind blew across No Man's Land.

The air was cold and the men coming off dawn stand-down made haste to their can of soup, blowing into the wrists of their gloves. In the night there had been the murmur of guns to the north where the Allies had crossed the Sambre; but nothing here was changed: daylight fell thinly across the littered wastes and there was no movement anywhere.

An hour later a signal was received in the Battalion H.Q. dugout of a British unit holding the line not far from Beauvoir-les-Hauts. It was read by Maj. J. M. Bull, temporarily in command during his Colonel's absence at Brigade.

Hostilities will cease at 1100 hrs today. Until that time the battalion is at one hour's notice to advance, should the Allied terms of the Armistice not be accepted. In the event of attack, or of any situation giving rise to suspicion that an attack is expected, the enemy will appropriately be engaged, if necessary at the discretion of local commanders.

To Maj. Bull this came as a disappointment. Shortly due to retire, he had found himself ordered on active service at the front only three weeks before, a 'stroke of luck' – as he had told his colonel – that would give him the chance of 'being in at the death' after so many years at the War Office. The signal now fluttering in his hands as he stood outside the dugout would have ended this chance had he not decided to interpret its meaning to suit his personal convenience.

The enemy lines were a mile distant. From the bleak horizon there could be seen smoke rising, and sometimes movement was heard in snatches of sound borne on the November wind. The smoke could be from the cookers and the sound could be that of the transport lines in the rear; on the other hand they could jointly be considered as *giving rise to suspicion that an attack was expected*. Further, he was temporarily privileged with the *discretion of local commander* and empowered to decide whether or not *the enemy should appropriately be engaged*.

At 0845 hours No. 1 Platoon was summarily ordered to raid

335

the enemy's position and bring back prisoners. The action was primarily intended to discover whether in fact a German attack was imminent; the capturing of prisoners would satisfactorily establish the operation's success.

The enemy, though taken by surprise, was holding his lines in some strength; and of the fifty-seven troops sent out, thirteen returned alive. There were no prisoners taken.

Major Bull had observed the action through his field-glasses and afterwards saw the remnant of the platoon coming in, shocked, demoralized and severally wounded. Stretcher-bearers attempted to bring in the mutilated who lay in No Man's Land crying for help, but a machine-gun drove them back.

For the major this was a second disappointment, though the action had stirred him greatly and more than once he had lowered his field-glasses to cheer his men on. Most of them were conscripts and many still in their boyhood, this their first action in the field; and as he watched the survivors dropping exhausted into the trench his regret at their defeat was overlaid by his admiration for their bravery. Turning to a young captain he raised his voice a little so that they should hear, and be consoled. 'Well, such are the fortunes of war. They fought damned hard and they've proved themselves to be soldiers. It was a grand show, a very grand little show.'

In the afternoon the sea off Dover lay calm under light haze. Across the harbour and farther out in the roads the ships were motionless, vague shapes isolated in the mist, as if suddenly abandoned. But some of the bells in the town were still ringing and people were in the streets, gathering in groups, an air of bewilderment about them as if day had come in the middle of the night, bringing them from their beds.

From the railhead there still marched numberless troops to swell the American units awaiting embarkation at the docks where the ships would take them to France. The eleventh hour had passed but machinery so gigantic would take time to run down; meanwhile under the peaceful sky their will to war could be acknowledged, and the cheering from both sides echoed among the buildings and faded across the sea.

The children of the Chalet School were among the crowds;

at eleven o'clock they had been told that a holiday was declared and now they stormed the shops for flags and sherbet-fountains.

At the station Hugh had found a place on the London bound train, jammed between a soldier and a fat woman who sat devouring bread and cheese; for some reason tears trickled at intervals on to her pasty cheeks but she ate with gusto. He'd had no idea, before eleven o'clock this morning, that he'd be sitting in a train soon afterwards; the Head had called him into his study to tell him the news first, and without thinking about it he'd asked if he could use the telephone.

A soldier passed the carriage with a little girl on his shoulders and Hugh remembered what had happened at the dockside this morning. He'd gone down very early, just for the walk and to watch a troopship coming in; there was nothing official yet, but there didn't seem to be any doubt left and he felt the stirring of the times in him, as so many did today. From the barrier where relatives and friends were these days allowed to wait he saw another ship just leaving for France, stern down and decks packed and the Red Duster limp at the mast; and he felt awed, being in the presence of so great a mercy. Those many men would go on living, because by the time they reached the slaughter-house the gates would be shut.

It was a leave-ship just docking, a salt-blistered hulk with red rust staining the grey of her plates. One of the first off was a big infantry sergeant, his blunt face weathered by the war and his eyes seeming uncertain what he was doing here and why people were cheering so. Hugh had seen this look in the eyes of soldiers before as they came off a ship, and knew what it meant: they were puzzled for a minute or two by the strangeness of the scene – people in clean clothes and no skulls grinning on the ground, nothing in the air to blow your head off. A woman called to the big sergeant and suddenly a small boy ducked under the barrier, his school cap flying off; and the sergeant lifted him until he was the taller, and looked at him against the morning sky, laughing and saying his name. The cap was near his feet and he picked it up; it looked a new one and had a bold yellow ring on a blue background. He put it on the boy's head, his great rough hands making ceremony of it, then stood back and looked at him with pride.

Hugh came away; there was nobody on this ship, or any ship, he had to meet.

Tom came through the gates and stopped for a moment, looking at the house. The day was very still and there was no particular sky above the tall chimneys, just a greyness. He felt awkward in the new blue suit; it didn't seem to fit very well though the man with the tape measure in the army depot said he'd 'grow into it' soon enough. He'd got his new mackintosh draped over the attaché-case because that was the arm he couldn't use properly; the M.O. had said the nerves would get better as time went by, if he exercised it enough, though he was no more use to the Army.

He could feel the sprig of hair sticking up again from his crown; he'd put water on it in the railway toilets and walked some of the way with one hand clamped on his head but it was no good. The smell of burning leaves was in the air and he could see the blue-white smoke from somewhere behind the potting-sheds; that would be Mr Willis making a bonfire and he wanted to call out *Mr Willis!* at the top of his voice, suddenly frightened that it wasn't real and that if someone didn't see him and say his name it would all vanish before he could touch it.

'Steady,' he said softly, 'steady, Tom.'

He went forward again, a careful step at a time, breathing as slow as he could, almost not breathing at all, but the sweet smell of the smoke was getting at him, making him remember other Autumns, and the red and gold and yellow leaves poured over him till he couldn't see properly.

'Steady. You've got a place here. Mr Kemp said.'

A window high in the house flashed as it swung and he heard it bang against the frame; a face showed and disappeared. He went on again, and in a minute someone came running down the front steps on the other side of the fountain-pond and stood there, slender in a blue frock, as if making sure who was coming.

In the evening a drizzle fell in the streets of London but nobody stayed indoors. Big Ben had been set chiming again this morning and now the lamps came on.

Pearlies were dancing arm-in-arm the whole length of

Commercial Road where the naphtha flares of the cockle-stalls made oases of light. A bus swayed through the crowds, the top deck a flutter of waving flags; a bottle of beer spun high and burst in a brilliant shower against a lamp-post; a little man with a crutch stood laughing fit to bust outside his shop – *Wilfred Bennett, Antique Dealer* – as three sailors and a policeman danced ring-a-roses round a horse-trough where an Irishman was having a bath with his clothes on. Ships hooted in the docks, competing with each other.

In Piccadilly the traffic had come to a stop and Eros was festooned with streamers already hanging limp under the fine rain; a colonel of the Dragoons, perched on top of a taxi, blew a hunting-horn with great vigour; soldiers were being carried shoulder-high round the monument, one of them waving to a pretty young WAAC in uniform – 'Hello Dolly! Say, can you'n me go on manœuvres together tonight?' Pickpockets flitted like sparrows where the crowd was thickest; at its fringe a woman in black stood alone with head lifted, her eyes closed against the sky and her lips moving.

'Are you cold?'

'No.'

They had come out on to the balcony to watch the street. This was the hotel where there had once been a fancy-dress ball and Vic had played the drums.

'London's gone mad,' Diana said. People thronged below with rattles and hooters and flags.

'Yes. It does that rather easily.'

Posters hung above the news-stands, the rain making the hand-painted letters run.

ARMISTICE SIGNED!

Aubrey wondered where it was and what it looked like, the document itself, signed in the name of ten million dead; and he remembered going into the house a few days ago, discharged from the convalescent hospital, and the feeling that had come to him once before: of awe and humility, the realization of the tremendous luck that had let him come home alive. He was still in uniform and carried the ashplant that in four years of peril had not often left his hand; Charrington took it from him with a deference more properly due to a silver-knobbed cane than to this battle-scarred stick. By chance Father was there, coming out of his study, and heard him tell Charrington:

'You can dump it.'

'Dump it, Mr Aubrey?'

'Burn it or something.' There'd been times when its closeness had kept him sane, reminding him of a saner world; but from now on it would only remind him of a past he'd sooner forget: already its scars and bruises had the look of something crippled.

'Very good, Mr Aubrey.' He went to the hearth with it; some logs burned there.

'Charrington,' in low tones.

'Sir William?'

'Do it with ceremony.'

And so the stick was taken in both hands, to be laid across the flames in the manner of a sacrifice; and Charrington stood back a few paces and for a moment kept still. Aubrey could make nothing of his father's expression as he watched the first flame curl and leap from the stick itself and then take hold; there burned away, perhaps, the ever-present agonies of mind, the fear of news and – worse – of no news, that had plagued this house for so unconscionably long. This at least Aubrey had been spared, and no amount of understanding could let him share it now; obliged to witness this theatrical little ceremony he had felt the kind of irritation of the healthy for the sick, and had been relieved when his father turned and said in matter-of-fact tones:

'So you're home at last. I hope you'll join me in a glass of sherry.'

A Red Cross ambulance was nosing its way towards Trafalgar Square; small chance that it was Pam's, though she was on duty somewhere: there were more ambulances than taxis in London at this year's end. She'd rushed home today for a snatched lunch with him 'to share the historic hour', but they hadn't talked about it; there seemed nothing to say. A cable had come from France while they were pecking at some of Cook's shepherd's pie: *Freddie and I totally unscathed and now liable to remain so. Lord bless us all. Vic.* The battalion had been in a minor action south of Ostend during the final week and it was a relief to know they were all right; he sent Charrington straight across to Mrs Kemp with the good news.

'Hugh's coming up from Dover,' Pam said.

'To see his mother?'

340

'No. The last time they met was at the funeral and she cut him dead, no joke intended; I could have slapped her chops instead of saying how sad I was for her.' She cut into an apple with slow care. 'It's me he's coming to see. Anyway that's what he said. He rang me at the unit though God knows how he found the number.' Her tone was off-hand but Aubrey saw the excitement in her dark eyes.

'It's the first thing he'd think of doing, Pom-Pom.'

'What is?'

'Seeing you.'

She didn't look at him. 'He's never come to see me before. Not specially.'

'The war wasn't over, before. There'll be no white feathers or dirty looks when you're seen together—'

'My God, he knows I'd rather be seen with him than – than a lot of people I can think of.'

'Perhaps he didn't believe it.'

'Why on earth shouldn't he?'

'Perhaps because he wanted to, a bit too much.'

She'd gone straight back to her unit after gulping some coffee. More people had come on to the balcony, some of them tearing up their menus and tossing the pieces like confetti into the street. A champagne cork came popping through the open doors and a cheer went up. A woman stood by herself at the end of the balcony, pressing her fur collar tightly together and looking without expression at the crowds below; she was one of so many, Aubrey thought; for them the war had been lost long ago and today meant nothing.

He had been to see Mr and Mrs Tuffnel as soon as he'd heard the news from Col. Rokesley; and last night he'd followed it up with a short letter.

I am only repeating what I told you when you were kind enough to receive me yesterday, because if you have it in writing it may help to remind you that when Geoffrey's trial comes up he will have the strongest support I am able to give him. He has proved himself before us all as a man of the highest courage, and though he is officially listed as a deserter his war record alone will automatically dismiss any charge that his act was one of cowardice. The high moral principles he has always held so tenaciously were clearly responsible both for the action that won him the Military Medal and for his final decision to lay down his arms.

Even if the court fails to recognize the value in such a man, we can hope that in the general thanksgiving for the ending of a brutal and fruitless war, leniency will be shown and mercy freely given. I shall of course keep closely in touch with you about events; and when the time comes I shall consider it an honour to assist in the defence of your very gallant son.

Someone in the crowd had found some balloons and people jumped at them to bounce them higher as they went floating above their heads. A fight seemed to have started near the pub opposite: there were dark milling figures and a woman screaming.

From the distance Aubrey heard a chime from Big Ben, and felt Diana shiver. He drew her closer against him.

'You're getting cold.'

'No. Did you hear Big Ben? I was there when it chimed before, when it all began. Were you?'

'Yes.'

Singing had started but it was overwhelmed by cheers as a chorus girl in tights and a feathered hat waved from a balcony.

'What was it about, Aubrey, the war?'

He thought how strange it was to talk of it in the past tense, when it had been their very life for so long.

'National greed, military pride; the need for something more exciting than driving a bus and doing the washing-up.'

'And it did no good, anywhere, to anyone at all.'

He looked down at her small cold face. 'Yes. I found you.'

She turned, pressing against him, and he tried to shut out of his mind the voice of the crowds; but it was insistent, surging among the buildings and rising to the dismal sky, where it lost all meaning. He'd heard this voice crying in joy for war; now it cried in joy for peace. It was a voice to beware of, wherever it was heard.